Anecdotal

For bulk orders please call Dog Ear Publishing at 1-866-823-9613
First published by Dog Ear Publishing
4010 W. 86th Street, Ste
Indianapolis, IN 46268
www.dogearpublishing.net

ISBN: 0-9766603-5-0
Library of Congress Control Number: 2005924184

This book is printed on acid-free paper.
This book is a work of fiction. Places, events, and situations in this book are purely
fictional and any resemblance to actual persons, living or dead, is coincidental.

Printed in the United States of America

Anecdotal

A Novel By

J. Brooks Dann

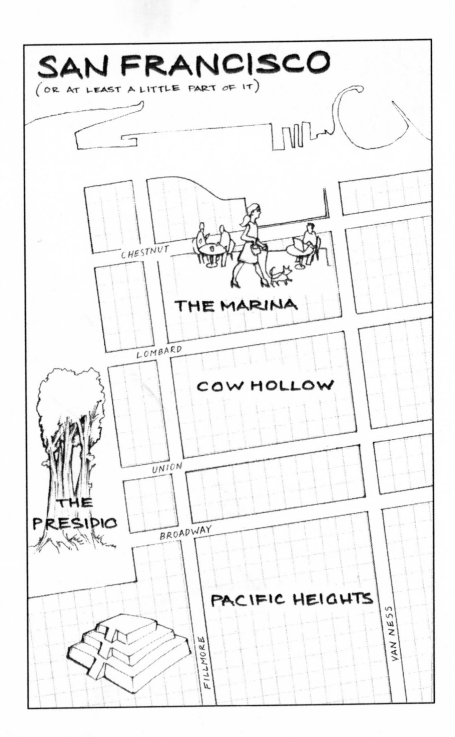

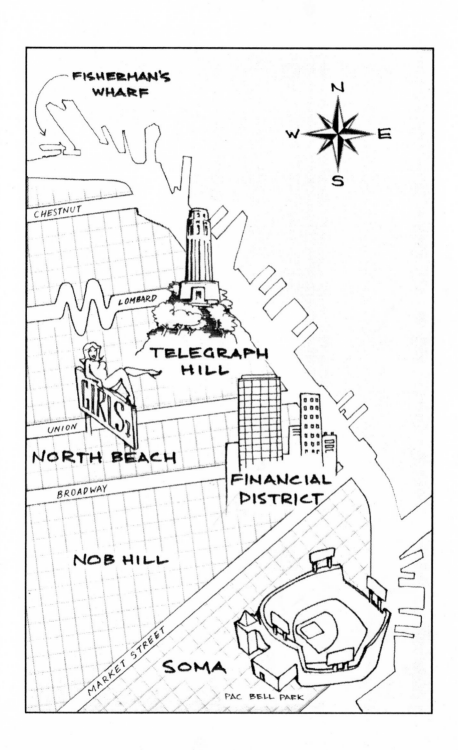

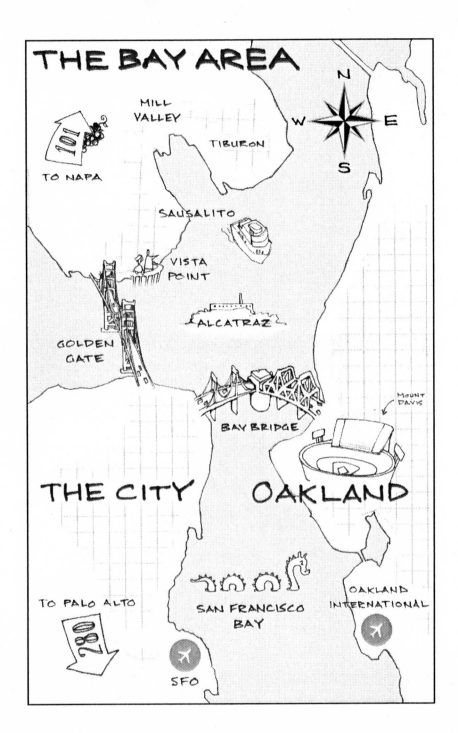

1

Falling

"Let me do your butt," she said.

"No. You just did it an hour ago," I replied.

Gabrielle set the bowl of water and the washcloth on my bedside table. Ribbons of steam glowed, illuminated by candles and dimmed lamps. REM's *Life's Rich Pageant* played softly on my stereo.

"Why not? Let me do your bum, you bum!" she demanded as she slinked up onto the bed and rested her head on my chest, taking care to avoid my elevated and bandaged knee.

"But, I'm already fresh as a country lane after a spring shower. You did such a good job with my first bath."

Gabrielle had flown in from Los Angeles four days before to take care of me after my knee surgery—where Dr. Rajiv Balakrishnan bestowed unto me a brand new ligament following my highlight reel fall on the basketball court in the Marina. Gabrielle relieved my mother, who had flown to San Francisco from Indianapolis the day before my procedure and served as my resident nurse for the first three days post-op. But, where I bathed *myself* with microwavable towlettes while my mom was in town, my current caretaker virtually insisted on providing the best medical care money can't buy.

She raised her head from my chest and planted a playful kiss on my nose. "Jacob...pleeeease," she pleaded.

"Hmmmm, I'll have to take it under consideration," I replied. G's powers of persuasion are legendary. She began kissing me again, much less playfully than before. After about thirty seconds, she slowly pulled away. I could tell she was about to whisper her next set of entreaties into my ear. She shifted her weight and moved toward my left side.

"Ooooow!" I squealed like a puppy as her knee smashed with the fury of ten thousand out of control freight trains into my hidden surgical wound. By reflex, my stomach muscles tensed and my upper body jetted skyward. Our foreheads and the bridges of our noses collided, making a sound reminiscent of the dying breaths of doomed melons, dropped by David Letterman from ten floors up. Twin "Ows" followed my original utterance a second before.

And then laughter. From both of us.

And then groaning. From me.

"Oh. Oh. G, you need to get me another hit of the Vicodin."

She was already on her way to get the amber bottle. "You just took some a couple of hours ago..." she commented as she consulted with the dosage directions on the label.

"But I wants it. I needs it. Ya gotsta gives it to me!" The humor was contrived, but the pain was, indeed, all too real.

"Okaaaaay, but it'll cost ya." We quickly brokered our deal. I got my painkillers and she got to give me my third sponge bath of the day. A fair covenant all the way around.

I yielded to the placebo effects of the small white pills immediately, sinking contentedly back onto the large shams at the head of my bed. The stereo paused for a brief moment as Michael Stipe prepared to sing track 3. I emitted a quick and nearly silent chuckle as tinny guitars announced the beginning of "Fall on Me."

"What's so funny?" asked Gabrielle as she looked up from my steamy feet, which hadn't touched the floor since my 9 p.m. sponge bath.

"Nothing. Just good memories from this tune." It was my favorite song. *Still* my favorite song, after all of these years, probably because I had never had a favorite song up until the point in my youth when it came out. When I discovered REM back in the mid-80s, I must have been either the last of the cool kids who found them while they were still underground, or the first of the mass-market muckety mucks who latched onto the group when they traded a few chits of indie cred for radio airplay.

I laughed because, in spite of the fact it was my favorite song, it took me years to figure out what it was about. I've always been lyrically challenged…even with songs I like…even with songs I love like "Fall on Me". One didn't enjoy the best vocal comprehension listening to well-worn tapes in a friend's topless 'Vette during midnight summertime drives. Playing scratchy records borrowed from 15-year-old proto-punks didn't help either.

Years later, when I went to college and purchased *Life's Rich Pageant* as my first CD, I started to listen more carefully. I had always thought "Fall on Me" was about supporting other people. You know, something like, "Hey, baby, you can fall on me…I'll be there to catch you…so don't you worry about falling."

After a few plays on my circa 1989 CD player, I began to realize my fallacy. The song is actually about the sky falling on your head. Asking the sky, begging the sky, pleading with the sky, "Please, don't fall on me."

Oh, well, it's still my favorite song. And I still can't sing the lyrics.

Gabrielle moved up from my feet toward my delicate knee. She carefully removed the outer support wrap and washed the still-swollen and bruised skin beneath. Her long hair was held up in the back by two crossed pencils—one from a luxurious conference center and resort and the other a well-chewed yellow implement I think I had used to take the GMAT years before.

My little geisha wore a pair of blue pajamas she had bought for me for Hanukkah almost four years ago. Our first Hanukkah together and her first Hanukkah, period. I had worn the flannel bedclothes a couple of times, but mostly valued them for the way she looked in them.

In case you're wondering, I was wearing an Indiana University sweatshirt and a pair of Harvard Business School boxer shorts. Indiana covered the heart, Harvard covered the aforementioned and oft-washed butt.

I took off the sweatshirt so Gabrielle could wash my chest. As she came closer, I noticed she smelled faintly of baking. Of blackberry pie. Which of course, made sense, since earlier in the evening we had spent several hours baking three fruity pastries—two as yet untouched and unspoiled, the other ravaged by our greedy appetites. On the bedside table next to the bowl of hot water rested our purple stained plates, each boasting a vanilla pool of melted *a la mode* where flakes of crust played.

We had harvested the blackberries earlier in the day—my first outing since the operation, with the exception of a one-mile ride to the doctor for follow-up two days before. G and I had ventured to a semi-secret spot in Marin County, just north of San Francisco, to procure our wild berries. Though the year before we had hunted and gathered our weight in free fruit, on this Sunday I picked only about one baggy full as I attempted to balance on my crutches and avoid falling into the brambles. Prior to Sunday, I had stood upright for only about 5 minutes at a time at most. Our little berry gathering expedition caused my knee to blow up to the size of a cantaloupe.

When we got home, I popped a few Vicodin and Gabrielle prepared the pies. She did most of the work, but I helped. I seemed to remember a mixing bowl and a spoon in my hand as I sat in the corner with my leg icing...but I *may* have just been using the implements as an improvised drum set while I floated on Vicodin. I'm not sure.

"What's this?" inquired Gabrielle as she pointed to my neck.

"I don't know; I can't see it."

"I think you have blackberry on your neck. How do you get blackberry on your *neck*?"

"I don't know." It might have been the blackberry pie filling I had smeared there 15-minutes before, when I heard her filling the bowl of hot water in the tub. But since I couldn't see it, I obviously couldn't know for sure. In my painkiller-induced haze, I also couldn't be certain if there were any *other* unseen and unsightly blackberry blemishes on my person.

She shook her head disapprovingly and then moved her mouth down to the mystery stain on my neck. "You are such a dirty, dirty boy," she winked as she followed up the initial cleansing with a swipe of the steamy towel.

"Do your lines for me again," I requested. In about three weeks, Gabrielle would be making her fabulous Los Angeles stage debut in a 20-seat theater in Encino. She was missing three days of rehearsal to be my naughty nurse, much appreciated by me, but I imagine not the most popular decision with her cast mates. "Do the scene with the kiss."

"Naaah. I really haven't memorized them yet…and besides, my script's already packed away."

"Then how about tomorrow night…over the phone, once you're back in LA."

"Maybe…I have rehearsal until like 2 in the morning."

Gabrielle's rolling bag was resting in the corner of my bedroom, packed and zipped up, her change of clothes for Monday resting on top. It was nearing 10:30 p.m.; Gabrielle would have to be up at 4 a.m. and on an airport shuttle at 4:30 a.m. so that she could catch a 6:30 Southwest flight and get to her job by 9 in the morning. Her "job job" she called it—the holding pattern… the mindless drudgery an aspiring actress engages in in order to keep the electricity on in a small Santa Monica apartment.

Monday would be hellish for her, an especially extreme day in a relationship filled with over four years of hectic travel schedules. The SF to LA commute was a mere milk run compared with the trans-Continental treks we had done for almost two years. She had traveled tens of thousands of miles to see me over the last several years. I had logged hundreds of thousands of miles—but I, of course, received double mileage credit because I'm a Premiere member.

However, Gabrielle far exceeded me in terms of sheer tonnage transported across those multiple circumferences of the earth. Her rolling bag was nearly exploding, filled with clothes and curlers and accessories. Busting with two dresses, just in case we ended up going for a night on the town. But, that's the *typical* girl thing, if what I see on *Sex and the City* is true.

I love Gabrielle because of the *atypical* girl things. Case in point: the *massive* planter in the far corner of my room. She tugged this huge hunk of masonry all the way from Toronto to bring to me as a house-warming gift when I moved into my flat in San Francisco. G persuaded Air Canada check-in officials, gate attendants, stewardesses and even a pilot to let her carry it on the flight. I don't know how she did it, but they let her strap that terra cotta titan into the seat next to her to fly the 2500 miles to Oakland. *Actually*, she had to carry it to her connecting flight. *Plus*, she had to lug that mother on the train *and then* on a bus to get it to my apartment [please note: as a dutiful boyfriend, I *certainly* would have left work early to pick her up at the airport if I knew the burden she was toting, but she had wanted to surprise me with the gift].

The planter is nice, but is by far *the* most ridiculous gift I have ever received. I still make fun of her for it years later.

It is also by far the most beautiful gift I have ever received. It's a daily reminder of the value of each and every one of those kilometers we have traveled to be together. And an affirmation of the value of every mile we may have to trek in the future. But, I think we're almost there.

✳   ✳   ✳   ✳

I didn't even remember falling asleep. Slumbering through the night for the first time since my operation, I didn't even stir when Gabrielle left three hours before. She must have placed a light blanket on top of me and my elevated and well-padded leg before she went to sleep.

Gabrielle had scrawled a note and left it at the foot of the bed.

> *J—*
> *You went out like a light. I guess that Vicodin really*
> *works. I can't wait to see you in LA in a couple of weeks.*
> *Maybe we can finish your bath then. I checked you out*
> *after you dozed off, and you're just the messiest eater I've*
> *ever seen…you dirty boy.*
> *I love you,*
> *G*

Underneath the note were my….*her* blue pajamas, folded neatly.

1.5

Dedication

Hey. That was pretty cool. That may have been the first short story I've written since I crafted the critically acclaimed "Galactic Warrior: The Quest for the Cosmic Imperium" for Ms. Sweet's fifth grade English class. It was my follow up to "Galactic Warrior: The Revenge of the Photon Brigade."

For the past few years, basically everything I've written has:

- Dealt with cold, hard business strategies,
- Sorely lacked any humor or emotion whatsoever, and
- Been littered with clumps of three bullet points…

…so, it will be a welcome release to write about something else for once. And without any of those bullet points or analytical tables or stock performance charts to spoil the page. I think I finally have a subject truly worth writing about. I'm pretty damn inspired right now.

At least *I think* the thing I completed a few minutes ago was a short story. I mean, it had some characters. It sort of had a plot. It even had some symbolism—did you catch it? It's been a *long* time since I've written anything with symbolism. There wasn't much conflict, though. Not much drama. I have to work on that. All in all, though, I think my morning Vicodin helped me give it a sentimental soft glow that I'm really pretty pleased with.

The plate next to me has turned from a sweet, soupy mélange into a hardened, gummy mess. I'm still just lying here with my knee elevated on the same pillow and in the same B-school boxers. Of course, right now my notebook computer is broiling my greater groinal area and about to burn a hole right through the aforementioned boxers—I really do need to check on this whole laptop computer-sterility linkage. I'm pretty dedicated to my little short story project here, but not that dedicated. So, I guess there's a little drama.

Hey, maybe even this trifling note could be a short story. Yes. That's one more story in the bank. Next story.

2

Consistency

Crik-fwam!

Crik-fwam!

Crik-fwam!

"Dude, you're hooooorrible," laughed Billy as he teed up a range ball three hours ago. "Someone's going to get hurt."

"What are you talking about? In about two months these shots will be flying 200 yards, straight and true," I said as I gingerly bent down to set up my next little white target.

I was reveling in this, sweating up a storm in one of the least demanding sports there is. Billy—one of my best friends from business school—was currently "between engagements," unemployed and killing time after two years as a high-powered investor. He convinced me to set aside my work for the afternoon to join him at the driving range. It was a great call.

In the almost four weeks since my knee surgery, I'd ridden prodigious distances on the exercise cycle and lifted somewhat less than prodigious stacks of weight with my left leg during physical therapy. However, this was the first activity I'd done that required coordination, and I, for one, thought I was doing pretty well.

Crik-fwam!

My left knee was still lacking several degrees of extension. Even with ideal stance, body rotation and arm motion, a perfectly struck ball was out of the question until my knee loosened up. But that would not be for several weeks, and, until that time, I would be launching an extraordinary number of balls into the metal divider that separated my little Astroturf tee box from Billy's.

Crik-fwam!

Crik. No "fwam."

"Hooked it," I laughed.

About 10 bays down, I saw a couple of other patrons talking to the facility's manager and pointing in my direction. They probably thought I was behaving like one of those idiot teenagers who shot put their 12-pound balls down the lane at the bowling alley on a Friday night. I gotta tell you, it kind of looked like that.

The manager walked down to my bay and asked that I refrain from shooting into the metal divider. I apologized, but assured him I was not doing it on purpose and pointed out that my recently repaired knee prevented me from hitting straight shots.

"Why don't you just turn out that way?" the range pro suggested, as he pointed out a set of targets 45 degree to our left.

"Then how will I know if I'm hitting the balls correctly?" I responded. Billy laughed and shook his head; the manager furrowed his brow in confusion. "No, I'm just kidding. I'll aim...out there somewhere," I said as I adjusted my stance.

Plenty of Criks. No more Fwams. Slice after slice after slice. White pellets shot away from my club; I tracked them with my peripheral vision.

"So, how is the writing coming?" Billy asked as he put away his 5-iron and pulled out his Big Bertha Driver.

"Really good. I'm making solid progress," I replied. *Man, I gotta write some new stories—today! I've wasted three weeks as a semi-ambu-latory pseudo-author. Guess I've been building too many PowerPoint decks lately...*

"Good. Good. So, what exactly is the theme of this...*thing* you're writing?" he asked.

"It's about all of the little things that combine to make up the big things in life. Well, you know, it's kind of about...*this*. This is what the book is about," I said, incorporating my best George Costanza hand gestures and voice, imitating the scene from the *Seinfeld* episode where George suggests to Jerry they should write a show about nothing.

"Huh?" Billy doesn't watch nearly enough TV. It's probably his greatest character flaw.

"I guess the main thing is this: I'll be writing about a man's point of view on women, friends, relationships, etc."

"Oh, kind of like *Swingers*?" he asked, referring to the classic 1996 "guys being guys" movie that reshaped the flow of rivers of testosterone in this country.

"Actually, no. Let me put it this way: I want to write about *A* woman, *A* guy, *A* relationship…and all of the necessary etceteras."

"Got it." Billy had become all too versed in a lot of the ins-and-outs of relationships over the last several months. He and his girlfriend had recently gotten back together after a break of several months. I'd spent a lot of time talking about it with him. At the driving range, back when my shots flew a little straighter and farther. Over cocktails after work, when he had a job. At parties, out on the fire escape, away from all of the people. "Make sure you have something in there about your boys, my friend."

"Oh, I'm sure I'll find some way to work you guys in," I answered as I gingerly bent down to tee up the ball for my next lame golf shot. *Note to self,* I thought, *make sure this thing is* not *like* Swingers.

Crik!

✳   ✳   ✳   ✳

After scattering a bucket of range balls in every possible direction, I joined Billy as he partook in the best thing about being an unemployed San Franciscan: drinking a beer in the afternoon sun. I decided to take advantage of the opportunity to engage in a little market research.

"Ever read any short stories?" I asked him.

"Yeah…in junior high," he replied.

I understood what he meant. During the first couple of days of my convalescence, my friend Erica brought me a collection of anecdotes and short stories. At first I thought the book might be a multi-pak with bite-sized nuggets of entertainment and wisdom, but I soon came to view it as the ultimate brain wave neutralizer—a potent sleeping agent when used in combination with Vicodin.

I was overwhelmed by the massive tidal waves of subtlety that ripped through the stories. I'm sure, somewhere out in the world, maybe in a secluded writer's bungalow in Maine or in some dank Hell's Kitchen apartment, there's a writer who is aggressively and potently using the short story form to convey truly powerful, meaningful tales. But as far as I can see, it's just a world where every spider's web glistens with dew, every flickering candle illuminates the mysteries of the heart and every sunrise presages a new world of unlimited potential.

In my readings of these little slice of life tales, I ran across so many people who made their own fruit preserves in their quaint New England kitchens that I thought Erica might have given me a cookbook by accident. Maybe there's just a lot more jam, jelly and marmalade hobbyists out there than I imagined, toiling and boiling and preserving little portions of their lives into hand-sealed jelly jars. But my kitchen isn't any sort of symbol. I'm the kind of guy who has no oven mitts, but seven spatulas.

These short story characters all seem to live in houses populated by antiques of untold value, property that is fading in color—or turning various shades of yellow, gray or brown—even as it is imbued through the decades with more and more meaning. My oldest possessions are the plastic milk crates I stole from behind the Freshman Union during my first year in college. They have been the one constant in my life, protecting my meager assortment of worldly possessions as I moved them from episode to episode: freshman year, sophomore year, junior year, senior year, resume-building job one, resume-enhancing job two, business school year one, resume-rounding-out summer job, business school year two, post-grad job debacle and present-day-career-in-limbo-pay-the-bills status quo.

But short stories have their appeal—especially to a writer. Some writers (and especially *potential* writers) are intimidated by the blank page. I love the blank page; I'm intimidated by the *full* page. That's why I always want to know the ending before I write anything, and often pen the conclusion first. Then, I've found, it's pretty easy to find your way from the beginning to the ending, whether the path is straight or circuitous.

In a way, my life is just a series of short stories right now—I'm sure a lot of people my age feel the same way. There are some constants, threads that tie together the various episodes in our lives, but in general we're a transient lot, jumping from school to job, then sometimes from job to school, and then, all too often, from job to job to job. Apartment to apartment, car lease to car lease, date to date, diet to diet and anecdote to anecdote. I feel I'm a short timer in the extreme, hop-scotching from gig to gig, consulting project to consulting project in this new millennium economy of ours.

I'm living a life with little permanence, and not much in the way of consistency. An existence light on plot, but rife with anecdote. I don't think I'm alone.

I hereby reclaim the short story for its rightful owners. For transients with credit card bills forwarded from four addresses. For twenty- and thirty-somethings who can't quite explain to their mothers what they do for a living. And, in general, for those with short attention spans and poor reading comprehension.

After our beers, Billy and I headed back to our cars, parked right next to each other outside the driving range. "Wanna come with me to a Giants game next week?" he asked. We both peered off a few hundred yards away to sparkling Pacific Bell Park, the home turf the San Francisco Giants needed to defend over the next month in order to squeak into the postseason.

"I think I can rearrange my schedule," I answered.

We both popped our trunks. His ride was a leased VW Golf, the perfect car to fit into the tight spots in parking-challenged SF. My vehicle was my second oldest possession: the vintage, cherry red, original equipment, immaculately maintained 1994 Ford Probe. The most unfortunately named car in history—the best automobile a marketing department ever demolished. Mine was the perfect car to bash its way into the tight spots on the streets of San Francisco, where parking is a full contact sport. *El Probo Rojo* was not exactly a showpiece amongst the fleet of Jags, Beemers and Benzes that sailed through the Bay area, but every parallel parking bruise and bash on its pointy nosed face made it all the more beautiful. To me, at least, these imperfections were the perfect complements to the collection of insectoid freckles the Probe accumulated every few weeks when I drove the 400 miles to Los Angeles to visit Gabrielle.

Billy slammed his hatchback shut and got ready to drive off for a few hours of career networking and 'net surfing. "Well, let me know about your progress on the book."

"I will," I told him. My next destination would be a café, where I'd put in one billable hour and then three hours writing my second short story. "Tell the little lady I said 'hi,' and that I can't wait to see her again soon," I said as I began to close my hatchback.

"Sure, and tell…dude, don't!" he shouted as I pushed the hatch down. Two of my clumsily stowed golf clubs protruded from the trunk. The metal on metal crack made both of us wince. My three iron was fine, but the pitching wedge's head was lopped clean off.

"Well, looks like no chip shots for me for a while," I laughed.

"Dude, you can get that club head put right back on."

"Yeah? You know what? I think this club and I both need a few months to heal."

3

The Most Romantic
Night on Earth

Higher. Higher. Lower. Wiggle and re-adjust. Gabrielle was trying on different sizes of cleavage in preparation for our Sunday morning brunch.

I admired the whole scene from her unmade bed, where I was reclining, my frail leg elevated and my throbbing knee crowned with a Safeway bag full of ice. Watching Gabrielle get ready for any sort of social event was pure entertainment—on every level. Part comedy, part drama, part porn. I could watch for hours...and usually did.

"So, who are these people again?" I asked for the third time in three days—I'd driven to Los Angeles to spend the long weekend with Gabrielle and to see her play. She patiently retraced the branches of the family tree in question, taking me through the various twists and turns until we reached our dining companions, Uncle Bob and Aunt Terri. Gabrielle herself had just been briefed on the connection by her grandfather a few weeks before. She was excited to meet these long lost Los Angeles relatives; it's nice to find a little bit of family in a distant corner of the country.

"OK, which one?" Gabrielle inquired, pointing to the three dresses laid out neatly at the foot of the bed and then the one on her body.

I got up on my elbow and eyed all of the dresses. "The first one," I answered, as if there were any question. Of course, I always said "the first one," because any other utterance would set a dangerous precedent. I would be forced to turn in my Guy Card if I ever said anything else.

But G knows my game. She turned back to the mirror and reshuffled her stuff. "Are you sure? I hear Uncle Bob is rich and that he *loves* cleavage! I think this might be the one."

"I think you need the dress that says: 'Trust me. Invite me over for lobster and steak dinners frequently. Loan me your Range Rover when my boyfriend is in town. Let us swim in your pool, drink your Mai Tais and luxuriate in your hot tub.'"

"See, I think *this* one ad*dresses* your last point [author/boyfriend's note: she emphasized *dresses* since we were talking about dresses. She is so cute]. They have to know the high quality of the people they'll have out by their pool," she chuckled. Then, she shook her head and crinkled her nose. "Eeeew, I'm pushing the 'naughty niece' humor a little too far, aren't I?"

"Shmoopie, you can never push that kind of humor too far. It's a boundless reservoir of mirth."

She unzipped dress number four and let it drop to the 15 year old carpet. She wiggled into the sundress she modeled 15 minutes before and when it was in place, raised her arms and flashed a "Ta-da" that would put Bob Barker's *Price is Right* "Showcase Showdown" models to shame. "So, is this better?"

"It's not a matter of 'better.' It's just a different flavor of perfection."

"Hey! I must have you trained pretty well."

Once we'd reached consensus on the dress, we consulted about shoes, earrings and purses.

"The first ones."

"The first ones."

"The first one."

Finally, with all major issues dealt with to the satisfaction of both parties, Gabrielle turned back toward her mirror and began to sort through her palette of lipstick shades—my cue to get dressed. I donned my "sophisticated enough for LA in the afternoon shirt," my "always appropriate flat front black Dockers" and my "multi-use, all you need is one pair while traveling" shoes. My complex preparations complete, I came up behind her and rested my head on her shoulder and my hand on her stomach. G tried to get me to flinch by wielding her lipstick dangerously close to my mouth.

"Do it. *Don't even doubt* that I'd go to brunch with ruby red lips."

"Oh, I *don't* doubt it," she declared. Then looking at her watch, she gasped. "C'mon, you're making me late. We need to get out of here."

We drove from G's Santa Monica apartment to Beverly Hills. "Do you think they'll have Egg McMuffins at this place?" Gabrielle asked. She always brought up our mutual preferred breakfast whenever we went to a trendy brunch venue.

"Well, it's after 10:30 a.m., so I don't think so. You know full well you can never get an Egg McMuffin after 10:30! But, I'm sure there'll be something you'll like."

"I think that's them over there! Oh, look there's a parking spot right in front!" She clapped. Since we both grew up in cities—or more precisely, hellishly idyllic suburbs—where parking was plentiful and free, we had a visceral distaste for valet parking. We circle blocks endlessly looking for a luscious parking spot. It must be in our genes. I fear for our children.

Bob and Terri ended up getting a good look at my filthy, bug spackled Probe as we pulled up not fifteen feet away from them. I was sure I'd have plenty of ways to redeem myself at brunch. Maybe Uncle Bob and I could exchange some cutting edge business buzzwords.

Gabrielle hugged her family: Bob, Terri and two brand-spanking new second cousins twice removed, ages four and three. I extended warm handshakes to the two parents and squatted down to offer up mini handshakes for the daughters. My knee roared in pain, and I'm sure I looked like an old man when I placed my hand on a fire hydrant to get enough leverage to stand up again. No more squatting for a couple of weeks.

"We thought we'd go to another place a few blocks away. It'll be more fun...and easier with the kids," said Uncle Bob.

"So we'll meet you over there," I responded, flipping my car keys around on my index finger.

"No, we can just walk. It's a few blocks."

I wanted to ask the exact length. After my deep knee bend, if "a few" meant two blocks, I would probably be in only excruciating pain in a few minutes. Four blocks would probably mean blinding pain. Six blocks would most likely feel like an acid-blooded Alien being born right through my six-week-old scar.

"Actually, Jake just had surgery and—" Gabrielle chimed in.

"No, I'm fine. Let's just head over. Get to know the neighborhood," I interrupted. This was G's family—I wanted to make a good impression. *What if Uncle Bob hates wimps? I think she said he's from Texas. Man, I gotta make a good impression. I want to be out eating lobster by that pool.* "I think I can make it, *if* you'll let me push Cindy in the stroller." Ah, a chance to work in a little bit of chivalry—nice. Leaning on the stroller, I thought I might be able to hobble a few hundred yards.

"Aren't you sweet?" declared Terri. And then, turning toward Gabrielle, "Where did you find this one?" It's the question female family members are required to ask to buff up the ego of the boyfriend during a potentially awkward first meeting.

"Oh, that's a very involved story," G answered. *And* a very clichéd literary device. I know, I know.

It might sound weird to say it, but I'm proud of the way we met. We're both proud. And we're *very* proud of the story we've crafted together over the last several years. We have different versions for different audiences. For Bob and Terri, I was sure she'd want go with the sweetest, sappiest version of the story. She'd leave out "I was really much more interested in his friend, at first." I'd omit my retort: "I was just looking for a cute chick and a vacation hook up."

Gabrielle dove into her tale. "Well, I was traveling back from a two-month trek in Africa, but I decided to spend a few days in France before my flight home…" she began. I knew she would cue me when she wanted me to jump in. We walked the *eight* blocks to our new brunch destination, regaling aunts, uncles and little cousins with the tale of the genesis of our relationship.

But in these pages, I think I'll break from the script Gabrielle and I co-wrote and teamed up to perform a hundred times, and instead try out a new take on a couple of interesting nights in Paris.

✳   ✳   ✳   ✳

After two years of business school, a student has probably read 100 case studies dealing with debt and borrowing. Corporate bonds and notes. High yield debt. Junk bonds. Convertible debt. Bank loans. Small business borrowings. Prime rate vs. LIBOR arbitraged derivative debt instruments. Treasury bonds, bills and notes. Leveraged buyouts and recapitalizations. Bankruptcies. Foreign debt, national debts, budget deficits, trade deficits.

We were taught so much, but did we learn anything?

"Hey, I'm already $60,000 in debt. What's $70,000? *Nada*!" I said as I toasted with my buddies somewhere over the North Atlantic. Most fresh MBAs, still warm from the oven and many with their hair still smushed with imprints from their graduation caps, accelerated their debt-o-meters by embarking on outrageous post-school travels. Sample itineraries of some of my classmates included:

- "Let's go on Safari and climb Mount Kilimanjaro and take pictures at the top in our tuxedoes!"
- "Let's do the Appalachian Trail, the Oregon Trail and the Inca Trail!"
- "Let's fly around the world and stop in every country that starts with 'A'!"

My motley crew and I were on our way to Europe to start our six-week trek across the continent, the centerpiece of which would be two weeks in France for the World Cup. My travel-mates were Dennis, a friend from B-School, and Kenneth, my roommate and boon companion from undergrad days, also a newly minted MBA from Wharton.

Paris was spinning with activity. The airport, the train stations, the bars and every little *Place, Boulevard, Rue et Avenue* was filled with the sights and sounds of the World Cup. Around the soccer venues [author's note: call it "football" in international editions], you could always catch the distinctive whiff of *la Coupe du Monde*, an intoxicating mix of cigarette smoke, beer, urine and pepper spray. You could bottle it and call it *Eau d'Hooligan*.

For three glorious exhausting days we followed our routine to the letter (notice the cool European-style timetable):

11 h.: Wake up

11:30-13 h.: Go someplace cultural and write mother postcard from there.

13-15 h: Eat ham and cheese baguette sandwich for lunch. Drink beer. Watch soccer on TV.

15-17 h: Nap and scratch

17-18 h: Stuff selves into subway car with small Tunisians and large Germans.

18-20 h: Watch soccer game in stadium. Drink beer. Try to learn the insulting soccer chants from both nations.

21-22 h: Eat ham and cheese baguette sandwich and/or steak with pat of butter on top for dinner. Drink beer. Watch soccer highlights.

22-23 h: Unload extra tickets for next day's matches. Find Norwegian dudes and take 'em for all they're worth—they're young, naïve, drunk and loaded down with North Sea oil money.

23- 4 h: Journey from club to bar to club to bar searching for some place where men do not outnumber women five-to-one.

On our fourth day, we decided we needed to take a sabbatical from our demanding sporting, social and cultural routine. Plus, we were a little emotionally scarred, after being subjected to a terrifying exhibition of pimply Scottish asses, caught in the crossfire as kilted Glagowers showed their various wares to a covey of English football supporters. We caught a train out of Paris for a day trip, eager to experience the best French culture had to offer. Our destination: EuroDisney.

Our day was filled with wondrous journeys through animatronic and semi-hallucinogenic attractions. We retired to our room at the *Maison de Mickey* for our standard late afternoon nap and the requisite televised football match. Our nighttime agenda included a visit to the mega dance club just outside the theme park's entrance. We hoped that with Paris and its hordes of football devotees 32 kilometers distant, we could find a spot with better social prospects than the testosterone and methane-filled venues we had visited the previous few days.

When we entered the club, we were awestruck by the colorful display before us: a dazzling array of colorful costumes and perfect multi-hued facial frescoes. Unfortunately, the colorful characters were all sweaty men. It had to be either the Gay Olympics or yet another blasted crowd of World Cup fans. Either way, it was not good news for our prospects of finding some female companions.

Trolling through the nightclub was an exercise in futility. Any groups of young women near the bar or dance floor were surrounded by a multicultural mass of malehood. All of the women in the place were surly, which was understandable—they'd been hit on and groped by Spaniards, Italians and Moroccans all night. Scowls were omnipresent. "Jeeez…this is Disney—isn't everyone supposed to be smiling?" I asked my friends.

The packed club was just an international bazaar of body odor. After an hour of being squooshed and pushed, we decided we had had enough.

"This place is ridiculous," said Kenneth. "The ratio here must be 10:1."

"Definitely not a target rich environment," added Dennis. "Should we get out of here? What are we going to do? Go back to the hotel and watch French 'Spanktravision'?"

"I don't think they have that particular pay-per-view channel on Disney properties," I answered. "Look, I'll get us a last round of beers. Let's just go sit in that corner, watch some World Cup highlights and just forget about talking to any more chicks tonight."

"Good call," they both nodded. They fought their way toward the nearly deserted far corner of the club while I pushed through to the bar to order a final round of Budweisers—the drink of choice for the true American in Paris.

By the time I had weaved my way to the rendezvous point, Dennis had already deviated from our agreed-to plan. It looked like he was attempting to insinuate himself into a group of about four women and six guys—well, it *was* the highest concentration of females we'd found all night. His back to Kenneth and me, Dennis was chatting up a young brunette on the edge of the neighboring cluster of twentysomethings. And basically, due to the social geometry of the tables in the corner of the club, Kenneth and I had only each other to talk to.

"So this is a real upgrade," I said to Kenneth. "Didn't we just make a plan? Aren't we going to stick with the plan…one agreed to by all concerned?"

"Eh…whatever," he returned. He'd already powered down his social motor and was content to just sip his beer and stare at the Italy vs. Cameroon highlights. I joined him in staring at the TV—it was either that or stare at Dennis' back.

After a few minutes, Dennis moved so he could try his best lines on another woman on the far side of the group, leaving a yawning gap on the padded bench between the brunette and me. She and I looked across the 3-foot vinyl divide and gave each other matching half nods and half smiles. I aimed my gaze back up at the ceiling mounted TV as the broadcast moved to the clips from the Italy vs. Cameroon match. I'd seen this highlight package three times already, so I took another sip of my Bud and turned to the brunette again.

"Did you try the escargot?" I asked her.

"Excuse me?" she laughed.

"I figured EuroDisney would probably have some good escargot booths. We should have tried to find some. You know…experience some fine French cuisine…"

She nodded and laughed. A little.

"Sort of an awkward gap here. Do you mind…?" I asked as I motioned toward the vacated butt impression between us.

"No, not at all. Please…"

I skootched a little closer. Not as close as Dennis had been, but closer. "I'm Jacob."

"Gabrielle." *Quel joli nom.*

"So you…this whole little party you've got here…" I gestured in the general direction of the other folks in her group.

"Oh, y'know, I just really know my girlfriend Annie over there," she answered, nodding in the direction of the woman whose palm

Dennis was now reading. "These other folks, they're all Annie's friends. They perform in the shows here. She's Cinderella."

"I see. So do we have a Chip or a Dale among us?"

She pointed to the fellow next to her. "Nigel over here is a Donald Duck. Just be thankful he's wearing pants now." *She's funny. Tres drole.*

"And so are you auditioning to be Daisy Duck or something?" I asked, implying two questions.

"No. Oh…NOOOOO!" She answered, shaking her head clandestinely and rolling her eyes. I'd noticed that Nigel was none too happy that outsiders had encroached on his little corner of the club.

"So you just figured you *had to come* to EuroDisney to ride *Les Pirates de la Caribbean…?*"

"I've been traveling through Africa for about two months. I just routed my return trip to Toronto through Paris so I could visit Annie. We worked together on some shows a few years ago."

Hmmmm, an actress. Tres interessante (as long as I was over there, I made a special effort to think in French as much as I could).

We chatted for a few minutes about her visits with the Masai and a close encounter with a hungry hippo during a rafting trip. We watched some of the World Cup highlights and she asked which teams she needed to pay attention to. We talked about the multinational mob scene Paris had become.

I noticed that Dennis had just about exhausted his best material and was getting nowhere with Annie. He looked my way and pumped his thumb back over his shoulder me—the international sign for "I've been shot down. Are you ready to go?" I looked over at Kenneth, watching the highlight reel for the fifth time and beginning to nod off in spite of the club's pulsating music. I nudged him and gave him the same sign. He was very eager to shove off as well.

"Listen," I said, turning back to my new friend. "We're getting together with a few folks tomorrow night in Paris. If you'd like to join in, give me your number and I'll let you know where we're meeting." We'd met a few interesting non-hooligans during our afternoon visits to Paris' cultural attractions and had planned a dinner in the Latin Quarter. A French business school classmate had loaned me his cell phone, which served us well for coordinating the social calendars of new friends we met in Paris and all over France (when I later received a $1500 bill for three weeks of calls, I wished I had learned the French phrase for "roaming charges").

"Yeah. That'd be fun. Annie's working all the time and hasn't been able to go out at all in Paris." I handed her a pen and stole the Disney drink special menu from its plastic holder for her to write her info on. She scrawled her name and number. "So, I'll hear from you tomorrow afternoon."

"Count on it."

And that was it. Ten minutes. Very mundane stuff. Dennis, Kenneth and I trekked back to the hotel. We didn't even do a post-game wrap up of the night—nothing more was said of our discussions with these Disney characters and the random Canadian visitor until the next afternoon.

During our afternoon *baguette, jambon et fromage* sandwich break, I retrieved the scraps of paper bearing the names and numbers of the Anglophones we had met during our first few days in Paris. We had the phone numbers for two great Kiwi couples on the free English language guide to the Louvre. On a map of Paris' Jewish Quarter, we had the number of four Australian women Dennis had chatted up outside of a Holocaust art exhibit. And, of course, there was the number of the young Canadian scratched on the back of Disney's drink menu.

I connected with the New Zealanders and the Australians in their hotel rooms after a couple of tries. When I called Gabrielle, a French answering machine politely requested that I leave a message. "Hi. This is Jake…from Disney…I hope I'm reaching the right person, and I hope you're still able to meet up with our little group tonight…" I entrusted the answering machine the directions to our chosen restaurant.

"Do you think she gave you a real number?" asked Kenneth.

"Who knows? Maybe some pair of married 50-year old Parisians will be joining us for dinner," I answered.

At around 7 p.m., we reached the eatery—a cramped Tapas joint flooded with wafts of garlic and charred meat—and immediately ordered up a pitcher of sangria. Within a few minutes, the Aussie quartet arrived, squeezing in around our table in the middle of the restaurant. We started comparing notes with them about our travel experiences. As was usually the case with Australians, the time each of them had spent trekking and working overseas was astounding. *How does anything get done in that country? Does anyone between twenty and thirty actually live there? Is every scuba instructor in the world an Aussie?*

After pouring a round of sangria for the table, I noticed a woman with a sheer dark blue top and tight black pants standing near the entrance to the restaurant, scanning the tables. The retreating sun backlit her through the ancient lead-paned windows. It took a moment for me to realize it was Gabrielle. We had both been jammed in behind tables at EuroDisney, so I hadn't gotten a full view of her. She was intimidatingly beautiful.

Gabrielle didn't recognize our band of chatty travelers upon first inspection; she probably wasn't looking for a table with four bronzed blonde women. I gave her a wink and a two fingered "we're the ones you're looking for" wave.

Her face lit up and she responded with a wave of her own. Gabrielle's hand slammed into the bottom of a tray loaded with a pitcher of sangria and ice-filled tumblers. The waiter valiantly tried to secure his cargo, but a hailstorm of ice exploded from his tray and the tumblers tumbled to the floor. As the pitcher slid back toward him on his unbalanced tray, crimson liquid sloshed onto his pristine white shirt. Slices of lemon and orange whizzed by—just like on that old Froot Loops commercial. The *garcon* managed to catch the half-filled decanter, wedging it in between his chin, his chest and the dripping tray. Gabrielle relieved him of the pitcher with one hand and stole a napkin from a pair of diners at a nearby table. She began to wipe the sangria from the waiter's face, her own face contorted with the most adorable expression of terror I'd ever seen.

"She's with us," I announced to the Australians, who along with the rest of the diners had been gawking at the wreckage.

It was a shot right out of a dozen sitcoms, but it was the first time *I* had seen it performed live. After the flawlessly executed scene of slapstick, Gabrielle wove her way to our table, half-filled pitcher and pink and white napkin still in hand. "Sooooo…I guess drinks are on me," she said, placing the remaining sangria on our table and dabbing away at her forehead with the white corner of the napkin. She introduced herself to the august assemblage.

God, she was freaking Goldie Hawn. The young Goldie Hawn. She was Jennifer Aniston. She was a gorgeous comic genius. And she was topping off my glass with sangria.

"You make quite a second impression," I laughed as she filled me up. "Good thing we didn't go to the fondue place we originally picked out. Boiling oil, bubbling cheese…"

"Yeah. My entrance was already *cheesy* enough," she said, regretting the attempt at humor even before she had finished the sentence.

For the next two hours our group shared plate after plate of ceviche, patatas bravas and paella…and massive volumes of sweet sangria. Gabrielle was—by several years—the youngest member of the table, but more than held her own even when the loquacious Kiwis arrived on the scene. Everyone was digging her stories from her recently completed excursion to Africa.

We flung a huge pile of francs on the table and then marched as a group—a pretty serpentine march after our night of imbibing—to a quiet bar in the Quarter. We brought the party with us; our troop drank and gabbed and sang for hours. I think one of our number even knew the French national anthem, *La Marseillaise*—the rest of us just boomed out nasally syllables as we joined in.

Around 3 a.m., it was obvious folks were just about *finis*. Dennis asked Gabrielle if she wanted to share a cab with us—her lodgings were about a mile from ours. Like a fool, I opened the door to the cab for Gabrielle and my traveling companions. As they piled in, my sangria saturated brain realized that I would be riding shotgun. *Merde*.

Dennis, Kenneth and Gabrielle had a gay old time in the backseat of the taxi. I just watched the scenery go by and marveled at the brillo pad like mustache worn by our driver, Hassan. *That thing must weigh a pound at least.*

We reached Gabrielle's billet after about 15 minutes—I think Hassan took the scenic route. She gave Dennis and Kenneth huge hugs and climbed over Dennis to get out of the car. Hassan started to roll away, but Gabrielle tapped on my passenger-side window. I cranked the window down.

"Jake, thanks so much for inviting me tonight. It was so much fun!" she said.

"Well, I think most of the people are getting together again tomorrow. Are you in?"

"Yes! Ring me here!" she said as she backed away toward the building's front door. Hassan started rolling again.

Gabrielle leaned back toward the car and extended her hand toward the open passenger side window. *Ah, great. A nice firm handshake.* I reached my hand out the window to grasp hers. I don't know whether it was the sangria or the motion of the car, but I ended up grabbing her fingers not with the normal handshake hold, but with the "charmed, I'm sure, m'lady…may I kiss this lovely delicate hand and then work my way up to your sublime neck and glorious lips"-sort of grip. You know the one.

"Well, yeah…nice hanging out with you," she said.

"Me, too. I mean you, too. I mean *nice hanging out with you, too*," I responded, pumping her hand a couple of times in spite of our strange grip. Gabrielle jingled her keys in her left hand, gave a final wave to everyone with her right and then bounced up the stairs toward the apartment's entrance.

The next day, Dennis, Kenneth and I stuck with our normal routine, with the exception of substituting roast beef baguette sandwiches for our normal ham and cheese. During our afternoon soccer break in a local pub, I put in calls to our crew from the previous night. One of the Kiwi couples—Julie and Rob—planned on joining us at 8 p.m. for dinner and the France-Saudi Arabia match on television. Two of the Aussies said they would come by for a few pints. And Gabrielle called back to say she planned on coming by around 11.

While Dennis, Kenneth and I rode in the Metro to our dinner venue, I coordinated with them on a plan for the evening. "Hey, guys. I think I might try to get some alone time with that girl Gabrielle tonight," I stated. "So, if I get separated…if I get lost…accidentally-on purpose…don't try to find me."

"So you automatically get the cute one?" asked Kenneth.

"Yeah, what's up with that?" added Dennis.

I was prepared to put forth my airtight well-reasoned argument, predicated on the "guy code" logic that I was the one who had gotten her number originally. Oh, and I was the one who was paying for this cell phone. Oh, and I had made all of the arrangements for our World Cup excursion. But before I had advanced more than a few words into my diatribe, my friends interrupted.

"We're just messing with you. Go get her," said Kenneth. "Geez, you couldn't have been more obvious last night."

"Yeah, don't worry. We've got your back," added Dennis.

We exited the Metro very near our destination, an anonymous little restaurant whose only qualifications were its many television sets and its proximity to the Champs-Elysees, Paris' main thoroughfare, filled with history and drunken rabble. After dining on *steak frites* with Rob and Julie, we were joined by the two Australian ladies during the second half of the soccer match. France was destroying the Saudis, and the French dining in our midst were already dancing around the restaurant celebrating the team's advance into the second round of the World Cup. As the final minutes of the match ticked away, my cell phone vibrated.

"Hi.......ielle.....find....crowd...." I could only make out scraps. She was obviously calling from a payphone in the midst of some mob scene.

"I can't hear you. I don't know if you can hear me…" I began. I gave the name of the restaurant and the Metro stop and told her the group would wait outside for her.

"….leven....there.....wearing......ello?"

"I really can't hear you." I repeated our location information again. "Hello?" There was no more crowd cacophony on the other end of the line. She had obviously comprehended the info, or had given up.

Our merry band ventured out the doors of the eatery after the game, where we joined tens of thousands of other merry bands who were descending on the Right Bank. The partying commenced in earnest as mobs crowded the wide sidewalks, and fleets of Citroens and Peugeots jammed the Champs-Elysees, their pubescent horns squeaking out the most grating of honks. We purchased some Heinekens from a street vendor and watched the parade of waving tricolors for several minutes.

"Do you have one for me?" inquired a voice not two feet away. I wheeled around—it was Gabrielle. "Any more Heinies?"

"Uh, oh yeah. Hi, by the way. C'mon, the beer guy's right over here. Hey everybody, Gabrielle's here!" I yelled to the rest of the group, a few meters away.

"We know! She already came by to say 'hello'!" said Dennis.

She did? I'm the last "hello"? Wait...I didn't even get a hello. Am I just the guy holding the cell phone? Am I just the guy closest to the beers?

Once we'd procured a beer for Gabrielle, our gang started proceeding en masse west on the Champs-Elysees toward l'Arc de Triomphe, the focal point for every French victory celebration [note to reader: please insert your own French military joke here]. Just like the night before, we got the chance to boom out a few bars of *la Marseillaise* with various huddles of drunken Frenchmen and women as we ambled up the boulevard.

I approached Dennis, and confided, "I think I'm going to try to get lost now."

"So, game on? Godspeed to you."

"Thanks. Maybe you guys could find some festivities on the other side of the street...or maybe near the Louvre..."

"Gotcha."

"So who needs another beer," I asked as I turned toward the group. Almost everyone had grabbed one about three minutes earlier from a vendor we had just passed. Gabrielle and I were the only ones with empties.

"I'm out," responded Gabrielle. *Excellent. It's all falling into place.* "Wanna go get some more?"

"Yeah, let's grab some from that one guy. I think he's like 20 meters back up the street." I always tried to use the metric system whenever I was in France.

The sidewalk next to the Champs-Elysees had become a swamp of humanity; it took five minutes to trudge down to the beer vendor, about 50 meters up the street. I loaded my fleece's pockets with beers—supposedly for the group—and we started back toward the street lamp where our mates had been congregating.

Then I spied an opportunity. "Oh, look, a juggler. Don't you love jugglers?" I asked.

"I guess. Only if they're flinging chain saws, though."

"Well, let's give this guy a minute. Maybe he'll get to the dangerous stuff soon." This gambit would buy me precious minutes. By the time we got back, Dennis would have the group in a jumble of soccer fans far, far away.

"Ah, screw it!" I said after a few minutes. "No chain saws. No flames. No ginsus. Whatta gyp. These guys need to import some American juggling know-how!"

"I agree. And they call themselves 'cultured'..." Gabrielle deadpanned as we traveled the final few meters toward our old gathering spot. "Where is everybody?"

"They probably just went to buy some nachos or corndogs or something. Kenneth is a big fan of French cuisine. We should probably wait here." And thus, we were lost...

...for all of three seconds. "Oh there they are!" said Gabrielle, pointing to a spot on the far side of the avenue, directly opposite our location. "I see Dennis and Kenneth's hats."

"Well, let's get over there." My travel mates were wearing their red Team USA hats; their *chapeaux* might as well have been signal flares. Gabrielle and I froggered it across the bustling avenue toward our group.

"We thought we'd lost you," we said to Dennis and Kenneth, almost in unison, she with a relieved smile, me with a "fuck you" scowl.

"Here, I got beers for everyone," I smiled, handing some to our friends from down under before tossing a well-shaken can to Dennis.

Gabrielle chatted with Julie and Rob while Dennis entertained our two Aussie guests. I pulled Kenneth aside. "Five hundred fucking thousand Frenchies out here and you guys get lost *right across the street*? C'mon, help a brother out here."

"What's in it for me?"

"The last half of this beer. Resale value: 3 francs. Minimal back-wash."

"You're a persuasive bargainer. OK, I'll do it. Just go talk to your lady."

Gabrielle was a few meters away, drawn by the commotion as some cops busted a couple of Algerians for selling knock-off World Cup merchandise. The contents of the police paddy wagon idling nearby looked like an all-star squad of soccer hooliganism, with your requisite array of German, English and Dutch lads. Once the authorities packed up their newest cargo, Gabrielle and I turned back to the spot where we left our posse.

"Where did they go?" asked Gabrielle, as we examined the group of French teenagers now occupying our former sidewalk space.

"I have no idea. Yow! Let's move!" I yelled as the teenagers ignited a battery of Roman candles in the midst of the crush. As sparks lit up the sky and danced on the sidewalk, I hustled us off toward the Arc de Triomphe.

"So, should we look for them? It's a nut house here, but we found 'em once," stated Gabrielle.

"Well, I have the phone. If they really want to find us, they'll call," I said, shaking my Nokia. "I think Dennis might have wanted some privacy. He's taken quite a shine to that Julie."

"And I think Kenneth has taken quite a shine to that Rob—big strapping rugby guy that he is."

"Exactly."

"Or maybe your buddies are just trying to get rid of you. Maybe they don't like you so much…" she said as she crinkled her nose.

"I've had my suspicions. Those bastards…jettisoning me *deux fois* in one night."

She laughed and shook her head. I laughed, shrugged my shoulders and held my palms up in the classic "I dunno" pose.

"Well, it wouldn't be so bad to get lost with me, would it?" I asked her.

"No, not so bad at all. C'mon, we have a lot of Paris to get lost in," she smiled as she tugged me toward a nearby fire breathing performance.

Over the next hour, we continued our scavenger hunt for freaks throughout the Champs-Elysees crowd. The throng was noticeably thinner but still rambunctious as we ventured east on the avenue to find a quieter locale. We found a café in a strategically placed enclave which allowed us to observe the remnants of the revelry but still converse at a sane decibel level. When the somnambulant waitress finally decided to come by—though neither of us was in any hurry to get out of there—we requested a bottle of Pinot Noir and an order of tira misu to share.

We drew out our dining experience, taking tiny, infrequent bites from our dessert. Our conversation meandered easily through topic after topic, pausing only to deal with a rose peddler. And then another rose peddler. And then another rose peddler. The salespeople came in many shapes and sizes—adorable children, hustling teens and older ladies—and shoved their bountiful bouquets in our faces every two minutes or so.

"Is there a horticultural convention or something around here?" I laughed.

"Maybe you just look like a real sucker."

"We'll see about that!" I waved down a member of the rosy horde and beckoned her over to our table. "*Je voudrais acheter la rose la plus belle pour cette femme, s'il vous plait.*" Actually, I'm sure I butchered the grammar, but I know my accent was impeccable.

The flower saleswomen handed Gabrielle the red rose. Definitely the best purchase of the night. Whenever an overeager entrepreneur approached us after that, I borrowed the rose from Gabrielle to repel the interloper. A silver cross fends off vampires; a fresh rose—wielded properly—fends off flower peddlers.

Gabrielle and I stayed at the café for an hour and a half all told, watching the post-game parade wind down to a trickle of tricolors. We then hailed a taxi to take us to…wherever.

Our cabbie sped though wide avenues and ancient goat paths, not applying the brakes until we reached the destination he chose for us. Sacre Coeur's dome glowed in the pitch-black sky; a swarm of punkers, skateboarders, backpackers and Franco-gangsta rap types orbited the site like moths drawn to a porch light.

We sat down on the stairs, and soaked in the scene. Pulling out a tumbler I lifted from the café, I poured Gabrielle a small glass of wine from the midget bottle I had purchased from a Champs-Elysees street vendor. Nearby, an unwashed sweatshirted teen with dreadlock nubs worked feverishly on a chalk drawing that could only have been the work of an acid addled mind. The artist ascended from the sidewalk as his oeuvre expanded, bringing his colorful scene closer to us minute by minute.

"I think we're about to become a work of art. Or something that *kind of* looks like art," laughed Gabrielle as she eyed the nascent Rasta drawing behind us on the steps. Just before we were enveloped in the scene, we skipped out through the last gap in the Technicolor chalk explosion around us.

Having polished off our small bottle of wine, we sought out our next adventure. Just down the hill from Sacre Coeur, a fenced off park beckoned. We turned over a trash can so we could climb over the wrought iron barrier before us. A merry-go-round stood motionless in front of us, Lippenzaners frozen in mid-cantor and Appaloosas captured in full gallop. I tried to find the power switch, but the control panel was protected by a heavy padlock.

Gabrielle and I climbed atop two horses that were neck and neck in their static race. We talked for about ten minutes and then, in mid-sentence, she descended from her gray nag and jumped on a speedier looking mount just in front of her. I, in turn, advanced to the powerful Arabian a few feet away, pulling even in our glacial pursuit. Gabrielle then moved up to a braying white stallion. As I jumped off the Arabian, she quickly dismounted her steed, and the race was on.

Even as we continued our conversation without pause, I started chasing her around the carousel. Each of us thought we could gain the upper hand if we could get the other talking, stealing precious breaths from the competition's lungs.

"So tell me about your life up until now…" I huffed.

"You know, I was born, I grew taller…and here I am. Tell me about…all of your…hopes and dreams."

"I believe…the children are our future.   So, you're an actress…what are your favorite…fifty movies of all time?"

"All 27 James Bond movies…the 12 Rocky sequels…eight *Star Trek* flicks…four *Star Wars* films…and *Casablanca*." Her math was off, but her strategy was brilliant. "So, what…are your thoughts…on the Middle East?"

And so it went. I thought it best not to work up too much of a sweat so early in our evening—it was only 4 a.m. after all—so I decided to graciously bow out. "You win. Your athletic prowess is astounding," I admitted, dabbing my sweaty brow with my sleeve. "You even managed to hold onto the rose."

"Ah, I could never let this go," she said earnestly, bopping me on the nose gently with the bloom. "What if another gypsy flower peddler tries to harass us?"

We walked down the incline of the hillside park and came upon another iron gate, a little more intimidating than the one we had already scaled. I climbed up to the cornice, wedged my foot between the fence's heavy iron bars, and helped Gabrielle ascend. Ornamental spears dug into my skin as I guided her over the top of the fence, providing a little pain to help keep me awake as I prepared for the next phase of the evening/morning.

Once we descended (and after I confirmed that I had not committed romantic or reproductive *seppuku* on the fence's sharp posts), Gabrielle and I checked our location on a street map.

"Hey, I think we're actually pretty close to some fun and games," I declared as I pulled out a pamphlet foisted upon me by a greasy and aggressive tout a couple of hours before. I pointed to the ad for the all night party hosted by DJ Krazeee, featuring Blaq Attaq and *Deux Jacques Chaque Heure*. "Look, this place is just a couple of blocks away. Sounds like a good way to wind down the evening."

It took us only two minutes to find the underground club, which was…underground. We descended into the smoky cavern, a wall of body heat welcoming us inside. Though probably less crowded than a couple of hours earlier, the club was still hopping. DJ Krazeee was in full effect, although, from what I gathered, only one of the deux Jacques was still hanging around.

I went to the bar to get us drinks while Gabrielle hovered on the periphery of the dance floor. When I returned with cocktails in hand 90 seconds later, she was talking with a very drunk Argentinean gentleman. "Oh, this is my favorite song! Let's dance," exclaimed Gabrielle as she pulled the drinks out of my hand, set them on a vacant table nearby and pulled me onto the dance floor. I think DJ Krazeee was spinning a techno-rap version of Air Supply's "Making Love out of Nothing at All."

About 90 seconds later, our friendly neighborhood Argentinean was doing a one-man *lambada* right next to us. "Can I...to dance you?" he asked over the booming bass line.

"Sure thing," I answered as I put my right hand on the small of his back, grabbed his right hand in my left and waltzed him in the direction of the bar. I pulled out a chunk of crushed franc notes and asked the bar tendress to get him two of whatever he was drinking. I gave him a pat on the back, wished him *bonne chance* and returned to Gabrielle on the dance floor.

We danced for about 90 seconds more, our sweaty, shiny foreheads imitating in miniature the light show in the steamy club. I slowed down our dancing pace by a beat, and then by another beat; we were nearly slow dancing in spite of the fast, grinding tempo. I looked deeply into her eyes and touched her cheek as our dance continued decelerating. I leaned my head down and she angled her mouth, awaiting our first kiss. But her eyes stared off twenty feet into the distance.

"Eeeeww. He's still watching us," she winced, jutting her chin to point back in the direction of our *amigo*.

I walked back over to the bar, shaking my head and doing the international sign for "tssk, tssk, tssk" with my fingers. "Friend, I have danced with you *and* bought you *dos drinkos*," I explained as I put my arm around the Argie's shoulders. "If you stop watching us, I promise you: I will cheer for Argentina if you play England in this World Cup."

"Yes! Beckham sucks!" he responded.

"*Si*! Beckham sucks!" I agreed, ten days before I found out who Beckham was. "So, we're agreed." The Argentinean took his two drinks and found another nice couple to stalk.

I returned to Gabrielle and recommenced our slow/fast dance as "Baby Got Back" shook the club. I pulled her closer and leaned my head down again. She could feel the weight of the moment. "I don't know if I'm the girl you're looking for tonight," she said as our mouths were two inches apart.

"Maybe that's why I found you," I answered.

Hey, that's pretty damn good, I thought. I had drawn my response from the "I'll just baffle you with a reversal of drunken logic" school of thought.

You know…"We're being so bad"/ "Then how come it feels so good?".

Or…"This is so wrong."/ "Then how come it feels so right?".

"Maybe that's why I found you." The words hung out there. Or maybe I said them a second time, in case she didn't hear me the first time. I don't know.

She put her hand on the back of my head and pulled me closer. We shared the first of our thousand kisses.

After a few more dances and a few more embraces, we left the club. The streets of Paris were humming with the activities of garbage men, newspaper delivery trucks and shopkeepers. The pitch black of the night we shared together was transforming into a steel blue, foretelling the sunrise maybe an hour away.

As we examined the scene, the rusted steel gate shielding a bakery/café noisily sprang off the ground a few feet away from us. "Bonjour," the proprietor said to the two startled North Americans. We ordered *café au lait*, croissants and brioches and watched the Paris morning take shape by the edge of some *boulevard* the street sweepers had not yet visited. We ate in relative quiet. I looked over at her. Again and again.

My experience in the world of romance was not so profound. I'd dated—not so much, but I'd dated. I understood the progression of first, second and third dates. I had gotten numbers at parties, pulled digits at bars. I'd done dinner. I'd done dinner and a movie. I'd done dinner and dancing.

There had been times…on vacation…at a wedding…in New Orleans…where I'd gone through the progression of first date through *sixth date* all in one night.

But I realized, as I stole glances at this woman next to me, I had no idea what romance was until that night in Paris.

"Cue the violins," you say. But that's my point. There were no violins. There was a rose, yeah. But there were sweaty soccer fans, fire-eaters, gypsies, acid-crazed freaks, Parisian hip-hop wannabes and leering Argentineans, as well. There were grand plans, schemes gone awry, calculated moments of spontaneity and accidental flashes of brilliance. This was the first time I had embraced every twist and turn, everything beautiful and funny and embarrassing and stupid.

Pardon my hyperbole, but as I looked over at Gabrielle again, I had the warm feeling that I might have enjoyed the most romantic night on earth. Before this, that thought had never crossed my mind as I kissed a woman goodnight or turned out the lights to join someone in bed.

But, if there were an essay contest for the most romantic night on earth for this particular square on June's calendar page, I felt for the first time in my life, I had a legitimate entry. Maybe the most romantic night on earth on another evening belonged to a couple in a run-down tenement in Beijing, who stared into each other's eyes after both feeling they'd conceived the one child allowed them by law. Some other night in the past, it belonged to two German lovers, reunited after 20 years when the Berlin Wall crashed down.

But, I'm sure at some point, it belonged to two teens in rural Iowa experiencing their first kiss. Or two strangers at Club Med who found some real connection after winning the limbo contest. Maybe, on this night, it belonged to two people who were brought together by soccer hooligans, Donald Duck, Budweisers and "Baby Got Back." Two people who strolled the Champs-Elysees, enjoyed fantastic red wine, danced like children around a carousel and shared breakfast as the sky above them transformed from steel blue into a gorgeous tableau of pink and salmon hues.

Maybe we were quiet because we could both barely keep our eyes
open. After almost landing face first in my *café au lait*, I looked over
at Gabrielle as she nearly replicated the maneuver. Our night was definitely over. I ruffled her hair in a move that might have been a little
too familiar and said, "Let me hail you a cab." One raised arm and
five seconds later, a taxi screeched to a halt in front of the bakery.

I opened the door for her and we shared a quick kiss, maybe both
feeling a little more awkward in the light of the approaching morning.
She held out the rose, shook her head just a little and grinned a "what
did we just do?" grin. "I'll call you," she said.

"I'll have the phone," I responded, as I reached into my pocket
and turned the Nokia's power back on.

✳ ✳ ✳ ✳

"Eat your French toast!" ordered Aunt Terri.

"I don't like French toast!" retorted Cindy, in much the same tone
as she said, "I don't like oatmeal" thirty minutes before.

Uncle Bob had already paid—I had made the perfunctory grab
for my wallet, but, he'd been just a little too fast for me…damn! The
two parents each smooshed one child's face roughly with wet naps to
remove all traces of jelly and syrup from the pudgy cheeks.

I earned some points again for pushing the stroller back to our
original rendezvous position, my knee creaking and wailing every step
of the way. But, I thought we'd accomplished our mission and would
soon be dining poolside as cabana boys and girls attended to our every
need. We exchanged hugs and hearty handshakes as appropriate, and
said goodbye to G's new Los Angeles family.

"So, I guess I'm driving back…" she said as I practically forced
the keys into her hand.

"You better believe it!" I answered as I fell into the passenger seat,
rolled down the window and propped my leg up on the external
rearview mirror. She put the car in gear and pulled out of our nearly-
primo parking spot. "Y'know, you forgot the part about the rose this
time," I told her.

"I know, I know," she laughed as she bounced on her seat and pounded her forehead, ever the perfectionist actress. "I'll make sure I get it right."

"You better, or I'll have to jump in next time. And you never know what compromising details I'll throw in," I lectured with my best headmaster voice as my knee throbbed with every heartbeat. "Man...I picked the wrong week to give up Vicodin."

4

Working the Leisure Circuit

This morning, my commute began at 7:42 a.m. and ended at 7:45 a.m. It took longer than usual—I had to open up a new tube of toothpaste before conducting my normal en route oral hygiene regimen. My office—a.k.a., the kitchen nook—looked like a mini-Stonehenge, with tall stacks of articles, research reports and presentation decks circling my small desk.

The first order of the day was an interview with the co-founder of an aggressive Midwest technology company about which I was writing an article. My typed list of questions and possible follow-ups sat at the top of the shortest paper monolith. I dialed the big guy's assistant. My highest priority of the last several weeks had been to develop a strong rapport with this woman, a critical task in getting on this fellow's calendar during the current millennium.

"How's the ankle doing?" she asked. For the last several weeks I had kept her up to date on my knee rehab—her sister was a physical therapist. "Those ankles can be tricky." Ankle…knee…whatever. At least she takes pity on the infirm.

"The ankle is recovering just great. Thanks. I'm going to do my rehab exercises right after this call," I replied.

"That's excellent. Stick with it! Well, I'll get him right now. He's ready."

The local radio station stood in for the normal hold music. A commercial for the Illinois State Fair. The fair had always been a bittersweet event during my boyhood in neighboring Indiana, a blast of fun in the waning days of our summer vacation. Elephant ears. Corn on the cob. People in John Deere caps. The fair kept you in touch with the real world.

Click. "Aaaaallright, so what are we doing here?" boomed the entrepreneur.

I explained what his company's PR department had probably already explained to him: who I was...some of the work I'd done...some of the people I'd worked with...the background of the article I was working on. Basically it boiled down to: *If you talk to me, you'll get to have five quotes and your picture in another national publication.*

"Can I put you on speaker phone...so I can record and take notes?" I asked.

"No problem."

And so our game of verbal tennis began. A 15-second question, followed by a 3-5 minute answer, then back for the next 15-second question. Of course, I had to chime in regularly with a well-timed "uh-huh" or "right, right."

"The company's original product was timed perfectly and hit a sweet spot in the marketplace, but how would you respond to critics who say that all of the bells and whistles on version 2.0 make it too expensive and too complicated for most customers?" I had no idea if any critics had actually said that.

"Well, they just don't understand where technology's headed these days. You have to have more features, more speed, more power..."

I snuck a bite of toast as he started his answer, well before I would have to chip in with a "right, right." *Oh, man!* A large dollop of grape jelly slid off and fell right onto my boxer shorts. A couple of purple globs landed on my big toe.

"But is your company going to be a player in the emerging small and medium sized business marketplace?" I asked.

"We really see the Fortune 1000 as our main targets right now. There will be all kinds of smaller software firms who will slap together something for medium-sized businesses, but we..." I took notes while I wiped the Smuckers from my toe.

After 45 minutes of business-speak and then a little Midwest-bonding, we wrapped up the call. I grabbed my black ballistic nylon Tumi briefcase and packed up my laptop, some enthralling journal articles and a few other papers I would need during the day. I was going to bust out of the confines of the kitchen office and see the world. The prototypical wireless-enabled-mobile-business-warrior of the 21st Century, that's me.

In my room, I donned my new Dri-fit workout attire and the first pair of shorts I saw, a freebie I received from one of the clubs at business school. After cramming a few "smart casual" basics into the expandable compartment of my briefcase, I limped off to the gym.

My cell phone rang as I was heading out the door. Ah, the perfect traveling companion for my 10-minute walk to the gym. "Jacob Tanner," I answered crisply—Gabrielle loved the no nonsense business greeting.

"HIIII-iii," she exclaimed. Even though I'd used the term in innumerable marketing consulting projects, I didn't really understand what the word "resonate" meant until I heard Gabrielle's "HIIII-iii." It just fit well in my ears. "How did the interview go? Did you really nail him? Did you kick his ass?"

"No, I'm a total pushover—no ass-kicking today. I just want YOU to think I'm a tough bastard," I responded. "He's from Illinois—we talked a little Big Ten basketball at the end."

"Illinois, that's next to Idaho, right?" she joked. She knew I had a complex about the way people from both coasts saw the middle of the country as a flat checkerboard of wheat fields, cornfields and strip malls. She had worked hard to memorize the placement of all of the "I" states, a level of geographic knowledge that had somehow escaped most of the young intellectual elite in our country. "Listen, I need to get back to work now, but just wanted to say 'hi.' I have a *dentist's* appointment during lunch today and it might run over into my afternoon."

"Is this a commercial 'dentist', a voice-over 'dentist' or a theatrical 'dentist'?" I asked. I worried her boss might take her off of the company dental plan before she lined up an agent.

"Hmmmm…I'd have to say I would choose number one," she said in her cryptic workplace code. I heard her other line—actually her boss's line—ringing. "OK! Gotta go! I I—"

I hoped the other caller didn't get the "—ove you" intended for me.

I arrived at my gym, the minimalist Titan Fitness on the Marina's Chestnut Street. At this time of day, Titan was populated by stay-at-home moms and dads, a few grad students and a couple denizens of home offices like myself. Plus, a few unemployed young professionals, emerging from their dank job search caves. Actually the mid-morning crowd was lightening up a bit—maybe San Francisco was getting over its two-year post dot com hangover. In the early evening, the place was packed with young professionals—I-bankers, venture capitalists, brand managers, retail buyers and the like. You have to wait so long for any apparatus, there is more than ample time for any professional, social or romantic networking you care to do. I'm just fine with the mid-morning scene, low-profile in the extreme.

I grabbed a few computer printouts and then stowed my mobile office/gym bag in the locker room. I began reading the background material for a new consulting project as I sat down at the stationary bike. The plan was to spend a billable hour reading and rehabbing on the bike and the elliptical trainer. Drops of sweat pooled with orange highlighter ink as I ratcheted the resistance up to the highest level I had attempted since my operation.

Then, I hit the weights, putting up stacks of plates that would put most fourth grade girls to shame. I hoped the Frankenstein-like scar bisecting my kneecap would signal to passers-by that I'm usually much more studly.

After nearly a hundred minutes of exercises and billables, I showered up and pulled my change of clothes out of the satchel. I donned a dark blue pullover and well-creased khakis—jamming them in my bag added horizontal creases to the factory-installed vertical ones.

My next stop was the Grove, a densely packed afternoon hotspot. Mobs of stroller-wielding mothers jammed the tables outside the café, periodically feeding bits of marble cake to their writhing human cargo. At least a half dozen dogs—ranging from Dachshunds to

Dobermans—usually guarded the exterior, whether tied to parking meters or huddled beneath tables. This was quite the sniffing hotspot as well.

Inside, an impressive array of laptops dominated the entire western wall of the place, power cords extending like vines from outlets six feet off the ground. I ordered a Cuban sandwich and Diet Coke and then secured my own place amongst the Dells. My own laptop humming, I started writing about the time I dropped jelly on my boxers during a phone interview with a technology bigwig.

A high number of the usual suspects were back for lunch again, gaggles of quasi- and pseudo-employed San Franciscans—most of the purely *un*-employed have moved back to Minneapolis or embarked on a six-month sojourn to Laos and Cambodia. The *quasi*-employed spend at least some of their time doing something *approximating* work—maybe helping a rich investor scope out a few entrepreneurial opportunities for ten hours per week. Perhaps diving into community service activities—the sort they hadn't engaged in since they filled the gaping holes in their grad school applications by tutoring immigrants or painting over graffiti on the walls of public schools.

The *pseudo*-employed put up more of a veneer, an obfuscating curtain of grand plans. They always seem to be working on a *huge top secret* project, often e-mailing friends cryptic messages to see if anyone has connections in the plumbing supply industry or knowledge of the bituminous coal mining sector or experience dealing with the Chinese space program.

Me? I'm *semi*-employed. I'm actually doing real work...and actually getting paid. I'm just not doing it all the time—I don't know, maybe I'm just living up to half of my potential. But, I've done it for almost two years now, staying "flexibly" employed while many friends were laid off from investment banks or bolted doomed technology companies before the bitter end. I was "on call" for my friends when they found themselves out of work for a few months. When folks needed a pal to kill an afternoon with, I was their man. More often than not, an article or PowerPoint deck could be pushed off 'til the weekend when truly great social opportunities came up.

Upper deck tickets for Giants versus Expos? Count me in!

Margaritas at noon? I'm there!

Ferry ride across the Bay to God-knows-where? Who could resist?

For the last few years, one could inevitably find hordes of MBAs, lawyers, web developers and other professionals at the ballpark, driving range and various outdoor drinking venues. Life on the leisure circuit was good, if you could set all the career angst aside for a couple of days a week.

Most importantly, my "have laptop will travel mode" allowed me to trek frequently to see Gabrielle, in Toronto and LA and all kinds of long weekend destinations in between.

Wait…I thought I heard the word "eyeballs" from across the room. Three years ago, pretty much everyone at the Grove and places like it all over the City was trying to "aggregate eyeballs," "disintermediate the industry" or fling some other impressive buzz-phrase in the hopes of recruiting naïve, starry-eyed employees or bamboozling naïve, starry-eyed venture capitalists. This fellow on the opposite side of the Grove spouting about eyeballs was either an ophthalmologist or a living anachronism. Ah, definitely an anachronism. He was wearing a denim shirt embroidered with the logo of Grilldude.com, one of the biggest flameouts of the Internet bubble period. One of the company's founders had tried to recruit me when I first arrived out West. After signing a non-disclosure agreement about the "stealth mode" "Project Blaze," I got the full run-down.

"Look, Jake, the American barbecuing public spends an estimated *$40 billion* per year on meat, grills, charcoal and other supplies. If we can get 10% of that market, we're going to be living large," proclaimed the founder, who three months before had been living large at Stanford Business School.

"But, that's only the beginning," he confided, his timbre perfect for a career in late night get-rich-quick infomercials. "We have the opportunity to fundamentally grow the market…to build up America's interest in grilling…to give them the resources they need to grill better and smarter."

Then, he dropped his voice and leaned in. "But, the real payoff is down the line. America's barbecuers are a *very* attractive demographic, representing over $4 *trillion* per year in consumer purchases."

Leaning in closer. "We want to lock up the eyeballs of the American grilling public and take advantage of their loyalty and their purchasing power to become one of the Net's retailing powerhouses. That's our 'secret sauce,' and why this company is red hot." He smiled triumphantly. I wondered if he practiced that line in front of a mirror, because, though comical, it was delivered masterfully. I also wondered how Project Blaze attracted $10 million in venture capital. Nine months later, the founder was touring Laos.

The sole remaining traces of Grilldude.com were the denim shirts on the dude across the room and on the racks at Goodwill locations all over the City. The blue denim shirt sections at Goodwill, the Salvation Army and a half dozen Haight Ashbury vintage clothing boutiques read like a hall of shame for the self-indulgent, power drunk San Francisco of the late 90s. So many people descended on the region like locusts—I can say that, because I guess I was one of the locusts.

Stock options were the currency of the realm. I would say the options game was like playing with Monopoly money, but too many other writers have employed that line already. Besides, it's a pretty insulting thing to say about Monopoly money, which can at least be used to purchase Indiana Avenue and provide your family and friends hours of wholesome capitalistic entertainment.

After touting the "market opportunity" and the "upside" associated with their companies, smiling recruiters—usually a founder in an early stage company or a polished HR professional in venerable *later* stage firms (outfits 3-6 months old)—would pile on extra selling points. Earlier in my career, companies had stressed perks such as matching 401Ks, educational loans, training programs and paid gym memberships. In San Francisco in the year 2000, however, a load of dot coms competed tooth and nail to be the most dog friendly workplace. *You would not believe* how many companies featured frolicking dogs on the "Why Work with Us?" pages of their web sites. *You would not believe* how many dogfights I saw in the luxurious converted warehouse offices South of Market, and how much dog crap I saw lying among networking cables on the floors of these new millennium Taj Mahals. *You would not believe* how many times my crotch was sniffed during job interviews—usually by canines.

Most start-ups planned their launch parties before they planned their strategies. If you were a single guy, you really never had to stock your refrigerator—hungry scavengers of the information age could chomp on pot-stickers, quesadillas and crudités at dot com launch parties almost every night. Someone must have been harvesting the Redwoods in Marin to manufacture the long pointy sticks for the tons of chicken satay we devoured every night at these events. Maybe the sticks were gathered and ground up and squeezed through some Dr. Seuss-inspired machine to create the torrent of business cards rampaged through any gathering of 20- and 30-somethings in the City. Maybe the business cards were Seussified into the cardboard sleeves which protect our hands from the hot coffee at the Grove.

After a couple of hours of intense work at the Grove, I journeyed to Starbucks, where I started writing about the Grove. Though one Starbucks waited a mere two blocks from the Grove, I instead trekked to one a full *six* blocks away. Lighter and airier than the Chestnut location, the Union Street Starbucks was definitely the preferred location for regulars on the Leisure Circuit; several lunchtime diners from the Grove were already there pounding away on their keyboards or enjoying a late afternoon perusal of a well-used *New York Times*.

"Medium caramel macchiato, please." I refuse to allow the brain trust behind Starbucks to remold my vocabulary. Tall, Grande, Venti—get real. This is America.

"Kareem!" a barista called out, letting me know my frothy drink was ready (I always employ pseudonyms at Starbucks). I sipped as I began tapping on my keyboard. I've never had a "real" cup of coffee in my life—the kind Flo from the diner pours into your white china cup after you flip it over. The only coffee drinks I can swallow are the ones that taste like the microwaved remnants of a hot fudge sundae.

After writing with somewhat questionable wit and flair for about two hours within Starbucks' friendly confines, I spent the next hour typing out a dozen e-mails which I would unleash on some East Coast colleagues when I returned home. I knew my night would be free if they headed out of the office before they could respond to my responses to their responses to my questions.

Not a bad day on the job all told. I jammed my papers into my briefcase next to my high-tops and powered down my laptop in preparation for my six-block walk home down Union Street. My knee was throbbing—I probably needed to ice it down after such a hectic day on-the-go.

My cell phone buzzed—my favorite traveling companion was phoning in.

"Dominos Pizza," I answered.

"HIII-iii. How was your day? Did you kick any more ass?"

"I can't kick anything these days. So, how was the 'dentist'? Any potential commercials for Crest or Colgate or Listerine?"

"Yeah, I probably have a cavity. *I need to go in tomorrow to find out if I have to have it filled*," she said, raising her voice a little bit so her boss in the next room could hear.

"So, any other big happenings today?" I asked as I kept walking.

"Well, no, not re…Hey, they got me a letter opener today!"

"Well, that's an exciting development. See? I told you the world of big business can be fun," I told her.

"I knoooow. I really like this thing. I'm opening up the mail so fast it's amazing. I can't believe I've never used one of these before," Gabrielle marveled.

"They really are a wonderful piece of technology aren't they? You wonder what people used to do before they were invented. I forget if it was Thomas Edison or Henry Ford…"

"Yeah. Y'know, we should buy matching *his* and *hers* letter openers, and then start writing each other a ton of love letters! I always *love* it whenever you write something for me."

I think I could work in some time to pen some lettres d'amour. *I'll have to pencil that into the calendar, after tomorrow's workout, but before the ballgame.*

We continued our wonderful conversation about nothing as faster-moving shoppers and stroller-toting mothers passed me on the sidewalk. Paying the price for not elevating or icing my leg all day, I limped down Union Street. Without Gabrielle, the evening commute would have been hell.

5

Clarity

"I went for the emerald cut diamond…she's always said she likes that shape. Her grandmother had an emerald cut engagement ring, and it had just always defined elegance for Paulina. So, I wanted to make sure I got something with that really elegant look from the 1920s, but also to give it a little bit of a modern feel as well," he said.

"It really sounds beautiful," replied Tiffany as she delicately folded a $20 into her G-string before ratcheting up the writhing once again. "And for the setting?"

"White gold. It's a little more understated, and plus it can go with so many more pieces of her jewelry," said Tim. He was one of my first college friends to get married—almost seven years ago. Even though I was sitting right next to him at his bachelor party in 1995, I was in a totally different place. I was worried about my softball team's upcoming semifinal game, and about what kind of personal ethical dilemma I could discourse upon for my business school applications.

"Any baguettes?" Tiffany seemed to know her diamonds, but I couldn't figure out why they were talking about bread.

"Oh, I forgot to tell you. Two on each side, four in all, to symbolize the four years we've been together so far."

"Awww, that's so cute," she said as the song ended, patting Tim on the head, folding her twenties and sliding on toward another table.

I've always seemed to be a couple of conversations behind in life. During junior high, when friends sitting with me in the back of the school bus engaged in ribald dissertations about their first French kisses and then their initial forays into the world of heavy petting, I had nothing to add. Just when I'd gotten some good back of the bus banter material, the rest of the world had moved on to locker room conversations, which always seemed to begin with "Well, her parents were out of town…". And then, just when I accumulated a little bit of locker room-suitable stuff, frat house tales seemed to rule the day. At that point, I didn't care if I kept pace or not.

Most of my friends from business school were those who showed up single. After graduation, however, a number of them started spending their signing bonuses on engagement rings. At a post-graduation drunken romp, I remember glazing over as a buddy, who had months before been torn between hedge fund management and investment banking, told of his painful quandary choosing between white gold and platinum.

Two years later, at a Jazz Fest junket in New Orleans, I worked feverishly to escape from a debate between two fellows with very different opinions on pear-shaped diamonds. I was worried it would come to blows.

At a Giants game about a year and a half ago, one buddy told me of the touchy in-law situation he was attempting to unravel. His girl-friend's sister—his future sister in-law—had just received a 1.5 karat engagement ring from her philosophy grad student boyfriend. He, as the six-figure per year MBA-type, would probably need to step up to something a little larger, but he worried a bigger stone would look monstrous on *his* girlfriend's finer, more delicate hands. What a conundrum!

✳   ✳   ✳   ✳

Many of the friends I studied with in business school are totally jaded—so to speak—on the whole diamond-buying process. We had the misfortune of reading a case study during our first year on De Beers, the gem-marketing colossus that controls the international diamond trade.

In the late 19th Century, Cecil Rhodes came to dominate the mining of diamonds in South Africa through his monopolistic control of the pumping systems used to suck the water out of mine shafts.

He snapped up the diamond mines of prospectors who couldn't pay their debts, gaining control of almost the entire supply of South African jewels.

Rhodes calculated the worldwide demand for diamonds by projecting the number of marriages in rich industrialized nations, especially the United States. He slashed production within his carat-filled mines by 30% in order to ensure that diamonds would retain their cachet as rare and sought-after tokens.

Did you know that diamonds are an incredibly common stone? You can walk through certain parts of the world and virtually trip over them. De Beers' diamond dealings represent the biggest marketing scam this side of the cola wars. Rhodes' corporate progeny controls the supply and flow of diamonds worldwide with an iron fist. Cecil died a single man in 1902.

In the last six months or so, I've fought off my cynicism about the injustice associated with the international diamond cartel. I have actually begun listening attentively to the diamond diatribes going on around me. I *even* know what baguettes are. Even if diamonds aren't rare, they are part and parcel of something very precious.

Recently, I've been studying up, trying to gain some usable knowledge of diamonds beyond the worldwide levels of supply and demand. A few weeks ago, I Googled "diamond engagement ring" for the first time. I really felt like I was crossing some new frontier as I waited in anticipation for the full 0.29 seconds it took for the results to be displayed on my screen ("0.29 seconds"—those Google guys are pretty cocky, aren't they?). The data dump was enormous; I've been reading about the "4 Cs" ever since. *Carat, clarity, cut* and *color.*

Carats are pretty self-explanatory: the weight of the diamond. In business school, we studied the millions of carats—the raw tonnage—of gems marketed each year. Once you start studying carats by their ones and twos, it's a whole new ballgame.

As I continued my readings on the Web, I was a bit surprised by the meaning of clarity. According to one engagement ring expert:

> Clarity is often mistakenly believed to be the factor
> that affects the amount of sparkle and brilliance. This is

not true. Clarity refers to the presence of microscopic features that formed within the diamond as it crystallized. If
readily visible to the eye without magnification, poor clarity will greatly reduce value, but otherwise, clarity has
minimal impact on beauty or desirability.

Now, the seventh grade science fair honorable mention winner in
me was intrigued; my faulty knowledge and faulty assumptions were
thrown out the window. If clarity was not the characteristic that
caused diamonds to sparkle, what was it then?

NOTES FOR 'CLARITY'

- cut—round, oval, sapphire, marquis, pear. heart shaped?
  heart shaped only appropriate for the type of guy who would
  propose at baseball game
- color—system starts with D? who came up with that?
  marketing geniuses at de beers should fix… gradations from
  white to yellow. all the way to Z. even schmuck like me can
  notice a Z diamond yellow. what about other colors?
  champagne, green, blue, etc. do people use these?
- balancing act. $$$ Budget. keep up with Joneses or take
  extra trip to Hawaii?
- How do you get size w/out revealing plan? steal another ring
  from Gabrielle?
- setting aside $$$ for last few months. might have to drive
  Probe a little while longer. might actually have to wash it.
- going to NYC in couple weeks. might go to diamond
  trading district. check out dudes with beards—hasidim.
  "Got a B'Nai B'rith discount?" Is there a secret handshake?
- might go with Money.

My studies are, as yet, incomplete, but there's one thing I know:
Clarity is the most important thing of them all.

6

Stupid Fuck

you stupid fuck

7

We Were on a Break

Hello again. I apologize for the profanity. The "you" in "you stupid fuck" was not addressed to *you*, but, rather, was aimed squarely at myself.

I also apologize for being away for a while. Of course, to you, it seems like I've only been away for one page, but it's been longer than that. I thought maybe inserting 15 or 20 blank pages could show the passage of nine days, but that runs counter to all of my instincts as an environmentalist.

I also apologize for leaving an earlier short story unfinished, but I'm not going to get back to that one for a while. You see: Gabrielle and I are on a "Break."

I have no idea what that means.

✳ ✳ ✳ ✳

We had taken advantage of Gabrielle's boss' vacation by traveling during the middle of the week for two nights to Santa Barbara, about two hours north of LA. My workload was pretty light, and I had an upcoming trans-continental flight where I knew I could get a lot done. Good times were had by all. Etcetera, etcetera.

We returned late to her apartment on Thursday night. Well after *Friends*.

I washed up a little bit and then joined her in her bedroom. She'd been crying, and I was worried she'd gotten some bad news in her voicemail.

But it was I who received the news.

I actually remember very little of the next couple of hours. Neither of us communicated with great coherence. Our conversation was bereft of any eloquence or profound statements. I seem to remember gushers of "I love you so much" emanating from us both. I recall an ocean of "I don't know, I just don't know" flowing from Gabrielle as one of two reasons for going on the "Break." It's not that she didn't know the reason, it's that the *reason* was that she didn't know, according to her. That last sentence—I'm not even sure if it would even qualify as *pidgin* English—may be pretty difficult to understand for people who don't know the complexities of "Breaks." I count myself among them.

The other reason she mentioned was "Timing." Timing. Timing. It came up time after time. I couldn't stand to hear the word uttered one more...time. In the nine days since this regrettable Thursday evening, I've had the chance to talk to a number of people about "Timing" in relationships.

- "Oh, Timing is the most important thing."
- "Yeah, Timing can be so important."
- "Timing is very, very important."

So, it seems a lot of the world knows about Timing. I'd always heard that love was the most important thing. It's extolled in songs, books, poems and films. Where's the movie entitled *Timing Story*? Where's the song "All You Need is Timing"? Is Timing a many splendored thing? How are the rest of us supposed to learn about how Timing can be everything, or be the end of everything?

Actually, now that I think about it, *Romeo and Juliet* is sort of about Timing.

Anyway, I just cannot, for the life of me, recall actual sentences we uttered during this three-hour period we lay on Gabrielle's bed. I remember the pain of my heart pounding in my ears. I was just so hot…just sweating…and my eyes burnt.

And the crying. The sheer force of tears. The pain I felt when little used tear ducts were forced to churn hour after hour—it was profound. I don't mean a pain in the soul; I mean intense, grating pain emanating from my tear ducts.

And I remember the snot bubbles. If anything, Gabrielle cried harder and longer than I did. As is my way, I tried to make her laugh, attempting to make her comfortable as she continued on about "Breaks" and "Timing." I learned during our session that intense combinations of emotions mixed with unexpected laughter produce snot bubbles—she inflated about five of them that night.

Gabrielle's roommate returned about an hour into our "Break" extravaganza. Her apartment had extraordinarily thin walls and highly conductive heating ducts that moved voices better than fiber optic cables. "Noise control" had been an issue before, and now it was arising again during the end of—or the "Break" in—our relationship. As she blew her nose, she reached for her stereo remote control and queued up the one CD in the changer.

I don't think I will ever be able to listen to James Taylor again. For five consecutive plays, I was forced to persevere through the gratingly soothing tones as he sang about Carolina, fire, rain, sweet babies named James, country roads, friends, Mexico and showers.

I examined our surroundings. I was everywhere. The nightstand I bought her, where my wallet, watch, keys and glasses laid. I hope I haven't given you the impression that I'm stupid; I have no illusions about that nightstand remaining bare. But, just seeing *my* possessions there for potentially the final time was utterly debilitating.

I felt the bed beneath me. The bed I had carried into this room when she moved to Los Angeles. The bed beneath me.

And then I looked up at her dresser, one which I also helped her pick out and move into her bedroom. On top of the dresser was a bud vase. I'd gone to a "Paint Your Own Pottery" studio on Union Street three years before to make her birthday present. Amidst the gaggle of mug and plate painting women—I think I may have been the only male to have ever set foot in the establishment—I worked for hours to depict small symbols of our relationship on the white ceramic surface. The women—a *bachelorette* party, if you can believe it—hovered around asking me questions about the tiny images I was crafting. For that moment, for that group at least, I was the paragon of the committed male.

Viewing the bud vase shattered yet another emotional barrier, and I was overcome with the most powerful wave of misery I'd felt yet. I couldn't believe the sense of betrayal I felt. I laugh right now as I type this, but I could not believe that someone I had painted pottery for could ever do this to me. And I laughed then, too. But I didn't blow a snot bubble.

"What's so funny?" Gabrielle asked as she wiped more tears away and tried to smile.

"I can't tell you. I'm just so tired. I need to sleep. Will you turn off the light?"

As she clicked off the black halogen lamp, I took a final look at the bud vase—and the lone dried red rose inside.

As tired as I was, I couldn't sleep. I had listened to Gabrielle sob for hours. Her crying was a sound which grabbed at me. One which four hours earlier I would have done anything to make go away. I would have done anything to soothe her and take away her pain. However, at this moment, I forced myself not to care.

In the next moment, however, I felt the cruelest blow of all. A wave of nausea and anger enveloped me. I got out of bed and noiselessly walked out to the living room, still fully dressed, but barefooted. It was four in the morning, but at this point I was wide-awake and furious.

My lap top computer was silently mocking me. Like Edgar Allan Poe's "Tell Tale Hard Drive."

I turned on the computer, the screen serving as the only illumination in the room. I purposefully clicked three times and opened up a folder containing a number of completed short stories, one incomplete short story, and notes for a dozen more.

I'm sure my face at the moment, bathed in a blue-gray glow, belied the rapture of rage I was experiencing. It was greater than the sensation I felt earlier, when I was almost overcome with regret and humiliation that I had ever painted pottery for Gabrielle. I was experiencing a new emotion, one on the other side of anger. Still, I must have appeared placid.

I opened up a number of the computer files. Red and green squiggles reminded me I had yet to spell check or edit my work. I read about sponge baths and chance encounters in Paris. For a moment, I entertained the vision of bringing my computer into Gabrielle's room and sharing the anecdotes and short stories with her.

She wanted some love letters. I'll show her some love letters. She'll really enjoy reading these sweet and entertaining passages. I'd like to watch her read these.

But then I thought the better of it. I didn't want the drama at the moment. I didn't care if I upset *her*—I just knew I wanted to spare myself another crying jag.

I closed the computer files and dragged all of those words and sentiments to the "recycle bin." It was the first time that I'd noticed that Microsoft had renamed it. It used to be the "trash can," didn't it?

I opened up files in another folder. Articles I "clipped" from websites on diamonds. On engagement rings. Those were also "recycled."

Maybe that was how she knew. Maybe that's what scared her. Maybe I had the stench of someone who had been contemplating a major purchase. Maybe I had stared a half second too long in the window of some jewelry store as we walked holding hands down the main drag in Santa Barbara.

Maybe Gabrielle had borrowed my computer to conduct a Google search on "Diana Ross" or "Diatom Paleolimnology" or "diagnosing heart disease" and was shocked when the search bar displayed the recently completed query on "diamond engagement rings." Undone in 0.29 seconds.

Finally, I looked at my notes for future stories. I think my face was still blank. I read the page full of abbreviations, quips, quotes and ideas. Mere computerized scrawls, but things that had been so fully thought out that, in a way, I had almost come to believe them as real. I nearly laughed, but I think the chuckle might have only come out as the arch of an eyebrow on my deadened face.

What a fool. Was I planning a book—or planning a life—with this document of 6,562 words? Was I a fourth grader sticking pins in the map, showing the places I wanted to visit? Maybe, but it was as if, by sticking the pins in the map, I had pierced the landscape and destroyed the places.

I placed my cursor at the top of the document and clicked. I dragged, and the screen turned mostly black, the text standing out in negative like words on a chalkboard. It seemed like it took forever for the black to reach the bottom of the document.

I'd envisioned a thousand scenarios for a life with Gabrielle. No, not paternalistically planning some Ward-and-June-Cleaver sort of future, but seeing so many ways we could make each other better throughout so many random and planned journeys through life. Each and every one of these visions seemed so solid, like it was built on a real foundation. One thousand gleaming futures.

But what had I really been constructing in my mind? I'd thought too far ahead and I knew it. What had I actually been building? Had I been building beautiful towers or shining bridges stretching toward the future? No. I was a kid, making miniatures with Popsicle sticks. Gluing together buildings that would just lie in splinters at the end of the day when someone decided to play Godzilla.

I took a moment to read the last white words on the mostly black screen. They were actually some of the first words I had typed into the document—just notes, rife with misspellings and abbreviations. I wrote about a ceremony. Short and sweet. Filled not with quotes from religious texts, but with statements of faith from the people that mattered. And maybe with some readings from *Where the Wild Things Are*.

The screen was still black. I typed, and the black disappeared. In the darkness of the room, my eyes took a moment to readjust to the brightness of the white screen. I read:

"you stupid fuck"

I pressed save.

✳   ✳   ✳   ✳

It's difficult to convey how thirsty I was, so I won't try. But I had never been so thirsty.

I walked into Gabrielle's kitchen, my nose very aware of the battle between the Glade Stick-up deodorizer and the rotting trash, the removal of which had become a cause celebre between her and her two male roommates. I knotted up the trash bag and took it out to the dumpster, laughing at myself all the way.

What is a "Break," anyway? What does that really mean? How significant is it, really? Had I overreacted with all of my diligent work on the computer a few minutes before? I returned to the kitchen and poured two glasses of water from the filter/pitcher I had bought for G. *Two* glasses. I laughed again at my own habits.

Billy had gotten back together with his girlfriend after a 6-month break. There must be other people who take time apart, and then figure out what's really important in life. Fortunately or unfortunately, with my high schooler's knowledge of dating and relationships, I'd never been on a break before, so I had no idea how these things worked.

I walked back to the doorway of Gabrielle's room. Her face was illuminated by a small streetlight from the alleyway her room bordered. From a distance, the dried remnants of tears made Gabrielle's skin look like travertine. I looked at her for a moment and sipped my water.

Then I backed out of the room and walked out the front door of her apartment. I just felt like looking at the stars, but all I could see was the glow of the LA night sky.

Timing. I'm seven years older than Gabrielle, and it never mattered until this night. Maybe she's a bit of an old soul and maybe I'm a bit immature. I've never known two people who got along better.

I live right next door to the world of permanence, but still in a world where most of the *things* that are important to me can fit into my collection of milk crates. My friends are leaving my world day by day for a whole different existence. Every day, more of my friends become my acquaintances. They have new concerns—building a life, having babies, raising children. They move; they move on.

Gabrielle lives in the world where people stress about getting an agent. Day by day, she meets more fellow travelers who also stress about getting an agent. Her world is growing; my world is shrinking. I didn't mind at all, when I thought we'd be living in the same world.

Billy lives a mile and a half away from his girlfriend. I live 400 miles away from Gabrielle. I'm never going to bump into her at a party. I'll never see her on Union Street in a chance encounter. Distance. Timing. Is this a "Break" at all, or is this just the term of art, the easiest nomenclature that can be employed to end an inconvenient relationship?

I drank the second cup of water I poured.

Once back inside, the strangest idea popped into my head. I had an overwhelming urge to steal Gabrielle's car.

I'm dressed. I'm packed. I should just go.

I'll take her keys—they're lying five feet away on the coffee table. She has a spare set. I'll leave her a $20 bill to take a cab to pick up her car at some airport garage.

I had visions of living out the lyrics to some Sheryl Crow song about love and pain and redemption in Los Angeles. I would ride on 'til morning and then ride on 'til LAX. I just thought it might be healthy to watch the sunrise.

And I didn't want to wake up next to Gabrielle.

I knew enough about LA to know where some of the 24-hour diners were, and I even knew where some underground clubs were. I'd find those establishments, have my first-ever cup of scorching black coffee and then move on for some vodka shots and then drive to some isolated and beautiful and un-LA spot to watch the sun come up.

But then, I had another thought, one which made me laugh and hammered home my level of exhaustion at the same time. I've had cocktails at Sky Bar at dusk. I've been to dinner parties in Manhattan Beach. I've barbecued at twilight in the Palisades.

I'd watched the sun set dozens of times over the Pacific Ocean in southern California.

But—and I can't believe I'm writing this—I didn't know where to find the sunrise in Los Angeles.

Weak beyond words, I forgot all about the car keys and Sheryl Crow, and, still fully dressed, lay down next to Gabrielle, on top of the covers.

8

Big Mo in Vegas

I was actually in line in front of the Southwest ticket counter at LAX before it dawned on me how miserable I was going to be for the next two days.

My e-ticket printout reminded me of the terrible truth; I was traveling to Las Vegas.

Now, I'll leave it to others to debate the merits of Vegas as an institution within this American civilization of ours, but one thing I knew for sure—it was exactly *not* the place I needed to be going mere hours after the clock started on my "Break" with G. But, I had already paid my money for the room into the kitty, and the norms of my little group of friends allowed no refunds for "pussing out." *And,* my non-refundable, non-changeable ticket to the east coast for business was originating in Las Vegas. So, Sin City, here we come!

This congress of overeducated Neanderthals—all friends from business school—was tabbed the "No Bachelor Required" Party. It had been a full three…maybe even four months since the last major bachelor blowout, so you can understand why this bunch of noble fellows needed to blow off some steam.

As I advanced in the queue, fresh tears dripped down my already saline stained cheeks; I was a little worried about erosion. The check-in agent did a triple-take at the sight of my swollen, salt-scarred face. I almost asked her if the airline offered bereavement fares.

After advancing through security, I found an ATM and withdrew $300, the maximum my bank allowed. Not a huge gambling stockpile, but I'm not a huge gambler. I used the ATM receipt to blow my nose and limped toward an airport lounge, where I planned to elevate my leg, watch some SportsCenter and kill the remaining hour before my flight boarded.

After propping up my throbbing knee on my rolling bag in the bar, I checked my voicemail messages. 8:22 a.m.: "Goooooood morning, JT!" screamed Billy, chants of "JT! JT!" echoing in the background from a couple of backup singers I knew very well. "I think you're getting into Veeeegaaaassss a little before we are, so just wait around the Southwest baggage claim for me, EZ and Beef. We'll meet you there and share a cab to the Hard Rock. Oooouuut!"

I'd never been a part of a nickname crowd my whole life. But given names rarely make an appearance among this group of friends. I guess we're kind of like superheroes in that way—maybe our nicknames are more like our high-powered alter egos. You'd never hear Captain America and the Green Lantern call each other Steve and Hal if they went to Vegas. Then again, they're from warring comic book companies, so they'd probably never be seen in Vegas together, anyway.

You've met Billy—a.k.a. Todd Williams—former naval officer, former dot com-er, former venture capitalist and current member of the Leisure Circuit. The "E" in EZ is for "Evan." Evan Riley is currently an investment banker, but was among San Francisco's most eligible bachelors from 1992-96 and 1998-2000. Oh, my, how times have changed though, since he met his current (and we all think *permanent*) love interest. Beef is Bo Farmer, 250 pounds of horseflesh and a native Minnesotan who excelled in hockey for Cornell's Big Red. Now 34 and a strategy consultant, Beef's 250 pounds are distributed a little differently than they were during his days on the ice.

Dehydrated and exhausted, I irrigated and caffeinated myself with two of whatever they call the airport equivalent of the "Big Gulp." I shook out my leg to restore circulation and headed out of the lounge. On the way to the gate, I stopped by the men's room to wash off my tearstains.

✳   ✳   ✳   ✳

I emerged through the jetway in beautiful Las Vegas, fresh off of flying an hour on a packed jet backwards facing a six-foot-six beanpole with sharp knees. On the way to the baggage claim area, I stopped by the men's room to wash off my tearstains.

Finding a seat near the baggage carousel for incoming flight 1833 from Oakland, I propped up my leg again and tried to work in 30 minutes of billables reading some article for a consulting project. My powers of concentration were in shambles and I retained none of the content, so I decided to charge the client for only 15 minutes.

The area was nearly deserted, except for some high-rolling septuagenarians milling around the Oakland flight's baggage carousel. The stainless steel contraption lurched to life as more tourists entered the vicinity, some already beginning to pick up duffels, stroller or golf bags.

"JT! Wattup, brother?" boomed EZ as he approached from the side. He extended his hand for a side slap—the hybrid between a high-five and a handshake. I slapped heartily and used the momentum to help my weak legs lift me from the vinyl waiting room seats. He laid his duffel bag down. "I gotta go get my clubs. I don't know where Beef and Billy ran off to. Back in a sec."

Feeling the effects of dehydration yet again, I located a drinking fountain nearby and tried to drink beyond my fill. In mid-glug, I was yanked off the floor and hugged by a not so mysterious bear. "Yo, beeeeyotch!" Beef roared.

"The knee! The knee," Billy and I proclaimed in unison. Bo set me down with tender loving care, apologized for the rough-housing and then punched me in the shoulder. "Man, how've you been? Haven't seen you out for months."

"Well, I've been laying low, y'know, with the whole not-being-able-to-walk- thing and all. And I've been...traveling for a bit...for business."

"You good?"

"Pretty good."

"Good. Hey, we'll go get our golf bags and be right back." They both went to join EZ by the carousel.

Pretty good. Yeah, I have my health...sort of. I wasn't going to tell anyone on this little junket about the "Break." I didn't care to be the lead weight around the group's collective ankles. In Vegas, if you're not adding to your troop's momentum, you're taking away from it. If you're not out there kicking ass, you're killing someone's buzz. If you mope, you kill the "mo."

The last thing I wanted was for someone to be on cheer up duty for me. Actually, *the* last thing I wanted was for the entire group to be on cheer up duty for me. I would have loved to just fade into the woodwork, although I wasn't exactly sure if there actually was any woodwork in the marble and neon empire that is Las Vegas.

Once the team had collected its belongings, we boarded a mini-van taxi to the Hard Rock Resort and Casino. I stretched out my knee on the back bench. "JT, the tee time's in an hour. You hitting the links with us?" Beef inquired from the front seat.

"Are you kidding? This guy is haaaaacking. His game has more slices than his knee right now," Billy inserted.

"Yeah, I think $120 per round is a bit too much for my game as it stands right now. Although that's probably only 50 cents a shot…" I laughed. Money *was* a little tight, in reality. I hadn't been able to travel for consulting projects for a couple of months, cutting into my billings. Insurance deductibles and physical therapy co-payments had eaten into the reserves. *Plus*, I had a couple of good friends' weddings on the calendar for October, so there goes another thousand for travel and gifts (ugh, I hadn't thought about the weddings yet).

This group of bulge bracket I-bankers, top tier VCs and high-powered consultants were among the biggest spenders I knew. Money would flow like water this weekend, a flood of liquidity in the desert. I was resigned to this fact, but hoped to limit my own personal drain.

On the bright side of the financial picture, however, at least I didn't have to contribute to the engagement ring fund for a while. So, I had that going for me.

"So, JT, what do you think you'll do today?" asked EZ.

"I'll rally some non-golfers. Maybe we'll hang out in the sports book or catch the Siegfried and Roy matinee."

"It's all good, JT," Beef smiled, "'Cause we're in Vegas, baby, Vegas!"

"Vegas, baby, Vegas!" EZ and Billy both thundered, drumming their hands onto the top of their seats. I was surprised that it had taken 17 minutes, 22 seconds for "Vegas, baby, Vegas" to join us. This rallying cry was a memorable piece of the movie *Swingers*—for many late 20s/early 30s American males, the Canon, the sum of all moral codes and all noble aspirations. The Tao Te Ching…the Gospels…the Talmud…the Kama Sutra…all rolled up into one. I think I told you a little about the flick a month ago.

I knew a couple of guys in the 80s who tried to pattern their lives after *Ferris Bueller's Day Off,* infusing an air of well-calculated insouciance into their characters. But I knew *dozens* of guys in the 90s who tried to live by the credos of *Swingers.* The impact of the film has been immense, rippling through all segments of society. I love the movie—I just didn't want to relive it this weekend.

"JT, I don't think you gave us a 'Vegas, baby, Vegas'…" Beef prodded.

Don't bother me. "I sort of got a sore—"

"VEGAS, BABY, VEGAS!" all three Harvard men roared, pounding the roof of our minivan.

I held out. They pounded. I held out. Held out.

"OK! OK! VEGAS, BABY, VEGAS, you motherfucking freaks!" I yelled, wanting to ram their Big Berthas down their throats.

"That's better, JT," Beef stated in his soothing older brother tone.

Our foursome was among the first to arrive. We checked in and all stowed our stuff in one room. I was relieved I would be shacking up with these guys for the two nights in Nevada. Sometimes you might not get too much sleep with these gentlemen around, but there were hidden risks with some of the other fellows who would be showing up for the "No Bachelor Required" Party. Sharing a bed with some of the other dudes could be a crap shoot.

Almost literally.

Let me make this clear: when traveling with a bunch of guys for a bachelor party…ski weekend…whatever…you MUST get to know the luggage. You MUST know who has staked a claim to the room—

and especially the bed—you will end up sharing. Sphincter discipline and bladder control are not strong suits amongst quite a few 30-something men once the Tanqueray and Ketel One have worked their magic. One ignores this universal truth at his own peril.

EZ, Billy and Beef hustled to get out the door while I dialed the cell phones of some of the guys who would be skipping the golf outing due either to late arrival or lack of coordination. I left six or seven messages and then walked downstairs with the other members of the San Francisco contingent as they went off to hail a cab to take them to the course.

"Don't go crazy, JT, and tell the other fellas we'll catch up with them laaaaterrrr," said Billy as he slammed the taxi's trunk. I headed back into the Hard Rock, which buzzed with a surprising level of non-check-in activity for just after 12 noon. Probably cadres of lapsed Gamblers Anonymous members either just starting or just ending their wagering day.

I settled in at the Hard Rock's small sports book, a chantry chapel off to the side of the cathedral of craps and cards. This time of day, it's pretty slim pickings for the sports fan, but luckily, there were a couple of East coast baseball games starting up. Otherwise, the only new sports entertainment would have been a preview of the Aussie rules football final from Melbourne. On one of the sports book's 20 screens, I watched San Francisco Giants highlights for the second time. It was looking like their current win streak had all but assured them a spot in the post-season.

And there I sat, for nearly two hours. It was a little too much time to be left alone with my thoughts, with only a worthless Pirates-Cubs baseball game to keep me company.

My cell phone finally buzzed around 2. It was Carson, an SF-based venture capitalist and the only one of our sobriquet-saturated group without a nickname. "Yo, JT!"

"Yo."

"Have you had lunch yet?"

I was about to say, "It's after two o'clock...", but then I realized that I had forgotten to eat lunch.

"No, I haven't had time. It's just been a whirlwind of activity around here. Let's grab something."

"Good. I'm with Balls. We'll see you down there in ten minutes." Balls was Greg Ballantine, a hedge fund manager residing in Boston. In 15 minutes, they both ambled into the sports book, each chatting on his cell phone.

"I don't believe those earnings estimates for Q1 and Q2. We should dump that motherfucker and ride the short," said Balls as he gave me a quick hug and pat on the back.

"No, they can't get in on this deal. What do they bring to the table besides $20 million?" Carson asked as he winked and offered up a high five. With a wordless confab comprised of pointing, shrugs and headshakes, the three of us reached the conclusion we should dine at the Pink Taco, a Tex-Mex joint just off the casino floor. They continued with their "buy low/sell high" conversations while I closely examined what the Pink Taco had to offer.

Carson wrapped his conversation first. "So what's shaking, pal?"

"Ah, just watching some enthralling baseball this afternoon." Again, I stuck with the non-answer, in order to avoid discussions of current events.

"Well, at least the Gigantés are kicking ass. The firm has a suite for the playoff games; I can't wait."

"Yeah, a lot of good my Red Sox season tickets are doing me!" said Balls as he snapped his mobile shut. "Looks like they're choking their way out of the playoff picture...*again*. So, what have you been up to, JT?"

"Living the dream...rehabbing the knee...that sort of thing."

We ordered and then gorged ourselves on the culinary delights of Texas and Mexico. I drank two of whatever the Pink Taco's equivalent of the Big Gulp is. About twenty minutes into our meal, Carson's cell phone buzzed to life.

"This is Carson...yo, beeeeyotch! What hole are you guys on?....Just making the turn? You spending a little too much time with the beer cart girls?" I could tell from the reverberations of the tiny cell phone that Carson was talking to a well-sauced Beef, although I couldn't make out any distinct sentences—if indeed any were being uttered.

"Hell, yes, I'm in! I got the info right here," continued Carson as he pulled a folded laser printed page from his breast pocket. "I called the dude. I had to call *a lot* of places, my friend. The place I found is pretty far away, and it's expensive. You still up for it?...."

Balls shot a puzzled look my way as he scooped up the last of his black beans with a tortilla chip. I answered him with an "I dunno" shrug of the shoulders as I sucked down the last of my Diet Coke and swirled around the ice water remnants.

"OK, game on, baby. We'll go get the stuff...You *better* be ready! Giddy up!" screamed Carson as he flicked off his phone. And then, turning to his dining companions, he decrypted the preceding conversation. "So, Beef and I are dressing up as full-on Vegas Elvises tonight, boys. We gotta go get the costumes. I think the place is like 20 minutes away."

Balls and I looked at each other with mirrored looks of puzzlement. "We haven't even done anything yet here in Vegas. Maybe we should hang out at the pool, or go ride that roller coaster at New York, New York," said Balls.

"And I meant to get an hour of work done..." I chipped in.

"C'mon, it's cloudy; the pool scene will suck. And 'work'? JT, who are you kidding? Just come with me! Keep me company," Carson prodded. Balls and I both shrugged to signal our grudging assent, tossed away our wadded up napkins and threw down a couple of wads of cash on the table for our lunch.

We all walked out the front door of the Hard Rock, where a cavalcade of cabs was waiting. Carson opened up the front door of the minivan cab and presented the driver with the printout as Balls and I climbed into the back. "Do you know where this place is?" Carson inquired.

"Yes. Is far," replied Manuel, the driver. "You have rental car or something? Is better..."

"No, we're good. If you know where it is, let's just head on over," Carson told Manuel. Then, turning to his pals in the backseat, he cheered, " Vegas, baby, Vegas!"

*   *   *   *

Thirty minutes later, we arrived at the costume emporium. Carson told Manuel, "Wait right here, we'll be out in a few minutes," and then bounded out of the van.

Balls and I thanked the driver and walked into the costume store. "Great to see all the sights Vegas has to offer, huh?" he laughed.

"Don't knock it man…You got attractions galore out here. Look, there's an Arby's *right over there!*" I replied.

We overheard the tail end of Carson's conversation with the manager as we approached the Elvis department. "So, we normally got about 20 of these things, but we're down to our final four," the tattooed man said as he motioned toward the sparse rack behind him.

"OK, guys, I'm just going to try these on and we'll be out of here in like…two minutes," said Carson as he walked into the dressing room through a tie-dyed curtain. *Why try them on?* I thought. *If there's an extra large and a medium, let's just take 'em and get the fuck out of here.*

Balls and I amused ourselves for the next fifteen minutes trying on Rasta wigs and Cat in the Hat *chapeaux.* Carson came by wearing the original red jump suit and carrying a blue one. "OK, guys, these two fit me, and I've gone back and forth on it. Which one should I go for?"

"The first one," Ballantine and I declared as one.

"OK, which shades?" Carson asked as he fumbled with a couple in the crook of his arm.

"Those!" answered Balls as Carson placed the first pair of garish golden sunglasses on his face.

"All right, let me just go pay for this and we'll head back." Carson walked back to the dressing room to put on his non-polyester attire. He emerged a minute later, tucking in his shirt with one hand and fumbling for his wallet with the other. "So how much, all told?" Carson asked as he draped out the sequined white and crimson jump suits on the counter.

The manager told Carson the total cost as he pulled out the accessories for the jump suits: two massive mutton-chop-adorned-jet-black Elvis wigs. "$30 for the glasses. $40 for the wigs. And then we also got a $60 deposit for each of the costumes—you pay the rental charge when you return 'em."

"Do you take Amex?" Carson inquired.

"No, just Visa and Master." I should have remembered seeing this establishment on the Visa commercial—"they don't take American Express." Between us, Carson, Balls and I had Black, Platinum and Gold Cards, respectively, but they wouldn't do us any good here.

"Guys, I just have my Amex card…" Carson opened his wallet and pulled out a meager sheaf of bills. "I think I have enough for the wigs and shades. Do you have a credit card we can put the deposit on?"

What kind of ass comes to Vegas with just $70? Not that difficult to find an ATM in the airport these days.

"I left my wallet in the room. I just had a little cash for lunch," said Balls.

What kind of ass goes out in Vegas without his wallet? It's like going into the desert without a canteen.

"I have some cash for the deposit," I said, pulling six crisp $20 bills out of my wallet.

"Great. We're good to go," Carson said as he transferred the money to the proprietor, who had already put the jumpsuits in plastic for safe transport. Carson grabbed the hangers and the bag with the supporting paraphernalia and led us out of the costume store.

By the time we returned to the Hard Rock, Manuel's meter registered $73. Carson contorted his body in order to grab his wallet. "Do you take Amex?"

"Yes, but credit card machine is broken," replied Manuel. "You have cash?"

"JT…?" Carson invited.

I had already folded four $20 bills for such an eventuality. *Ah, how the money flows in Vegas! Just yield to the torrent of spending,* I thought. Yes, I do find myself thinking metaphorically a lot these days.

I handed the cash to Manuel, also delivering a little "keep the change" nod for good measure. He offered up his own "*gracias*" nod and then rolled off to take his place in the Hard Rock's taxi queue. Our now cash-strapped threesome entered the casino, noticeably more alive with the sounds of rock music, slot machines and bachelorette parties. Out of the corner of my eye, I noticed the sign pointing to the hotel's automatic teller machines.

"Hey, Carson. Could you hit the ATM and get my money? No reason for me to be in this whole Elvis transaction anymore," I said.

He continued hustling through the lobby. "Dude, I have a conference call I need to jump on in a couple of minutes. I'll getcha later…"

"Carson, I'm practically out of money now. Could you just get the $200, man?" The math was easy: $120 for the two jumpsuits and the $80 necessary for the cab that took us on his errand.

"$200?" asked Carson as he broke his momentum temporarily. "What…?" I could see the calculator in his head working immediately, and it wasn't displaying the same answer as mine.

Oh, no. This is going to suck, I realized immediately. From the look on his face, I could tell that he was annoyed not only that I had asked him for the money right away, but that I had the gall to ask him to repay me for the cab ride. I could almost hear the wheels turning in his head. *Carson thinks the 90-minute excursion to the costume store was a fun field trip, shared by all! He thinks we all had a wonderful Vegas adventure that we should all be chipping in for!*

"Look, there's an ATM over there," Carson stated, pointing toward the sign I was about to point him toward. He renewed his momentum toward the bank of elevators. "Go get some money for now and I'll give you what I owe you later."

Balls and I slowed down and then halted in the middle of the casino. "Do you?..What did?..Is he going to?…." I asked him.

"Dude, I don't want any part of this," replied Ballantine, backing up as he raised his hands and shook his head.

I fumed. *Carson! That motherfucker! That motherfucker! I want my $200!*

Ah, the day was going along splendidly. Nothing like good times with good friends to take one's mind off heartbreak and misery.

✳   ✳   ✳   ✳

Four hours later, our cabal of 25 merry men had assembled for dinner at the steak house in the hotel. I had been seething about the $200 for *only* about 3 hours and 42 minutes; I wasn't going to let that Carson spoil my 18 minutes of fun!

Within the next few years, it was a good bet that the exploits of at least a few among our troupe would hit the front page of *The Wall Street Journal*—their achievements and/or indiscretions memorialized in pointillist portraiture by some financial sector Seurat. But with my current rate of earnings, I certainly didn't plan on sitting for that particular sketch artist anytime soon. When our mega-bill arrived—I think it was six pages long with a supporting deck of financial exhibits—I was one of three "punk ass bitches" who opted out of "credit card roulette," preferring to plop $200 on the table rather than risk my credit card being the last one pulled out of a chef's hat by the waitress. Last card in means *you* pay for this entire herd of drunken bastards, and even with Enron-like accounting skills, I knew I couldn't make those numbers work with my bank account. I felt that after the events of the previous 24 hours, I should not tempt fate.

The petite redhead extracted card after card, calling out the owner's last name before EZ flicked the plastic wafers across or down the table to each potential payor as he was let off the hook. The first fifteen or so cards emerged without much fanfare, but the owners of the final ten credit cards really started to sweat as the final countdown began. Surrounded by the aroma of fine cigars—an aroma that had just begun to metamorphosize into a stench—and in the midst of plates laden with remnants of fat and butter and red steak drippings, the final seven…six…five fellows started to exude a very tannic sweat, perspiration composed almost entirely of the Cab Franc and Shiraz they had just imbibed in massive quantities. Some of the dudes with cards still in the mix really couldn't afford this kind of bill, big time degree and high-profile jobs notwithstanding. Retribution from wives and fiancées is swift and without mercy.

Waitress: "Johnson."

Group: "Ooooh!"

Waitress: "Gomez."

Group: "Ooooh!"

Waitress: "Two left. So I guess the last one pays, right? Our runner up is…Goldman! And the 'winner' is…Brady!"

Group: "OOOOOOOOOOOOHHHHHH!"

In the end, the "winner"—the owner of the final card remaining in the hat—had to take the *major* financial hit for the team. DB—or Dog Breath, a leveraged buy-out specialist from New York—ended up laying out almost $4000 for this night of red meat and cigars. This would not be the first time he had to cancel his summer share in the Hamptons due to a round of credit card roulette. DB had been hexed by bad karma for years, starting with his unfortunate moniker. "That's what happens when you try to make up your own nickname, my friend," I told him once.

✳ ✳ ✳ ✳

Money, money, money. As we headed from the steakhouse back to the Hard Rock's central bar area, I retrieved $300 more cash from the hotel ATM. Of course, my transaction had to be a "cash advance," not a withdrawal, because I had already reached my daily ATM withdrawal limit of $300 in Los Angeles. Automatic finance charges. Transaction charges. Bank fees. The cash just flows. Just a little more capital I was laying out for *Carson's* costume. Just a little more salt on the financial wound. Just a little more fun and merriment in Vegas.

So, here was our group at the hotel bar, breaking up into little clusters, some talking business, some talking babies, some talking *to* babies. Balls, DB and Wonger had insinuated themselves into a bachelorette party, and were proving to be quite the popular gents. Back in the day, invading bachelorette parties used to be one of my favorite pastimes, but these days, I wouldn't even know where to start.

I drifted from cluster to cluster, stopping occasionally by the bar to silently watch TV for a few minutes at a time. "JT! Order up some drinks, brother!" thundered EZ from about 20 feet away, as I watched some Giants-Astros highlights. The other clusters came to life, becoming aware of my presence and location once drinks were an issue.

"Yeah, you got this round, JT!"

"Over here, too, JT!"

"Tanqueray and tonics for us, JT!"

The last order wasn't necessary. After years of partying with these fellows, I knew everyone's drink of choice. I ordered an assortment of a dozen drinks for the guys who were within earshot of EZ's original decree. I made the mistake of laying out cash for the cocktails, since afterwards my wallet was nearly running on empty again. The cash just flows.

After I had delivered the drinks to the various clumps of friends milling nearby, I spied Beef and Carson, clad in their gold-trimmed jumpsuits, on the other side of the bar. They were whooping it up with a group of women, one of whom wore a snakeskin cowboy hat—I never know what to make of urban cowgirls. I walked over to the Laurel and Hardy Elvises.

"JT!" they both boomed, shooting up their beer bottles in a toast.

Carson put his arm around me. "Hey, guy, there's some people here you should meet."

"Yeah...great. Hey, I was just wondering...did you have a chance to grab that money? Between shelling out for the dinner and buying a round for the drunken fools over there, I'm just about tapped out."

"JT, do I look like I have any pockets in this thing? Balls has my wallet. You don't need money when chicks are buying you drinks all night, my man." I could see why people would treat these twin Elvises to drinks. Their costumes were so original...why there were only four or five other Elvises I could see from my position at the bar.

"Yeah...some people are hitting the tables...I thought I might join them," I suggested.

"Just hit the ATM. I'll catch you tomorrow," he commented as the snakeskin-cowboy-hat-girl put her trademark snakeskin cowboy hat on his head and began a-hootin' and a-hollerin'.

"Hit the ATM." I'll hit you in the fucking skull, you bastard. "You don't need money when chicks are buying you drinks." That's my suit, you

shit head! I paid for it! Those drinks should be rendered unto me until all of your debts are paid in full, you cock sucker!

"Yeah…well, I'll see you guys…I'm just going to…" I drifted off as one of the bevy of babes mounted Beef's back and he began galloping around like a Clydesdale. It was still 48 minutes until midnight, the magical hour at which time all cash advance fees and finance charges would be waived. I could just mill about for a while and then get some cash and join the crew at the $5 table. Was there even a $5 table at the Hard Rock? Would anyone in my group be caught dead at such a low roller table?

Then, I had a change of heart. *Fuck 'em. Fuck 'em all.* I went up to my room, had a glass of water and went to bed.

※　※　※　※

I awoke at 7 a.m., staring right into the face of a drooling Elvis. Beef was still clad in his white jump suit, clutching his disheveled mutton chop/pompadour wig like a tiny teddy bear. I rose up, fresh as a daisy. Running out of money at 11 p.m. might be the best hangover preventive there is.

Over in the other bed, EZ spooned Billy. Both clad in their boxers, they looked like an Abercrombie and Fitch catalog gone horribly awry. From the looks of it, and from the distinctive smell of stripper perfume emanating from Beef's get-up, I figured they rolled in at about 4 a.m. after a little individual attention from the local *titterati* at Club Paradise, an establishment right across the street from the Hard Rock.

After limping over to the far wall of the room, I unzipped my rolling bag and pulled out my workout clothes. I silently got dressed and left the room, taking time to grab a couple of articles from my briefcase.

The workout room was empty at 7:12 a.m. I guess I was the only guest of the Hard Rock Hotel and Casino ambitious and/or lame enough to try to get in an early morning workout. I set the timer and started pedaling the exercise bike.

The stationary bike's internal mechanism whirred and purred, interrupted periodically by chirps from the machine's computer brain.

I tried reading the article I needed to finish off for a meeting on Monday, but this was again an exercise in futility. Hanging out last night with the guys might have been an annoyance, but at least it was a distraction. Left alone with only the humming and beeping of the bike, my mind drifted every ten seconds or so to thoughts of Gabrielle—I even tracked the increments on the exercise cycle's red digital timer, just for fun.

After finishing 30 minutes on the bike, I tossed aside the article, tuned the gym's television to MTV and started lifting some weights. Still, Gabrielle was there. My confusion. Humiliation. My tears mixed with my sweat.

My entire workout took about an hour and a half. I washed up in a nearby bathroom and went down to the Hard Rock's main hall for breakfast in the hotel's diner. The electronic blings and pings of the slot machines cried from a distance. I thought I might see some of the business school crew in the diner or in the sports book, placing bets on Saturday's college football games. But, it seemed none of my compatriots were as restless as I.

I considered treating myself, ordering a massive breakfast with all of the early morning basic food groups: eggs, bacon, ham, sausage and pancakes. Then, I thought the better of it and just order one fried egg and a piece of rye toast. Saved a couple of bucks. I drank glass after glass of water. I couldn't get enough water. Though sober as a judge, I still felt dehydrated, weak and wasted.

When I returned to my room, it was nearly 10 a.m. As soon as my card key clicked in, I heard the chorus of "JT" from my friends. All three were awake, lying in bed watching east coast college football. "What happened to you last night, man?" asked Billy.

"Ah, you know, I was hanging out for a while, but I've been under the weather. Thought I would rest up for tonight."

"You better *get it done* tonight, baby," declared my bunkmate, Beef, his face still shimmering with the body glitter from one of Club Paradise's Ambers or Tiffanys or Fantasias. He was once again coiffed with his Elvis wig and adorned by gaudy sunglasses, even as he dined on a breakfast of Toblerones, Doritos, Fritos, Cheetos and Bloody Marys from the honor bar. EZ and Billy were also partaking in the buffet: pistachio shells, M&M wrappers and discarded Absolut mini-bottles were scattered on the floor in the proximity of a trashcan.

"Sooooo...are we, like, tracking what we eat from the honor bar?" I inquired. The night before, I had thought about taking a Twix as an almost-midnight snack—until I saw the price. My question drew puzzled looks from my roommates.

"Y'know, write everything down on a pad. Or, say, Billy, you put your wrappers over there." The phone rang, but I continued. "EZ, you put yours on the desk. We can add it all up at the end..."

Beef answered the phone. "Bunny Ranch Whore House and Spa, how may I help you?...No-ho way!...No-ho way! Are you shitting me? If you're shitting me, I will fuck you up!"

EZ, Billy and I exchanged confused looks.

Beef continued his exchange. "Are you fucking with me? If you're fucking with me, I swear I will shit down your throat!...No-ho way...No-ho way! OK, see ya." He hung up the phone and started cracking up, his belly shaking like that of a rock and roll Santa Claus. "That was Carson. He just got a call from Rat. He's getting married." Rat was Larry Rattner, another business school classmate, based in LA. He usually attended events like the NBR Party, Jazz Fest in New Orleans and ski weekends in Lake Tahoe, but was not in Vegas the previous day.

"Married? Cool! When's the date?" Billy asked.

"Today!" Beef replied.

"No fucking way!" said EZ. "Where?"

"Here...in Vegas...in a Chapel in the Bellagio! We're all going! Everybody's here, so he figured, 'Why not?'" laughed Beef.

"Dude, that's awesome!" Billy yelled as he pounded the mattress, causing a pile of pistachio shells to leap skyward. "A wedding!"

"Awesome...a wedding," I echoed, as I turned away to go take a shower.

❋   ❋   ❋   ❋

While most of the group hit the links, Monkey, Balls, Wonger and I spent the early afternoon at the Hard Rock's pool. I should say *they* spent the early afternoon *at* the pool and *I* spent the afternoon *in the proximity* of the pool in an abortive effort to get some work done. After a few hours, we headed inside to watch some baseball at the sports book.

While I remained at our table in the sports book for the entire time, my companions were constantly on the move. They had jam-packed agendas:

- Getting in a few hands of blackjack
- Returning voicemails from senior partners
- Going to the front desk to find out if a FedExed contract had arrived for review
- Approaching a few young ladies at the corner table
- Buying face cream—but in accordance with the edict "What goes on in Vegas, *stays* in Vegas," I shall never disclose the purchaser.

"Can you guys believe it? Rat is eloping! That's hardcore," said Monkey. Monkey was Pat Maloney, dubbed with a simian moniker because he *insisted* we should call him "Money," as his collegiate friends had done. He was persistent in spite of the fact we already had a "Money" well entrenched in our group. Again—never try to pick your own nickname; it can lead to disaster.

"It was probably easier for them to elope than to deal with a lot of the hassles involved with intermarriage. Family, priests, rabbis, churches, synagogues…" Balls commented.

"Well, this is going to be an all-time classic. What are you guys wearing?" Monkey asked.

"This," we all said in unison.

By 5:30, our foursome arrived at the staging area in front of the designated chapel. It appeared all of the other foursomes were running late. None of the golfing contingent had turned up yet for Rat's 6 p.m. ceremony. We loitered in the lobby, listening to snippets of the 5:30 wedding and watching the frantic preparations for the 5:45 p.m. nuptials.

"Anybody want to be a flower girl?" a voice called out behind us.

"Rat! My man, this is fantastic," declared Balls as we all converged on the tuxedoed groom. Manly hugs were exchanged, with special care taken so as not to crush Rat's lovely boutonniere.

"Larry, I'm really happy for you and Tina. It's great that you're making it happen," I said as I pulled away from our hug. I figured that on the man's wedding day, I'd break away from the rodent nickname.

"Thanks. I'm glad you guys could be here on short notice. Y'know, with this interfaith couple thing, stuff can get pretty complicated, so we just wanted to go out and get it done," he commented as he patted me on the back. *Oh, God, please don't let that be a cue for them to ask me about the latest in my flailing romantic life.*

"Mr. Rattner, if I could have a moment…" a clipboard toting wedding wrangler interrupted. Rat excused himself and went off to attend to the logistics of the impromptu celebration.

The 5:45 wedding party loaded into the venue and the 6:15 connubial contingent gathered nearby in the chapel lobby. We wondered if our group of four would be the extent of the Rat wedding party.

That notion was quickly dispelled. "Yo, look, it's the four stooges!" declared Beef as he entered the lobby with EZ and Billy. Their golf spikes clicked on the white tiles in the elegant lobby.

"Where's everyone else?" Monkey asked.

"They should be coming up right behind us. We were in the first foursome to finish up, but the other guys were on the tee and on 17," said Billy.

"Well, this looks like it's going to come together just like clockwork," I said. "Is someone going to roll in here with the beer cart girl?"

"Oh, she was *strong*, JT, *strong*. We can only hope she's here as a bridesmaid," laughed Billy as he dug dirt out from under his fingernails with a golf tee. Over the next few minutes, a few more of the golfers and a couple of the non-golfing gamblers arrived, but we were still about two foursomes short of a wedding. Amidst the talk of stock picks and Sunday NFL picks, I began to hear the canned music in the chapel getting louder. The French doors opened and the blissful couple emerged, being showered with rice as they walked toward the casino. Once they were out of earshot, a dexterous vacuumer quickly removed all reminders of the most holy and solemn occasion that was the 5:45 p.m. wedding.

"You'll want to take your seats; we'll be starting in about two minutes," commented the high priestess of the clipboard as she scurried by. Our band of around twenty shuffled and—because some were still shod in their spikes—clicked its way into the chapel. The venue was actually much more tastefully appointed than I imagined—but then again, this is the "*New* Las Vegas."

We didn't have long to wait for the ceremonies to commence. Within about two minutes, Rat had taken his place near the...God, what do you call someone who marries people in a casino? Rat had taken his place near the...*guy*... at the front of the chapel, and the cutting edge Muzak system began to play the wedding march.

The French doors at the rear of the chapel opened. From my angle, I could see Tina laughing and giving some hidden figures the international signal for "hurry up." Carson and five other late arrivals hustled in as "Here Comes the Bride" continued, a couple of the duffers taking time to stow their golf bags just outside the chapel. I motioned to a couple of the latecomers to take their hats off. They complied, revealing sweaty foreheads and receding hairlines.

As Tina began her walk down the aisle, the distinctive sound of Velcro ripped through the room as one of the golfers decided to remove his forgotten glove. A few seconds later, another of the late arrivals decided to remove his golf glove as well, but, cognizant of the racket caused by his friend, tried unstrapping the Velcro band very slowly. The slow tearing sound was tantamount to fingernails being scratched down a chalkboard. Billy reached over and yanked off the other fellow's Velcro strap with one decisive tug.

Just as Tina arrived at Rat's side, I felt a tap on my shoulder. Billy, sitting a row behind me, was passing along something from Carson, two rows back. It was the money he owed me. I almost waved it off because of the inappropriate timing, but then just decided to grab it, giving him a two-fingered "thank you" salute and then turning back around to observe the ceremony. I noticed the

Mona Lisa-like face of Ben Franklin on the outermost of the two bills that were handed to me. I shoved the money into my breast pocket.

"Friends, we are gathered here today…" the officiant began.

I began to wonder if Carson had given me the full $200. What if the middle bill was just a fifty-dollar note—just the deposit refund and his portion of the interminable cab ride to the suburbs of Las Vegas?

"Tina and Lawrence have shown true love throughout the years…"

I had to check it out. Did he stiff me? Did he really think Ballantine and I were sharing in some fun adventure with him?

"Tina, do you take Lawrence…"

I reached back into the pocket to extract the folded bills. I pried them apart in the same way an old west poker player might covertly examine the hand he had been dealt. Beneath the placid portrait of Benjamin Franklin lay the tousle-haired likeness of Andrew Jackson. A total of $120.

"Speak now or forever hold your peace…"

My face must have turned beet red in an instant.

That motherf—…that little shi—…that jerk! That total as—…that co—…jerk! I didn't know if a casino chapel counted as a place of God, but I didn't want to tempt fate thinking italicized obscenities.

"Do you have the rings?…"

My fuming continued unabated. *Does he think this cash will just all even out? "Catch ya on the flip side." What, I buy the $80 cross-country cab ride and he pays for the $5 taxi back to the Hard Rock from the wedding?* I understood the "let it slide" mentality of picking up a gin and tonic here, or a vodka tonic there, for somebody else. Those transactions usually equaled out amongst a group of friends. But this was beyond the pale!

"By the power vested in me by the state of Nevada, I now pronounce you man and wife. You may kiss the bride."

I slid the bills back into my shirt pocket and clapped with the rest of my friends. Though the first to arrive, I'd actually missed the whole wedding.

✳   ✳   ✳   ✳

After the ceremony, Rat and Tina shielded themselves from a hailstorm of rice and ran beneath an archway of Ping irons, held aloft like sabers at a West Point wedding. The 6:15 p.m. wedding party weaved past our bulky group into the chapel as a couple of our mates pulled beers from their golf bags.

The "reception," such as it was, took place at Shintaro, a Japanese restaurant in the Bellagio. Rat and Tina came by for about half an hour, even imbibing a celebratory sake bomb with the crew. When it came time for credit card roulette again, all of the conscientious objectors from the night before were peer pressured into participating, one by one. Chants of "JT! JT! JT!" in the middle of a crowded restaurant shamed me into flipping in the old Amex after I'd flipped off the group.

My card was pulled out third, so I only had to sweat for about one minute. It may sound hateful, but I prayed to whatever Shinto gods watch over sushi restaurants that Carson's card be the last in the hat. His Amex was pulled out third from last. Beef ended up taking the hit for the team, shelling out over $2000.

Our cabal descended on the Bellagio's casino by 10 p.m. like a Mongol horde. We weren't much for subtlety.

Since I hadn't gambled at all the night before, I figured it would be sacrilege if I didn't blow a little spare change at the blackjack table. I hoped $200 would last me for a couple of hours, if I followed my normal low-profile betting pattern. I walked around to get the lay of the land, trying to find a $5 table to which I might recruit some of the other "low rollers" in the group.

I strolled. I wandered. *Does the Bellagio even have $5 tables? Does it even have $10 tables?*

I returned to party central. It wasn't hard to hone in on my group's shouts of "Vegas, baby, Vegas!" I sat down at a $20 minimum table with EZ, Wonger, Monkey and Dog Breath, asking the dealer to change five $20 bills.

"You gotta go a little stronger than that, JT," suggested EZ as he stacked and restacked his chips.

"Just starting off with this. I want to see what kind of night it's going to be." My friends all had fresh drinks; it might be a few minutes before a hostess came around to take my "free" drink order.

I kept craning my neck, trying to find one of the fishnet-stockinged hostesses. For the next twenty minutes, I bet the minimum—and had a minimal level of success. Still, I was "in the game," with $60 still working for me. Finally, a hostess arrived, and each of us placed a drink order.

After about six more hands, my remaining $60 was exhausted. Not that big a problem, I still had an additional $100 of risk capital I was willing to part with, if necessary. I extracted Carson's $100 bill from my breast pocket and held it out while I waited for the dealer to shuffle the new decks and start the new shoe.

"Oh, excellent call, JT. We should bust out Club Hundo!" smiled EZ as he reached back to grab his wallet.

"Actually, I was just going to change—"

"Strong move, JT. *Club Hundo is in session!*" Wonger exclaimed.

"No, I just want to—"

By this time, all of the guys were digging multiple $100 bills out of their wallets. *Multiple* $100 bills.

"Guys, I really don't—"

"JT, this is now a Club Hundo table! You go large or you go home!" EZ laughed.

And then the Chorus pitched in.

"Yeah, bring that Hundo, JT!"

"Catch Hundo fever, JT!"

"Strap it on! It's Club Hundo, JT!"

"Fine! You fuckers. Long live Club Hundo!" I screamed as I slammed the portrait of ol' Ben down on the table. They all clapped as the dealer flung out our cards.

Well, as it turns out, Club Hundo was not that long-lived for me. My 19 was no match for the 20 the dealer gave himself. Five $100 bills disappeared from the table; four new ones appeared in an instant, is if by magic.

"Thanks, guys. I'll always cherish these wonderful times we shared together at Club Hundo, but I'm afraid my bank is closed." I stood up from my chair and hung out a few feet behind the foursome. *Where's that drink? $200 gone in 40 minutes and not one watered down drink to show for it?*

On the second Club Hundo hand, the house dealt itself a blackjack. EZ turned around. "JT, you gotta leave," he said, trying to telekinetically shoo me away without touching me or looking directly into my eyes.

"I'm just waiting for the dri—"

"No. No. No lurking, JT. It's bad karma," EZ declared. "Club Hundo's got a lot riding on these hands!"

Athos, Porthos and Aramis amplified his point.

"What's with the lurking, JT?"

"Don't be a lurker, JT!"

"Survey says, 'Eeegggghhh' on lurking, JT!"

Gotta love that Las Vegas! Don't get in the way of that big mo'. "Guys, I'll just head over here to the bar…to watch some TV…could you have her bring the drink over there?"

"We'll take care of that drink, JT. Just move along," said EZ.

✹　✹　✹　✹

Three large waters and 58 minutes later, I stared up at ESPN SportsCenter, which I realized was about to start *again* with the same show I had just watched. Look, I'm just pathetic enough to watch SportsCenter for an hour *in Vegas*, but not so pathetic as to watch the same broadcast a second time.

I returned to the area where my crew had been playing. Almost all of them were gone. I caught a glimpse of Wonger and Dog Breath hustling toward the exit, and I wondered if I should go after them.

"Jake, have a seat." It was Money—Nick Monroe, an investment strategist based in Manhattan. He was at an abandoned $50 minimum blackjack table.

"Where'd everyone go?" I asked as I sat down on the stool.

"Some went back to the Hard Rock. Some went to see the ladies at Club Paradise."

"Should we go chase 'em down?" I asked.

"Fuck 'em," he answered.

Yes. Fuck 'em. Fuck them, indeed.

"Let's just chill out in the bar for a minute," he said as he stood up and waved me toward the nearby bar. I got up to follow him. "Man, I've barely talked to you on this trip."

"Well, I'm a little gimpy for golfing, and I was sort of sick last night…"

"I've been watching you…" he said. *Watching me?* In Vegas, guys usually only watched their cards, or the dice. Sometimes they watched the large screens with the football over/under they had $500 riding on. Sometimes, they watched the game of silicone pong that bounced around in front of their faces in smoky strip joints. *Watching me?*

"I've been watching you," he repeated as we sat down at a table in the bar, "and you're acting pretty pathetic. You're not yourself."

"Ah, it's just this Club Hundo thing, man. Sucked me dry in like thirty seconds…"

"No."

"It's just this thing with Carson. I didn't want to get into it. I just got a little pissed off with him about some cash he owes me…I'm letting it get to me too much."

"No. Don't lie, JT. It's Gabrielle, isn't it?"

Maybe this was why I'd been avoiding him. Had I consciously been *avoiding* him? Money was, along with Billy, one of two people who knew I was working on this book. Knowing that he had been shopping for rings, I had talked with him about two weeks earlier about the process of getting engaged. The 4 Cs and all of that.

He was the one person who knew I had been preparing to propose to Gabrielle.

He continued, "You know, a group like this gets together to see each other…not to gamble or get lap dances."

"Could have fooled me," I chuckled.

"Well, *some* of the guys are in it for that," he nodded. "But the point is: people are here to catch up, on the good and the bad. You don't have to keep everything bottled up and walk around like a zombie. Lord knows, you've been there for other guys over the years…in spades.

"Let your friends be your friends, man."

I decided to unload. "OKOKOK, Carson committed a major party foul man. He owes me eighty fucking dollars and I shall have my recompense!" I proclaimed.

"That's a start…"

"And I think G and I just broke up. We might be on a "Break"…I don't know. Four and a half years. I don't even know what a fucking "Break" is. I'd rather know. I'd rather *know*. I'd rather be able to decide whether I love her or…hate her." The last words drew a tear out of my eyes. I was very embarrassed I'd said them.

"I've been there," he said. "You'll sort all of this out. Just remember, buddy: 'You're money…and you don't even know it.'"

Another line stolen unabashedly from *Swingers,* but hearing it was much more pleasant than being regaled by a 500th rendition of "Vegas, baby, Vegas". Coming from Money, it was the ultimate compliment.

"Nah, dude. I know it," I laughed. Of course, I was lying.

We talked for about 20 minutes, which included a two minute recap of the official onset of the "Break," and eighteen minutes of just shooting the shit. Our Vegas momentum had come to a screeching halt, but it was by far the best time I'd had on this trip. A waitress finally came by to take our drink order.

"God, I'm so parched…I'm such a waste. I think I should just have some water."

"Two large waters," Money declared to the waitress. Then with a wink in my direction, "And two scotch and waters. Easy on the water."

We both laughed, and then we talked. We would have shut down any other joint. But Vegas never closes.

9

Tales from the Couch Patrol

I exited the Yellow Cab as Eartha Kitt's recorded voice purred a fond farewell and reminded me to get a receipt. Hurrying inside under a light rain shower, I pulled my rolling bag up the building's ramp and into the lobby.

"Why hello, it's good to see you again. How are you?" asked the attendant at the desk.

"Doing well, thanks," I lied. "It's been a few months since I've been in New York, but it's good to be back."

"Well, I'm sure you'll have a great time. Here's the key."

"Great. Hey, if he has any dry cleaning down here, I can take it up."

"Ah, yes. Thank you," he said, turning to a rack behind the reception desk. "Are you sure you can carry all of that?"

"No problem. Hope to see you tomorrow."

When I was 22 and working for McKay & Associates, the consulting colossus which stands astride the world of international commerce, I used to stay in some of the posher venues known to man. The Waldorf in New York. The Four Seasons in Boston. The Ritz Carlton in Atlanta.

Now that I'm 32, with a top-flight graduate degree and years more work experience, the nature of my homes away from home has changed dramatically. When you're "doing your own thing," the T&E experience is quite different. I'm decidedly less pampered during my travels. Never is the fresh, white embroidered robe laid out for me. And, rarely is room service on the menu. Now, it's all couches, all the time.

I must live the least glamorous "jet set" lifestyle known to man. Already within these pages, we've traveled to San Francisco, Paris, Hollywood, Las Vegas and New York. Soon, if I actually keep writing this thing, we'll journey together to Boston and even to Indianapolis, Indiana, the Crossroads of America. Ain't nothing the least bit posh on my current travel docket.

"Hi honey, I'm home," I said as I opened the door to Kenneth's empty Greenwich Village loft apartment. I flicked on the lights, hung up Kenneth's dry-cleaned Boss and Aboud on a doorknob and walked into the phone-booth sized kitchen. Like many Manhattan kitchens, this room was pine fresh and unspoiled. But the refrigerator was an international bazaar of Chinese, Thai, Italian and Mexican leftovers. I recognized the Chinese food containers from my last visit, almost three months before, and decided to go with different fare. In the freezer was a Stouffer's French bread pizza I purchased during my last stay with Kenneth. I cranked the oven and ventured toward the living room.

Blankets, a pillow and a towel were already laid out there for me—sure, no robe, but the service is decent. I cracked open the *This is Spinal Tap* DVD I had bought for Kenneth as a "thank you" for an earlier billet and let the entertainment commence. Over the last several years, as I've trekked from couch to couch throughout this great land of ours, I've bestowed gifts upon my generous hosts along the way. DVDs, CDs, books and booze were usually the trinkets a poor traveler traded for a warm room and a bath. I would often cook for my hosts as well; with some of my Manhattanite friends, I think I knew their kitchens better than they did.

"Hi honey, I'm home," Kenneth called out as he almost tripped over my rolling bag in the entryway.

"Hey, man. I'm just chilling in my room," I said. Per an earlier message to me, he was coming back from a Sunday evening date, probably his 20th first date of the year. *God, first dates. I don't even* *remember how to do that. Ugh...*I thought as I saw him toss his keys and credit card receipts on his desk.

"Glad to have you back here," he said as we exchanged a quick hug. He slapped me on the shoulder as we plopped back down on the deep, deep couch. While fantastic for sleeping, the pricey piece of furniture was a dismal failure as a couch. It was impossible to avoid sliding down and slouching. "So, how's Dennis doing? I haven't talked to him for a while, but I was just thinking about him today."

In addition to bearing economical gifts, the budget business traveler on Couch Patrol was also expected to purvey information. Like a wandering minstrel during the Middle Ages who told of events in towns over the hill or in the next valley, I was often the transmitter of news.

"He's good. Last I saw him was when he visited me after my surgery. It's pretty much the same update as always, though: new job, new date, new yoga routine. It's bikram now."

"So, what are you up to this week?"

"I have a couple of meetings, but mostly I'll just be working out of here. I'll catch up with some of the B-School friends a couple of nights...and then I have the wedding on Saturday."

"Well, we have to get a squash game in!"

"Y'know, I think I'm still at least a few weeks away from being able to run around like that. Next time." Kenneth and I had a squash series dating back to college. He's kept track of the overall results via paper, PC and now, PDA. Our record is 69-30, in my favor.

"But I just got a new racquet and some Dri-Weave shirts and shorts I want to try out. C'mon, man," he pleaded.

"Dri-*Fit*."

"What?"

"It's Dri-*Fit* clothing..."

"What did I say?"

"Dri-*Weave*. That's the stuff they use in panty liners."

"Whatever. Well, we should get in just one match. Maybe Friday...you can exercise your leg all week—"

"So," I interrupted, "Gabrielle and I are on a 'Break'."

"What? No...are you serious? 'Break'...what does that mean?"

"I have absolutely no idea. You want a little pizza?" I asked as I rolled off the "couch" to retrieve my meal.

"Well, when will you know what it means? Are you going to talk to her about it…the 'Rules,' I mean?"

The "Rules" of the "Break". Will we be seeing other people? Are we going to still see each other at all? How often are we going to talk? What is it fair to ask? How long is it going to last? There are probably a lot of other parameters for said "Break," but I knew very little of this milieu and I hadn't had time to get to Barnes & Noble to buy the instruction manual yet.

"I bet we'll talk near the end of the week," I said as I came back with my cheesy and tomatoey loaves.

"Oh, right. Well, all you can do between now and then is raise the roof in NYC."

"Oh, yes. *I Am The Man*. The roof: it shall indeed be raised," I replied with loving sarcasm, before returning my attention to the life and times of Spinal Tap.

Over the next few days, I had my two meetings, watched a dozen DVDs and shuttled around Manhattan having coffee, martinis, beers and/or baby formula with a number of chums and chum-ettes. On Thursday, Money invited me to join in on a semi-regular billiard night with the boys: DB, Wonger and Monkey. I had played pool with friends several times in smokeless San Francisco in the last year, but the carcinogenic atmosphere in this SoHo venue made the experience seem all the more genuine.

Though Money knew about the "Break", the other fellows had, as yet, not heard about it.

"Oh, no. Dude!"

"Oh, dude. Man!"

"Oh, man. Dude!"

For the next hour, I forced myself—because I needed the knowledge—to listen as the guys briefed me on "Breaks." I sipped my beer and took it all in. Knowledge gathered from their personal experiences, passed on through urban legend, or gleaned from anecdotes told by siblings, cousins, second cousins, friends, ex-girlfriends, coworkers and schoolmates. The multitude of flavors of "Breaks" confounded me. So many confusing combinations of time frames, progress milestones, communications protocols, notification standards and romantic/sexual alert boundary points. A dizzying array of possible endings: marriages, rekindling of dating, lifelong friendships, lifelong acquaintanceships, total silence, total hatred...the list continued.

"Well, I know how we can get you through this thing man, whatever it ends up being. When you're ready to hit the scene, we gotta get you back to NYC!" said Money.

"Oh, you'll rip it up here, baby!"

"Oh, man, some damage *will* be done!"

"Oh, JT, you'd be a dangerous man in Manhattan!"

"Well, thanks. I don't know how 'dangerous' I'll be for a while," I laughed before taking my last sip of beer.

"Just remember," said Money, "*Mi casa es su casa*...or *mi couch-a es su couch-a!*"

✱ ✱ ✱ ✱

Kenneth and I stumbled back to his apartment at about 11:45 on Friday night. It had actually ended up being a pretty fun night on the town. Or, maybe mildly entertaining. Well, at least tolerable.

Kenneth went off to his bathroom to brush his teeth and wash up before bed. I kicked off my shoes and plopped down on my couch/bed. The remote control almost knew by itself to turn on SportsCenter. I sat through a couple renditions of "boo-ya" and "back, back, back", and then noticed my cell phone was ringing. I walked out into the corridor to take the call. It was 11:58 p.m.

I pressed the "Talk" button. "Ah, just before the buzzer..."

"Hi," Gabrielle said plainly and quietly. "I just wanted to call to say 'Happy Birthday'."

"Yes, it is indeed my birthday. For...72 more seconds. It seems like just yesterday I was 31."

"Did you and Kenneth go out?"

"Of course. He was such a lovely date; he wore my favorite pink dress." During college and when possible in our post-collegiate years, Kenneth and I took each other out to dinner for our birthdays, which are only four days apart. He pays for my dinner and drinks, and I pay for his. Aren't we just adorable? "So, how are you?"

"Good...I guess. How are you?" she asked.

"Oh, you know."

"Yeah."

"Yeah."

After a few more antiseptic exchanges, we continued my "Happy Birthday" call by discussing some of our rules for the "Break." Actually, we *discussed* just one rule really—I already knew she planned to date other people, and I knew that I did not plan on visiting her during this period. But, we jointly decided we would stay in touch, and would try to talk every two or three weeks. From two or three times per day at least to once every two or three weeks. Happy Birthday.

We continued talking for a few more minutes—about my trip to Vegas and other random matters. Then she asked me a question.

"So, which 'hotel' are you staying in this time? Are you crashing with Kenneth again?"

"Yeah."

Then she asked another question.

"Are you sleeping on *our couch*?" she sort of laughed.

I was incredibly surprised by what happened next.

I squeaked.

It was a sound unlike any other I had ever emitted. A feeble, but shrill sound, signaling the start of a sudden and unexpected crying jag.

Her quip recalled a trip to New York four years earlier when, after a night of theatre and club hopping, Gabrielle and I retired for a good night's sleep on Kenneth's odd-looking couch, acquired just days before. In the middle of the night, we conferred and decided to perform a dedication ceremony for the new settee—one definitely not covered under the manufacturer's warranty. It was my only violation of the Code of the Couch Patrol, and a grievous one at that. The episode became a running joke, one which Gabrielle and I cited whenever we visited Kenneth—or whenever another friend purchased any new furniture.

"Jake...what? Are you still there?" she said after a few seconds of silence.

Sniffling hard and steadying my voice, I asked her, "Why would you bring that up?"

"*I don't know!*" she bawled from 3,000 miles away. We both persisted sobbing and sniffling for the next minute. Actually, the periodic sniffles and whimpers were probably our most effective mode of dialogue during this late night exchange.

The harsh lighting in the corridor hurt my eyes and the buzz of the high-powered fixtures hurt my ears. Leaning against the plain white wall and seated on puke-colored commercial-grade carpeting, I composed myself before she did.

"I have to go," I announced coolly. Not for any pressing appointment, or to catch the encore broadcast of the night's SportsCenter. I just *had* to get off the phone. "I have to go."

"I do, too," she said quietly.

I flicked the phone closed without a "goodbye" and went back inside. I returned to the couch and lay down in the Jake-shaped crater.

10

So This is Why They Cry at Weddings

Actually, don't worry: there is *no* crying in this story. Yeah, I know; I'm a little relieved myself.

I got an early start the Saturday morning after that first call with Gabrielle. I rolled out of my indentation in the couch and pulled a white dress shirt out of my rolling bag. Cursing myself for not unfolding my dress shirt and suit in the six days I'd been in New York, I just hoped the steam from the shower would do an adequate ironing job on my clothes. Kenneth doesn't own an actual iron; every scrap of his laundry is sent out.

After drying off, I tugged at the creases in my dress shirt and did a passable job of de-wrinkling. Following my shave, I poked my contact lenses into my eyes. I donned my dark blue Hickey Freeman suit, the one suit I had bought since business school. I had worn it very rarely in this era of the Dockers-dominated workplace.

Consulting with the Metro North schedule I had printed out a few days before, I checked the times of the early afternoon trains to Greenwich, Connecticut. I was traveling north for the day to celebrate the wedding of Jose, a business school classmate. Woo-hoo.

The Supremes' Mary Wilson bid me a fond farewell as I got out of the cab at Grand Central Station. Inside, I grabbed a copy of Friday's *Wall Street Journal*—neatly folded on a bench—and walked to my train's departure platform. *The Journal* was good company on the hour-long ride, as we traveled beyond Harlem, New Rochelle and Rye, and into Connecticut.

I grabbed another cab at Greenwich station and headed over to the church. I would be about an hour early, but thought it might provide a good opportunity to catch up with some of my business school classmates. Quite a few familiar faces were milling about when I arrived.

None of my friends from the Vegas extravaganza would be at this event. No, this wedding would be populated by the "double kissing" crowd, not the "double fisting" crowd. There would be a smattering of Americans, but most of the invitees originally hailed from Latin America or Western Europe. The son of a Bolivian cement magnate and the daughter of a Swiss Consul General, both currently I-bankers on Wall Street, were two of the first classmates I ran into. It's not that hard to hang with this crowd if you speak a little French and have memorized the capitals of all of their countries. After that, you just do the patented "fake kiss left/fake kiss right" move, and you're like one of the regulars at Davos.

The October sun beamed down on us with August-like energy. As the appointed hour approached, the steps of the church teemed with sundresses and sunglasses. "*Ciaos*" and "*holas*" were exchanged with vigor.

This was looking like it might shape up as a strong afternoon and evening. I even received a few "save me a dance" requests from some of the ladies among the crowd. I was considering resuming my dancing career at the post-wedding reception, maybe after a couple of cocktails to numb the sore knee.

About ten minutes before the ceremony, the group started to flow into the chapel. Conversations about bond yield curves and the recently wrapped up Hamptons social season continued seamlessly as people elegantly sidestepped into the rows of pews.

"I think it's really going to be a lovely night," said the friend sitting next to me, Thom, a British Manhattanite who worked for an LBO fund during the week and tried to gain leverage against the scrum in his rugby matches every weekend. It never ceases to amaze me how British guys get away with saying the word "lovely," but they really can pull it off.

"I hear the club where they're having the reception is absolutely brilliant," I responded. *Man, I can't even pull off a "brilliant,"* I thought as my mate smiled knowingly at my attempt at Anglophilia.

I pivoted away from the chap next to me and craned my neck in order to get a better look at some of the late arrivals. Amongst the "Where's Waldo?" forest of faces, I picked out a few additional old friends from business school. There was Ian, with whom I teamed up on a project for a corporate finance class. There was Renata—a woman I had dated for a total of three weeks before total incompatibility and corporate recruiting season came between us. There was Diego…with whom I think I had a beer …once.

The bride's side of the aisle was a zone of mystery. I had actually never met Jose's bride-to-be, Stephanie, so I had absolutely no idea who was friend and who family. I scanned the crowd of Greenwichians, Danburyites and Stamforders to get the lay off the land. Near the back of the chapel, I spied what I thought was a familiar face. I focused in on the man with the bearded countenance and realized he was focusing in on me. I couldn't for the life of me place the face within any context.

Did Jose invite an old professor of ours? Did one of his family members visit us at business school? Is this some famous financier who was busted for insider trading?

After a few seconds, the bearded man nudged his neighbor, who looked up from the wedding program she held and squinted in my direction. Then she smiled and waved. And then I knew.

It was Uncle Bob and Aunt Terri. *Gabrielle's* Uncle Bob and Aunt Terri.

I smiled and waved back at them. *Holy fu—…holy sh—…what the he—…are they doing here?* I exclaimed within the confines of my brain, taking care to maintain my prohibition against swearing on holy ground. Aunt Terri began to squeeze out of the pew when the church's organ came alive with the bridal march. She stopped midway and returned to her seat, smiling again and transmitting a set of hand signals which I think translated to: "How funny is it that *you're* here!?! What a coincidence! Let's meet out front after the ceremony so we can exchange big hugs!"

I returned the smile and my own set of Marcel Marceau Morse code, one with a basic message: "Yes, see you out there afterwards! Unless, of course, the floor of the church opens up and vicious minions of Satan pull me down into the depths of some horrific, noxious and fiery level of Hell all my own."

Terri nodded and smiled back, giving me the "OK" sign.

I turned back toward the front of the church, where the entire wedding party had assembled. As the organ emitted its final few notes, I grinned and shook my head. "Lovely."

❊   ❊   ❊   ❊

I couldn't stop laughing during the ceremony. Laughing at this most absurd of situations. Laughing at the sublime torture of the slow-moving service. My English friend Thom and a couple of other nearby schoolmates were variably amused and annoyed. Thom elbowed me; "What's the deal, mate?"

"Sorry, sorry," I whispered. "I just can't believe Jose's actually getting married. I was thinking about the time I locked him out on the roof for two hours in just his boxer shorts."

They all nodded and giggled in fond recollection of the episode I had concocted on the spot.

❊   ❊   ❊   ❊

"How funny is this?" Aunt Terri asked, after we shared the afore-mentioned big hug.

"I know! *How funny is this?*" I said as I shook Uncle Bob's hand.

"This is the last place we would have expected to see you…way out on the East coast. But I guess it is your old stomping grounds," commented Bob.

"Yes. Much stomping gets done out here, that's for sure," I laughed.

"So you obviously know Jose from business school. How funny? You see, I used to work with Stephanie at a television station in

Phoenix, and we've just stayed in touch throughout the years," Terri said.

"How funny!" I returned.

"So Gabrielle didn't come with you?" asked Bob.

Without a pause, I went straight to the answer I formulated during the whole "I pronounce you man and wife" part. "I was coming out here for business after some other travels. You know, with her schedule, it's tough to make the 3,000-mile trip for just two days. I don't think her boss would give her any time off, either." I would let Gabrielle inform all of her relatives and friends of our current status—whatever it was—as she saw fit.

Though a few people had their own autos or rental cars, most of the business school crowd had come to the wedding on the train and was reliant on the wedding shuttle bus for transport to the reception. Terri, Bob and I were standing near the front of the bus when the driver released the air brake and began to shut the door. I knocked on the door and he reopened it. "One sec; I'm riding over there," I said to the driver. And then to Terri and Bob. "So, I'll see you over at the—"

"You should ride over with us. We can catch up some more," asserted Bob.

"*Honey*, he wants to talk to his old friends. You take the bus and we'll see you over there, Jake," Terri smiled. She took Bob by the hand and they stepped away from the bus. "Oh, and Jake…" she said as she glanced back over her sholder, "Save me a dance!"

✳   ✳   ✳   ✳

And that's the moment I knew: there's just way too much potential comedy in this "Break" stuff. I just can't pass it up. It's the gusher of giggles. It might be *the* mother lode of mirth.

Where else can you get such emotional confusion? Random crying jags are always good for a laugh. And snot bubbles are always— *always*—amusing every time they pop up.

The morning after the Greenwich wedding reception, back at Kenneth's Greenwich Village apartment, I turned on my computer and pointed and clicked my way into the depths of the "recycle bin."

I pulled several short stories out of the bin. You remember—the one about the sponge bath…the unfinished one about buying an engagement ring…and all the rest. And then I wrote the anecdote about that longest of nights in L.A., when snot bubbles abounded. On the plane flight back to San Francisco on Monday, I wrote another story about a trip to Las Vegas. On Tuesday, I penned the tale of a couch in New York City and the man who slept on it. Today, Wednesday, I've been working on a story about the lovely wedding in Connecticut and the fellow invitees I unexpectedly ran into. I've almost finished it.

❉   ❉   ❉   ❉

Near the end of the evening, just before I planned to hitch a ride with Thom back to Manhattan, I finally caught up with Jose and got a chance to congratulate him on his marriage. He asked me about the current events in my life, and I updated him, omitting the "Break"— it's just not something I felt like talking about a man who had been a husband for a grand total of six hours.

Just when I was about to impart a final congratulatory man-hug to Jose, Aunt Terri and Uncle Bob approached. "Jose, do you know—?" I asked.

"Of course, we met earlier tonight," he responded. "And how do you know each other?" Jose asked.

"We're related to Gabrielle! We're her aunt and uncle," Terri beamed. I had spoken to them several times throughout the evening—I was the only person they knew there, other than the bride, after all. I did, however, beg off on dancing. The knee, unfortunately, prevented any dancing that evening. "We met Jake a few weeks ago in LA. Here Jake, have you had one of these? They're *fantastic*. I grabbed the last one…"

"No, I didn't try one." She lifted a mini-mousse tart from a plate with small desserts. I reached out to take it from her, but the chocolaty treat continued its upward trajectory past my hand and toward my mouth. I either had to turn away like a recalcitrant toddler avoiding his dosage of Gerber's smushed peas, or open up and welcome the dessert. I opened up.

"Yummmm. Thanks, that *is* delicious," I said after I swallowed.

"Well, if you think that's delicious, you ain't seen nothing yet. We have some great restaurants to go with you and Gabrielle when you come back to LA," said Aunt Terri as she dabbed a bit of chocolate off of the corner of my mouth with a cocktail napkin. She and Uncle Bob were in their early 40s and eager to hit the town with a fabulously social couple like Gabrielle and me. "Oh, and you guys have to come by for a swim some time soon!"

"Well, thanks. My travel schedule is a little up in the air right now, but I'm sure Gabrielle will let you know," I smiled.

"Terri...Bob...I have a question," said Jose as he put his arm around me. He reached across his body with his other hand and squeezed my cheeks between this thumb and fingers. "The real question is: how does a guy who looks like this get a girl who looks like Gabrielle? All of America wants to know!" Everybody laughed.

I smiled the best I could with my face mashed between Jose's fingers. "You know, I ask myself the very same question every day."

11

Packing Up

In addition to allocating hour after hour of "ass time" to chronicling the 10 days I'd just experienced, I did a little house cleaning upon my return to San Francisco. I'm sure this scene is repeated around the world a million times a day, but it happened to be the first time it has happened in my world.

I took Gabrielle's drawer out of my bureau and placed its contents into a plastic milk crate. Clothes of all types, work out attire, little bits of Canadian money. I removed all of the pictures of her and of the two of us from their frames, and replaced them with pictures of my family and friends. Assorted knick-knacks, baubles and trinkets, meet the milk crate.

Moving into the bathroom, I grabbed the various lotions, lipsticks and eyeliners that were littered among my things. I removed bottles of nail polish and nail polish remover. Herbal conditioner? Loofah? Into a second milk crate they went.

I journeyed to the kitchen. On the counter was a note from my flatmate declaring he had eaten two of my cans of Chunky Soup and drunk two of my cans of Diet Coke. Underneath a washed out Chunky can lay a note and a $20 bill. "Sorry we missed each other. One day, our schedules in SF might actually overlap! I look forward to catching up."

From my cupboards, I removed some random ingredients for some dishes she had made or intended to make. Canned peaches? I never eat them—gone. Coriander (what the hell do you put that in)—gone. Other various and sundry foodstuffs—gone. Frozen left-over blackberries—well, I kept those.

Down in the garage, I checked out my car for traces of Gabrielle. My glove compartment was populated with a surprising number of lipsticks and cosmetic pencils, although I wasn't sure if they were the kind women used for their eyes or their lips. Is there a difference? In the trunk, I found a ball cap and a sweatshirt, two articles of clothing she took with us on our blackberry picking outing weeks before.

I came back up to my place with an armful of Gabrielle, and paused in the hallway. My flatmate had put on display an array of pictures from his travels over the years, beauty shots of pyramids, towers, canyons and the like. I stopped in front of one in particular, a shot which I had stood in front of many times in the past. It was a gorgeous shot of Cinque Terra, an area on the Italian Riviera. When this particular photo was shot, the city absolutely glowed under a per-fect sun. I had never heard of Cinque Terra until I asked my flatmate about the photo. It had seemed to me like the perfect spot to get engaged…or more likely to honeymoon, once the finances were replenished.

I can't tell you how much I wanted to rip the photo from the wall. I left it there, however; it wasn't *my* property. Maybe if I ever ended up seeing my roommate again in person, I'd ask if he had another 8 by 10 that could fit into the frame.

The items from the car topped off the second green West Lynn Creamery crate. I placed both plastic milk crates at the back of my closet.

When I turned around, I started to snicker when I realized the lone item I'd forgotten to pack away: the giant planter. It was obvi-ously too big for any milk crate. Plus, the flora inside it had grown so large in its sunny corner, the massive ceramic piece would be exceedingly difficult to move, much less store, anywhere in the apart-ment.

The planter was given a reprieve. It would continue to occupy the corner it had owned for years.

12

The Laundry

I'd come up with a bit of a plan, a sort of timetable.

I had two weeks to be pathetic. Seek solace from good friends. Drink too many beers and explain my heartbreak to buddies while playing the most depressing game of billiards ever. That sort of thing. The male equivalent of sitting around in sweatpants eating entire cartons of Haagen Dazs.

I decided that at the two-week mark, I had to allow the extrovert in me to reemerge. Meet some new people. Specifically, talk to random women. I had been dating Gabrielle for over four years—it had been a long time since I had been under any pressure out on the social scene. I was totally out of practice in dealing with the awkwardness and mild nausea associated with "breaking the ice."

Figure 1: "Break" Timetable

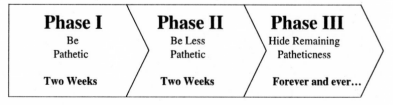

Then at "B Plus One" ("Break" plus one month) I had to start dating again. I was sure Gabrielle would be a tremendous hit among the swell fellas down in Los Angeles and that she would have no shortage of preening suitors. Dating heavily would be the only hope for salvaging my sanity. I just needed to remember how to date—and it's something I was never too accomplished at in the first place.

Thursday marked 14 days since the official commencement of the break. The prescribed two weeks of wallowing was over. The new Era of JT would soon be inaugurated.

But first I had to do my laundry. I was flying out of town on Friday, and had reached the end of my underwear rotation.

I bagged up my dirty clothes and tossed them into the hatchback of the Probe. Launderland—my wash-eteria of choice—was only six blocks away, but I never walked; doing a Santa Claus impression over the hills of San Francisco held little appeal.

I threw my garments into the industrial strength washers. Now, I just had to kill 24 minutes, but I realized that I had forgotten to bring my briefcase with me, so it would be impossible to dispatch a load of work while I did my loads of laundry. That was truly unfortunate, because I did a lot of my best work at the laundromat, and I always loved working in a billable hour in between the loading and the folding.

My only companions during the wash cycle were an *US Weekly* magazine and half of a *Sports Illustrated* that was resting pretty close to the top of the laundromat's trash can. Luckily, the remaining semi-soaked half had the article about the San Francisco Giants I'd been meaning to read. They're going to win the whole thing this year, and we're gonna burn a whole lot of cars. I'd always wanted to live in a city with a post-championship orgy of car burning. Maybe…some day…

After the thorough cleansing, I appropriated a laundry trolley and rolled my soaked clothes over to Launderland's wall of dryers. Unfortunately, I couldn't find two contiguous dryers, so I had to propel my whites to the opposite end of the building.

When I returned, I spotted a corporate finance book in the seat next to that occupied by my *US Weekly*. I dove into an article about celebrities' pets, but was able to tear my eyes away from the pages when the owner of the corporate finance tome returned. A stunning blonde sat down two seats away, having just started her own clothes tumbling in a nearby dryer. She pulled another book out of her back and commenced reading…

Whoa, this could not be better, I thought. She was reading *The Ten Commandments of Innovation,* probably the top-selling business book of the last five years—a book I knew backwards and forwards. I'd worked with the author for three years on various strategy consulting and writing projects. From the looks of it, she was an aspiring MBA. *I'm going to rock her world. She's not going to know what hit her.*

"That's a pretty good book, huh?" I asked. Game on.

She glanced at the book's front cover and then briefly up at me. "Yeah, it's pretty good." She gave me a quick close-mouthed smile, a double nod and a shrug, and then commenced reading again.

Oh, lady. Don't you know the whole new worlds I could open up to you? I could enthrall you with business tales beyond imagining. I could captivate you with stories of creativity unleashed and legends of raw capitalism unbound. I could make you shiver…make you sweat…make your toes curl…for hours at a time with stimulating exchanges of knowledge.

"It's pretty interesting…" I commented, inviting her back in.

"Yeah, it's got some interesting stuff." She looked at the back cover and then up at me. Eager to get back to her reading, she said, "I sort of have to…" She gave me the double nodded shrug and buried her face back in the volume.

Oh, baby. Don't you know what I could do for you? I'm in the acknowledgements, my sweet. The author thanked me. I found a typo in the last proof that had eluded even the most skilled editors. I suggested rewording two sentences and they were indeed reworded. I developed a new categorization scheme for exhibit 16 on page 187, allowing five ungainly categories to be collapsed into three elegant ones.

I'm a glutton for punishment, so I continued, trying to engage one last time. "So, you're in business school? You're reading these for class?…" I motioned to her paperback and the blue hardcover finance book.

"Yeah, getting my MBA," she stated, giving me the briefest glance of them all.

Oh, sweetie. Don't you know I'm awash—virtually drowning—in business education? Would that I were folding my laundry! You would bear witness to a collection of Ivy League paraphernalia the likes of which you've never seen. You would see sweatshirts from clubs and T-shirts from student bonding activities. Ah, and the corporate logos! Such an array of elite companies who had years ago tried to recruit me, back during a bygone era when I had some measure of real career focus. All of it, sartorial testimony to…something.

Well, this first foray back into communication with the opposite sex was just going gangbusters. My skills were razor sharp. My confidence was virtually exploding.

When it came time to fold, I found a space by the far away dryer and went to work. After about two minutes, I realized how nauseous the fluorescent lights and piped-in easy-listening rock music were making me. I stuffed the multicolored pile of warm unfolded clothes into my cavernous laundry bag and headed home.

13

407 Miles

"Your sister needs some black cock."

"Excuse me?" I demanded, flicking my headphones down around my neck and halting work on a short story entitled "The Laundry."

"Just tell your sister black cock will solve her problem."

"Wha…?"

"There are a lot of places you can get it close by." Well, this I knew for certain. I was back in LA for a wedding and crashing at the West Hollywood condo of my sister and her fiancé. Santa Monica Boulevard seemed like it might boast quite a bit of the commodity in question.

"Here, let me show you," the man said. Curious, I followed. Where was this going? "You see the gap between the metal plate and the tiles? I think it loosened up with people turning the shower on and off. That's why it's leaking downstairs.

"You could go with a clear silicone caulk, but I'd say with the black tiles here, your sister should get black caulk. It'll look better," opined the live-in superintendent of my sister's building. "There's a hardware store four blocks up Santa Monica."

"Thanks, I appreciate it. You're right; the black is the way to go. I'll make sure we get some later today," I said as I escorted him to the front door.

Shaking my head and laughing, I returned to the guest room, sat back down at the desk and grabbed my cell phone. Then, I placed the cell phone on the desk, got up from the chair, lay down on the bed and stared straight up at God in misery.

I had palmed my cell phone with the intention of calling Gabrielle. Instinct. Reflexes shaped by a four and a half year relationship. We'd interrupt each other several times a day laughing about the absurd things we saw in the world. We loved double entendres—and relished the rarely executed triple entendre.

But there was no way I could call her. That would be too comfortable and familiar.

Maybe I could drive over there. It's just seven miles from here. That would be funny. Hugely entertaining.

The wedding yesterday was fun and hugely entertaining. Yay! My third wedding in three weeks! I love weddings these days. I'm a really excellent wedding guest these days. I'm fun and hugely entertaining.

I had called my buddy ten days before to tell him that in spite of the blood oath I had sworn on the RSVP card, I would be attending only as one—and we would not need a second beef plate. "She'll be out of town," I lied. "Family thing...we got the dates messed up." I didn't want to burden him with all of my trauma while he was on the final approach to matrimonial bliss.

"Wow...dude...we just finished all of that...the seating and the numbers..."

"Awww, man. Hey, just throw me at the 'singles table.' It'll be fun to do some dancing," I said.

So, when the man-and-wife-to-be made the final adjustments to their numbers, I ended up as their rounding error. I was on the opposite side of the room from everyone I knew at the wedding. Far away from the "singles table." Miles removed from the "cute young unmarried couples we hope get it done soon" table. Light years distant from the "breast pump and mortgage discussion group" table. A vast expanse of barren temporary dance floor separated me from all of them.

Instead, I completed the circle of eight at table 14. Three sets of aunts and uncles. The priest. And me.

I did, however, get to make the rounds among my friends later. It was fun and hugely entertaining to give my "we're on a 'Break' right now" speech 15 or 20 times. I laughed the six times a pal said, "Here, let me buy you a drink" as we stepped up to the free bar.

In about two hours, a blue van will pick me up and shuttle me to LAX. The same type of blue van that picked me up at the airport on Friday. That was a novel experience for me in LA. One of the things I used to enjoy about flying into the city was trying to spot my usual chauffeur as she'd pull up outside of baggage claim. Usually running late, she'd inevitably be applying lipstick with one hand and shoving discarded granola bar wrappers into the glove compartment with the other when I'd sneak up on her. She would explain the three unexpected things that had happened to her in the previous hour that put her behind schedule. Then she'd exhale, bounce up and down in her seat, kiss me and say, "We're going to have fuuuuun" as we passed the monstrous glowing "LAX" sculpture at the airport's exit.

I'd flown the 400 mile distance from San Francisco to Los Angeles so many times, driven it even more. The reason I traveled those 400 miles was seven miles away. With the urgency of proximity, I lay on the bed thinking about her, unable to get her smile and those damn granola bar wrappers out of my head.

I just couldn't wait for my ride to the airport.

14

The Least Datable Man on the Planet

I thought of boycotting the event in protest of the grand and gross injustices committed against the downtrodden by the organizer.

"JT, thanks for coming by!" said Carson as he led me into his Pacific Heights apartment.

"Hey, I brought this to pitch in; it looks pretty interesting," I said as I handed the bottle of red wine to Carson. "It's from the Midwest. I thought it would probably be the only wine with a pig on the label." I considered not bringing any wine to the wine and cheese sampling party, but since that would only harm other innocent wine samplers at the event, I decided to leverage economic pressures through other means. I resolved that I would start to earn back the $80 due me by eating extraordinary amounts of cheese, all of which, I knew, had been purchased by Carson.

"Well, get on in there. I think you know most of the folks. See ya in a bit," he said as he peeled off to talk to a tall blonde whom, I gathered, he was chatting up before.

"Catch you in a few," I returned, as I poured a glass of wine and headed for the cheese table. I knew about half of the people in the room; a few were business school classmates, while some others I just knew from other parties in other apartments with other Bay views.

"Mr. Tanner, always a pleasure to see you," said a voice from behind me. It was Tamara, a business school classmate and a director of merchandising for the Gap. She clinked my glass and delivered a quick kiss on my cheek as I finished chewing a few cubes of gouda. "So, I see you're actually up and around again. I haven't seen you out in a while."

"Well, once I was finally ambulatory again, I was on the road big time. LA, Vegas, New York. Weddings, work, the whole shebang."

"In LA? So how is Gabrielle doing? Is she coming up here for the Halloween parties?" asked Tamara.

"Well, no. Actually, she and I are on a 'Break.' We're taking some time off, probably about six months."

" 'On a break.' Kind of like Ross and Rachel from *Friends*?" she almost laughed. It was only about the twentieth time I'd heard the comment in the last week. "I'm sorry. You guys were great together, but I just hope it works out for the best."

"Thanks," I said. I should have clinked glasses, taken a sip of wine and then moved on to a conversation about the weather or about the triathlon training everyone seemed to be involved in. But I continued. "You know, she's such a special person. She's really just so beautiful and talented and smart. I'm really going to miss her during our time apart. I think we're an exceptional couple and we have a unique bond—over four years of a long distance relationship. Four years. I hope this time apart can be good for her...good for both of us. But, you know, the most important thing for me right now is to be out there. I'm really looking forward to meeting some new people and having some new experiences."

"Uh huh."

"So, anyone interesting I should be meeting down at the Gap?"

"I'll let you know if I think of anyone. I'll see you in a bit," she said as she patted me on the shoulder before going off to grab another glass of wine.

Just as Tamara left the frame, a star performer emerged to take her place. "Hey, baby!" screamed Erica as she slapped me hard on the ass. She gave me a rocking hug that a few weeks before would have been dangerous for my mending knee. She put her hand on my face and contorted her own into a comical frown. "Are you happier now?

No more moping? It's good to see you out mixing it up again with all of the cool kids."

Erica is a great old friend, a fantastic companion throughout both my undergraduate years and in business school as well. She's an investment banker in the City, one of the few who had survived round after round of layoffs during the two-year IPO drought. Erica was the first person I called when I started proactively informing people of my new relationship status.

"Yeah, I'm getting out there again. You know, telling people that I'm on a 'Break,' but ready to have some new experiences."

"'Have some new experiences...'? Are you telling people the same sad-sack shit you told me last week?"

"Well, no...uhhh..." Actually, I had refined the speech a great deal. It was much more succinct, now.

"Jake, don't be a dumbass. You've been *dumped* buddy, and the sooner you realize it, the better. C'mere, Auntie Erica has to straighten you out." She retreated to a set of paired chairs in the corner.

"Uhhh....yeah; just one sec," I said as I grabbed a handful of assorted cheese cubes and followed her to our private little alcove.

✳   ✳   ✳   ✳

To be honest, even before Erica opened up her can of emotional "whoop ass" on me in the corner of Carson's apartment, I had begun to think I needed to tweak my approach to the "Break." Or, more specifically, my approach in *explaining* the "Break." Actually, I came to realize, I was probably an idiot of monumental proportions for explaining the "Break" at all.

Maybe I was cushioning my own ego. As if it's less damaging to say, "She dropped me like a hot potato for a period of not less than five and supposedly not more than six months" than to say, "She dropped me like a hot potato."

Or, maybe I didn't want the emotional side of me to believe what the intellectual side of me had come to believe.

Regardless, my post-"Break" PR campaign was ill conceived and poorly executed. Exhibit 1 describes where I went wrong.

Exhibit 1: Weaknesses of the Post-"Break" Strategy

WHAT I SAID	WHAT I MEANT	WHAT THEY HEARD
You know, she's such a special person. She's really just so beautiful and talented and smart.	Hey, I'm Mr. Mature and Magnanimous. Isn't this the kind of thing we adults say? Look, not a trace of bitterness anywhere.	He's totally infatuated with her. No one else stacks up in his eyes.
I'm really going to miss her during our time apart.	I'm not afraid to admit the way she's affected me. Further evidence I am a mature adult.	"Time apart"? He really thinks he's getting back together with her...
I think we're an exceptional couple and we have a unique bond—over four years of a long distance relationship. Four years.	I'm a committed kind of guy. No fly by night operation here.	Four years? That's a long time to be dipping your toe in the pool. Is he commitment-phobic? Or is he just so pathetic that he can't land his woman after four years?
I hope this time apart can be good for her…good for both of us.	Yes, maybe there is some re-prioritization needed, and some emotional healing. I'm a mature, new millennium kind of guy. I'm not afraid to admit it.	So, anyone I might even consider fixing this guy up with might be set aside like yesterday's news at the end of this "time apart."
But, you know, the most important thing for me right now is to be out there. I'm really looking forward to meeting some new people and having some new experiences.	I'm really looking forward to meeting some new people and having some new experiences.	This guy really wants to get laid.

During the weddings in Greenwich and Los Angeles and the other social events I'd been to over the last couple of weeks, I'd probably delivered a variation of this speech 25-30 times. I am, indeed, clueless beyond comprehension.

"Are you guys making out in this corner or what? Should we put on some *Led Zeppelin IV*?" asked Billy as he nudged his face into our conversation.

"I'm just trying to educate our little friend Jake here on the way the world works," said Erica as she slapped my cheek a couple of times. "I'm afraid he's not ready for the mean streets of the dating world."

"It can be cooooold out there, JT. Take it from me; I did not enjoy my time out there at all during my little break a few months back. Are you getting out on the scene again already?"

"Probably...in a couple of weeks. You know, just meet some new people and have some new experiences..." I said, tossing in the last clause for the sole purpose of needling Erica, who had spent the previous 20 minutes imparting the collective dating wisdom of the ages to me.

"I'm gonna nail you in the nuts if you keep talking that way," she laughed.

"Seriously, dude. You have 'cut the cord', right? You're not talking with Gabrielle, are you?" asked Billy.

"No," I lied.

"Good. It's hard, I know, but it's probably for the best," he nodded.

"Hey, listen, I don't know about you guys, but I'm starved," I said, hoping to avoid any further delving into these matters. "Anyone want some of the brie?"

A couple of weeks ago, Gabrielle and I discussed our limited set of rules for this "Break." It occurred to me—after this conversation with Erica and Billy as well as other discussions with friends over beers or via long distance—that it was probably even more important for me to have *my own* list of guidelines.

Exhibit 2: JT's Rules for the Break

RULE	RATIONALE
1. Don't tell anyone else you're on a "Break."	Whether you're in the "just face reality" camp or the "just try not to look so pathetic" camp, it's the smart move. I've been convinced.
2. Don't make any promises you're not going to keep...which probably means don't make any promises.	There are millions of people out there enjoying each other's company who haven't confided every hope, every dream, every deep, dark secret during dates one through ten. Plus, I'll probably be better off if I just start planning my life, say, one day or one week into the future.

3. Don't be afraid to break hearts.	Look, I know I'm much more Don Knotts than Don Juan. I don't know if I've actually ever broken a heart in my life. But the point is: if you're afraid of ending something, it means you're also afraid of beginning something. I don't want to be afraid of starting something that could be exceptional if the situation arises.

I'm not expert in these matters, at all. I'm learning this as I go along. As I've mentioned before, I have a high schooler's knowledge of this sort of thing—dating, relationships, etc. Well, maybe everyone in the world feels that way about himself or herself.

So, I guess, the best thing we can all do is just start to move forward. It would help if we could just tell which direction was forward.

"So, Jake, we're agreed on the general outlines of a plan?" asked Erica.

"Yes."

"And what are our three rules?" she demanded.

"Number One: Don't be Mr. Mopey. Number Two: Don't be a whiner. Number Three: Go get some tail." Obviously, her suggestions for my grand plan were a little different from the guidelines with which I'm moving forward. But I take all suggestions under advisement.

"Good, good. We'll get you back in the game yet!" Erica said as she, once again, slapped me on the buttocks. I tried to dodge her playful swat and felt a little twinge in my knee. "And, once we get rid of that limp, you'll really be a catch!"

" 'Once we get rid of that *limp…*' *what*? I didn't think that was his problem!" Billy laughed.

"Todd [Erica never stoops to using nicknames], welcome to the world of real *a*-dults," she said matter-of-factly as she plunked Billy square in the forehead with a chunk of blue cheese.

"Hey, I'm going to go get some more cheese," I said, as I backed toward the table o' munchies. "I'll get you guys some."

Carson had recently placed out a couple of new varieties. *Maybe I'll take a doggie bag*, I thought as I piled the cubes, chunks and slices on my plate.

"Why, hello Jake," said a voice from across the cheese table.

"Hey, Cassie, I didn't see you there. How have you been?" Cassie was a...she, uh...well, I guess I just know her from chatting with her for 30 seconds at a time over cheese tables at various parties, really.

She told me about her triathlon training and the group she was putting together for a ski house at Lake Tahoe this coming winter.

"Alas, all of those things are unattainable for me for a while. I just got ACL surgery a couple of months ago."

"Ooooh. Ouch. Well, how are things other than that?"

"Well, getting by...getting by. Having fun...work is good..." I said. "But, my girlfriend and I recently broke up—"

"Oh. I heard you were just on a break," she said as she put a few small pieces of cheese and bread onto her plate. "Have you tried the brie?"

15

Mini Wheats

Actually, it wasn't such a bad conversation. Most definitely civil. Pretty darn cordial. At times, friendly.

In a few rare moments, even funny.

Three weeks post-Break, Gabrielle and I were having our second conversation. Our first, you may recall, ended up with me on a feeble crying jag in the hallway of a New York apartment tower.

This time was different. I was extremely proud of myself, as I maintained total control even when we began to talk about some new topics.

"So, I got cast in my first job. It's voice-over for a radio commercial," she said.

"That's good. I'm really happy for you," I said. I had always planned to fly down to Los Angeles immediately to surprise her after she had been cast in her first "Hollywood" role, no matter how small. Another trivial grand plan—gone. Oh, well.

"It's for an Indian casino outside of San Francisco," she continued.

"That's good," I said. *So, now I'll get to hear her voice several times a week, transmitted right into my car radio. 100,000 watts of fun.* "I'm really happy for you."

"Thanks."

"Yeah."

"Yeah.

"Oh. There's something else. It's sort of funny, if you think about it…"

"Uh-huh?"

"Well, Chloe and Darrell moved in together," she said.

"Oh, really? I'm happy for them." Chloe is Gabrielle's sister, a recent transplant to LA. Darrell is a college friend of mine who lives in Hollywood. I had introduced them about seven weeks before, when I went to LA for G's play. "You know, it's about damn time! I was wondering when those two crazy kids were going to settle down together!"

She laughed. "Yeah."

"Yeah."

"Yeah."

Our "yeah, yeah, yeahs" were followed by sighs from each side of the telephone line. Then, I heard some crunching from her end of the connection.

"What's that? Are you having a snack?" I asked.

"I'm sorry. Acting class was *so* long, and I've had nothing to eat all night; I'm famished. I just grabbed something really quick from the kitchen. Do you mind?"

"It's all right. Whatcha eating?"

"Some Mini Wheats."

Oh God Oh God Oh God Oh God! Don't lose it! Don't lose it!

And then, of course, it was lost. For the second time in my memory, I emitted that totally foreign and, before this month, unknown "squeak" that I had discovered in Manhattan. I covered up the receiver and left Gabrielle alone in silence for a few seconds. The tear ducts started churning again.

"Hello? Jake, are you still there?"

Mini Wheats. My, my, my—a whole lot of symbolism can fit inside that tiny orange box. My cereal purchase of choice is the Kellogg's Variety Pak—usually the adult version with Special K and Corn Flakes, but every once in a while the kid's variety, with Froot Loops and Apple Jacks. Over the course of a couple of weeks, I eat my way through the progression of cereals, but I always stop before I eat the Mini Wheats. I really can't stand 'em.

But G loves them. Whenever she'd come over, there'd be an ample stock of frosted Mini Wheats for her to have for breakfast or to snack on. Sometimes, she'd take a couple boxes back to nibble on during her plane flights to LA. We had joked that Mini Wheats were the ultimate symbol of our extreme level of compatibility.

Still covering up the receiver, I wiped my eyes and blew my nose. I let out a meager laugh, but it was stifled by another wave of despondency.

"Jake? Jake?" Gabrielle called out.

"G...I threw away the Mini Wheats."

"*What? Why would you do that?*" She started sobbing on the other end of the line. From 400 miles away, I could see her face instantly streaked with tears. The sound of her crying and the vision of her contorted face intensified my bawling, which, in turn, caused Gabrielle to double up her wailing.

I couldn't look at the things, the garish orange packs taking up shelf space and mocking me every morning. I knew that from this point forward—for the next six months at least—I would have to buy the General Mills variety pack instead of the Kellogg's.

"Why would you do that?" she asked again. At this point, I think we were both laughing and crying, but the crying ruled the day. I was sad that we couldn't laugh *together*, because it was all pretty damn funny.

"I didn't know if you'd ever...It might be a long time before...I just can't be..." I responded eloquently. And then, I finished, "G, I have to go."

"I have to go, too," she sniffled.

And then: silence. No more crying—or crunching.

16

Mind Control... or Lack Thereof

Author's disclaimer: I provide the following information solely in the hopes that it can further medical science's understanding of the workings of the human brain. Or at least one particularly pathetic human brain.

✳   ✳   ✳   ✳

I've always been an indifferent dreamer, but a *day*dreamer of considerable intensity.

Those characteristics have become all the more pronounced over the last several weeks. I've kept a little notebook around to scrawl any random self-mocking thoughts I might have. I started keeping the pad by my bed at night in case anything interesting came to me while asleep.

I'd try to scribble some thoughts in my little dream notebook, all of the rememberable items, day after day. The snow-white pages revealed to me more than any notes could.

I'm not dreaming.

It sounds incredibly dramatic, the way I phrase it—like my soul has been stolen. I probably am dreaming, but I most certainly *cannot* remember one dream from the last several weeks. When I wake up from a long night's sleep now, I feel like I did when I emerged from anesthesia after my knee surgery three months ago. My eyes and my mind click on all at once, emerging in an instant from a tableau of total black.

During the day, just the opposite is true: it's like my brain is on steroids, speed, LSD, and probably some of the hip new drugs the kids are taking these days. A half hour of rehab on the exercise bike seems to take hours, because my mind jets off on any number of tangents. Then I pause for 15 minutes in between sets of leg presses...just thinking.

Another case in point: just this morning I experienced a particularly hilarious episode.

I called into the office of the founder and CEO of one of the hottest names in retailing in the world. I'd been trying to get this interview for months for an article I'm writing. Quite a coup.

"Is it OK if I put you on speakerphone, so I can record our conversation?" I asked him.

"That's fine," he said, as his gaggle of PR staffers also assented in the sonic background of his speakerphone.

For the next 45 minutes, we talked about his company's stellar brand, new product lines and the impressive level of growth internationally. My final question would drive some final critical points home.

"You've talked a lot through the years about how your employee culture is the company's key strategic asset. Your company has tripled in size over the last ten years. You've opened thousands of new stores worldwide. With such tremendous growth, how have you been able to transmit that corporate culture effectively?" I inquired.

"It's a good question. I'm going to answer you with the way I talk about this challenge internally—I hope it comes through well in print," he began.

"Uh-huh."

"Jake, do you have children?"

"No."

"Well, growing this company...and developing our incredibly unique culture...it's been a process a lot like raising a family."

"Right, right," I nodded, just before taking a bite out of a Pop Tart.

"For me as a father, there have been values I want to imprint on my kids as they've grown up. You're not sure how to impart these values, whether you lecture your children about the values, or whether you just make yourself an available, active father, so they see your actions and learn these lessons in their own way. So, Jake, you can just imagine the challenge."

"Uh-huh." *Family…active father…got it.*

"In my own life, as my family has grown, and my kids have grown older, I've had to evolve how I've tried to demonstrate these values…these boundaries…these ways we behave. Eventually, your kids leave the nest, so you have to hope you've given them a good way to learn on their own about the ways to do the right thing. You see the picture I'm painting…"

"Right, right." *I can see it. Kids…growing older…getting bigger…learning all the time.*

And then, disaster struck. In one instant, I realized the family I was picturing in my mind as he spoke was my own.

And Gabrielle's.

I'd never experienced a wave of psychic pain like the one I felt at that moment. Tears shot from my eyes—I mean *shot*, like the fiery liquid out of a flamethrower. They burnt and blinded me. Before I started squeaking again, I desperately reached for the mute button on the speakerphone.

The whole time the CEO had been speaking I had been visually narrating my own story. It was populated by these cute little sprightly amalgams that perfectly blended Gabrielle's and my features.

I rushed across the kitchen office to the sink and spun off a dozen sheets from a roll of Bounty. I wiped my eyes and blew my nose, which was already stopping up. Knocking over one of the massive article piles next to my desk, I returned to the phone.

"…so, it's not just about some 'employee handbook' or a set of 'company values' inscribed on some tablet, you have to get out there, with the employees, let them see how you treat the customers."

I unmuted the speakerphone. "Uh-huh." I remuted the speakerphone.

The waterworks continued. *Thank GOD this is a phone interview.* I shot across the kitchen again to pour myself a drink of water, hoping to clear my throat for the interview summation I knew I would have to deliver in about a minute.

They were still in my head. Little Jimmy, playing with his die cast cars, assiduously avoiding any valet parking fees by dutifully cranking his new Hot Wheels-brand Powershift Garage Playset. And then little Bettina, her tiny fingers molding a huge multicolored pot behind her Play-Doh-brand Creativity Table.

"...so when you've built the loyalty amongst your employees, you're rewarded by extraordinarily high levels of loyalty among your customer groups."

I unmuted the speakerphone. "Right, right." I remuted the speakerphone.

I was a minute into my...episode...but beginning to pull myself together. I decided to punch the wall next to my desk, just to put a little "manly" exclamation point on the last 60 seconds of fun. I blew my nose one last time and took another drink of water.

"...so any investment we make in developing this culture...in building this family feeling...is repaid back many times over. For us, loyalty equals profits, which we share within our entire family."

I blew my nose and unmuted the speakerphone. "Well, thank you so much. It's been just great stuff. Our readers are truly going to enjoy this. Is the PR department still back there?"

"Still here," a woman said, several feet away from the CEO's speakerphone.

"Well, Bettina, I just wanted to thank you again for putting this together..."

✳   ✳   ✳   ✳

In college, I was depressed for a grand total of five days, three of those attributable to the end of a two-month "relationship" with a woman named Dawn. During this taxing 72-hour period, Erica invited me to have lunch with her at her dormitory's dining hall.

As we walked outside, I confided one last thing to her. "It's just hard to get certain visions out of my head."

"What? Her—naked, on top of you?" she laughed. That Erica; what a cynic! There was the vision of the way Dawn ate pudding, taking the spoon into her mouth twice for each bite, the second time turning it upside down to lick away the remaining tapioca—so cute. And, the picture in my mind of Dawn in a certain nightgown, which imbued her with an interesting "Horny Holly Hobby" appeal. *And, finally,* yes, her naked on top of me.

"You know what you have to do to begin the healing process, Jacob?" she asked, all tones of joking aside.

"What?" I inquired. She was a psych major after all.

"Get some other chick naked…and on top of you." Such wisdom from such a young woman.

My problems now are amplified by a few of orders of magnitude. I know I'm not saying anything particularly insightful to the tens of millions of people in the world more experienced in relationships than I, but the hardest thing is knocking these visions—this daydream fodder—out of your head.

With Dawn, I had three pictures that were burnt into my brain. With Gabrielle, it's tens of thousands. Pictures of the past and images of the future.

And then there's the question: should I even be trying to forget? Are Gabrielle and I done forever? Is this just a temporary thing? Is this "Break" a transition, or is it a termination? Will the "Timing" work out…come due…align…whatever the hell "Timing" does?

✳   ✳   ✳   ✳

Another exciting and intriguing development I've noticed—one which I'm sure will confound brain researchers—is that I've actually begun to understand music lyrics. The portion of my brain responsible for processing sound waves seems to be more highly attuned to the particular wavelengths employed by popular musicians. And the segments of the cerebellum that cogitate on the meaning of lyrics is on some whole new plane of awareness.

In my entire life up until this point, I've memorized the lyrics of only four songs longer than the "Itsy Bitsy Spider." This eclectic jukebox includes "The Reflex" by Duran Duran, "The Star Spangled Ban-ner" by Francis Scott Key, "Jukebox Hero" by Foreigner, and "Foxy Lady" by Jimi Hendrix.

But I'm the fucking lyrical Rain Man these days. Songs come on the radio that I've heard a hundred times, and I finally understand the chorus. I hear something two or three times, and all of a sudden I'm singing it in the shower like some teenage girl. Especially if it's some horrific song about breaking up.

A couple of nights ago, Dennis and I walked into a club South of Market that was playing all of the hits of the 80s. After "Melt with You" died out, the DJ queued up "Always Something There to Remind Me" by Naked Eyes. Yes, I said Naked Eyes.

> *As shadows fall, I pass a small cafe where we would dance at night*
> *And I can't help recalling how it how it felt to kiss and hold you tight*
> *Well, how can I forget you, girl?*
> *When there is always something there to remind me*
> *I was born to love her, and I'll never be free*
> *You'll always be a part of me*

A few lines into the song, I had to sit down. "Something in my contact lens," I told Dennis.

Naked Eyes? Are you fucking kidding me? You are truly descending into the depths of madness if Naked Eyes is messing you up! But the next day, there it was: a new addition to my library of memorized lyrics.

There's one song in particular that I've been trying to avoid at all costs. But, I actually just played it on my stereo to get enthused to write this passage. It comes from my favorite album, *Ten*, by Pearl Jam. You know the record; it's the one with "Jeremy."

I used to avoid playing this CD when I was with Gabrielle. You see, in only 999 of the 1000 scenarios I'd envisioned did Gabrielle and I end up together. I did entertain one future vision of us apart, and it sometimes crept into my consciousness. The soundtrack for that 1000th scenario is "Black," the fifth track on *Ten*.

I know some day you'll have a beautiful life
I know you'll be a star in somebody else's sky
But, why can't it be mine?

Actually, when Eddie Vedder sings it, it sounds more like, "But, why-hy, why-hy, why-hyyyyyyy can't it be, can't it beeeeeee miiiiiiiii-iiiiiiiaaaa-haaahiiine?"

One time, Gabrielle and I drove together in a rental car on a five-hour trip. She had brought along a few CDs, *Ten* among them. As "Black" was about to come on, I advanced the CD, skipping to track six "Jeremy" from track four, "Why Go." She had a quizzical look. "I don't really like this song—too depressing. It reminds me of something," I said.

Shaking her head, she said, "Someone must have really hurt you in your past."

And with that, I close this passage examining the strangely fascinating world that resides in my mind these days. Thank you for your time.

17

Bridget Fucking Jones

I've done my time in bookstores. I've browsed, perused and wandered. For the last several years, as a devotee of biographies and histories, I've stuck mostly to those sections within the aisles of my friendly neighborhood book purveyor. Recently, I've had to troll the business buzzword bin for my job, checking out the latest flavor of the day financial gurus.

Tonight, however, after Erica and I shared a coffee at the Grove, we ventured into a nearby bookseller. I had just told her of the little chronicle of my life I'd been tapping on the past couple of months.

"See, you're just like Bridget Jones," she said, pulling a book from a particular rack with which I hadn't been acquainted. Oh, I had made the acquaintance of Ms. Jones, having read the first 50 pages at Gabrielle's house over a year ago while I waited for G to get dressed. I had also read a few of the other books in the section, and watched the movie versions of a couple more. *High Fidelity* was good.

But seeing this array in front of me, this panoply of vibrant colors unlike anything I have ever laid eyes upon, stirred new feelings within me. As I ran my fingers over the bright spines with even brighter 48-point type, new questions emerged within me, questions like:

What the Hell am I Doing?

I hadn't realized until that moment that my life had become a genre, which is even worse than your life becoming a cliché. I was smack dab in the middle of the "second coming-of-age angst" genre, also known as the "my relationship is a shambles, I think too much, and I have some issue with my body" school of literature.

Oh, yes; it's much like the Lake Poets, or the Beat School. Except with the "second coming-of-age" school, the covers are much more colorful. When they are displayed all together, you begin to think that you're in the gift shop at the end of Willy Wonka, Inc. Factory Tour. My God…the yellows—canary, maize and saffron. The blues—turquoise, aqua and robin's egg.

And the pinks. The pinks. The Eskimos have about one thousand words for snow, but in the publishing industry right now, they're working on their ten thousandth version of pink. I think whole new shades of pink are being invented every day by teams of chemists to adorn the exteriors of these books.

Leafing through a few selections from the Technicolor display, I quickly found some other universal elements found within the finer works of the genre. By far the most critical element is "love of shoes." Characters don't seem to qualify for personal redemption unless they discover the perfect pair of shoes. In this way, this genre borrows from some of the classic works across the ages. We can see parallels with the pursuit of the Golden Fleece and the quest for the Holy Grail, the stuff of plot and parable for hundreds of works of literature. But, when you think about it, those stories merely chronicled the search for the perfect pashmina and a lovely knick-knack that "just makes the room." And of course, the expedition in L. Frank Baum's *The Wizard of Oz* takes the whole shoe quest to a new dimension, as said shoes are actually imparted to the heroine at the beginning and become crucial to the fulfillment of her critical mission. Now this stands in stark contrast to the masterpieces of such great authors as Mark Twain and J.R.R. Tolkein, in whose works the likes of Tom, Huck and assorted Hobbitses actively eschew shoes in the course of their noble and manly undertakings.

Can we trace the other antecedents of this extraordinarily colorful genre? Well, Gregor Samsa in Kafka's *Metamorphosis* definitely had body issues. And, certainly, few shoes would have fit him. His chitinous shell, squirming legs and giant antennae also interfered with all of the important relationships in his life. Plus, as an added bonus, Kafka wove in ample material on career angst—it's hard to hold down a sales job when you're a cockroach. Brilliant stuff.

I scanned the back covers of about a dozen books on the Technicolor rack. It seems that reviewers—at least according to their little blurbs—find these books "wickedly funny." It seems that being "wickedly funny" is a prerequisite for getting a little shelf space these days. Oh, God, please bestow upon me wickedness, and grant unto me funniness, that I too might be "wickedly funny."

You know, I didn't originally intend to be a visitor to this overcrowded land of shopaholics and manic-depressives. I didn't decide to write this thing to chronicle a "Break" or a break up or whatever the hell this is.

I had actually planned on telling a very different set of stories.

Like the one where the guy and the girl don't have enough closet space, so she wants him to get rid of ratty old T-shirts, and he wants her to pare down her dozens of pairs of seldom-worn shoes. They develop their own barter economy, where five disgusting T-shirts equal one pair of scuffed pumps. But then they each rescue their old clothing—all of it reeking with sentimental meaning—from the trash heap. "Heh, heh, heh," the reader would have said. "It's funny 'cause it's true."

How about the one where the guy donates seven spatulas to Goodwill, and the guy and the girl go out and get a *brand new spatula*. "How cute," the reader would have said. "What excellent use of symbolism."

And the one where the guy and the girl have to go pick out china patterns, and the guy is *way* more into it than the girl. "My, what a humorous and unexpected twist," the reader would have said.

Yeah, readers love those unexpected twists.

I begin to wonder, as I am now back in the Grove typing away, what are all of these other people with laptops doing in here? Three years ago, you could have been assured that they were coming up with brilliant ways of selling cotton candy or fishing bait over the Internet. But now, I wonder…

As I look up from my tiny table—I'm essentially crammed into a square yard of space in the darkest corner of the room—toward other sippers of cappuccino and machiatto, I begin to wonder what they could possibly be working on. What could they be typing so feverishly on a Sunday night, these graduate students, with their worn out overcoats? And why are these un-, quasi- and semi-employeds toiling with such urgency? It only takes an hour to clean up that resume. Are they too trying to channel their angst into a 350-page trade paperback with a fuchsia or salmon or bubblegum cover? Have they ruined enough relationships to fill the requisite amount of chapters? Do they really think their body issues are significant enough to warrant a spot on the rainbow rack?

Just a few days ago, I thought keeping up with my little creative project might be therapeutic; now I ponder if I've embarked on some terrible literary death march.

Did I describe a "death march" as "terrible"? I think in my paranoid and caffeinated state last night, I succumbed to exceedingly redundant hyperbole. "*Terrible* death march"…as if there's any other kind…

18

Ripped

"Do with me what you will. Mold me. Shape me. Use me. Abuse me…I don't care," I said earnestly.

Giggles. "You're funny," said Meritza, as she handed me my pants. Or at least pants that would soon be mine, once Meritza rang me up and I left this gallery of semi-haute couture.

I'm a buyer, not a shopper. It makes me fairly popular with the Meritzas of this world. On this afternoon, I was replacing a good portion of the slacks and jeans I had accumulated over the past five years or so. My rehab work on the stationary bike and elliptical trainer had melted two inches from my waist, so it was either get new pants or hope suspenders come back in style. Meritza had earned my business by responding positively to my practice flirting.

"Oh, yeah, those are much better," she said as I walked out of the dressing room wearing slacks that left very little room to grow. She brushed something off of the seat of the pants—a loose thread perhaps.

"Hey, anytime you want to touch my ass, you just go ahead and ask," I commented oh-so-smoothly. "It will always be there for you." Giggles. I was enjoying my afternoon.

"Here, try this on, too," said Meritza, offering up a stretchy pullover very similar to one I already owned. I put it on directly over the T-shirt I was wearing, peered into the mirror and gave the pinched mouth *I don't think so* expression.

"God, we're good looking," she cooed as she sidled up next to me at the mirror. Unable to maintain her sexy face, she broke down giggling again. I decided to buy the stretchy pullover. "OK, so we said we need to get you a couple of pairs of jeans...I'll be right back."

Inside the dressing room, I unzipped the black slacks I'd be purchasing in a few minutes and awaited Meritza's next delivery. Within a few seconds, two pairs of jeans flopped themselves over the changing room door. One was a pair of weathered, gray denim and the other was... *Wait a second. What the...?*

With the black pants re-zipped, but unbuttoned, I hustled out of the dressing room. "Uhhh...Meritza...do I look like the kind of person who would wear these?" I asked, holding up the pair of *ripped* blue denim jeans in front of me.

"Oh, those will look great on you. That cut is really what you should be wearing," she responded.

"No, I mean..." I realized I could easily blow the whole rapport we'd built up in the past half hour. Not everyone held such strong views as I on the issue of ripped jeans. I had decided long ago—or at least a couple of years before when they first came into fashion—that I would not buy a pair of *pre-ripped...factory ripped* jeans. I always tried to be flexible in life, but I did have a few hard and fast rules.

[Please see my analysis in Exhibit 3]

But I digress.

"No, I mean...well, do people like me *really*...I mean, a guy my age...I just don't think I'm a ripped jeans kind of guy." I added a little dash of laughter to the end so that Meritza wouldn't see how deeply I was struggling with the proposition that someone thought I was indeed a ripped jeans kind of guy.

"No, all kinds of guys wear them. It's just the style. Besides, the jeans you had on when you came in here were pretty well worn. They had a couple of rips, didn't they?"

"Yyyyeeeeessssssss, but...y'know, those jeans are seven or eight years old. Those are *real* rips. You break the jeans in yourself...they're comfortable...each rip has meaning." I was absolutely going over the edge and I knew it. I had never had to elucidate my theories on pre-ripped jeans to another human before. Maybe the foundations of my philosophy were a little shaky.

Exhibit 3: People with whom to Avoid Close Association

THE PEOPLE	WHERE YOU FIND THEM	RATIONALE
Those who wear pre-ripped jeans	• Art openings attracting young professionals • Literary readings attracting young professionals • Dilettante bowling nights attracting young professionals • Always at the Grove on Chestnut Street…and sometimes the Grove on Fillmore Street	My God, could they try any harder to get some cred as carefree quasi-Bohemian types? They fall more easily into the trend du jour than did Dr. Seuss' star-bellied sneeches who inhabited the beaches. I just want to see what happens when the "Bedazzler" self-sequining kit becomes all the rage again.
People who say, "Don't hate the player, hate the game"	• MTV • Eminem and Limp Bizkit concerts • Las Vegas—primarily in the clubs where one can get one's freak on • The pick-up basketball courts in the Marina	They had the bad taste to latch onto one of the worst catch phrases of 2001. This pithy little statement could be used to justify…oh, pretty much anything any stupid bastard wanted to do. I decided I hated the playaz and the game.
Individuals with the motto "Work hard, play hard"	• Self-help courses…oh, and courses on how to get rich in real estate with no money down • Radio station ad sales departments • 3:30 p.m. happy hours • Pretty much every personal advertisement I've ever glanced at	Statisticians from MIT employing multivariate regression analysis have demonstrated an almost 100% correlation in the use of this phrase with those who actually just play hard. Those who really do play hard and work hard rarely find the need to adopt a motto. Indeed, I'm considering extending my disdain to anyone who maintains that they have a motto.

"Look, honey, you shouldn't think so much about it," Meritza said as she pushed me back into the dressing room. "Just put your pants on."

She was right. I *should* be able to embrace the pre-ripped jeans lifestyle and everything it entailed. Maybe I'd been too dogmatic in my denunciation of pre-ripped jeans and those who wore them.

The craftsmanship on these jeans was, indeed, exquisite. The company must send the pants from a factory in Mississippi to a bustling couture workshop in SoHo...or maybe in West Holly-wood...to have fashion experts rend the garments in just the right way. Delicate white threads trickled off the end of each pant leg. Though the silver buttons on the fly were bright and shiny, they were hidden by a masterfully frayed flap of fabric. And the front pockets looked like they might lose a rivet at any moment, heightening the overall sense of intrigue associated with the jeans.

I donned the pre-ripped pants and they were as comfortable as the well broken-in pair I'd worn in—perhaps more comfortable. When I emerged from the dressing room, Meritza nodded.

"See, don't you look nice?" she said in a tone very similar to the one I remembered my mother using when I reluctantly tried on my first "big boy" suit about 25 years before.

"OKOKOK...you're right," I admitted.

"You should wear them out," Meritza suggested.

"Well, they're already pretty worn out," I said.

"No, you should *wear them out of the store*, silly." God, I am truly, truly daft about 22 hours each day.

I snapped my Amex down on the counter as Meritza folded up my old Levis and put them in the bag, which was already bulging with my new purchases. We exchanged a final bit of banter before I hoisted up my new costumes and headed out to take on the world in my pre-ripped jeans.

19

Rehabilitation

I awoke yesterday and immediately felt the pressure of trying to be a reasonably productive player in our 21st century economy. Rarely these days do I feel the demands of having not enough time in the day to execute all of my grand plans and herd all of the irksome details, but yesterday was stacked with activities. Back to back to back—wait, is that anatomically possible?

Between 7 and 9 a.m. I had two conference calls. Colleagues on the east coast debated if we should present a 25 or 30 page deck next week. In a mere 45 minutes, we agreed to cut and paste the material from various slides onto other slides, thereby leaving us with a masterfully crafted 25 pager. We congratulated ourselves on an elegant solution.

Then, I talked with a client about how we really needed to excise the term "vision statement" from a document we were working on with them. It seems that last year the firm's management team was nearly torn asunder by an incredibly rancorous discussion about a possible vision statement. The client and I agreed to change the section heading to "mission statement" while leaving the rest of the content as-is. Another crisis averted.

For the next hour, I knocked over e-mail dominoes, chipping in my opinions on virtual discussions that had been developing between colleagues in the early morning hours. "Where should we convene as a team to talk about the deck? Any suggestions?" read one e-mail query, copied to everyone who had touched the project. "How about in the hotel restaurant of the Hyatt where we're all staying," I creatively suggested. It was an incredibly productive morning.

At 10 a.m., I decided that I'd take advantage of a break in the schedule before some other heavy commitments kicked in during the afternoon. I wanted to squeeze in my knee rehab workout and hustled to get ready to go to the gym. Grabbing a book I needed to get through for my current consulting project—always good to work in a billable hour—I rushed out the door and down the long hill toward my gym.

When I reached Titan Fitness, I quickly stowed my fleece and cell phone in a locker. I checked the time on my handset, and noticed the date. *Huh…one month exactly since the "Break". My deadline for shedding all basket case personality traits.* More specifically, I had promised myself that it was the day I had to start lining up some dates. It was a Friday—I was pretty sure I'd meet some interesting young women at the two parties I planned on hitting that night.

I'd have to cut my routine on the stationary bike short if I wanted to get in my weight training. I opened up my book and blindly walked toward the row of machines.

"Whoa there!" exclaimed a petite young woman as she pirouetted away from a collision with me.

"I'm sorry, I didn't see you. Sorry," I returned. She was gorgeous. Her beauty struck me immediately. I was actually lucky I didn't say the clichéd: "I'm sorry, I didn't…see you…sorry," the extra pauses, of course, giving time for the camera to cut from my face to her face and then back again as our eyes meet, our expressions conveying a sense of earnest, but wonderful confusion.

But by the time my second "sorry" worked its way out of my mouth, I was already mounting the exercise bike.

"No problem," she laughed. She gave me a quick almost-wave and progressed on to her chosen quarter of the gym.

I started pedaling while programming "30 minutes" into the electronically enhanced cycle. *Have to keep it short today. Gotta get back to work.*

Having read a good seven or eight lines of my book, I decided to take a break from my work. *Let's see, who's in the gym today? Ah, there's*

"Black Sabbath T-shirt wearing guy" two bikes down. *I hope you have about seven of those T-shirts, man, or we're going to have to declare your torso a toxic waste cleanup site. Oh, "three-karat diamond wearing lady"…there you are. The diamond is looking as beautiful and inappropriate as ever in the gym. Let's see, who else? Hmmmm…oh, "amazingly beautiful pirouetting girl," you're still here?*

She was dressed in a tight fitting spandex top that left her midriff open to the glances of the four guys whose workout regimens happened to take them to her immediate vicinity. Her ponytail flexed as she curled her dual 15-pound dumbbells.

I gotta get back home and get to work. I should just do 20 minutes on this thing.

In between sets, she pressed her hand to the side of her jaw, turning her head back and forth periodically to each shoulder in a contrived, but exquisite, neck stretch.

Man, I have the big Customer Interview Project I need to get started on this afternoon. I really should just do 15 minutes.

I read another three lines of my book. I decided to take another break. She was talking with *"perpetual Don Johnson stubble dude,"* who was next to her doing curls even though he had just done curls yesterday—in blatant disregard of the maxim you should always give your muscles a day to rest and recover.

OK, four minutes twenty-two seconds. That should just about do it. Time to hit the weights.

I bee-lined to the drinking fountain for a quick swig. Removing my glasses, I wiped my sweaty face—that was a tough 4:22—with my shirt. It was just then I noticed how slovenly I looked. Roughed up black Nike high tops I planned on replacing within days. Non-matching white socks—one Adidas, one generic—each having been jilted by their mates months earlier, but now finding a home together at the very end of my athletic sock rotation. A dark blue "Harvard: The Michigan of the East," T-shirt, scarred by a huge bleach stain ripping through the stomach and up to the chest. And my glasses! I never wore my glasses to the gym. They were sliding down my face on the thin film of sweat that was emerging. I had to Poindexter them back up onto the bridge of my nose every 15 seconds of so. Oh,

God. My hair. I hadn't even looked in the mirror that morning. Who knows what strange swirls and cowlicks had taken over?

Fuck it. One month. I'm going in.

I thought I would work in a quick set of curls or some other exercise requiring dumbbells. I moved around the corner from the drinking fountain to the free weight area and...she was gone. Where was the little pirouetter? Mr. Stubble had moved on to the cardio area, which is where he should have been in the first place. Had that jackass scared her off with his ham-handed attempts at small talk?

Disgusted, I returned to the area by the drinking fountain, where the leg exercise machines resided. *Well, it looks like I will get some real rehab in. This sucks.*

I started with leg extensions, gingerly extending my lower leg up to exercise my still painful knee. A tinny "clang" after each rep announced to the gym that I was indeed a wimp, still capable of putting up only a small stack of weights.

I fumed as I attempted to read my book again.

Doesn't she know she was supposed to be the one? I'm supposed to make a valiant attempt at hitting on the most beautiful woman in the gym...and go down in a blaze of glory...that will serve as testament to the fact that I'm emotionally whole...and that I'm ready to be shot down by countless women all over the City.

Although I had never hit on a woman in the gym, Titan Fitness was known for being the launching pad of quite a few relationships. Actually, I'd really never even met anyone in Titan in the three years I'd been a member. I had talked to plenty of people: "Are you using this bench?"... "Is that a good book?" ... "Do you know what time the yoga class starts?" I'd chit chatted with members whom I had met in other venues: "Great party at Carson's, huh?". But I'd never really *met* anyone new at the place. Well, I was friendly with the gym's membership director, but that really didn't count, since he was sort of paid to be my friend.

I moved on to my second exercise, still reading while I lifted. I rose up out of the apparatus to increase the weight for my next set— and bumped into the beautiful midriff again.

"Hey. Hi. Sorry....again," I managed.

"No worries...again," she smiled as she doubled up the weight stack and began to use the machine I had vacated one minute before.

So, now the clock was ticking. I had 12 reps—about 30 seconds—to think of something to say to this woman. In spite of the notion of equality between the sexes, it was still usually the responsibility of the guy to break the ice in social situations. Like most men, I was still trying to decipher the best means of opening up a conversation. I rifled through the file cabinet of my mind to try to locate some openers that had worked in the past.

- "So, how does that new Zima taste?"
- "Hi. Will you sign my friend's birthday card?"
- "You guys are rooting for the Gators, too? We love the Gators!"

(OK. OK. Before you paint too harsh a picture of me, just let me say these things. First, Zima had just been launched weeks before and was sweeping the nation like a cool and refreshing wildfire. Second, my buddy Kenneth's birthday *was* actually the next day and *I did* give him the card. Finally...well, this one *was* contrived. We really *did not* want the University of Florida to win a damn thing, but it just seemed like the best thing to say at the time if we wanted entrée into a group of six young alumnae.)

Eleven...Twelve. I noticed the weights behind me had stopped clanging and rose from my vinyl perch.

"So, did you get knee surgery, too?" I asked. Pretty good for such short notice, eh? If she possessed any shred of the Florence Nightengale complex, she'd be very interested in my healing process. *Plus,* it explained why I only put up half the weight she was lifting.

"What? Yeah...no," she laughed, paused, shook her head and then extended her hand. "*Hi.* I'm Angeline."

Of course you are.

I shook her hand. "I'm Jake. Hi. I just meant, you know, you're back here in the dark part of the gym, doing the same exercises I'm doing. Y'see, because I had surgery a few months ago," I informed her, raising my scarred knee for show and tell.

"Ouch! Not fun, I imagine. How did it happen? Was it basketball? It's usually basketball with guys."

"Yeah, that's what happens when you drive the lane into the 'land of the giants,'" I said, hoping she understood the technical sporting terminology.

"A friend of mine ripped up her knee back when we were in training, God, nine or ten years ago."

"Training for…"

"Rhythmic gymnastics. We were getting ready for an international competition and she slipped, and…" Then she made a sound effect for ripping and tearing that I have no idea how to spell—even though I know exactly what it feels like.

Rhythmic gymnastics. The kind where women jump around with streamers and juggling paraphernalia. Nice…

Though rhythmic *gymnastics* bored me to tears, rhythmic *gymnasts* had always fascinated me.

"So you went to Michigan?" she asked, motioning toward the T-shirt I should have thrown away long ago.

I told her "no," and then we proceeded to swap vital statistics on education, birthplace, career highlights, etc. We recounted our wanderings around the country, listing the cities we had called home because our mail was sent there.

Surprisingly, we talked about September 11th. She had been visiting New York at the time, staying less than a mile away from Ground Zero—I had just been in Boston on business, flying back three days earlier on an early morning non-stop flight to San Francisco.

We rhapsodized about the places we'd traveled. I'm usually not a "rhapsodizer" as such, but she seemed so moved by her travel experiences that I figured I better juice up the "emotional impact" portions of my stories.

After an hour it dawned on me: We'd been talking for an hour. *What the hell is going on here?* I figured this discussion would go pretty much the same as my crash-and-burn session two weeks earlier at the Laundromat. Much to my amazement, I seemed to have found someone who actually wanted to listen to me. I had certainly given her plenty of outs— "You probably need to get on with your workout…" and such—but she hadn't bitten. All in all, this looked like it *could* be a successful foray back into the world of dating. Only one way to know for sure.

"So, we should definitely get together soon. I'd like to get your number," I said.

"Yyyyyeah. Sure," she nodded. I wasn't sure I liked the way she spelled her answer.

"Gooooood," I returned, imitating her pause and her nod.

"No, no, no! I'm sorry. I just…I…yes, we should get together."

"You had me worried. It's very intimidating, you know? I'm not very experienced in this area—trying to approach women in the gym."

"I could tell…"

"Oh, well thanks!" I declared, with a dash of mock embarrassment.

"No, no! In a *good* way," Angeline responded as she leaned in and gave me a little reassuring shake of the arm. Even though I was way out of practice in the field of courtship, I could definitely recall one of the major tenets of flirtation: touching is good. "Definitely give me a call!" She walked over to the bulletin board nearby and quickly perused the attached notices for "Lost Cat," "Spanish Lessons," "At-Home Massage," and the like. Finding the least worthy of the fliers— a bright red "1999 Porsche Boxster For Sale" poster—she ripped it down and scrawled her info using the pen strung up on the bulletin board.

"So, take this, my number's on here, give me call…"

"Hey, I'm kind of lame with gym pick up lines, but I do know how these things work," I said as I held up the slip of paper. "Wait, so I have to dial all seven numbers, right?"

"Smarty!" she exclaimed as she punched me in the stomach. She slugged me in the stomach! I think she even accompanied it with some sort of kung fu movie sound effect! Punching is even better than touching. *What the hell is going on here?*

"So, I'm going to head out now," she said, smiling and slowly backing her way toward the front of the gym. *"You'll call me.* You may have to key in a 415 at the beginning. If you're using a pay phone, make sure you insert some change first." She grabbed her fleece from a hook on the wall, gave me a final wave and then bounced her way toward the exit of Titan Fitness.

I stood in stunned silence for a few seconds. I thought it was going to be much harder than this. But there it was, in my right hand—the folded scarlet flier with Angeline's number. I snatched the string and pen combo from the bulletin board and transcribed Angeline's info from the piece of paper onto the bookmark of the tome I had thrown aside an hour before. I needed backup...multiple redundancies...to make sure I didn't screw this thing up. Once I finished my workout, I would store the number in my cell phone.

I decided to clang for just a few more minutes on the leg exercise machines; I didn't want to blow my schedule for the whole day after all. As I walked toward the locker room to reclaim my belongings, I took a quick look at myself in the gym's curling vanity mirror, my first glance into a mirror all day. My hair was a spectacle. An Alfalfa sprouted from the left side of the top of my head, while a Buckwheat bristled just above my right ear. I started to finger comb the rascalous anomalies out of my hair.

"I got a ticket," said a voice behind me. I whirled around and saw a none-too-pleased Angeline brandishing a notice from the Department of Parking and Traffic. "We were talking so long the meter people got me."

She handed me the ticket. I took a look at the $45 buzz killer; the meter people loved ruining good days. "I'm so sorry. I totally lost track of time. We should have...you know...please let me..."

"Don't worry about it!" smiled Angeline. "I'm just foolin' with you. It was totally worth it. I got to meet *you!*" She reached up with both hands and mussed up the hair I had just started to put back in order. "Talk to you soon. Bye."

"Bye," I managed.

What the hell is going on here?

20

World Series

I had a tremendous amount riding on this Sunday's game. The pressure was enormous.

Sunday was the seventh game of the 2002 World Series. The San Francisco Giants were squaring off against the Anaheim Angels.

The Giants should have finished this one off already. Saturday, during Game 6, they squandered a 5-0 seventh inning lead. They choked. But I was partly to blame as well.

Barry Bonds and company blew the game wide open Saturday night with a huge fifth inning. That was all well and good with me—I loved blowouts when my team was the one dominating. The run-away victory in the making was most welcome on this night in particular. Although we were still several days away from the 31st, Saturday was going to be a massive night for Halloween parties in the City. I could watch the blowout in progress out of the corner of my eye while I was finishing up work on my Halloween costume.

I was almost delirious with happiness as I pondered the combination of World Series Victory and Halloween debauchery. It would be an intoxicating cocktail, one that could have been mixed by Bacchus himself. The excessive victory toasts with buddies who had been cheering for the Giants for anywhere from 30 years to 30 minutes. The needless smooches with women who *actually* knew and cared that there was a World Series going on—plus many from those who didn't. And the car burning. Oh, the car burning.

In the seventh inning, I got the most fantastic idea: I should get some Giants World Series Championship gear. With the Giants pitching a shutout against the Angels, both legal and illegal silk screening operations must have been springing to life all over the City. Although sports paraphernalia wouldn't exactly blend in with my costume, if I were clad in the *vetements de victoire*, I would be more of a focus for both the excessive toasts and the needless smooches. Sheer genius.

I pulled out the Yellow Pages and called a few nearby sporting goods stores. Either closed, or not stocking the championship gear. I tried a couple of T-shirt shacks in Fisherman's Wharf, the stomping grounds for San Francisco's uber-tourists. After three calls, I struck paydirt. "Yes, we will have the 'World Series Champs' T-shirts," claimed the entrepreneur, his Punjabi accent lending him instant gray market cred. "We have the silk screens set up already and we will start printing in a few minutes."

"Great. I'm there buddy," I assured him. "Hold the first one for me. The *very first one* you make."

Brilliant. Everything was falling into place. Jagdish was saving a primo championship T for me; I was the first person in the City to think of calling him. A quick detour in the taxi to get the first shirt off the presses and then I would be off to the masquerade madness.

But then the tide of the game began to turn. Revved up by their cursed (kur-SUD) mascot—the Rally Monkey—the Angels did indeed begin to rally. The crowd began pounding those damned red Thunder Sticks—the inflatable noisemakers produced a detestable racket.

I realized I had a made a terrible mistake. The Angels scored three runs.

I dialed. Jagdish answered. "Hello, I called about half an hour ago and asked you to hold a T-shirt for me. Please cancel that order right away," I ordered.

"Wha…who?" he said.

"Just do it!" I hung up.

I had been the first person to call Jagdish's T-shirt emporium. I had committed a massive violation of sports protocol and had set in motion a terrible series of events. I'm embarrassed as I chronicle the magnitude of my transgression. The heart of the Angels' order shredded the Giants' relievers, and Anaheim won the game 6-5.

Revelry still abounded at the evening's Halloween parties, but the festivities were a pale shadow of what might have been.

Every imaginable sports cliché was flying around the room when I arrived at the home of Billy and EZ for Sunday's pressure-packed game 7. Around 15 people had gathered for San Francisco's Game-of-the-Century-of-the-Week. I was a little disappointed with the crowd. You could usually count on a healthy population of women attending any event at the Telegraph Hill house, but in this case the bachelor pad was crowded almost exclusively with bachelors.

I settled into a comfortable black leather recliner, my sports viewing cocoon for the evening. *Focus. Focus.*

Pizzas were ordered. Beers were uncapped. Pringles were popped. I ate, but rarely talked, in spite of my friends trying to tap into my usually useless well of sports trivia. I didn't know if I was just the evenings' entertainment or if they really wanted to get some perspective on the game. "Dave Henderson ...Donnie Moore...Gene Autry ...1961...'79, '82, '86...Bobby Grich ...No...Zero," I answered tersely. *Focus.*

The Giants drew first blood, but our crew of San Franciscans had little time to celebrate; Anaheim notched the equalizer in the bottom of the inning. Then, the homestanding Angels knocked in three runs in the third. First, San Francisco's pitcher nailed a batter. *Take your base, wimp.* Then, our trusty hurler served up a meatball right over the plate, leading to a bases-clearing double. Some little girl pounded SF's defenseless outfielder with a Thunder Stick.

"Fucking fan interference," yelled just about everyone. The "fucking" is just natural—it's so alliterative.

A pall had been cast over the household. All energy had been sapped from our crew, in spite of the fact that six innings remained. "C'mon, let's go," one of the two women in attendance said to her boyfriend. *Good. Get that bad karma out of here.*

Billy tried to talk to me about something, but my thoughts were 400 miles south. Not 425 miles south in Anaheim, but 400 miles south—in the heart of Los Angeles. Inevitably, hordes of Los Angeles residents were adopting the Angels as their own. Probably hundreds of thousands more every inning. People who couldn't spell Anaheim. People who couldn't find Anaheim if you started them off in Disney Land's parking lot.

I started picturing a World Series party in Hollywood. Medium-sized apartment. Stained carpet (this is young Hollywood we're talking about). If you crane your neck, you can see the "Wood" in the Hollywood sign. The "Holly" is blocked by a billboard for *Jackass: The Movie*. Three people are watching the game, shushing the posers behind them. Another twenty are acting out the script couriered to every World Series party planned in Hollywood for that night.

Untucked-quasi-cowboy-shirt-wearing dudes circle the scene. Spiked-frosted-boy-band-hair abounds. Sunglasses-at-night-inside are rife, graduated blue or sepia covering carefully waxed guy-brows or perched delicately on the frosted crown.

They find Gabrielle. They bombard her with their inanities.

Fourth Inning. *I DO think I remember your* Highway to Heaven *episode. Are you still in touch with Michael Landon?*

Fifth. *I could shoot your headshots. I'd do you for free.*

Sixth. *I was a writer for* Angels in the Outfield. *Yeah, uncredited, but hey, it's Disney.*

Inning after inning, I sat quietly in the black chair. I had a stack of Pringles on my chest that I crunched every once in a while, but was otherwise silent. The Giants were doing nothing, absolutely nothing, to salvage my evening. I seethed.

Seventh. *My production company has the option on the* Rally Monkey *movie.*

Eighth. *Send me your reel. I have a producer friend who's looking for someone like you.*

Ninth. *You're going with us to the Sky Bar for some champagne to celebrate, aren't you?*

The Giants were blowing it. I couldn't stand the thought of revelers in LA. I couldn't stand the thought of the winning high fives and hugs that would be sought and given at Hollywood parties. It should be us taking to the streets. We thirteen guys and one gir...oh, the other woman must have taken off, too. We should be hitting the bars in between the seedy North Beach strip clubs on Broadway. We should be kissing random women who want to kiss us solely because that's what people reveling in the streets do. We should be getting so trashed that those of us with real jobs will show up at 3 p.m.—unapologetically. And the cars, oh the cars should burn. That's what champions do.

The Angels centerfielder caught a lame floater and the game was finished. And, with it, the dreams of so many San Franciscans who just wanted to get drunk and burn things.

Leather jackets were donned almost instantaneously and half the group was out the door within 30 seconds. Pizza crust boomerangs were tossed into the garbage. Domino's boxes were violently folded and smashed into the black lawn and leaf trash bags serious partiers are required to purchase.

Thunderstix pounded and fans continued screaming. Over the roar of the crowd, loud post-Game interviews praised teammates and Jesus Christ.

I rose out of the black chair for the first time in 90 minutes, brushing shards of Pringles onto the floor. I walked out to the deck, and looked out at one of the best views in San Francisco—Alcatraz, the Golden Gate, the lights of Fisherman's Wharf. It was so silent, I couldn't even hear the usual whelpings of Pier 39's sea lions. No extra buses filled with raucous fans rumbling by. No fire trucks.

My side had lost.

21

Little Princess

I traveled to Boston the Monday after the Giants' World Series loss. With the amount of work I had to do out east, I definitely should have flown out on Sunday, but I wanted to stay in San Francisco another night just in case the streets were flooded with revelers and riot police.

As I sat at the computer at 10 p.m. on Wednesday night, I was reeling a bit from two previous days involving near all-nighters. From across the office, I heard a happy cry of "Ooyaa" as Garrett locked his fingers behind his head, leaned back in his chair and displayed the smile of a job well done. Or at least a job...done.

I had introduced Garrett to the joys of "Ooyaa" two years before. "Ooyaa" was not only an orgasmic groan that ended a weary consultant's evening, it was an acronym standing for "Out of Your Ass Analysis." Loosely translated, it means, "I *should* spend about ten more hours of research and data crunching on this, but with a couple of assumptions, clarifying asterisks and wild guesses, I can end my work night right now."

"Good enough for this client, eh?" I asked Garrett without pulling my eyes from my screen. "I'm right there with you, buddy. Just a couple more bullet points and I...am...out of here."

"We should grab a beer on the way back," said Garrett. "We haven't hit the bars at all. You fly 3,000 miles and you're not going to the Cantab even once?" he asked, referring to a legendary bar about a mile up Massachusetts Avenue from Harvard Square. Garrett was a year behind me at business school and had worked with me on numerous consulting projects over the last two years. And, of course, I was crashing on his couch.

"I'll definitely go to the Cantab. But Jay has to come, too," I said. Jay was an intern for the small Boston consulting firm Garrett and I were working with on this project. He had sort of become our team mascot, keeping us entertained during this week's late night sessions.

Jay was taking a semester off from Brigham Young to learn about business. He had, indeed, learned a great deal about making plane reservations and changing toner cartridges. I hope delaying that graduation was worth it.

"I'll come. Just order up a Shirley Temple for me and I'm good to go!" Jay declared. "Does this joint have any music?"

"You better believe it. The best live music in the area," I replied. Jay was a huge music fan, a devotion that ran headlong into his Mormon faith at times. Case in point: the song that came on during this conversation, a little ditty by Tenacious D, Jay's favorite group.

As I finished up my last slide, comedian Jack Black, the group's lead singer, crooned out melodically from Jay's computer speakers. Even late in the day, this member of the Church of Latter Day Saints shielded his ears from every curse word Jack Black uttered. It gets to be a little difficult when the song—filled with the lovely tones of violins and acoustic guitars—is entitled "Fuck Her Gently."

> *And then I'm going to love you completely*
> *And then I'll* **[earmuffs]** *fucking fuck you discreetly*
> *And then I'll* **[earmuffs]** *fucking bone you completely*
> *But then I'm gonna* **[earmuffs]** *fuck you hard*

Sheer comedy. I had queued up the song three times in the past hour on Jay's computer jukebox. Jay's interpretive dance gave me the last little bit of energy I needed to polish off my analysis. "Ooy-aaaaaaaaaa" I bellowed, eliciting a look of satisfaction from Garrett as well. "Are we ready to rock, gentlemen? I just need to print and then take two minutes to check my e-mail."

I pressed print and heard the HP in the other room start humming with activity. It would take a couple of minutes to process the job, so I started clicking through my e-mails. The usual stuff from my mother, sister and a few members of the Vegas party contingent. And then I opened the last of the day's e-mails, from Angeline, the woman from the gym.

Although exhausted after a marathon work session the previous night, I was able to arbitrage the three-hour time difference and call her in San Francisco at a reasonable hour. We confirmed a plan for Thursday night. I was fairly pumped for this first date, which at this point was 24 hours away.

The laser printer whirred away in the other room as I started reading Angeline's e-mail. I got another late night chuckle from reading her missive. Her note was a belletristic opus, a cornucopia of SAT words from someone who had spent a fair bit of time with a thesaurus, either in the past or during the typing of this e-mail. "You missed a most exquisite All Hallows Eve soiree last weekend, an event of unparalleled magnificence..." the e-mail began.

I noticed the message also included a *large* attachment. I clicked "download" and went to retrieve my printouts in the neighboring office.

Oh, I forgot to change the date on the title page...ooooooh, I put the wrong source on this slide...I wonder if I should have used a different discount rate on these cash flow projections...man, I should have made this box a different...

"HOOOO-ly crap!" shouted Jay from the next room. Now, Jay assiduously avoided all potential demerits toward his status in the next life, so I hustled back into the main office to find out what had elicited such a reaction.

Both Jay and Garrett were bunched in front of the large flatscreen computer monitor I had been in front of a couple of minutes before. "Hey, Jay, where exactly does 'crap' fall on the—"

"Jake, I think you have some 'splaining to do," Garrett interrupted, his eyes still on the monitor. "Exactly what kind of stuff are you getting into?"

Is he talking about the presentation? It's all pretty standard stuff...

"How long have you known her? And does she have a sister?" asked Jay.

"What are you guys talking about? I have absolutely no idea—"

My late night office mates moved away from the computer screen, Garrett turning around with a Cheshire-style grin on his face and Jay remaining transfixed on the monitor.

"Oh, my God," I said.

On the outsized screen was an almost life-sized, high definition picture of Angeline. The shot was almost certainly taken at the Halloween "soiree" she mentioned in her e-mail. Angeline was "dressed"—if that's the proper term—in a minimalistic outfit, a loose confederation of fabric, leather and metal.

She was masquerading as Princess Leia…in the Gold Bikini.

As if the S&M-oriented scene from *Return of the Jedi* needed to become any more legendary, Leia and her totally inappropriate swimwear were elevated to mythic proportions during a particular episode of *Friends*—Season 3, Episode 1 (no, I am not *that* Rain Man-like; I just Googled it…). In this episode, Ross explains to Rachel his ultimate sexual fantasy, which happens to involve a certain Princess of Alderaan and a certain *barely* PG-13 bikini.

Angeline was posed next to someone I could only assume was a friend of hers; each of them had a cocktail in-hand. The friend wore a French maid's outfit, but looked demure and positively plain next to the Princess. I noticed that Angeline had styled her hair in the appropriate manner. On the *Friends* episode, Rachel arrays her hair to mimic Leia's strict, side-mounted hair buns. Angeline was truer to the spirit of the film, wearing her hair in a long braid that draped over her exquisitely defined collarbone and toward her equally exquisite…bikini. Her biceps were adorned with serpentine armbands, and her wrists with solid, golden bracelets.

"I think you might be in for an interesting first date," said Jay.

"Man, what kind of pickup line did you use? We need to bottle it and patent it…" laughed Garrett.

"I resent the accusation and take great offense, sir. I never use 'pickup lines'; I just try to break the ice," I said in a mock huff.

"OK, in what masterly, poetic way did you 'break the ice'?" Garrett inquired.

"Uhhh...I talked about knee surgery...ligament replacement...that sort of thing."

"Of course. Who could resist that?"

"Yeah. Yeah. Say, guys...guys," I said as I nudged Jay away from the computer. "Why don't I take a minute to do a couple of corrections, and then we can load up and head toward the Cantab?"

"Sounds like a good plan," commented Jay as I navigated the display back to the PowerPoint deck I had been working on.

"Jay, do you want me to delete this picture?"

"Uhhh, why don't you just finish up with the edits? I'll take care of the picture tomorrow," he said. I couldn't wipe the grin off my face as I made the last couple of corrections and pressed print.

When the printer completed the three new pages, I gathered them up, put away all of my stuff into my Tumi briefcase and said, "Gentlemen, your carriage awaits." Already clad in their coats and packed up, my officemates flicked off the lights and hustled down the stairs. I returned back over to the computer and navigated back to the Halloween photo. I took one final look, and closed the file.

I laughed and shook my head. *What the hell is going on here?*

22

The Most Romantic Night on Earth, Part II

I woke up at 3 p.m. today—Friday—at my flat in San Francisco. I missed a conference call, and I could not care less. For the first time in…God knows how long…I am not checking my "morning" e-mail as the first order of business once I boot up my computer.

No, I feel like writing. And although I considered penning a sonnet or two, I think I'll merely content myself to describe a night of twists and turns and karaoke.

Yesterday, I awoke in Boston after a pleasant but all too brief sleep on Garrett's billowing leather sofa—one of the finer couches I frequented. On this day, I awoke at 5:30 a.m., extraordinarily early in the morning for me—the guy with the 30-second commute.

Because I was trekking back to SF in the afternoon, my team was getting together for an early morning meeting to discuss our project findings. We'd done some fairly good work, but it was still pretty much the standard "align the organization," and "align the incentives" and "align the bullet points" conversation we always had. I particularly enjoyed the meeting, however, because of one particular exchange.

"I'm not sure if we're sending across the right message with page 6," I called out as we flowed through a deck put together by another team member.

"Why?" asked the head man, the professor with whom I had worked for several years. "Our findings are solid. We've seen this pattern in a number of industries." He said "we" a lot. It was royal, or near-royal.

"Uhhhh...." I wanted to give him and the others assembled a little more time to catch up. No luck, except for Garrett, who started to smile, but didn't want to steal my thunder. "We want to explain the three phases of the our process: 'Search Investigate Assess'..."

"Yes..."

"But I think we go a little too far with our new 'Search Investigate *Asses*' methodology..."

Some embarrassed "Oooohs" and some quick pecking into the PowerPoint presentation soon followed. Microsoft should do something about the ass. I've fallen into that same "ass-trap" before.

So, with all of the intellectual heavy lifting done with the team, I hurried to the airport. Boston's Big Dig was particularly agreeable that day, and I made it in record time. I had almost two hours to kill, and I don't particularly relish long periods of silent time. I don't really like to be idle and alone with my own thoughts, these days. My mind drifts too much while reading—I turn the pages for whole chapters without remembering one concept. I thought about writing a short story about the "ass-trap" and other similar anecdotes. I decided to go to an airport bar and watch the same SportsCenter all the way through...twice. Did you know that on this day in 1991, Magic Johnson revealed he had tested positive for HIV?

During most of the plane flight, I was lucky enough to have an escape from my own thoughts. Thank God for *Spy Kids*.

After the cinematic interlude, I pulled out a couple of journal articles I needed to read. I'd *try* at least to get through them. I was really looking forward to seeing Angeline tonight. I couldn't decide if I should load up on caffeine or dive into one of the well-footnoted sleeping aids I held in my hand.

I was going to have to be pretty energized to keep up. The one thing I knew from our meeting and a couple of telephone discussions was that she was all energy, all the time. Well, from the Halloween pictures she e-mailed me, I guess I knew a couple of other things as well. What were we going to do? We had our meeting place picked out—a hopping sushi place about six blocks from my home. Would we do anything after that? I don't think I just want to get drinks— I'd fall asleep right in my vodka tonic. Maybe bowling...she mentioned in her data dump at the gym that she loved to bowl. It's active, playful and it shows we can do the sophisticated Marina thing, but also go "old school" with the bowling league set. Maybe...

I'd read 20 pages of my journal article, and remembered not a word. Thanks to Angeline. *This is all right.*

A delayed connection in Denver. Something about a plane coming in from New York. I would still make it in plenty of time. I would have to make sure I squeezed in a nap on this 2-hour flight to SFO. While I can rarely manage to get 40 winks in my bedroom or a hotel, I'm an excellent napper in the air.

I made the wrong call employing my napping powers on the plane. I awoke non-refreshed. I was still not dreaming. At least not that I can remember.

By the time I navigated through SFO, long-term parking and rush hour traffic, I had about one and a half hours before I was supposed to meet Angeline. Not enough time for another attempt at a nap. Just time to:

- Watch a little SportsCenter.
- Do a hundred push-ups.
- Shave, shower—or maybe shower, shave.
- Listen to some Metallica.
- Shine cutting-edge-fun-yet-stylish-guy-of-the-new-millennium shoes.
- Get dressed in single dude garb.
- Down two shots of espresso on the way to sushi.

I passed leather jacket after leather jacket as I walked to Mas Sake, the loud, slightly grungy, hipper than hip sushi joint. I welcomed the cool early November weather; my Midwestern blood was still a bit thicker than most Northern Californians'.

Mas Sake was on Lombard Street, but not the curvy part made famous by *The Real World-San Francisco* and by 42,672,901 post-cards. This portion of Lombard was part of US-101, and thus boasted innumerable gas stations and motels—some with a stubborn seediness that metaphorically pissed on the stoop of the tony neighboring districts. Lombard Street was the dividing line between the ultra-fluffy white bread Marina and the slightly toasted, butter top white bread of Cow Hollow, my neighborhood.

Per my custom and due to my ultra-short social commute, I arrived at the boisterous sushi joint about ten minutes early. Music boomed. Wherever you went in the establishment, you were surrounded by exposed midriff; Mas Sake's geishas were clad in cut off Jack Daniels T-shirts, Daisy Duked 49er gear and the like. Tips tended to be excessive, and often delivered directly…by hand…with a smile…to the wait staff.

I quaffed down a Diet Coke at the bar and watched SportsCenter—the captioning wasn't on, as it was in many loud bars, but I was getting pretty adept at reading the familiar anchors' lips. 8:05—Angeline's running a little late. I had an excuse to start the cocktail hour, but decided to stay with the caffeine.

8:18.

8:27.

8:28.

8:29. Actually 11:29 in my biological time zone. OK. I had to fly 3,000 miles, but I was there on time. Should I have called to confirm? We'd exchanged e-mails 24 hours before; wasn't that within the bounds of modern dating etiquette?

I decided to walk outside—although I'm not sure why people do that. What…just in case one's dining companion had trouble finding the door and was searching the environs of the restaurant for some secret passage? My strides toward the exit were purposeful, long and brisk. I opened the door and smashed into Angeline.

"That excited to see me, huh?" I laughed, my hands cradling her elbows in a post collision near hug.

"I was going to say the same thing!" she returned, making our quasi-hug into the real thing. She laughed and play-punched me in the stomach, delivering more adorable combat sound effects, to boot. "Did you get a table? I'm staaaaaarving!"

A few seconds later, we were at our table in the rear of the dark, cacophonous restaurant. Angeline chose the seat in our booth facing back toward the kitchen. I, therefore, had to face out onto the main floor of the restaurant, where distractions abounded. It looked like a casting call for *I Dream of Jeannie: The Movie* out there.

The place was bustling, packed to the rafters. God, it was deafening. Our table was extra wide—we had to shuffle the edamame bowl back and forth. I had to lean forward just to make out every third word. "…television…deciding… lifestyle…university… balance…Washington… yellowtail…" she sort of said. I guess I could have tried to read her lips a bit, but instead, I chimed in with profound responses like: "Ah, television!" and "Washington? You know I lived there for two years…" If this were, say, a *fourth* date, I would have used the clamor as an excuse to join her on her side of the table. But I was pleased with my current perspective on our dinner. Watching her during the meal was like observing performance art. The deftness and grace with the chopsticks. The endearing double eye-brow arch every time she delicately brought her sake cup to her mouth. The enthusiastic childlike table pounding as successive rounds of our insanely expensive dinner were brought out to us.

Plus, the non-stop smile. And the regular bursts of laughter for no reason.

She jumped over to my side of the table as we awaited the check, and locked her left arm into my right. "I know what we're doing next!" she said playfully.

"What are you suggesting? I'm not that kind of boy!" I huffed, feigning to pull my arm away from the link with hers.

"Noooo!" she pummeled my stomach again, adding a different sound effect than earlier. "I'm taking you somewhere…," she started shaking her head, "…and, I'm not telling you where! No matter how much you beg!"

I guessed that was my cue to beg. "Don't hurt me that way. You have to tell me. You have to."

Her head shaking continued. "Uh-uh-uh."

She insisted on paying, her Amex hitting the plastic tray before I could even react. "Waaaait…" I said.

"Uh-uh-uh," Angeline declared.

After autographs were signed and carbon copies safely filed away, we proceeded through the maze of crowded tables back toward the front of the restaurant. As we approached the raised bar area, a familiar voice bellowed. "There's the man! JTeeeeee!" It was EZ.

"JTeeeee! Wassssgoingon, brother?" asked Billy, as he slapped a quick man-hug on me.

I couldn't have planned it better if I'd tried. Running into good friends while on a date was one of the best ways to add momentum to an evening already rocketing in a positive direction—if the friends played their roles right. Judging from the red glow on EZ's face, they were only two cocktails into the evening. They'd be on good behavior…well, *pretty* good behavior.

"Angeline, these are two of my best friends from business school—Evan and Todd," I said, electing to use their real monikers instead of their *noms de boire*.

She was no wallflower. Angeline got right up in there, shook their hands with the aplomb of an insurance salesman, and went to work. "It's *very* nice to meet you. So you two can confirm that this guy actually *graduated* from an educational institution?" she joked, locking her arm in with mine again. "I really like brainy guys and he doesn't seem the like the academic type…" she said, flaring her left nostril and looking up at me in mock disgust.

"Well, we had to help him out a lot. Y'know, private tutoring on the multiplication tables…flashcards…" EZ deadpanned. Good, good—right on cue. Let the irreverence commence.

"Writing papers for him…taking his tests…passing him notes so he had something to say in class…" chimed Billy.

"Staying with him while he waited for the short bus…teaching him how to play nice with the other kids…helping him with his bathroom skills," EZ continued. Yeah...a little too much irreverence there. Maybe EZ was three cocktails into the evening.

"So tell me, what do I need to know about this guy?" Angeline asked as she pivoted around our linked arms to get closer to the boys and push me away. EZ and Billy talked downward in semi-secretive, stage whisper tones to Angeline. Although I was only about four feet away, I could barely make out a thing. But then again, I wasn't really trying.

I stole Billy's Sapporo from the rail at the border of the bar area, trying to maintain my sake buzz lest I descend into a spiral of drowsiness. EZ and Billy gave Angeline the download, and she would turn around periodically with different looks—mock horror, faux disgust, simulated shock. And then smiles. Real smiles. They must have been getting to the more serious stuff... "great friend"... "pillar of the community"...that sort of thing.

Then she started in, delivering her analysis to my buddies—what did she know about me anyway? Who knows what she said, but it elicited gut busting laughs and high five invitations from EZ and Billy.

"Gentlemen, it was lovely meeting you, but I'm afraid *JT* and I need to be departing now. Our evening's just getting started," said Angeline. She gave Frick and Frack hugs and told me, "I'll see you outside in a second," evidently wanting me to listen to the glowing reviews my friends were obviously about to bestow upon her.

"Strong work, JT," stated EZ, extending his drink-free knuckles for a fist knock.

"Out of your league," said Billy. "But she's way into you. Get it done."

"Not bad for the first first-date in almost five years, huh?" I replied. Then, moving outside the bounds of the male bonding lexicon, "I'm happy."

It was a departure from the normal script, but EZ raised up his glass to me and Billy patted me on the butt. I returned the toast with Billy's Sapporo, took a final swig and joined Angeline outside.

She began pushing me up the sidewalk immediately, striking a Sisyphean pose as I leaned back against her hands. "Fun, fun, fun! We're going to have fun! Guess where we're going…"

I'm pretty good at guessing games, and when the answer is literally right in front of me, I'm even better. "Uhhh, are we going to Silver Clouds?" I inquired as I extended my hands to prevent crashing into the doors of the karaoke joint a mere 50 yards away from Mas Sake.

"Yessss," she answered as she dropped me off at the bar and started to advance through the crowded room. "I'll be right back. Don't move." I summoned the bar tender and ordered myself a vodka tonic and her a…I had no idea her drink preferences, other than "sake after sake." I ordered her a vodka tonic, the rational thing to do considering I could double fist it if she wanted white wine or some umbrella-laden drink.

Coming to Silver Clouds might not have been the best call; I was hitting a wall, and with all of the regulars in here for their Thursday night Laura Brannigan fix, we might not get up for an hour…or two.

"You're on in ten minutes," said Angeline as she plopped a packed black binder into my lap.

"Uffff! How…?"

"I have friends in high places here. Quick, pick out your song and write it down. I've got to see how you perform."

"You're not—?"

"I was just here last night. *Tonight* is *your* night."

I opened the tome of song choices and found the obvious choice immediately. The only choice really. I wrote the song number down, faked letting her read it, and then delivered it myself to the karaoke song-meister. Now, karaoke was not my thing, but I'd done it eight or nine times over the years, and enjoyed it well enough. One thing I realized though: I was good. I was the idiot savant—the Rain Man—of karaoke. It was a useless skill, one that I usually shied away from. Slightly less useless, however, than my *most* developed skill— flipping quarters off of my elbow and catching them in one lightning-fast motion. I had discovered quarter catching while watching a 1977 *Happy Days* episode that featured a mutant like myself, and was shocked when I realized the scope of my incredible and utterly super-fluous talent.

But, back to karaoke.

"And now, let's bring up JTeeeee!" Angeline must have asked the MC to call me that, because I put "Sven Johansson" on the sheet. She was the lone clapper welcoming me to the stage—the big groups that populated the place really only took care of their own. Little did they know I was about to enthrall them like they'd never been enthralled before.

I surveyed the room. *Ah, all of the elements are here. This is set-ting up nicely.*

Jimi Hendrix would be backing me up once again, or at least some session musician trying to pay homage to the God of Feedback.

"Foxy...Foxy."

(Hell, yes, I stole it from *Wayne's World*. But, c'mon, every karaoke performance is a blatant theft.)

To my mind, *Foxy Lady* is the ultimate karaoke song. You can belt it out, even if you have a terrible voice. If you have a sore throat, it sounds even better.

First step in performing *Foxy Lady:* Look for the Bachelorette Party. Given this was a Thursday night, I went to plan B: look for the gaggle of horny 40-something women. Bingo. Just to the left of the stage. I chose one lucky lady and started the serenade.

"You know you're a cute little heartbreaker—Foxy." Don't worry, if you try this maneuver, she'll be into it. She'll sing the "Foxy" into your mike. This woman—replete with one helluva fuzzy perm—per-formed magnificently, writhing like a music video vixen.

Next, if you can spot 'em, head for a group of tourists. Don't look for paraphernalia from far away colleges like Iowa or South Car-olina—look for people wearing hats or sweatshirts from the city you're in. Perfect. A big table with an ALCATRAZ fleece and a sweatshirt featuring the adorable faces of Pier 39's sea lions.

"You've got to be all mine, all mine. Ooh, Foxy Lady." If you hold your mike in the middle of their group, they'll join you in singing the "Ooh, Foxy Lady."

Now, if that's all you got, don't be afraid to go back to the well maybe one more time with each. Lather, rinse, repeat. But then stop.

But, scan the crowd again, and you may have the elements for *Advanced* "Foxy Lady." Look for a drunk dancing woman—it's probably about 50/50 there's one out there. Boom, there she is. Get over there.

"Foxy Lady, here I come." She *will* dance right next to you, like she's being featured in a music video. Don't laugh no matter how bad her dancing is. If you have a bad-ass expression on your face, she'll get into her moves even more, and grind you like you've never been ground before.

Then, if you're really going for the gold, you might choose the move with the highest degree of difficulty: getting the reluctant surly group of frat boys to join in. Sometimes you can get them to hop along with you like they're in the pit at Woodstock 2001. But this is tough. I spotted a group, but they were far away and didn't look like they'd be into it. I was running out of time. I decided to head back to the stage and stick the landing.

A final recommendation: if you happen to be singing "Foxy Lady" in the presence of a date or a hopeful future-date, don't sing in her direction too often. Let her know that you remember she's there, but also make it clear that, right now, she's sharing you with the world. I delivered the next couple of lines in Angeline's direction.

> *Yeah, get it, babe—You make me feel like…Feel like*
> *sayin' foxy*
> *Foxy*
> *Foxy lady*
> *Foxy lady*

The applause was pretty loud, but was cut short by the grim tones of the MC announcing, "Tonya and Margaret, you're up." I was glad when I reached the end of my command performance. A set of keys hit me in the chest. Room keys? I bent down to pick up the BMW key chain at my feet and then looked up at a giggling Angeline, her arms cradling her stomach.

"Room 330!" she yelled, as she ran up to tug me off the stage. I had actually been thinking of joining in with Tonya and Margaret for "Love Shack."

Angeline pulled me outside and locked her arm in with mine once again as we hustled toward nowhere in particular. "We have to get you on *Star Search*, or…is the *Gong Show* still on?" she said.

My teeth were starting to chatter as my coating of Jimi-sweat mixed with the rising wind. She began to rub up and down my arms, the friction creating some much welcomed heat. "So where to now?" I asked as I pulled her keys out of my pocket. "Maybe a nice, leisurely midnight drive?" I was joking—in spite of my recent on-stage exertions and now the bracing wind, I was fighting back fatigue.

She responded quickly: "Of course! Maybe Napa. Or down the Pacific Coast Highway to a beautiful moon-lit beach…"

"…someplace secluded…" I continued.

"…so we can make out…"

"…if you insist," I finished.

We arrived at her car and both hopped in. "So which is it, PCH or Napa?" she queried.

"PCH. Definitely. We can go for a swim." I furthered our game of verbal chicken, even though I knew I would have to veer off first since my central nervous system was shutting down.

"We're off." She looked me directly in the eyes as she peeled out from her parking spot on Lombard, a Volvo swerving to avoid us. The convertible top sprang to life, yielding its position to the perfectly clear night sky. The jolt of hypothermia perked me up again temporarily, but it was soon replaced by the most wonderfully warm warmth I'd ever experienced.

What is this wonderful warmness that's warming me? Am I asleep?

"Are you feeling that? The heated seats? They're great when you have a convertible!" she yelled over the rushing wind that no longer seemed quite as icy. The wonders of German engineering. *What'll they think of next? I don't think they have these in Ford Probes.*

"I like 'em," I said to Angeline, not turning her way since my eyes were flickering closed in spite of the hot and cold *and* the potential of making out within mere minutes. We sped off of Lombard and into the Presidio, a closed military base in the western part of San Francisco that was now a national park. The Presidio was the setting for a spectacular movie featuring an under-appreciated dramatic turn by Mark Harmon. Now, Angeline and I careened around the turns that Mark had negotiated during his epic performance 12 years ago, tall fir trees the only spectators for my date's high speed Grand Prix.

"Y'know, they have SFPD and Park Police and Military Police and CHiPs that all patrol this place," I said, perhaps with a little hyperbole. She gunned her vehicle's impressive engine even more, accelerating by a bank of bushes before our rapid halt at a 4-way stop. On the southern point of the intersection's compass rose was a Park Police patrol car. The officer flashed his lights, allowing us to go through first; Angeline waved in thanks.

We exited the Presidio near the ocean, Angeline's engine roaring through an otherwise quiet neighborhood. "There must be a beach around here. Or maybe some cliffs where we can listen to the waves crash in!" The BMW's headlights illuminated a sign reading: "Ocean Access: Private Drive." We stopped.

"Well we do want to go to the *ocean*..." she said.

"...and we do want some privacy..."

"...and we are *driving*..."

A swinging metal gate was begging to be swung; it looked like someone forgot to reinsert the padlock or thought the scary, scary sign would be enough to intimidate the likes of us. I was about to pop out of the car to clear our way when the "whoop" and red radiance of a cop car approached from behind us. "The fuzz. Stay cool," I said.

Angeline immediately waved to the driver of the SFPD cruiser. "We're looking for the Presidio, but it's all dead ends around here. How do we get out?"

SF's finest quickly imparted directions we already knew, and we were soon back on our way to the rolling hills and winding roads of the Presidio. "Oooh!" popped Angeline, stirring me from another doze. "I have just the place."

We drove. We owned the deserted roads of the Presidio. We owned the vacant merging lanes at its northern exit. We owned the full expanse of the glowing and undiscovered Golden Gate Bridge.

Angeline steered us off US-101 at the first exit in Marin County. "Vista Point," read the sign. I'd biked past the area many times before, but had never stopped to admire the view—it looked like the kind of place Japanese tourists and buses full of church groups visited.

We stopped at the southern edge of Vista Point's parking lot, looking back at our twinkling city some four miles distant. Our Golden Gate Bridge dutifully remained at its post, letting us know it was ready to carry us back to the City at the time of our choosing. We remained silent for a minute or so, as the revolutions of a tiny toy lighthouse on Alcatraz marked the time.

"It's really beautiful."

"It's pretty amazing." We talked in voices we had not used up to this point in our evening together.

"I feel like I'm in high school. We used to take the most amazing drives to nowhere on freezing nights—but before the snows, so we could speed," I said. "I loved the sound of tires rolling over the road on a cold night, and the sound a lone passing car makes…"

"I like it too, that's why I didn't turn on the radio."

We talked for a while, with not even a foghorn to interrupt us on this perfectly clear night. Our discussion moved fluidly from Italy to cheese to hot tomato soup to Andy Warhol to New York to September 11 to Israel to Egypt to diving in the Mediterranean Sea and back to Italy again.

My blinks were lengthening—only the powerful attraction I felt to and from this woman in front of me kept me awake. My fatigue and the remnants of my sake glow made everything seem dream-like…so at ease, with no inhibitions and, surprisingly, not plagued by any bouts of overthinking.

"I'm going to kiss you," I declared.

"OK."

We slowly leaned in, breaking the neutral zone of the BMW's center console. She was wearing vanilla perfume, and the tasty scent permeated our shared space.

I looked into her eyes, coming ever closer. I looked into her eyes…*Why aren't you closing your eyes, Angeline? If you start to close yours, I'll close mine.*

The momentum of our pre-kiss lean continued slowly…inex-
orably…but something was wrong. *Why aren't you tilting your head,*
Angeline? I'm ambidextrous; I can go either way. I subtly re-tilted my
head on final approach for a left-lipped kiss. It was down to the final
few millimeters…

OK, OK. We've knocked heads. We're forehead to forehead. I'm not
sure exactly what's going on here, but I've been in this situation before.
Just get it done…and don't look into her eyes.

I looked into her eyes, the tiniest tremors rippling across the
white surface. Then the microscopic tidal wave of a tear began to well
up in the lower regions. *Don't pull back. Don't ask her what's wrong.*

"What's wrong," I asked as I pulled back two inches, separating
our sweaty foreheads.

"I have a boyfriend," she whispered meekly.

I quickly leaned back against the heated seat. Actually, I pulled
back so far I was pretty much out the door. The dashboard's clock
read: 2:07 a.m. I looked up at the perfectly black sky and tried to
ignore the stars.

"Jake—" she tried to say something. My hand flew up to silence
her—I didn't look down, but it might have looked like the "talk to the
hand" gesture so popular among the kids these days.

I was so tired. Tired of this night and tired of everything. My
thoughts were so loud and my blinks were so long, almost mini-naps.
I didn't want to look into her face again. I would ask her to drive me
home and get out, never looking into her face. That face. Over the
last couple of hours I'd allowed my overactive brain to paste that face
into a couple of imagined photos I was *so sure* I'd take with her in the
next month, or in the next year.

I was so tired. *How did this happen? I don't deserve this. I'm in*
trouble. This is the last thing I needed. How did we get here? It looked
like it could have been so perfect. But I was sapped of all energy. I
couldn't fight for the attention of this woman. I was too depleted, too
wasted, too wrecked. *How did we get here?*

How did we get here?

I lowered my glance from the sky and rested my chin upon my
hand, staring at the orange bridge in front of me.

"You drove here," I said, breaking the silence.

"What?"

"*You* drove here…You *drove* here…You drove *here*."

Silence. She stared at the steering wheel.

I continued, at times talking to the side of her head, at times to the steering wheel, at times to the stars. "I don't know you very well. You don't know me very well. But from our first meeting, it was obvious there was something drawing us together. Everything we've done tonight has reinforced that. Every single thing. Every single second…"

She played with the key chain, still housed in the ignition.

"I don't know anything about the relationship you just brought up—obviously. All I know is: you drove here. Here, to one of the greatest views in the world. Probably *the* greatest view in the world. To possibly *the* most romantic spot in the world. Only you know why you did that—I'm not going to try to dive into your psyche to figure it out. My own brain's not even working right now."

She looked off in the direction of Alcatraz, directly away from me. Her hands still tickled the keys in front of her.

"You could have driven me home. You drove here. You're holding the keys." She dropped her hand away from the ignition. "You can drive home now if you want."

Silence. I wanted to convince her but I didn't want to convince her. I didn't target a woman with a boyfriend. I didn't want to joust for the attention of a woman with some guy I'd never laid eyes on. I didn't want to expose myself to the possibility of heartbreak and annoyance and wasted time—all of it. How did we get here?

Should I say something else? Should I just let it soak in and see what comes of it? What else could I possibly say?

Silence.

Silence.

"It's too bad we can't be together. I can tell we'd make the most tremendous lovers!"

"Oh, really?"

"Yes. Amazing. I can tell our bodies would fit together perfectly. I can tell there would be night after night of heat…passion…"

"Oh, really?"

"Yes. It's impossible to deny it's crazy I know it but it's impossible to fight it I know you feel it you feel it you feel it you feel it..."

"Oh, really?"

"Yes, I'm going to make you feel it."

And then we had our first kiss. You could probably see that coming. But there's a twist you might not have expected. I didn't expect it.

Angeline was the one who started the cascade of quotes.

"It's too bad we can't be together," she said. SHE said. I was still looking off into space wondering if I should try to say one last profound thing before she drove me home. Angeline then vaulted over the center console and gear shift. Yes, vaulted. Her athleticism was impressive, almost intimidating. She landed in my seat, her legs straddling on either side of my hips. Her head was higher than mine and she looked down intensely into my eyes. "I can tell we'd make the most tremendous lovers!"

"Oh, really?" Now, I didn't know what the hell was happening. But I *did* know that I shouldn't show total shock. I tried to keep my, "Oh, really?" kind of cool, kind of mischievous. I think I succeeded.

"Yes. Amazing." She removed the black scrunchy from her pony tail and shook out her long hair. God she looked beautiful, silhouetted against the clear starry sky. "I can tell our bodies would fit together perfectly." She cradled her flowing hair in her hand and, with a flourish, waved it away from her face, giving me an unobstructed view of her eyes. A note to the ladies out there: anytime you're considering meekly tucking in your hair behind your ear before a romantic encounter, consider this "flourish" move instead. "I can tell there would be night after night of heat...passion..." She moved her face closer to mine, and then peered to either side of the BMW, building anticipation by pretending to look for peeping toms who might be intruding on our moment.

"Oh, really?" I was ready for this one. I tried to be a little more roguish, disbelieving even. You know, like, *You've got to prove it.* It was her scene, I was just acting in it.

"Yes. It's impossible to deny it's crazy I know it but it's impossible to fight it I know you feel it you feel it you feel it you feel it…" She was shaking. It might have been the cold; her coat was balled up in the back and she had been away from the warm cuddle of the heated seats for a full 20 seconds. Her quivering added to the chaotic intensity of her passionate run-on sentence.

"Oh, really?" These things come in threes. This time I matched her earnestness and anticipation. I wasn't play-acting.

"Yes, I'm going to make you feel it." She leaned in and closed her eyes. I leaned back and closed my eyes. Vanilla enveloped me.

And then we had our first kiss.

✳   ✳   ✳   ✳

Angeline pulled her car into my building's driveway at 4:02 a.m. We smiled at each other. The night…the morning…it was all so unpredictable and unexpected. I left after one final short kiss.

I dreamt that night and remembered the dream. I was a child in an ice cream shop.

23

The Game
of Telephone

"Wait a sec. Let me see if I got this straight…" said Billy.

"OK."

"So you talked to her for *an hour* in the gym last week…"

"Right."

"She gave you her number…"

"Uh huh."

"Her *real* number, to boot..."

"Right."

"You talked a couple of times on the phone after that…"

"Yes."

"You made plans to go out…"

"Yeah."

"For *dinner*, not for lunch or a coffee or a visit to the 'Make Your Own Candle' store…"

"Uh huh."

"For a dinner at this hip, dark, sexy place with Playboy bunnies waiting on every table…"

"Right, right."

"And *she* paid…"

"Well, I tried to pay, but she seemed to have been palming her credit card and by the time—"

"OK, OK, JT; just stick with me here…"

"Sorry."

"So, then she suggests going on to *another* venue…"

"Yep."

"And after that, suggests going on a *midnight drive*…"

"Uh huh."

"And *she* drives…"

"Yes."

"…to freaking *make out central*, Vista Point…"

"Yeah."

"Where, in the midst of the perfect night, with, like, the most killer view known to man, she tells you she has a boyfriend…"

"Right."

"But starts going at it with you in a couple of minutes anyway. The end."

"Yeah, that pretty much sums it up." I think Billy has a real career ahead of him working for Cliffs Notes if he can't get a job anywhere else.

"Dude, I just have this to say: she had ample opportunity to stop that date at anytime if she wanted to," he said matter of factly. "You have nothing to be worried about. It was in her court…it was her call."

"Yeah. Y'know I thought—"

"Man, she could have gotten off the 'J Train' at any station, but she must have *liked the ride*. Heh heh heh. Yeah, baby!" he shouted. I had the sense a new nickname might be in the works for me.

"Yes, thanks. I think—"

"Love to ride that 'J Train'! All aboard, ladies, 'J Train' is leaving the station!"

" 'J Train'…got it. But do you think I—"

"Wooooooooo wooooooooo! It's the fucking bullet train coming through!"

"OK…yeah…thanks…you've been most helpful." Click.

✳   ✳   ✳   ✳

Of course I had to call Billy about the date. He was an integral part of the action, so I owed him an update. But there was another critical reason I called him.

There's a massive body of case law out there in the world when it comes to the rules of dating—drawn from a huge collection of detailed stories and sketchy anecdotes. Sometimes you want to find out if your situation and your actions fall within the bounds of precedent. Now, these rules can of course apply to the minutiae; you know, stuff like "How hard do I need to try to grab the bill on the first date if I'm the guy?" or "Isn't it all right if she pays for the dinner if she has a *much, much* nicer car than I?".

But the laws of precedent also speak to broader, and deeper issues as well. Questions like, "Did I do something wrong here?" or "Do I need to step back from this?".

Sometimes you need a consultation with a jury of your peers. In my case, my friends were much more knowledgeable about the cold, harsh world of dating precedent than I. They helped further my education on the "*Realpolitik* of Relationships."

✳   ✳   ✳   ✳

"*No*, you didn't do anything wrong. Not in the least! Are you kidding me?!?" said Erica.

"Hey. I'm just checking things out. It's always good to get—"

"But there's something else going on there, with 'Gym Girl' and that other guy."

"Well, *thanks*."

"No, don't get me wrong. She's obviously all over your shit. I mean you're just the most adorable little thing…"

"Thanks."

"I think they must be practically done already. If you're a woman, you *can't* put yourself in that situation—or I should say in that *series* of situations—unless in a way you've moved on emotionally. Or looking for an excuse to move on," Erica said.

"Yeah, but if you're a guy you never really feel good—"

"What, do you think all of these relationships that come to an end have nice, neat finishes all tied up in a bow?" she asked. "Does someone put a notice in the paper when there's an 'official' end? Do you file documents? No. It's messy. There's nothing definite."

"Yeah, I guess."

"Look, I was still sort of seeing Kevin when I met Jonathon," she said.

"Really? I don't know if I knew that—"

"And I met Blake when I was still with Jonathon…but I was tuning out."

"Wow, I never really put the whole timeline together," I laughed.

Erica went on to list half a dozen other examples off the top of her head—people we knew from college and business school who didn't have the neatest, cleanest beginnings to their relationships. Several of these couples were now married or engaged. I just hadn't realized the circumstances of their meeting. I guess I wasn't paying attention.

"Now, there is one very critical issue in this whole debate we haven't talked about," she said.

"What's that?"

"Did you touch her boob?"

"I'm not going to even get into—"

"He touched her boob!" Erica yelled out, possibly to the whole bullpen of bored investment bankers at her office. Then, she refocused her vocalizations back into the phone receiver. "No, seriously, I'm sorry. But the one matter we still need to discuss is this…"

"What?"

"Did she touch your thingy?!?" she cackled.

"JeeeeZUUUS! You are such a—"

"She touched his thingy!" Erica again crowed to the invisible peanut gallery.

"All I'm going to say is: I think I did pretty well on the first date, all things considered, for a guy on a break."

" 'Guy on a break'…Listen to this dude. You've been dumped. DUUUUMPED!"

"Erica, I'm just saying—"

"DUUUUUUUMPED!"

Click.

✳   ✳   ✳   ✳

"I mean I really don't understand the attraction—from her point of view, that is," I said.

"Sure, you're repulsive," said Kenneth.

"Totally. I'm still gimpy; I can't even really walk around well or dance..."

"God, yes. You looked like Quasimodo with the way you limped around here. You even used it as an excuse to not answer my squash challenge. You're practically deformed now."

"Exactly, that's what I'm saying. *And,* I have no idea what I might have said, in the gym, on the phone or in the restaurant to actually make her think I was worth dating..."

"Well, you're a terrible conversationalist...always going on about Indiana basketball or the evils of valet parking..."

"I know. I do have some good oral hygiene, though. No cavities."

"That's right, excellent brushing habits. Solid enamel. So you got that going for ya..."

"...which is nice."

"Listen, I think this whole thing could be good for you," Kenneth said, ratcheting down our sarcastic banter a few notches. "You just need to worry about one thing: having a good time. Don't think too much about it, just have a good time with it."

"Yeah..."

"Y'know, if it turns out to be a short fling, so be it. There's no law against that. Just let the pace of it evolve."

"Well, thanks. I think that's good advice."

"There are probably more convenient 'rebound girls' out there—ones with fewer attachments. Still, this sounds like it could be pretty interesting."

"Sometimes 'interesting' ain't what it's cracked up to be."

"Yeah. Just make sure you take good notes so we can figure out how a total basket case like you hooks up with a rhythmic gymnast."

"Bastard."

Click.

✳   ✳   ✳   ✳

"Should we be expecting any more pin up shots via e-mail?" Garrett asked.

"I'll look into it. It really would be a nice thing to do for Jay, wouldn't it?"

"It could be, or it might really undermine his whole worldview. He'll start just covering one ear when a dirty song comes on…"

"Yeah, I guess I should be careful. Eternal damnation sucks."

"So, what's your next step, Jake?"

"You know, I really have no idea. In a way, I guess I just have to let it come to me."

"So to speak."

"No, that's the *third* date," I corrected him. "No, seriously. You don't want to be a 'homewrecker;' you don't want to stick your nose in things. In a way, you just want to *be there…*"

"I don't think you really have to worry about that. Judging from what I've heard, there's no 'home' to be wrecked."

"Yeah, maybe. And I realize we're all just out there on our own, but you don't want to be hurting anyone."

"Jake…"

"I know…I know…"

"You were hurt. It sucks, but that's the way the world works. You worry about *you*. Everyone else takes care of themselves."

"I know."

"Dating…relationships…it's a full contact sport out there, man. And people get hurt…"

God, I hope he doesn't say, "Don't hate the playa, hate the game"! Please don't say that, Garrett! I so value your friendship and would hate to lose you over a cliché!

"…Just be a good guy, and everything will turn out for the best."

"Yeah, I think it's the way to go. Everyone's a grown up out there…"

"Exactly."

"And dating is a 'full contact sport.' I'll remember that one," I said. "Thanks, man. I appreciate it."

"No problem. Make sure you keep your East coast brethren up to date! See ya!"

"Bye."

"Full contact sport." Just like parallel parking. It's a vicious world out there.

24

I Guess

Her acting class. My knee rehab. Her "job job." My "work." Her family. My family. Los Angeles weather. San Francisco weather.

Within about 15 minutes we had pretty much run through the standard list of conversations.

"So."

"So."

"Yeah."

"Yeah." It really didn't matter who said which "so" or "yeah."

"So, how else have you been spending your time?" I asked.

"I went to the do it yourself car wash the other day and I had so many granola wra—"

"You know what I meant."

"I know…Yeah, I guess I've been seeing someone…a little."

"Yeah."

"What about you?"

"I guess I've been seeing someone…a bit." A "bit" was the operative word; since the mega-date, Angeline and I had just…*hung out*…a couple of times. I wasn't really sure what was happening on that front.

"Yeah," said Gabrielle.

"Yeah," I replied. During the next few seconds of silence and sighs, my mind kept working. I continued, "You don't have to answer this if you don't want to…I'll understand…"

"Uh-huh."

"I've met him, haven't I?" I asked.

I heard a few sniffles on the other end of the line, and then she answered, in a barely audible voice. "Yes."

"Got it." I had not a doubt in my mind who it was. Drama Boy. When I traveled to LA to see Gabrielle's play two and a half months earlier, I met her fellow cast members. Although the cast was in general very affable, one fellow in particular seemed all too eager to avoid any form of contact or communication with me. Drama Boy shared a scene with Gabrielle, one where they kissed. This was the scene I asked that she practice with me the last time she was in my flat, a scene which she begged off on performing. This was the scene I asked her to recite the time she gave me the sponge bath.

Silence.

"Well, why don't we call it a night," I suggested. "We'll talk in a few weeks."

Sniffle. "OK...Jake, I want you to have a good Thanksgiving. Have a Happy Thanksgiving," she said, or asked.

"I'll try. Bye."

"Bye."

25

The Moon's as Big as Your Head

"Where are you?" asked Angeline.

"I'm at the Grove, slaving away."

"Fillmore Street or Chestnut Street?"

"Fillmore."

"I'm coming over. Bye."

So, it looked like Angeline and I were about to embark upon our sixth date. After our whirlwind "I lived a lifetime in one night" first date, our succeeding get-togethers had been decidedly more casual affairs.

We sucked on the same milkshake at Mel's Diner on Lombard and smooched a little.

We shared a lunch at a great, but cheap, Chinese restaurant. This time I *insisted* on buying and had already prepositioned my credit card under my plate. She and I hung out at the Grove on Chestnut for a while after that. And, we did a little smooching in her car as we said goodbye.

Angeline joined me for a couple of drinks at a nearby bar one night. And, we did a little smooching in her car as we said goodbye.

She brought me lunch one day at my apartment, and stayed for a while to do some reading. She listened in on a couple of conference calls and interviews I conducted. Strangely, she seemed to really enjoy it. I enjoyed it, too; it's always nice to get a little massage while you're listening to someone talk about the future of telecommunications industry regulation. After that, we went on to enjoy a delightful afternoon.

Sometimes, it's difficult for me to describe my job...actually, it's probably better to call it my "current professional situation." I know my mother still doesn't understand what I do.

Now, I know how my mom must feel. For the life of me, even after our five dates, I still couldn't understand how Angeline spent her time. It seemed to be some combination of yoga instructor, freelance advertising copywriter, hand model, interior design consultant and organic basil farmer.

"Hi, honey. How was your day at work?" she asked me after she had snuck up to my table at the Grove.

"It was brutal. They attached electrodes to me! They made me stand on one leg for three minutes straight! They made me jump up and down 100 times!" I said as I pulled the ice bag off of my knee and lowered my elevated leg. This location of the Grove was just a couple of doors down from my physical therapist, with whom I had just shared my last formal torture session. He had, however, ordered me to continue my regimen of self-flagellation for the next three months.

I scooched over to make room for her in the well-cushioned and pillowed corner I had occupied for the previous three hours. She plopped her large purse/small tote bag down on the cushions (what do you call those bags anyway?) and snuggled up against me. "Mind if I take a nap here for a while?" she asked as she nestled her head on my chest.

"Be my guest," I said, even as she was making herself comfortable against me. Within one minute, she was asleep.

So there I was, with a woman sleeping on my chest, and with nothing to do. The only reading material within reach was an investment banking report on the future of the alternative energy industry. I worked in another billable half hour, taking care to highlight the report very slowly and quietly lest I wake up the sleeping Angeline.

Just as I reached the end of the section on high efficiency windmills, Angeline stirred and checked her watch. "Oh, my God! I really did fall asleep didn't I?"

"You were so cute with your snoring and the little conversation you had with yourself, I didn't want to wake you."

"No. Shut up!" she said as she clawed her nails into my stomach. Both of my knees slammed up into the bottom of our café table, but the pain was minor and I decided to concentrate instead on subduing her in a little close quarters wrestling match. "OK, you win! You win! Puh-leeeeease let me go, you big strong man..."

"What do I get if I do?"

"I'll buy you a coffee..."

"Deal," I said as I released her. "But make it a mocha or frappa something. I can't drink the real stuff."

"I'm getting a double. I gotta caffeinate!" she said. Strange...up 'til this point, I thought caffeine was the primary component of her blood plasma.

She came back in about two minutes with something large and dark for herself and something light and foamy for me. We chatted for about 30 minutes about her day of random work, my day of random work and current events. Then we transitioned to travel plans and the upcoming Thanksgiving holiday.

"So, are you flying home to the Heartland?" she asked.

"Ooooh, yeah. Wednesday through Monday of Hoosier hospitality and Boggle," I answered. "What about you? Are you flying back home?"

"No, I'm going to Europe for a few days."

"Oh. Oh, are you meeting your family over there?" I had, after all, seen many ads for off-season fares from San Francisco recently.

Pause. Pause. "No..." she said, starting to look downward. "I'm going with Trevor."

My plan since our first date had been to "be there." To be available, to see what could happen, but not to push for anything. As much as I was attracted to and intrigued by Angeline, I really didn't have the strength to get involved in some tussle over a woman. I had wondered for the previous couple of weeks if there was a break-up in progress. I guess I had my answer.

As I set down the cup with the detritus that was my mocha-something, I couldn't hide my confusion. "Listen, Angeline. I don't really…I mean, I can't figure…You've really taken me on one of the stranger rides…" As I spoke, I became very aware of how crowded the Grove had become. "Why don't we get out of here?"

"OK," she replied, beginning to look embarrassed. I packed up without looking at her and opened the café's door, holding it ajar as she followed me out.

We walked north a couple of blocks to a city park, only speaking a few words along the way. The park was terraced, rising high above street level like a Mayan temple. We took the stairs up several of the terraced levels, eventually stopping at a bench near the top of the park. "Good exercise. And I thought my physical therapy was done for the day," I said. She smiled, a little.

We sat on the cold stone bench and just looked at each other for a bit. Then we both started shaking our heads and laughing. A little.

I decided to begin. "Sooooooo, I'm a pretty educated guy, but I *cannot* figure out what's going on with us. I know why I'm here, and I think you do, too. But I don't know why you agreed to go out with me. I don't know why you're here with me right now. Can you tell me why?"

"I don't know," she said. The last thing I needed *in the world* was another "I don't know" conversation. Nothing ever gets accomplished in an "I don't know" conversation.

"I think you *do* know. You don't have to tell me if you don't want to. I'll tell you that *I'm* here because I haven't met anyone in my time in this city who has energized me and electrified me like you have. I haven't met anyone *nearly* as beautiful as you. I can't get out of my head the way you walk or chew or even nap on my chest. And there are other reasons, but you're awfully quiet right now and I don't care to continue without reciprocity…" She laughed. A little.

I continued. "I see a lot of potential here. I *thought* you must be breaking up with Trevor, but if that's not the case…well, I just can't be a part of...*this*. Whatever we might call what we've been doing the last couple of weeks."

"I know," she said. "It's just..." Silence.

Silence.

She finally continued. "It's just I feel so close to you already. I don't know what it is...I just wish...I could almost..." She hit me in the chest with the back of her fist, the "thud" the only sound for a few seconds.

I removed her fist from my heart and guided her hand down to the cold stone bench. " 'Almost' isn't very good for me right now, I hope you can understand."

"I want to see you, though. Couldn't we just be friends?" Ah, fair reader, you and I both saw this question coming from a mile away. The request to "just be friends" is like Kryptonite to the male of our species. I won't get into it too deeply here. The "just be friends" phenomenon has been documented in movie after movie and analyzed *ad nauseum* within the literary genre in which we now find ourselves.

I laughed for a second and then answered her. "Could you be my friend? Really? I know I couldn't be your friend. I mean, even after just the little bit of time we've spent together, wouldn't it just seem like some shadow, some weak facsimile of what we could have had? Could you *really* be my friend?"

"No. I guess not." She looked down, but I still stared at her. She looked beautiful in the lights of the park. Well, she looked beautiful anywhere. If this was going to be the last time I see her, I was going to get my money's worth. We sat silently for a minute.

"Sooooooo, where are you going in Europe? I hear Albania is lovely this time of year..."

She giggled for a bit and then looked up from the bench. "We're going to Italy," she said as she backhanded her long hair away from her face. "A few days in Florence, then the Italian Riviera for about a week...Cinque Terra and Genoa."

I nodded slowly as a tear welled up in one eye. My placid face belied the speed at which my mind was racing. *Florence? Cinque Terra? Cinque Terra! He's going to propose to her! He's going to propose to her! This can't be anything but an engagement trip. She must know.*

She must! What the hell is she doing here with me? What the hell has she been doing these last couple of weeks? What the hell was she doing at Vista Point?

I realized that as little as I thought I knew about Angeline's situation—about Angeline *and Trevor's* situation—I actually knew even less. The sheer volume of what I didn't know could fill up the Gulf of Genoa.

"Wow. That's a pretty cool area from what I hear. Make sure you check out the world's largest ball of twine," I told her, chuckling a bit to hide the subtle tremor I could feel in my vocal cords.

She laughed again and then stopped as she put her hand on mine. "I don't want to hurt you," said Angeline, looking up from our overlapping hands. When her eyes met mine, I arched my eyebrow and shook my head slightly. Softly, she said, "I'm sorry. I *didn't* mean to hurt you."

Just a little paper cut on top of a sucking chest wound, my dear. Don't give it another thought. God, right now, even my baggage has baggage. And the baggage for my baggage has little carrying cases.

"Are you OK?" she asked.

"Don't worry about a thing. Just another interesting dating anecdote, eh?"

"Yeah."

"Yeah," I said as I looked into her eyes until she appeared a little embarrassed by the attention. I pivoted away from her a few degrees and looked up at the sky. "Sooooo, it sure is bright out here tonight. It must be a full moon. I wonder where it is…" I stated as I scanned the sky above and behind me.

"What are you?…don't be silly…the moon's right over here," she said, thumbing over her right shoulder and glancing back.

And there it was. Low on the horizon, resting between the houses and apartment buildings that bordered the park, maybe thirty degrees away from my line of sight, which had been trained on Angeline's eyes. It was the largest, brightest moon I had ever seen.

I turned away from her again, letting her stare at my back while I laughed at myself and cried at my world.

"Jake. What's so funny? Jake, are you OK?"

I wiped away the remnants of the saline trail on my face and turned back around. "Aaaaaah, yeah," I said from the back of my throat before I cleared it. "That's just the most brilliant, dazzling moon I've ever seen. When you were talking, I couldn't take my eyes off of you. I just needed to look at you for these final minutes.

"The moon's as big as your head, and I didn't even see it…until just now."

She touched her hand upon her cheek and then covered her mouth with her palm. Then, without a word, she turned directly away from me, until I could see only her back and her long hair.

"I'm sorry, I shouldn't have…" I said. I hadn't really planned to say anything of consequence, but I think somehow I did.

She turned back toward me, laughing and sobbing concurrently. She didn't notice it, but as she started to speak, a snot bubble formed by her nose and popped in an instant. I think I might need to research this "snot bubble" issue in the Technicolor section of the bookstore.

"Oh…you…you…" she managed. She stood up and even before I could raise my head to look her in the eye, she wrapped her left hand around my right ear and pulled me up off of the stone slab.

And then, of course, we kissed. For a long, long time.

After the long, long kiss, she stepped back from me and wiped her eyes and her nose with her sleeve. I tried to pull a Grove napkin out of my pocket to aid her in this endeavor, but reached into the wrong pocket first and came out with the wad of napkins too late. I unfolded the clump and put a few in her hands.

"My darling, Scarlett. Here, take my handkerchief. Never, in any crises of your life, have I known you to have a handkerchief." I wondered if she got it. She took the napkins and wiped her eyes and cheeks. I was sure she would blow her nose a few seconds later, once we'd said goodbye.

"Soooooo…" she said.

"Soooooo…" I said, "I guess I'll see you at the gym. Remember: the world's largest ball of rubberbands…"

"I thought it was twine," she smiled.

"*Right.* I was confusing it with Venice…that's where the rubber bands are. Well, safe travels. Goodbye."

"Goodbye."

I walked away in the opposite direction of the steps we had used to climb the Mayan pyramid. As I traveled the six blocks down the hill on which rested the neighborhood of Pacific Heights, I barely noticed the pain in my knee. Once home, I cruised down the long hallway in my flat, flying past a whole world of travel pictures.

26

Thankful

The flesh popped and whistled as it was lowered into the roiling cauldron of scorching oil.

No, I'm not getting all Poe on you here; I'm just talking about my Thanksgiving. My sister, her fiancé and I joined my father, aunt, uncle and little cousins for the first of two holiday dinners. As children of divorce, my sister and I had to maintain a rigorous Thanksgiving schedule:

1 – 4:30 p.m. Thanksgiving with dad and his side of the family.

4:30 – 5 p.m. Transition period when we tried to digest our food as quickly as possible as we drove past suburban Indianapolis' strip malls and subdivisions (yes, yes, you Coast-o-philes: all of the malls and subdivisions *were* cornfields when I was a kid).

5 – 9 p.m. Thanksgiving with mom, and her side of the family, as well as assorted friends and "steps."

Although I had heard great things about the Thanksgiving turkey deep-frying experience, this is the first time I had witnessed or participated in the holy rite. I was looking forward to devouring a few crispy morsels at my aunt and uncle's house before I headed to my mother's home for the more traditional Thanksgiving fare. I checked my watch to see how my sister and I were doing on our timetable.

"Wait a second, how long does this thing take?" I asked the assemblage of carnivores.

My father lifted up his glasses to read the sheet with the cooking instructions. "Let's see…three minutes a pound…and we have a twenty pound bird…so probably an hour or a little more."

"Then why are we starting this thing at 3:53 p.m.?" I asked. "Why were we eating cheese and crackers for two hours? We have to take off. We're not going to get any turkey. Jeeez…" When I finished I walked in from the cold and wet outside air. *These people have no sense of time. No notion of logistics. Doesn't anyone plan anything?*

"Well, you could just stay a few…" my dad said as he followed me inside.

"Yeah, yeah, yeah. That would go over *real* well. We have twenty people waiting for us so that they can start eating at venue deux. I don't feel like incurring the wrath of mom. There's no time." *TIMING! Fuck Timing.*

We spent the next few minutes finishing off the cheese and crackers and listening to my aunt and uncle talk about the sporting exploits of my younger cousins. When 4:30 tolled, I hopped up, flipped the cars keys around my finger and thanked everyone for a lovely set of appetizers. My sister, her betrothed and I were off.

"I mean how many times have we done this split Thanksgiving? Everyone knows the drill," I asserted as I drove along the nearly deserted road. "People go around changing things and don't think about how it impacts the rest of the plan. It's not like I need any more turkey or anything. I mean I get enough turkey as it is. But, jeeeez, if you're going to make this big spectacle out of deep-frying a turkey, heat up that fucking oil and get the show on the road. You guys know what I'm saying?"

"Riiiight," my sister said, nodding.

"Sure thing," her fiancé said, patting me on the shoulder. See, they both agreed with me, too. The logic is infallible.

❋   ❋   ❋   ❋

"So, the Parkers called. They're going to be over here in about twenty minutes. We'll eat a little later," my mother said as we stowed our damp coats in the closet.

"Oh, that's fantastic. God, we have like twenty other people over here and they just…" I trailed off. "What are they doing? Finishing off their sweet potatoes or something?"

"I think they were returning an overdue movie to Blockbuster and running a couple of other errands," my mother said. "Don't worry about it. It's just more time for Boggle," she said as she tweaked my nose.

I've been writing a lot lately, as you know. My awareness and command of words, morphemes, and lexemes has reached startling proportions. Up until this point, I had harnessed this power only for crafting anecdotes and weaving short stories. On this night, however, I used my powers to annihilate and utterly humiliate my family in Boggle. I was ashamed of myself.

✳   ✳   ✳   ✳

Only the tiniest remnants of food dotted the plates at both the main dining table *and* the kids' table. In most households, it would be time to clear the table. But in my home, there was one final bit of business to take care of.

My mom tinked her glass with a fork. "All right, everyone. For those of you who have been joining us for years now, you know what we're about to do. For those of you are new, this is where we all go around the table and tell everyone what we're thankful for. Better get ready; you'll be on the spot in a minute."

Most veterans prepared something beforehand, usually about thirty seconds worth of sober, serious and heartfelt stuff. Even when boyfriends or girlfriends joined the festivities, they were often briefed and usually came armed with a couple of Post-it notes of material. My uncle was the granddaddy of all Thanksgiving speakers, though. My mother's brother in-law always recites a couple of meaningful articles and then speaks for about ten additional minutes about things like the minimum wage and the evils of NAFTA. Last year, however, he had most of the assemblage in tears when he spoke about September 11.

I usually deliver a pretty good performance when it's my turn. This year, though, I got nothin'.

Nothin'.

The dominoes were falling toward me, one every thirty seconds or so.

"...for my new grandchild, who was born six weeks premature, but is..."

"...that my team won the league championship and I got a trophy and I got a..."

In case you hadn't realized it, I was in a bad place. Even Thanksgiving, my favorite holiday by far, had failed to improve my mood. On the outside, I looked like a reasonably well-groomed 32-year old professional. On the inside, I stewed like some bitter 15-year-old Goth kid, dressed in black and boasting a bar bell piercing right through my nose.

"...my new dog, Hortense. She's just the most precious..."

"...for Republican control of the House and the tax cut that returns..."

My weakest instincts were the strongest force within me. The only partial smile I managed since my Boggle win came when I considered saying "Fuck Thankful" about 15 seconds before I was due to speak.

"Jake?"

"I'm just thankful I'll always have my family," I said feebly.

✳ ✳ ✳ ✳

Since I'm always with my father for the first half of the day and can't help my mom with Thanksgiving preparations, I try to make up for it by rallying the troops for the table clearing and dishwashing campaign. I recruited this set of cousins and a couple of the regular guests to various post-Thanksgiving clean up functions.

And, of course, while we cleaned, my sister and her fiancé danced.

In an act of utter disregard for the cleaning going on around them, they danced to the Frank Sinatra song being broadcast on speakers in every room. For ten minutes, as I cleared the table, dried the silver and put various leftovers in Tupperware, they danced.

As the cleaning duties wound down, I plopped myself at the kids table and continued to watch the swinging. I was seething. And then a thought came into my mind. *Why am I seething? I'm not a seether. I've never been a seether. Am I seething because someone I love is happy?*

I thought I had been ashamed with myself earlier when I destroyed my family in Boggle, but it was nothing compared to the wave that swept over me at the kids table. *How much have I changed? Is this permanent? Is this the "adult" me?* A tear tried to sneak its way out of my eye, but I snuffed it out with a quick scratch.

And then another thought entered my mind. *Why didn't I ever dance with Gabrielle after Thanksgiving dinner?* I had introduced her to what I thought was the proper post-meal ritual: lying down on the couch, unbuttoning one's pants and shoving a hand down the front of the slacks. In the two previous years we had shared Thanksgiving in Indiana, I had even been so considerate as to unbutton her pants for her and guide her hand down the front of mine.

Why didn't we ever dance? I can dance. I love to dance. I'd taken swing lessons with Erica during business school. I knew how to salsa. I'd been forced to go to cotillion in junior high and retained full knowledge of the waltz and fox trot. It would have been a great way to avoid clearing and cleaning duty, to boot, as my sister so ably demonstrated.

I should have danced with her to remind her what was important to me—what I was thankful for. Another tear snuck up on me. This one I didn't have time to scratch away before it jumped down toward my cheek.

I looked past "Dance Fever" and saw my mother gazing at me, with a look I'd never seen before on her face. She waved me over to the seat she had reassumed at the head of the table, and then asked me to sit on her lap.

"Have you been taking your calcium, mom? I'm 50 pounds heavier than you."

"Listen to your mother!" I sat down. "This is all pretty new stuff for you isn't it?" she whispered into my ear. I nodded.

From the time I was seven years old until I was 31 years and 359 days, I had probably cried a grand total of 10 times. I was lucky enough to have avoided academic angst. I was risk averse enough only to go after sure things on the adolescent romantic front. I guess I just glided along. As a matter of fact, one of the times I actually cried was when my mother screamed at me during her divorce for seeming so unaffected by it all. I had of course, been affected and depressed by the situation, but I never cried about it until she called me out.

Now, 10 times is just a pretty solid day on the ocular precipitation scene. I write so much about tears and crying that I regularly have to consult the thesaurus. I just had to resort to calling crying "ocular precipitation," for God' sake. I wasn't ready for this at all, from either a literary or an emotional point of view.

I think I might be feeling emotions more deeply on this Thanksgiving Day because maybe I had healed—if even just a little bit—during my brief time with Angeline. Having that taken away so quickly…

"Do you keep the turkey droppings?" my uncle called out from the other room.

"What?" my mom yelled out around the corner.

"Do you keep the turkey droppings…for soup or gravy? Or should we dump out this pan?"

"We keep the turkey *drippings* for gravy. You can put that in a Tupperware."

"Right…*drippings*…" he tailed off.

My mom and I looked at each other. "C'mon, you *have to* laugh at that," she said.

So I did.

27

Connections

So, I have a little time to kill right now on this fine Monday. When I called the airline this morning, all was copasetic; the automated voice swore on her life that my flight would depart on time. But, now it's obvious she deceived me, because my flight is going to depart Indianapolis two hours late. This delay will also cause me to miss my connection from Chicago O'Hare to San Francisco. Life is good.

I'm looking at a satellite picture of the entire United States of America right now, and there are no clouds of note near any of the cities that figure in to my trip. There *is* some crappy weather coming down from Canada toward the Midwest, but that shouldn't affect travel schedules for hours. What gives? Did some plane coming out of Detroit forget to load up on V-8 juice and have to return to the gate? Did a bird crap on the runway in Newark?

✳ ✳ ✳ ✳

You've obviously watched some movie at some point in your life where a little kid harasses some dude by shooting at him with his fingers and yelling "you're dead." The kid's parents make some half-hearted effort to control the rambunctious tyke, but his guns keep on blazing. That's happening to me right now, one hour into my delay in Indianapolis.

"Pssshhkew. Pssshhkew. You're dead! You're dead," he shouts as he takes cover. Well, why would he take cover behind his chair if I were dead?

This has happened to me twice before, actually, and I played along, once dodging the imaginary bullets and other time catching and eating them. This time, I'm not in the mood to be so animated. "No, I'm safe. I have a force field."

"No you don't! Wait…what's a 'force field'?" asks the six year old.

"It's a hard magical shell that bullets can't get through. Like what comes out of Green Lantern's ring," I say.

"Green Lantern? Who's that?" he asks as he comes toward me. *He doesn't know who the Green Lantern is? What are they teaching kids these days?* The kid presses his menacing digit against my chest. "See, now I shoot past your force field!"

"No, I have armor like Iron Man," I say. "Bullets can't hurt me."

"But I have Cop Killer bullets! They get through anything! You're dead!"

Jesus Christ! What the hell are they teaching kids these days?

"OK, you beat me," I tell him. "I'm all dead inside."

❊   ❊   ❊   ❊

Greetings from the tarmac of the Indianapolis International Airport. We're two hours into our delay on the sunniest of sunny days. But we've made progress; we've left the bars, TVs and ample restrooms of the terminal for the zero bars, zero TVs and two restrooms of the cramped Boeing sardine can. But, we have traveled a good 250 yards, which is nice.

So, this is what I'm writing about now. What a noble literary effort I've embarked upon. Maybe during the Chicago to San Francisco flight I can power up the old laptop and type in some choice material on airline food. It is not—as I have heard from several standup comedians—the least bit tasty.

Then, when I get back to San Francisco, I'll concentrate again on all the crazy, crazy fun-ness that is the "Break." Hey, maybe I'll write some good stuff about Internet dating. Lines like, "Hey, how about that Internet dating? That Internet dating is just *crazy!*" I'm really looking forward to it. I should *definitely* keep this little chronicle going. I could retitle it—maybe something like "Twenty First Dates in the Twenty-First Century." Kind of catchy, eh?

Oh, my God. Things have changed a little bit since I snapped my laptop shut an hour and a half ago. I don't know how they've changed…*exactly*. But they have, indeed, changed.

Angeline called.

She left a message on my mobile phone voicemail. My message indicator lit up just after I was informed by the gate agent that I had indeed missed my scheduled connecting flight to SF. Since I had a bit of time to kill, I listened to the message three times. Then I transcribed it:

> "Hello, young sir. *Surprise!* It's Angeline. I'm…*not* in Europe; I'm in San Francisco. If memory serves, you should be embarking on a flight today back to our fair city. If that is the case, I would most enjoy picking you up at the airport and serving as your chauffeur back home. Please call me when you get a moment. Ciao and *Shalom.*"

I called her back—immediately, obviously—but just got her voicemail. Now, I'm camped out in a Starbucks in the United terminal, with arguments aplenty between delayed travelers and gate agents piercing through the Dave Matthews song "Satellite" as it plays on my earphones.

I was originally scheduled to arrive in San Francisco at 12:24 p.m. Now I can't see getting in before 4 or even 5 p.m. As I hear delay after delay announced and watch the skies outside start to turn gray, one overwhelming thought throbs in my brain:

What the hell is going on here?

So, it's almost 5 p.m. in Chicago and I am four caramel machiattos into my day.

And I just spoke to Angeline. She didn't go to Europe *at all*. She flew home for three days to be with her family and then traveled back to SF yesterday.

"There's so much I want to ask you, but I want to do it in person," I said.

"There's so much I want to tell you. And I can't wait to see you in person," she replied.

So, now Canada's weather has definitely joined our little party here in Chicago. And, it really looks like it's going to be a slumber party. I thought I was going to get out of here around 6:30 or 7, but the little "DELAYED" lights are flashing all over the terminal like it's a freaking disco.

Angeline and I had originally talked about grabbing a late dinner when it looked like I might arrive just after 9 p.m. Now, it looks more like 10 or 10:30. I just called her to tell her.

"No worries. I'll be there no matter what time it is."

It's 8 p.m. in the Windy City and I am loving—*loving*—the fucking Monday Night Football game I'm watching right now. Fucking *loving it* like there's no tomorrow. *Cannot* get enough of that fucking Monday Night Football. Go Raiders.

Actually, the Oakland Raiders are looking pretty damn good. They could go all the way this year. And then we'd *definitely* have some car burning in the Bay area. Win or lose.

Still, I would give it all up to get on a freaking plane right now.

OK, so I'm very pleased with my decisions weeks ago not to swear in churches and casino chapels. I think God just helped me out a little bit here.

I came up and played it all cool and nice to the gate attendant. "Hey, this has been a rough day, hasn't it?" I said. I got her to smile, even. I think they're going to try to get a couple of flights off the ground, but I was far, far back in the computer queue. But, then I told her about the "Break" and about Angeline and the mysterious phone call. I'm now at the top of the standby list.

✳   ✳   ✳   ✳

It's almost 10 p.m. and some hardy and gallant souls are outside my window de-icing the plane's wings. Rumor has it that this plane might actually take off tonight.

I feel like I have a seat on the last chopper out of Saigon. People were practically handing me their babies to get them out safely. Desperate air travel refugees were waving fans of cash in my face for my seat—which I think is going to be on *the* last flight to San Fran, if not *the* last flight out of O'Hare.

My man in blue insulated coveralls is fighting desperately to help me out. The snow is coming down, but my man is battling hard, spraying this plane like he's never sprayed before.

There's an announcement. We're pushing back in a minute.

Just enough time to call. No answer. I leave a message. "We'll be there right after midnight. I'll understand if you can't pick me up. Bye."

"Sir, please stow your lap top," says the stewardess standing next to me.

"Sure thing. One sec, Sandra. Hey, look. You're in my book."

28

Little Whore

"So, how was the traffic coming out here?" I asked.

"Very light. They're doing some construction on the entry ramp though. It held me up for a couple of minutes," she replied. "So, how was the food on your flight from Chicago?"

"The steak tartare was just OK, but the Bananas Foster was truly superb."

Angeline and I had been at it for a couple of minutes, ever since she picked me up at SFO at 12:42 a.m. We were wrapped up in the smallest of small talk, giggling and shaking our heads in wonderment and befuddlement. I intended to get a more in depth update on the series of events that led her to call me, but that could wait for a little bit.

"And the Boggle? I trust the Boggle came off as planned," she said, as she pulled off of Highway 101 just a few miles from the airport.

"Oh, yeah! I was on a whole 'nother plane...a whole 'nother dimension with my Boggle game. Gosh, I was just seeing words...I even found 'truncated'—*nine* letters. Everyone else just found 'run' and 'cat.' I was scared by my own dark powers."

"That's just fantastic," said Angeline as she stopped her BMW in the parking lot of a marina on the San Francisco Bay. She moved the gearshift into park and then rolled over the center console, into my seat. "You'll have to tell me every little detail. Every little fucking

Boggle word…" Her hands cradled my face, pressing in on either side of my jaw.

"So, are you glad to see me?" I asked her under my breath. We both took a moment for one final, subtle giggle and headshake, and then she released the recline lever on the side of the German-engineered seat. From all evidence, she was glad to see me. Which is nice. Within about thirty seconds, all of the BMW's windows turned opaque with steam, nearby streetlights becoming fuzzy and barely noticeable. Unfortunately, we didn't get *that* much time to renew acquaintances.

"Booo-duup! Booo-duup!" Despite all of my Boggle acumen, I have no idea how to spell out the startlingly loud chirps projected by the police car that pulled behind us. Our car's back window alternately glowed blue and red. "Please stay in your vehicle," buzzed a voice from the cruiser.

"I guess I better reassume my position," smiled Angeline, her face two inches away from my nose. She skillfully executed a mini-cartwheel back over the center console and gearshift and into the driver's seat. Angeline rolled down her window a moment before the officer approached the car.

"How are you folks this evening?" as he looked into the vehicle and shined his flashlight onto each of our faces.

"Fine," I replied.

"Fantastic, thank you officer. How are you on this fine evening?" replied Angeline.

"Uh, yes…uh…fine, thank you. Ma'am, is this your vehicle?"

"Yes, what seems to be the problem?"

"I'm afraid we can't have occupied vehicles in this area after business hours. I'm going to need to see your license and registration."

She pulled her license out of her wallet. "Excuse me," she said to me as she leaned over my lap to extract her registration papers from the glove compartment, pausing for a moment to wink up at me.

"Sir, I'm going to need to see some identification from you as well."

"Wha?..Why do you need—" Angeline began.

"Here," I said as I reached across her to deliver my license to the trooper.

"Thank you. I'll be back in a few minutes. Please stay in your vehicle," he said as he walked back his cruiser, obscured by the steamed windows but viewable through the side-mounted mirrors.

"OK," said Angeline, as she used the electronic controls to move her seat back. She turned toward me and sat Indian style. "Why do you think he wanted your license?"

"He thinks you're a whore."

"Excuse me?"

"He thinks you're a prostitute and I'm your John," I laughed. "He's probably checking the databanks for 'priors', or 'calling it into the station' or something!"

"Hahhhh! You're right!" she said as she punched me on the leg. "But doesn't he know that I never kiss my customers on the mouth *when I'm on the job?*"

"Didn't he notice your 'If this Beemer's a'Rockin', don't come a'knockin'' bumper sticker? He's crossed the boundary...this is bordering on police brutality."

"Do you think I should save him some time and tell him to check under my whoring name, Roxie Vanderfoq?"

"That's good. That's too good. Let's just keep that one for ourselves," I suggested, just before a yawn ambushed me.

"You're tired. God, you've had a *long* day."

"I'm getting used to it."

"Well, don't worry sleepy head; we'll have you in bed in just a few minutes."

"Uh, ma'am," said the officer as he loitered outside Angeline's window. "Thank you for your patience. Here are your documents, and here is the gentleman's license. We'll let you off with a warning this time. This is private property and there have been some complaints about activities taking place here, so it would be best to avoid this place after dark. Some pretty unsavory characters..."

"Thank you officer, you have a good night. We'll be sure to avoid this place."

"Thank you, ma'am," he said as he returned to his vehicle.

"Let's go find another place!" she said as she put the car in gear and pulled away.

✳   ✳   ✳   ✳

Angeline pulled into the driveway at my flat. "Sooooo…"

"Soooo…Oooooaaawww," I replied, finding it impossible to fight back my second yawn of the evening—now morning. "Would you like to come up…help me carry my luggage, maybe..?"

"I'd be delighted," she replied, turning on her car's blinking hazard lights.

That's cool, I thought, when it registered she planned to return to her car within a few minutes, *no need to rush into Everything.*

"Hello? Anybody home?" I yelled down the corridor as we walked inside. However, the only trace of my roommate was a wad of my mail he must have rescued from our cramped mailbox, and an empty bag of my Milano cookies with a $5 bill and a Post-It beneath. "I thought you might be around this weekend. Oh, well. I'm off to Frankfurt for business. Hope to see you soon. Maybe during Chrismakkah." That's four months and counting without laying eyes on the guy.

Angeline had remained in the living room, sitting on the couch and thumbing through a four year old *Architectural Digest* my roommate kept around for pure affectation purposes. She held out her hand. I took hers in mine, intending to help her up, but she pulled me down to the couch with her. Both of us just lay there.

Her, staring at my chest. Me, staring at the cushion behind her. My head was a foot and a half further up the couch.

"Hey, you come up!" I demanded.

"No, you come down!" she retorted. Silence. Finally, "Halfsies?" she asked.

"OK," I agreed, squirming a little lower while she wriggled my way.

"There," we both said as we faced each other plain.

I began. "It's hard to know what to say right now. I don't envy you the week you've probably just had. You can tell me whatever you'd like to tell me about it later… tomorrow… whenever. All that

I know to say is that it's good to see your face again, because I honestly didn't think I would," I told her. "We can probably be ourselves a little more, now. I'm looking forward to being with you...and to being less guarded when we're together. I'm just *really* looking forward to getting to know the Amazing Angeline."

"Thanks. Me too. The Amazing Jacob..."

"No, you have to have something that starts with 'J'."

"I'll work on it."

"You can't use 'Jackass'; I've copyrighted that for myself."

She laughed and then kissed me. "OK." We just looked into each other's eyes, and mine began to feel heavy as sleep set in.

"Or 'Jerk-Off'!" I exclaimed, perking up again temporarily. "I'm reserving 'Jerk-Off' for myself as well. You think of something new!"

"I will," she said.

We continued talking—about what I have no recollection. All I remember is a soporific feeling, warm and cool at the same time, working its way through my body, brought on by her voice. The perfect tones...the complete NPR-ness of her voice.

The next thing I knew I was waking up after a hard slap on the butt delivered by Angeline. "Jake. It looks like all of these time zones have caught up with you. I'm going to go home now."

I got up and sleepwalked her the four feet to the front door. "There's a lot I want to say to you. I mean I know that you—"

"Not now. Not now," she said. "We can talk about all of that later. I'm just so glad we got to be together tonight."

"Yes. Me too. Good night."

"Goodnight."

"Oh, and thank you!" I said as she paused on the stairwell. "You're the best cabby I ever had."

29

Last Night

Last night I was extraordinarily lame. It was Friday night, but I planned on staying at home, alone, in front of my computer. The previous week, I had stretched my flexible schedule to its limits and had not put in nearly enough time on the work that pays the rent.

Obviously, I've been spending a lot of time with Angeline. I was discovering that there are many logistical and scheduling implications when the woman you're dating actually resides in the same city as you. Being so steeped in the methods and practices of long distance relationships, I was taking a little time readjusting to a more normal dating routine. *Normal...right.*

Just as I was about ready to whip off another slide with three brilliant bullet points, my cell phone buzzed. "Hey, kid," I answered.

"Are you still being a nerd?" asked Angeline, the cacophonous chorus from the restaurant making her almost inaudible. She had joined some of her friends for dinner at an Italian restaurant in the North Beach district.

"Yeah, unfortunately. I have a couple more hours of work I need to finish tonight so I can go out with *you* tomorrow night," I responded.

"OK, but you need a break," she said.

Yeah, like I really need a "Break," I thought. "I can't come out. I'm disgusting, and I really do need—"

"No," she interjected. "I'm coming over there for a little while! See you in five."

I worked for four, and then took one minute for a little personal grooming, so I wouldn't be quite the mess I had described. The doorbell rang and I returned to the front of the flat to answer it.

"Here is your Amazing Angeline to save the day!" said the aforementioned young lady as she gracefully sashayed directly by me and into the living room, toting a small paper bag in each hand. She sat down on the green velvet couch and carefully removed the contents from one of the brown bags. "I brought you some dessert. This tira misu is *soooo* good!"

"Thanks. It looks great," I said as she withdrew two forks from the paper bag and loaded up one with a bit of the dessert for me. "Mmmmm, bu' wasss i' da odda bag," I managed as I covered my overflowing mouth.

"Surprise!" she said with a flourish as she poured out the contents of the other sack onto the table. It looked like a Made-in-Sri-Lanka Hanukkah starter set. She started putting candles into a disposable menorah, and said, "It's the last night of Hanukkah. We need to celebrate, silly!"

"Thanks. I'm so glad you came over. You're the perfect study break," I said as I planted a kiss on her forehead. She was concentrating on finding a book of matches in her purse.

"Ah-hah!" she said as her hands emerged from the purse with a match already flaming. "*Ba-rukh Atah A-do-nay, E-lo-he-nu Me-lekh ha-o-lam, asher kidd'-sha-nub'mits-vo-tav, v'tsi-vanu, l'had-lik ner shel Hanukkah.*"

"Uh...wow!" I said, truly surprised by the display of Hebrew I just witnessed.

"The glories of the Internet. *Now,* you have to teach me how to play *dreidl.*"

At one time I actually knew the rules of *dreidl.* Each of the Hebrew letters on the four sides of the small plastic top actually had some game rule associated with it: take half the pot, add to the pot, etc. However, I found it was usually much more entertaining to make up rules on the spot.

"OK, so we each get 10 of these Hanukkah gelt," I said as I pulled open the plastic mesh bag and divvied out the foil-wrapped chocolate coins. "OK, so why don't you spin first, and we'll just go through the rules as they come up."

Angeline spun the *dreidl*, sticking out her tongue in intense concentration as she worked to get just the right English on it. When it finally fell, the upward facing side revealed the letter *gimmel*. "OK, so what happens now is you are commanded to give me half of yours," I informed her.

"All right," she said, reluctantly counting out five coins and placing them in my pile.

"Look, if I spin the same thing, you get seven right back from me," I said as I took the *dreidl* in hand. "...But unfortunately, I just got a *shin*, which means I get five from you. So...it looks like it's game over, and I win. Oh, well," I said as I pulled back my huge pile of winnings and started to peel the foil off of one of the doubloons.

"Wait, that doesn't seem fair."

"Hey, these are the rules that God handed down to Moses on Mount Sinai. I'm not going to argue with 5,000 years of tradition!"

"But what about sharing the winnings?"

"I'll have to check to see what Talmudic law says about that," I said as I started to put the piece of chocolate in my mouth. Angeline moved in before I bit into the gelt, timing her action perfectly so her lips and the chocolate rendezvoused with my lips at just the right moment. We shared a chocolate kiss.

"Strong move," I said as we finished up the first kiss. I grabbed another piece of *gelt*; we did, after all, have seven other nights of Hanukkah to make up for.

"We should go together to see a rabbi sometime," said Angeline.

"Uh...sure," I answered, more than a little startled. I swallowed the small chocolate coin, instead of waiting for Angeline to join me for another kiss. This statement might have been the last thing I expected to hear from Angeline, a Catholic school girl up until college. It was also a surprising request to hear from someone that I had only known for six weeks.

"I'm really interested in Judaism. I consider myself more culturally Jewish than anything else," she continued.

"Well…we should definitely go then. Probably in the New Year, though. As the Christmas season approaches, rabbis have their hands full trying to keep the Jewish youth from being lured away by the evils of Claymation holiday specials."

"Good. We'll go in January. Now, I'm going to rejoin the chicks," she said as she donned her coat. She then grabbed the plate with our dessert and fed me the last bite of tira misu. "Here, you might want to keep this for next year," she smiled as she pulled a printout for the official rules of *dreidl* out of her jacket pocket and flipped it onto my lap.

30

Long Distance

"So."

"So."

"How was your Hanukkah? Any good presents? Sorry I didn't call..."

"Well, it fell between our calls, right? Gotta stick with the schedule..."

"Right..." she said quietly.

"It was fine. Mostly checks, you know? No variety. It's not like the old days, like when you got a cool Rock 'em Sock 'em Robots one night and a lame pair of socks the next."

"You see, we never had to worry about that! It was just an avalanche—"

"Let's not do the 'Hanukkah/Christmas Compare/Contrast Routine' right now, OK?"

"OK."

"So, you're going back home for Christmas?"

"...and New Years. What are you doing for New Years?"

"Oh, I may stay here, but I may go to New York. Nick Monroe is having party."

"Oh, that would be fun. Gosh, I haven't been to New York since—"

"Yeah, I remember. We discussed your New York travels a couple of months ago." *Ah, "Our Couch." That was fun. I might be staying on it again soon.*

"Right."

Silence.

"Soooo…" she said, "How have you been spending your time?"

"I went to the do-it-yourself car wash the other day—"

"Stop!" she laughed.

"Oh, you saw through that one?"

"Yes! 'Cause I know you never wash that Probe!" she continued laughing.

"Are you implying something about my personal grooming?" I chuckled. "But, I've changed so much in our time apart!"

"Not that Probe! Wait, I'm confused, which Probe is which? Where were we?" she asked.

"I don't know! But I think we have a new routine!"

"Right!"

"But, to your question: *yes*, I've still been seeing the same person I mentioned before. We're just…eh, you know. We're going all right. Things are…good."

"Oh."

"And you."

"Well…no, I'm not seeing *him* anymore. It wasn't what I thought it was. He's not…oh, never mind. Do we have to talk about this?"

"No, of course not."

Silence.

So, G, should I feel bad I can't reciprocate and commiserate? What should I do now? Break out a little Cat Stevens, maybe? "Ooh, baby, baby, it's a wild world. It's hard to get by just upon a smile…" I bought you the CD for Christmas last year. You should know: "If you wanna leave, take good care. Hope you make a lot of nice friends out there, but just remember there's a lot of bad and beware."

Yes, that was another one of the songs the bustling lyrical center of my brain had memorized in spite of my best efforts.

"Well, I hope you get a lot of nice things to wear at Christmas," I said, breaking the silence. "So…have a good Christmas, and I guess we'll talk in a few weeks."

"Around New Years?" she asked.

"Yeah, let's talk around New Years."

"OK...bye."

"Goodbye. Have a good Christmas, G."

"Thank you. Bye."

Silence.

I sat up a little more in my bed and returned to reading the magazine article I had been glancing at before Gabrielle's call. It was almost 1 a.m. Reading this techno-speak riddled article in the dimmed light would hopefully put me to sleep in about ten minutes.

I looked over at my bedside table. I picked up the phone and dialed.

"Hello?" she said.

"G...I love you more than anything."

"I know. I love you, too," she cried.

Ah, but of course, I cried as well. What better way to cap off a perfectly lovely evening of conversation? Why get a good night's sleep when you can cry a little bit and stay up tossing and turning until 4:30?

God, this move will definitely earn me some demerits against my "Guy Card." So, we shared about five more minutes of sobs, sniffles and laughs, and maybe about three sentences between us.

Finally, I decided to take control. "OOOOOOOOOOK, so now that we've straightened out that issue..." I said.

She laughed.

"...I guess I *will* be bidding you a good night now. For real this time."

"OK," she sniffled. "Thank you for calling back."

"No problem," I said.

"And I *do* love you." Click.

31

It's the Most Wonderful Time of the Social Calendar

"So, we'll catch up later?" asked Angeline.

"Yeah, let's catch up later. I'll let you know if I get done early," I remarked. An impossibility—I would not be getting done early.

"Yes, and I'll let you know if my plans change." Her plans weren't going to change.

"Great."

"Great."

Angeline and I had spent the previous six hours trolling and grazing along Union Street in Cow Hollow. We'd shopped for Hanukkah (OK, I was going to be a little late with some gifts) and Christmas presents. We'd tried on leather coats, strappy shoes, sport coats, skirts, squash goggles and more strappy shoes. We'd foraged for CDs, an exercise designed to check out our musical compatibility—she's a little too Enya and I'm a little too rock and roll. We'd drunk Bloody Marys and eaten crepes.

Throughout our excursion, we'd engaged in a little verbal jousting about our plans for the evening.

"You should come to Billy and EZ's party tonight. *Best view in the City...*" I said.

"You should come down to Palo Alto for the Christmas party. *It's an amazing house...*" she responded.

"C'mon these are *my boys.* There'll be freshly bought *Christmas cookies and Doritos...*"

"*Or,* you can have a *catered seven course dinner...*"

"*Three* different kegs, each with its own distinct blend of the finest malt and hops..."

"Home-made egg nog..."

"Home-made *Jack* Nog..." I countered. Add a little Jack Daniels and any semi-drinkable sludge can become a veritable ambrosia of the gods.

"OK, OK, you got me there," she laughed.

Our social spheres did not overlap at all. And on this night, each of us had our "main event" of the holiday party season. Her small cabal of friends was getting together in suburban Palo Alto, about 40 miles away, for an elaborate dinner party with a late start time. My best friends were gathering about four minutes away for a Christmas rager. On this December evening, her event might as well been 400 miles away; holiday party traffic jammed up the highways and surface streets in the Bay area. We agreed we could visit some lesser events on the holiday party circuit *together* the following week. Tonight, we would both fly solo.

"So, maybe when you get back to the City..."

"Yeah, maybe..." she said right before kissing me goodbye, heading out of my apartment with the bags of Christmas gifts for her family.

I loitered around my apartment for a bit, watching the late college football games and writing the paragraphs you just read. Then, I took my second shower of the day, suited up in some of my recently purchased togs and donned my ever-faithful black cashmere jacket. Before heading out, I put some candy canes in my pocket, both for their breath freshening power and because they helped with a great holiday season joke.

During the party-hopping season, it can take an hour to get a taxi in San Francisco, longer on nights with inclement weather, like this one. Being less tied than most to the bourgeois luxuries of Yellow Cab, I decided to catch the number 45 bus to head cross-town to Telegraph Hill.

Billy and EZ's place was already packed when I arrived at 9:30. I worked my way across the large main room, where almost two months before our crew had commiserated over the Giants' World Series defeat. Tonight, however, it was all mirth and merriment, all the time. Our hosts for the evening stood in the glow of their Christmas tree.

"Gentlemen," I intoned solemnly, as I engaged in the customary holiday greeting with each: a hearty handshake followed by a man-hug with a little less hip-hop edge than those we exchanged at bachelor parties.

"JTeeeeee! What? No arm candy tonight?" EZ had obviously had his fair share of holiday spirits already.

"Yeah, seriously," Billy continued. "Is the lovely and talented Angeline joining us?"

"Unfortunately, no. A little bit of a social calendar train wreck. It's all so new, we haven't synched anything up yet. But I just had to be here with my boys..." I said as I pulled an ornament out of my pocket and hung it on a bare branch of the Christmas tree. The Kwanzaa ornament gave a little bit of pan-holiday cred to the tannenbaum; I put it near the Hanukkah dreidl ornament I'd brought the year before.

The Christmas tree boasted some of the hosts' favorite ornaments contributed over the previous five years; it stood as a tinselly time capsule of our years since business school. Miniature Budweiser cans hung as testament to the bacchanalian times just after our graduation (the first tree had not only been adorned by miniature, beer-themed ornaments, but by several real, post-shotgun empties as well). Two years later, nicer ceramic and intricate metal ornaments began to find their way onto the boughs as young venture capitalists and invest-

ment bankers sought to provide a touch of class. Now, the young parents within our social circle brought trinkets from their two year olds.
Sloppy—but cute—combos of construction paper, cotton and glitter.
Or Christmas-themed Shrinky Dinks made by kids still too young to
have heard the phrase "color inside the lines."

"JT, what's shaking man?" It was Carson.

"Just trying to shake the tree a bit, my man. Good to see you."
We shook hands and swapped holiday man-hugs. I boiled underneath the veneer of holiday cheer. *When am I going to get my $80, you
slug?!*

"I just came from Rex and Delilah's place. They had an amazing
spread. Thought I'd see you there. Some of us may hit Tammy and
Julie's place a bit later, you want to come?" Carson was much more
the man about town than I; I had no idea who any of these people he
loved to list were. He flung out unfamiliar socialites' names much in
the same way he casually ordered up $100 bottles of wine whenever a
group of us went out to dinner.

"You know, I think I might just hang out here for the duration.
Set up camp in a corner and let all of the party hoppers come to me."

"So, when are we going to get our squash rematch in? I gave you
a good run last time…"

"It *was* a pretty tight match. Of course, I *was* missing a ligament
in my knee at the time as well. I'll get out there with you soon. My
bionic leg is almost ready to go; gotta learn to walk again before you
can run…or smack into the walls of the squash court." When
healthy, my squash game involved many big time collisions between
man and the hard white enclosure.

"So, I've been hearing some stuff about some new 'dream girl',"
he said as he leaned in a bit. "Does this person really exist? I mean,
where is she?"

Like I can't get a dream girl. I can get a dream girl, punky!

"Well, unfortunately, we haven't optimized our social logistics
yet. She's with her good friends tonight. Maybe next time."

"And listen, dude," he pronounced as he put his arm around me.
"I was really sorry to hear about you and Gabrielle. Meant to talk to
you about it for a while. I really liked her and you two were a great

couple. But you deserve the best and it seems like you're doing a great job moving on." Carson was obviously a few chapters behind, but it meant a lot to hear this from him. He grabbed a couple of cups from a nearby tray of Jack Nog, handed me one and offered up a mini-toast, chinking his Dixie against mine. We gulped down our first cups o' Jack Nog, a holiday concoction best sipped. Then we shot down yet another cool yet scorching drink of the stuff.

"So, are you sure about Tammy and Julie's? We may also hit Gavin's thing…"

"I'm sure."

"And stop dodging me for squash. No more of this: *'My leg! My leg!'*" he squealed.

"I'll let you know. A few weeks." *And then I'll run your weak ass all over the court, you sorry sack of shit.*

Billy and EZ's holiday party had actually moved well beyond the Dorito fest I had joked about earlier in the day. EZ's girlfriend of two years—and fiancée of two weeks—had seen to that. I was thankful she had upgraded the party's fare, especially since I was counting on a full stomach to moderate the effects of the Jack Nog. I think she also had a hand in making the party look a little bit less like the "Elves Gone Wild" bash of a few years before—both with her tasteful tweaking of the décor and her prudent editing of the guest list.

Still, for me, the guest list was like a cavalcade of stars. Beef arrived with great fanfare, resplendent in his Santa beard and hat. He bear hugged me from behind—quite a compromising position, really. Beef lifted me up for what looked like might be a body slam on the hardwood floor. My feet almost danced on the ceiling, but, after two seconds he crashed both of us down on a billowy black leather couch as innocent, sitting bystanders scurried away. I was now sitting on the sweaty Santa's lap. "So, tell St. Nick what you want for Christmas, you little bastard," he ordered.

"Never. Doing so would be like betraying my people after 5,000 years of persecution."

He clamped down. "You're not getting up until you tell me your Christmas…yooow!" he screamed. A well-executed titty twister allowed me to leave the clutches of the demented Santa. I popped up right in front of Beef's escort, Renee.

"Well, hello, Mr. Tanner."

"Well, hello, Mrs. Farmer-to-be." I dipped her in time with the booming music (toward my good knee, of course). We exchanged a holiday faux-kiss. I clasped her left hand. "Gosh, I'd kiss your hand, but I can't seem to find a way around this rock." Precisely 2.25 carats of love and profit adorned her ring finger. Beef had proposed to her within an hour of arriving back home from Vegas three months earlier.

"So, tonight do we get to meet the new lady we've heard about?" asked Renee.

"Yeah, she'll sit down for Santa!" Beef chimed in, patting his lap.

"Alas, in every relationship aborning, there are the inevitable social calendar conflicts. She won't be joining us tonight." Beef and Renee journeyed into the crowd as the future Mrs. castigated the large man for his Yuletide roughhousing.

A few minutes later, Dennis, business school pal and former European traveling companion, strolled up to the penthouse, toting a confused and doe-eyed date *du jour*. "Jaaaaa-cob," he said as he approached and offered up a "snaps" handshake. I'm normally terrible at those, but this one seemed to come off pretty well. "So, is tonight the debut performance of the little gymnast I've heard about?"

"Alas, unfortunately, we had separate plans for tonight, but soon…hopefully soon."

"Excellent. Ah, Jack Nog," he said as he began to lead his petite Prada-wearing mannequin toward the bar. After a few steps, he returned as his date floated toward the general vicinity of the bar. "Listen, Jake, you know the last time I saw you and Gabrielle together was at last year's Christmas party here."

"Well, I…"

"God, I was there at the beginning…way back in France…I have a lot riding on you guys. I just can't see you two *not* being together," Dennis opined. Since the commencement of the break, Dennis and I had confined our conversations to global currency market arbitrage, the impact of 19th century colonialism on today's geopolitical instability and the best spot to hook up with bachelorette parties in San Francisco. We had avoided almost all discussion of Gabrielle and me—and of any potential of rekindling our relationship months down the line. But I guess the unspoken moratorium had expired. "After being long distance for so long...after everything...it just seems like the connection is too strong. I'm really rooting for you guys."

"Thanks, Dennis. I don't know...I just hope—"

"It's definitely great you're having fun right now. I'm glad you like this new woman; she sounds amazing...but I'm just still seeing you and Gabrielle getting back together. I mean, I *really see it.*"

I didn't know what to say. Dennis' diatribe was counter to the party line I had heard from most of my friends, who urged me to stay firmly rooted in the real world. But did they really know anything more about the "real world" than did Dennis?

"Well, thanks for saying that, my friend. I mean, all I can hope for is...what I want...all I want...is peace on Earth and goodwill toward men," I quipped, trying to change the subject with a little Yule humor. As a Jewish kid, Yule humor was never my forte. "Look, it's just all about the Jack Nog tonight. Merry Christmas," I said as Dennis' date came by with a fresh supply of the house Nog.

"Cheers, you two." I toasted the two of them and finished off the Jack Nog I'd been nursing; I then finished off the new cup in one quick shot. "Time to grab a little free dinner. I'll catch up with ya in a bit," I said as I ambled toward the colorful, well-candled buffet.

Ever the active hostess, EZ's fiancée had just brought up a plate of mini-quiches. The fifth course of my own finger food feast. I downed a couple of the hot-from-the-oven pies, and then heard the rumblings of a new arrival.

"I want me some of that!" screamed Erica.

"Ah, a tartlet for the tart," I responded as I popped a quiche into her mouth. It then dawned on me that the newly baked quiche might have been a little too hot for the aforementioned maneuver, especially when her mouth gaped open and she tried to fan the invisible flames. "Here, take this," I said as I grabbed a half-drunk Dixie Cup of Jack

Nog from the appetizer table. Germs be damned. She probably thought it was my drink anyway.

"Smooooth Jake. You try that with all of the girls?"

"No, just the hotties." It was the truth. Erica knew how to wear a dress. My mere association with her made me more appealing as a potential buddy for hundreds of dudes all over the City. Someday, I'll figure out a way to use that.

"You're the hottie tonight. I like the new pants," she said as she felt up and down my leg. And then a disappointed expression came to her face. "How many times do I have to tell you? No wallet in the back pocket!" Her hand dipped into my back pocket and pulled out my billfold. Then in a fluid motion, she flipped up the back of my black jacket and slapped my rear. "See, now you can work that ass!" Erica's over-the-top compliments and platonic PDA are always welcome and much appreciated. She's the biggest ego pumper I have.

"This ass is yours and yours alone," I said as I leaned in close and whispered into her ear.

"Now, I know that's not true. Where's my competition?" she whispered in turn, inserting my wallet into my jacket's inside breast pocket.

"Alas, due to the vagaries…aw, screw it. I've answered this question too many times tonight. She ain't coming."

Erica pulled back from our hug. "Is everything—?"

"Yeah, yeah. It's just *new*."

"Well, there'll be many, many other times…Happy Hanukkah." She nudged her chin toward a small mistletoe pin near her shoulder.

"Merry Christmas." We kissed and parted, but as I ventured away to get the next round of Jack Nog, I winked. "You might want to move that pin…unless you want someone to be kissing that left breast."

As I approached booze central, my cell phone vibrated. The green caller ID panel glowed with Angeline's number.

"Ho ho ho," I answered.

"I'm coming to your party!" she screamed across our bad connection. "I'm just getting off the highway. I'll be there in ten minutes."

"But, what about—?"

"Ehhhh, I got four courses in, that's all I need. I'll see you in a few. 'Ta.'" That's short for "ta-ta," which never seemed to me like it needed shortening.

Angeline is coming! I celebrated with another Dixie cup of the ever-present Nog.

After twenty minutes of small talk with a cascade of acquaintances, I was still awaiting Angeline's arrival. Parking on Telegraph Hill could take half an hour on a normal night; she could very well have been in the midst of a maddening scenic tour of the area while on a quest for a spot…any spot. I'd done it many times before, circling endlessly. *Look kids; Big Ben, Parliament, Alcatraz…*

But Angeline's parking karma appeared to be better than mine. She came up the stairway, arm in arm with Billy, her old friend from the Mas Sake adventure six weeks before.

"I found a party crasher. She said you invited her," laughed Billy.

"I think she's stalking me. You might want to have the bouncer get rid of her. You know these groupies. Uff!" She punched me in the stomach and laughed. Such is her way, I was learning.

"I'll leave you kids alone," said Billy as he ambled away.

"Thanks, Todd, save me a dance!" Angeline wrapped her arm in mine and smiled up at me in the perfect glow that only strings of cheap white Christmas lights can provide. She wore a tight burgundy sweater—flecked with gold and blue—that went all the way up her exquisite neck. Her cream skirt molded tightly to her legs, giving way near the floor to dark brown knee high boots. She took a sip of her red wine and drank in the room's activity. "So, do you know everyone here?"

"Yeah, most." EZ and Billy's own "mystery roommate" was unfortunately in full effect tonight, having invited hordes of random Euros. A German national, he seemed to have asked every consular secretary and copy boy in town to the fete. The smoking Europeans dominated the large deck outside in the San Francisco mist, lighting up Camels and bounding onto nearby rooftops, while the smokeless Americans inside steamed up the windows and imbibed way too much Jack Nog. To each his own vice.

"I want to meet your friends," she said, tugging on my elbow. As if I would have it any other way.

"OK, I guess. Just keep in mind: they think I'm married with three kids back in Indiana, so don't blow my cover."

"Your secrets are safe with me," she said as we approached the ravenous pack of MBAs near the window.

After the requisite introductions were made and about five minutes of chits were chatted, I quaffed my final bit of Jack Nog and looked over at Angeline's nearly exhausted glass. "I'm going to get a refill of the house special, and I'll bring you another...?"

"Cabernet," she smiled.

"Back in a couple. Just need to say hi to a few people..."

This was my favorite part. I took the scenic route over to the bar. Basically, I meeted and greeted folks all the way across the room, but always took advantage of our short conversations by stealing glimpses of Angeline over their shoulders. She owned her corner of the room. I had absolutely no idea what kind of stories she was animating with her expressive hands and face—well-practiced after years of training with the finest Ukrainian rhythmic gymnastics coaches—but I was totally entertained nonetheless.

Whatever Angeline discussed with Beef earned her a "punch it in" fist knock, 2002's version of the high five. From the motions of her pantomime, she and Dennis discussed some sort of climbing...or maybe swimming. A minute or two later, Angeline and Erica began an animated dialogue, using their hands like bookends to compare lengths. Just based on the eight, ten and twelve inch increments they displayed, I think they were discussing purse sizes. I *hope* they were discussing purse sizes.

After about ten minutes, I completed my appointed errand at the bar, by this time of the party a sorry display of empty Absoluts, half drunk cocktails, dessicated lime remnants and legions of discarded corks. As I pivoted to begin my return trip, laden with one of the final cups of Jack Nog and a glass of cabernet (or whatever red was open), a "White Christmas" dance mix from a group called the "Bing-Blings" began to boom from EZ's Bose speakers. Carson, a dancing fool if there ever was one, swept up Angeline in a frenetic swing as other party-goers dispersed to give the dancers a wider berth. His moves were precise and quick—the same robotic repetitions I'd seen scores of times. Carson was one of the City's pre-eminent swingers, and wasn't at all scared to break out his patented moves—but he was a one-trick pony. Swing was always the order of the day, whether the music of the hour was Billy Joel, Billy Idol or Billy Ray Cyrus.

"Refreshment break?" I asked Angeline as I dodged a particularly frenetic Outside and Inside Underarm Turn.

"Yes!" she beamed. "Pardon me, fine sir. My waiter…er, prince…has returned," she continued as she broke off the swing and curtsied to Carson. I handed her the overdue drink.

"So, am I going to get you on the dance floor, Mr. Tanner?" she asked in between sips.

"Maybe…if we could convince someone to put on Journey's 'Open Arms'. I think the knee is only ready for slow dancing for the next couple of weeks," I laughed. "Besides, I don't think this is the best venue for my comeback tour," I said, kicking at a puddle near our feet, undoubtedly a broth of dirty rain water, Jack Nog, gin and sweat.

"Well, you'll save the first dance for me," she declared.

"If you're good."

"If *I'm* good? *You* are the one who has to worry about Santa's 'naughty and nice' list," she lectured.

"Not a problem. I don't believe in Santa."

"No? What about the Little Drummer Boy?"

"No."

"The Grinch?"

"Of course, if Dr. Seuss wrote it, it must be true." Gotta love the Seuss.

"Do you believe in mistletoe?"

"I think I can be convinced."

"Rudolph?"

"Nah."

"Dasher or Donner or Blitzen?"

"No…but I do believe in Vixen," I suggested innocently.

"Really?"

"Oh, yes. I'm the high priest in the Cult of Vixen."

"Really?"

"Oh, yes. I make pilgrimages to worship at the altar of Vixen."

"Really?"

"It's my sacred and holy duty," I said earnestly before swallowing the last of the evening's Jack Nog. I surveyed the still bustling scene before locking back in on her eyes. "So this little gathering pretty much sucks. Maybe we should move on to the next stop on the party train."

"I completely agree. We need to find a more sophisticated crowd, one commensurate with our social standing. I tire of these boors," she grinned. I grinned right back at her.

Without another word, we headed to retrieve our coats from the upstairs bedroom. Jackets in hand, we skirted by the periphery of the party crowd toward the staircase. Across the room, Dennis and Erica each raised a glass as I glanced back toward the pack. I returned the gesture with my imaginary goblet, and descended the stairs, stopping only to thank Billy and EZ near the exit.

Angeline's parking karma was unparalleled; her car was waiting in the much venerated spot right outside of Billy and EZ's house. I opened the door for my gorgeous designated driver and hustled around to the passenger side. As I slid into the warm cuddle of the Beemer's bun warmers, I felt another wave of Jack Daniels tickling my brain. Life was good.

The BMW went west on Lombard, rain soaked streets crackling beneath the car. I looked at her face each time a streetlight illuminated it. "What? What?" she would ask in response to my stares.

"Nothing." Everything.

At this point in the evening, my smiles were contented smirks and my eyelids were heavy. As I lounged in the passenger seat, I said, "So, I bet every guy you've ever dated has called you 'Angel'. Am I right?" A slightly impolitic query, I decided a few seconds ago when I typed it. Still, she took it in stride, laughing at her inebriated inamorata.

"Yeah, pretty much. Kind of comes with the territory with my name."

"Ah, but no longer. I think I'm going to call you…'Jelly'. You know, like strawberry *jelly*."

"I get it."

"Like grape *jelly*."

"I understand," she laughed.

"Because your name is An-*jelly*-ne."

"Your logic is incredible."

"I know," I responded, nodding and then nodding off into a well-deserved three-minute nap.

I was roused by Angeline as she clawed and tickled my stomach. She had found another fantastic spot, just a few feet away from my building. *It's another Christmas miracle*, I thought.

We walked up to my second floor flat and went right inside without a word. As Angeline passed me, I put my hand on her shoulder to stop her, and then removed her damp coat. She shivered and laughed as I moved her hair to one side and kissed the back of her neck.

We proceeded down the long hallway to my bedroom. I flicked on one lamp once we were inside; a warm orangish glow welcomed us. Angeline set down her purse and began to look at some of the pictures displayed in my bookcase. New shots of me with my family. Five-year-old photos of tuxedo clad business school students brandishing Cuban cigars. A ten-week old image of many of the same friends—some with significantly less hair—at an impromptu Las Vegas wedding.

"Why don't I wash up a bit and get us some water? Just make yourself comfortable," I said as I switched on a Coldplay disc.

She nodded and continued perusing the artifacts of my bedroom—a collection thinned out dramatically three months before.

I journeyed back through the corridor to the kitchen and poured each of us a large glass of ice water from the pitcher in my refrigerator. Proceeding back up the hallway, I stopped in the bathroom. I popped a couple of Advil and then gave the teeth a quick brush. I cranked the "C" knob and splashed a few tidal waves of arctic water up onto my face.

I stared at my wet face in the mirror for a few seconds, because that's what guys do in books like this. Then, I dried off, gathered the huge plastic San Francisco Giants cups and headed back toward my bedroom. I took a large gulp of water as I entered my room…and was extraordinarily lucky I didn't execute a Danny Thomas-esque "spit take."

Angeline was lying on her side on my bed glancing through a magazine, her cheek resting on her palm. She was wearing blue pajamas. *The* blue pajamas. The ones I had donned twice, but which Gabrielle had worn a hundred times. The blue pajamas that G wore in dozens of images burned into my brain.

"I hope you don't mind. You said, 'Make yourself comfortable,' and these were in the traditional 'pajama drawer'," she said.

"No…yeah…you look great," I said as I sat down next to Angeline and handed her a cup of water.

Holeeeeeee….Of all the things not to put into "deep storage"! Why didn't I entomb those in a freaking milk crate. Those should be buried in the deepest recesses of my closet. Oh my God; did I even wash those things?!? Did I just shove them back in the drawer?

I wondered if she could smell Gabrielle's perfume or the lotion she used to put on nearly every night. I looked into Angeline's face and smiled what might have been a nervous grin.

She tossed the magazine off of the bed and tousled my hair. As we leaned against the large shams, I started to feel the color coming back to my cheeks. I started to feel the warmth of the Jack Nog flow through my body again—actually it probably wasn't the holiday brew, but something else altogether.

And, you know, I just decided not to worry about the blue pajamas. I didn't care if they bore the scent of a distinct brand of perfume or some imported lotion.

I stroked Angeline's hair and tickled her ear. I leaned in to kiss her lips and then her neck, and lost myself in a cloud of vanilla.

32

Almost the Best Day Ever

I normally don't write right now. This time of day. This late. Or this early. But there's this mix of caffeine and red wine and testosterone and cholesterol and adrenaline that's making the words ricochet around my head. I need to tell you about my day. Right now.

I have to tell you: I wrote the ending first. It's rife with passion and intrigue, and there *might* be some violence. However, I must request we all begin here, at the beginning.

✴   ✴   ✴   ✴

So, the morning appeared cloudy from my back window, but sunny from the front. Somehow I knew the front window would carry the day. Today (yesterday, actually) would be a beautiful day, I decided. An eventful day. Action packed and energy-laden. I would make it so.

My "work" To-Do list barely took up one Post-It note—one of the small ones. It was the kind of list that could take up a full day if I let it, or be crammed into two hours if I forced it. I resolved to finish all of this corporate minutiae in one hour, figuring I could save time by omitting any form of proofreading, fact-checking or other attention to detail in my work. I would rush through my list of e-mails, PowerPoint slides and spreadsheets with a devil-may-care ferocity and speed. I would unleash my creative powers and then unshackle myself from my kitchen table desk.

I gave myself one extra minute for an important call.

"Be here in 90 minutes!" I bellowed into the handset.

"What?...Hello? Jake?" asked a confused and possibly still asleep Angeline.

"We're getting out of town. You're driving. Get over here in the convertible. I don't know what we're going to do...but it's going to be something. So let it be written, so let it be done!" I really said that—I was emboldened by my early morning decisiveness. It was a small dose of over-acting in a day that would be dripping in drama in a few hours. She laughed. She agreed. Now, the clock was ticking.

I booted up my computer and went at my work with a precision, flair and efficiency that surprised me—even scared me. First came a prodigious amount of cutting and pasting of brilliant, semi-brilliant or at least grammatically correct things I had written before. Within 30 minutes, the bits and pieces of my Microsoft mosaic were fully assembled. Then, my fingers veritably danced around the keyboard and my mouse scurried around my desk as I de-fonted and re-fonted. I changed numbers to bullet points and bullet points to numbers. I audaciously experimented with new slide color schemes—like a modern-day Titian or Monet.

After 58 minutes, I had produced a masterpiece of management consulting. I was particularly proud of my font choices.

Quickly, I showered, shaved and got dressed. Since we would probably embark on some outdoor adventure, I figured the layered approach was the way to go. I realized my final layer was a top that Gabrielle had given me about a year before. *Uh, not today.* I tore off the sweatshirt and donned a pullover that I had purchased a couple of weeks ago.

Angeline pulled up outside my building 30 minutes after our agreed-to time, which was fine since I had actually factored a 45-minute late arrival into my master plan for the day. It was a wonderfully sunny December day in the City, probably around 50 degrees. It was the kind of December day when Bostonians wear shorts and San Franciscans wear parkas. After doing a head-fake on a Dukes of Hazzard jump-entry into her car, I eased into my customary position in the passenger side. Once again, I felt the warm embrace of her BMW's heated seats.

We looked like actors in a rental car commercial, ready to hit those winding roads they always seem to find. I pulled off my $5 gas station sunglasses and she pushed her $180 Gucci shades up into headband position. Without a word, we gave each other a quick kiss and started laughing. We gave each other a not-so-quick kiss and started laughing again.

"Well, where to, young lady?" I asked.

"Hmmm…I'm kind of thirsty," she said. "Maybe a little red wine…"

"Strong choice. Napa it is." As if there were any other choice for two crazy kids ready to live the day-trip dream played out in so many inspiring car rental ads.

Within 5 minutes, we were speeding across the Golden Gate Bridge toward wine country. As we neared Vista Point on the northern side of the bridge, I could feel Angeline's smiling eyes peering toward me. I kept my eyes straight ahead on the road as we passed the site of our first kiss. "I hear that Vista Point has some good views," I deadpanned. She giggled, snorted and then giggled again before we kissed at 72 miles per hour. Very irresponsible, I know, but she kept both hands on the wheel.

As we approached the exit to Sausalito, the first town north of San Francisco, Angeline merged onto the exit ramp and declared, "We have to make a quick stop. I need to get my car washed." Where my philosophy is to leave well enough alone and keep the protective layer of sap, soot and grime on my auto's exterior, Angeline maintains her car immaculately. The car wash was just a few hundred feet off of the highway. As we pulled into the lot, Angeline reached into her purse and pulled out her nearly full "frequent washer card" for this establishment (note to self—what happened to my Subway card? Did I leave it in my jeans? I think I'd earned a full sandwich).

It's always interesting to go to a place with a "regular," no matter what sort of venue it is. I've found that sometimes, in the world of dating, people reserve their regular hangouts—whether they be bowling alleys, restaurants, bars or foot massage places—for people with whom they've developed a strong comfort level. In a way, it's sort of touching that Angeline took me to sing karaoke on the night of our amazing, beautiful, interminable first date. Silver Clouds might have been her favorite place in the City, and she chose to share it with me.

And, as strange as it sounds, I began to feel that coming to this car wash was a milestone in our relationship. When we pulled in, several employees paused during the buffing, drying and wax-on/wax-off routines to wave to her. She drove up near the entrance of the car wash tunnel and stopped at the hut housing the big man of the operation—they greeted each other like old friends.

"Hello, Enrique! How did your daughter do in the Christmas show?" inquired Angeline.

The car wash manager grasped her left hand. For a second, I thought he was about to pull a Pepe Le Peu and kiss her arm all the way to the elbow, but he just gave her hand an emotive shake in the way that Latin *maitre d*'s and salsa dance instructors often do. "Oh, she was just like you: an Angel. She had her own solo and it was so beautiful. We videotaped it…"

"Well, I would love to see it," interrupted Angeline. "You'll bring the tape for me?" I had no doubt she meant it.

"Of course. So where are you two traveling today?" he asked as his eyes veered my way. A hint of confusion flashed over his face—he must have met Trevor sometime in the past. I think it was beginning to register with him that I was not the former occupant of Angeline's passenger seat.

"Enrique, this is my new friend, Jake." I smiled, nodded and gave him a half peace sign/half wave. "We're going to Napa Valley today to tour the vineyards and try some wonderful wines and food." She sounded like she was giving a voice-over for the sort of airline in-flight travel show that comes on before a two-month old episode of *Everybody Loves Raymond*.

"Excellent. Well, we will make sure your car looks spectacular," he declared as he opened Angeline's door with a slight bow. She and I walked toward a set of benches back toward the road, near the car wash's buffing and drying area. Around fifteen of what I presumed to be Mexican workers buzzed around several sparkling Lexuses (or is it Lexi??) and Benzes, toweling off and vacuuming the $70,000 rides of Marin housewives. A few of the workers nodded and smiled to Angeline as she sat down on a nearby bench—one even doffed his cap. She gave a cute little wave back to a couple of the members of the drying crew.

"Don't let me hold you back. You can go catch up with them on their current events, too," I told her.

"Thanks! I'll be right back," she squealed as she grabbed my forearm, kissed me on the nose and ran off to converse with her pals. I got the feeling she only knew a couple members of this crew—I don't think most of them stay too long in one place.

I could tell she was excited to practice her Spanish. Although Angeline fashions herself quite the linguist, the various befuddled and bemused looks on the workers' faces gave me the distinct impression that she was mangling their native tongue. A couple of them answered her queries in English, perhaps hoping that she too would decide that English would be the most efficient language in which to continue the conversation. Still, they were psyched beyond belief that she was there with them—a smoking hot San Francisco woman who was genuinely fascinated by their lives. It was probably all too rare an occurrence in the drive-up/drive-away industry they found themselves in. Most owners of the Lexuses and BMWs were in a hurry to drive away. We eventually drove away too, but not before Angeline had made three or four new friends.

Napa Valley lay 30 minutes ahead. Two hours later we were there. Angeline claimed she knew a great route to some of the best wineries—we ended up at an oil refinery. I really do hope I can eventually come to view this sort of thing as endearing. I'm working on it.

We eventually managed to locate the 797 square mile expanse of Napa County and spotted a stately manor that could only be a winery. We had no idea where we were or what vineyard we were visiting, but that was fine with us. Inside, a vanload of German tourists sampled some reds...actually "sampled" isn't the right word. These middle-aged mustachioed men and their wives were sloshed beyond belief. The men were beefy, the women ample. Mullets and proto-mullets abounded.

I squeezed past the chaotic jumble of Hessian jolliness and advanced toward the wine tasting counter. Before I could put in an order for whatever the fruit-of-the-vine-of-the-day was, the Germans had broken into song. I turned around and was not surprised to see Angeline—laughing almost uncontrollably—among the covey of tourists. A bearded fellow sporting a Bayern Munich soccer jersey and Adidas sweatpants had invited her to dance, and, of course, she was not one to shy away from a little intercultural exchange. Though she's as graceful as they come, it was hard to recognize what sort of dance this odd couple was attempting. Polka, perhaps? German square dancing gone horribly awry? Do Germans square dance?

Angeline hammed it up for the crowd. As the portly polka dude swung her my way, she flashed a mock look of horror. Actually, maybe not so mock. Polka Fever was in full effect—and their hopping was coming awfully close to large displays of wine bottles. I was actually a little wary of the whole developing scene, and, even as I chuckled along with the merriment, I watched the heavy man's every move. My worst injury in college—one that robbed me of two months of intramural glory—was an ankle that was badly sprained in a dancing accident. I was a bystander in that situation as well, just waiting in the beer line—too cool to do the Electric Slide. But there was no protection from that uncoordinated mass of humanity. Pivot left and "sliiiiide." An oblivious woman putting a little extra oomph into her "sliiiiide" crushed my ankle. But I digress.

Luckily, after about a minute, the huffing and puffing German had had enough, and gave a weary "*danke*" to Angeline. She danke'd him as well, and hustled over to my zone at the wine sampling bar before the next round of "Roll Out the Barrel" could begin.

"What are you doing? There are five more tourists who need their daily polka fix," I chortled.

She nestled up next to my arm, grinned and slugged me playfully in the gut. "Why didn't you save me?" I love it when she slugs me.

The rest of the afternoon was more of your typical Napa Valley fare. Of course, we received extra attention from most every wine-

and-cheese type at the vineyards we visited. Well, she got the attention, but I got most of the wine.

Loaded up with about 20 bottles of wine, seven wedges of blue cheese and three loaves of freshly baked bread (French or Italian, I'm not sure...I'm 32 years old and I don't think I know the difference), we headed back to the City after our 10 hour Napa Valley adventure.

We were famished, having never sat down for a proper meal the entire day, but, instead subsisting on pretzels and white wine mustard samples at various vineyards. As she drove south, I grabbed one of our recently acquired loaves and broke off several chunks of bread for us, creating a shower of crust crumbs in the process. Then, I dove into our cache of blue cheese and smushed off a few lumps from some of the varieties we'd purchased at the last winery.

We played a guessing game about the blue cheeses I was feeding her. Stilton? Danish? Gorgonzola? I kept her guessing and always declared she was right on her last query. I actually had no idea which was which—I hadn't bothered to glance at the wrappers when I broke off the masses of cheese.

We didn't speak much on the way back, other than during our cheese-themed game show. Our words per minute rate these days was almost definitely less than half of what it was a few weeks ago. We knew the names of each other's siblings. Our favorite classes in high school. Our favorite toys growing up. Our preferred deserts. Our most exciting travel stories. We had the pieces, the building blocks, the relationship Legos—we just needed to see how they all fit together.

I just kept staring at her face and her eyes. Polygons of light strolled and danced across her eyes, neck, forehead and hair as the headlights of vehicles in the heavy traffic bounced off of the BMW's rearview and side-mirrors.

During our ride out to Napa in the morning, we were infused with such a feeling of glee, almost childlike. Now, I was bathing in this tremendous sense of comfort. A day filled with red wine sampling tends to take the edge off, but that wasn't the source of the incredible sensation of well-being I was feeling.

For a brief moment, I was almost upset at how at ease I was, how much comfort I felt just being near Angeline. Should I be feeling *this* comfortable *this* soon? Was I so at ease because of her, or because of "the idea of her" (to borrow a cliché from several heavy, heavy relationshippy conversations I'd been a part of over the years)? There was still so much I didn't know about her, and even more I didn't know about us—together.

We approached Vista Point again from the north side of the Golden Gate Bridge. Seeing this particular promontory snapped me back into relationship reality. I remembered staring at the night sky during a moment of confusion seven weeks ago. I didn't want to be confused on this night, so I just told my over-active brain, "Please leave me alone."

Why overthink this? Why steal from yourself? Why cheat yourself? Stop fighting it. Just feel it, Jake. Be good to yourself, and be good to Angeline, by swimming with the current of these emotions you're experiencing, rather than against them.

We stopped at the end of the backed up toll plaza on the south end of the Golden Gate Bridge. Freed briefly from her driving duties for the first time in almost an hour, Angeline ripped off her safety belt, grabbed me by the hair and started kissing and sucking on my neck with surprising, but much welcome, gusto. Her other hand wandered down my chest, past my lap belt. She peeked away from the attention she was giving my neck, eased up on the brake and moved the BMW up to occupy the vacant two-car length gap in our line. Her hand kept meandering around my bread-crumb-filled lap. As we rolled toward the toll collection station, her lips moved from my neck to my ears.

"You know what I want? What I need?" she whispered. Before I could respond, she let out a gasp. "Ooooh, I have everything I need, now." She raised her head from her ear-licking detail, winked at me and displayed the sheaf of $1 bills she had pulled from my jeans pocket.

That toll: best $3 I ever spent.

So, back to real time with Jake about to do a face-plant onto his lap top computer at 5 a.m. I think it's time to turn the reigns of this narrative back over to the version of me from four hours ago, the version much more amped up on caffeine and adrenalin and hormones and toxins. Things are starting to get interesting. Get ready for some sex, violence and even some symbolism—if I remember correctly. Good night.

✳   ✳   ✳   ✳

We came back to my flat with arms full of wine bottles and fruit and baguettes. And cheese. Like twelve kinds of blue cheese.

"FEED ME!" roared Angeline as I kicked the door closed behind us. A quick left turn took us right into my living room, and she dove into the bag o'cheese.

"Should I see if I have anything else in the kitchen?" I asked, knowing that my normally well-stocked refrigerator and freezer boasted only Hot Pockets after a recent August expiration date purge.

"No, just get over here. You need to try this one!" she exclaimed as she cheesed up a chunk of bread with one of our blues. Angeline stuffed the open faced mini-sandwich into my mouth as I pulled one of our reds from my back pack. My mouth was too full of bread and moldy cheese to even taste anything. I was just trying to avoid choking. *Don't choke before the semi-drunken sex, Jake,* I told myself. I bit down hard to try to break up the mass, but I was mostly chewing with the roof of my mouth, the rock hard crust shredding the soft flesh.

"That's really fantastic," I replied as soon as I was out of danger. I took some strawberries out of the bag of fruit we purchased at an over-priced, organic, yuppie-farmer's market in Napa. I held out one of the largest berries. You know, trying to get the whole *9 1/2 Weeks* thing going in our 7 1/2 week-old relationship.

"C'mere," I beckoned. Still sitting cross-legged on the living room's Turkish rug, she butt-shuffled over to me to take the fruit into her mouth. While Angeline finished chewing the strawberry, I reached behind a pile of firewood—there mostly for show—to grab a small Duraflame log. I ignited it inside my shallow, much-too-small fireplace, the kind common in San Francisco flats. *Did I open the flue?* I thought. Unfortunately, in my time, I had killed more than one romantic interlude by flooding a room with smoke. This time, however, it looked like at least *most* of the chemically-laced Dura-smoke was wafting up the chimney.

I continued my manly duties by corking—corking or de-corking? Or un-corking?—one of the bottles of wine we bought at the impromptu Polka Festival.   I poured.   She wrapped two hands around her wine glass as if it were a goblet and drank her first $10-worth before I had even finished pouring my glass.

"More...*please*," she demanded...then requested.   Angeline had been our designated driver after all; she had to catch up.

We continued to gorge, kiss, chug and massage for the next half hour.   "Ooooh, I think I'm stuffed," she proclaimed, lifting up her sweater to pat the skin of her perfectly flat and toned stomach.   *Yeah, she's just busting at the seams.*

Leaving her belly exposed, she leaned back on one elbow toward me, taking a sip from her wine glass.   She then leaned her head back onto my right knee, her upside down face staring up at me.   I fought back a laugh and turned it into a smile.   We had partaken of our wine earlier with such abandon that Angeline had a child's grape juice smile on her upper lip.   I'm sure I boasted the same temporary tattoo.

She was a bit closer to the fireplace than I.   I looked down at her belly, faint dancing shadows showing the contour of the subtle but strong muscles of her perfect midriff.   In the firelight, her stomach started to glisten.   The sweat of wine-induced warmth?   The heat of the fire?

I needed to touch her sparkling skin.

So I did.

A tremor went through her body, and she pivoted away, rolling her head off of my knee.   Startled, I almost apologized.   No need, I quickly determined.

Angeline pushed me down and pounced on top of me.   Where normally our initial kisses were interspersed with chatting and laughing, now, an intense, resolute silence gripped us both.   We rolled through breadcrumbs, cheese wrappers and leafy strawberry tops toward the couch.   Breaking from our kiss momentarily, I gripped the cushions from the sofa and tossed them around the room.   We continued our rolling embrace around the living room, halting intermittently on the islands of green upholstery.

We spun toward the neighboring dining room. I had long entertained grand visions of sweeping off the accumulated mail, magazines and consulting presentations which usually covered the long dark dining table as prelude to making love, but while I was out of town a few days before, my flatmate removed all clutter from the area. Angeline and I slid around on the freshly Pledged surface, getting tangled in the red fabric runner that adorned the table.

Moving slowly, but purposefully, we gracefully stumbled out of the dining room and slammed against the wall of the foyer. She exhaled with the force of our collision, regained her leverage, and propelled us both toward the opposite side of the hallway, angling back toward my bedroom.

For five minutes, we breathed and kissed and unbuttoned and sweated as we ricocheted back and forth between the walls of the 70-foot hallway of my shotgun apartment. We came to a stop in the middle of my flat-mate's wall-mounted photographic travelogue. Angeline's arm shot up above her head in an exceedingly theatrical motion portraying "unbridled passion." Her hand dislodged one of the framed beauty shots, which glanced off of her bare shoulder. Responding with reflexes little dulled by our red wine binge, I caught the flying frame *Matrix*-like before it smashed on the ground.

"Are you all right?" I asked her as I kissed the red mark on her shoulder.

"Yeah," she breathed. "That was impressive."

"Yeah? You think so? Just wait."

I moved my mouth from her right shoulder to the left side of her neck and resumed my kissing duties, simultaneously remounting the frame upon its naked nail. I glanced up at the crooked picture.

It was Cinque Terra.

The phone started ringing. I had no doubt who it was. The moment just seemed to be taking on a life all its own. A microcosm in macro.

The writer in me leapt for joy—*Wotta twist! More material. This stuff writes itself.*

The lover in me was confused—*Am I about to get my eyes scratched out? Whatever you do, DO NOT stop kissing.*

The pathetic, heart-sick, depressed, emotional wreck inside of me was terrified—*I* cannot *hear her voice right now. I'm kissing Angeline. I'm staring at Cinque Terra. I think I'm going to throw up.*

The answering machine 30 feet away clicked to life. My silent recorded voice lied to the caller, telling her I wasn't home.

In about 8 seconds, I would really know just how pathetic, heart-sick and depressed I really am.

The tone and timber of the caller's voice were unmistakable—Gabrielle. *Should I start groaning to drown this out? You don't groan, you ass!* My mouth was afflicted by an instantaneous drought. *Find the reserve tank of spit. Lube up that mouth, you idiot.* Clutched in an embrace in the hallway, I tried to hear her every word while attempting not to listen. *You pause, you're a dead man. Smooch. Kiss. Nuzzle. Repeat. Do not stop!* I could only make out bits and pieces. "…going home…all of your things…New Years… thinking of you…"

It was like experiencing a train wreck in slow motion. But…hey, I was getting through it. Saliva crisis: averted. Kiss continuity: strong, nary a pause in there. Nausea: just the right amount—especially after a Chianti and two Merlots, and a few lung-fulls of Dura-flame fumes.

I'd been so focused on my own neuroses that it took me a second to notice that Angeline had totally stopped her grinding gyrations—she was barely kissing me at this point. *Oh, God. Do not look into her eyes. She'll start again. She has to.*

I had only been able to make out part of the answering machine message. *Oh, God. What did Gabrielle say? Did I miss something?*

The gene that makes us look at car accidents kicked in. I had to see her eyes. I pulled away from our one-way kiss.

Angeline was smiling. A very knowing smile. Roguish. Devilish, even. She ripped off my already loosened shirt and pushed me against the opposite wall. Her strength was impressive. She came at me hard, our kiss nearly a demolition derby of teeth.

My pants sprang to life, or rather, the vibrating cell phone in my front pocket. Again, no caller ID required—I knew it was Gabrielle.

She had paired her calls as long as I'd known her—first dialing the home line and then trying me on the wireless. She'd always leave a cute message on each. Never a paraphrased version of the previous message—always something new.

But, if I were the least bit curious about the message Gabrielle was about to leave in my voicemail, Angeline quickly knocked that thought out of my brain. She pushed herself hard against me…or, more specifically, against my phone. "Mine mine mine mine mine," she whispered and gasped, her feral territoriality doing nothing to dampen my mood and confidence. Ring after ring. Pulse after pulse. Was my growing enjoyment of the wonders of modern telecommunications testament to some sort of emotional healing process, or was it proof my mind was still irretrievably mangled? I'd worry about that later.

We tripped the final few feet into my bedroom, the final stop and terminus of one of the city's longest hallways. I was pleased my room was looking neat and well *feng shui*-ed. Only a discarded sweatshirt lying on the comforter detracted from the perfection. I took the pullover and tossed it over the blinking red light of the answering machine on my bed-side table.

Later, Angeline scurried out through the hallway, retrieved some of her possessions and went into the bathroom to clean up and change. She would not be staying the night; tomorrow, she and some of her friends were taking off at 6 a.m. for a long-planned trip to Vail. She was going to sleep at the home of one of her fellow travelers, a woman who lived near the airport.

While I chilled out alone in the darkness of my room, I decided to check my cell voicemail messages. No, I am not insane—I wasn't going *near* the answering machine until tomorrow, and I planned to skip over whatever recording Gabrielle left on the cell voicemail as well.

10:48 a.m., work-related: "…I like the corporate logos you pasted in next to the names…could you also bold the first two lines on slide 12?...I talked it over with my boss, and he wanted to see if we could do a 3 by 3 instead of 2 by 2 matrix..."

12:36 p.m., Mom. Love her, but I'm gonna skip that message in my present state.

4:12 p.m., Nick Monroe, a.k.a. Money, calling from New York: "Hello, sir. No excuses. *You...are coming...to the New Years' party.* Stop fighting it. Don't be a girl—book the ticket to New York."

8:15 p.m., Billy: "Yo, brooooo...It's Billy and Carson. We're getting a group together in your 'hood at the Mauna Loa for some beers...and some *chiiiiquiiiitaaaas.* We'll swing by your place when we get there to see if you're around. Probably about 10:30. If not, see you tomorrow for the big Raider game."

I squinted and read the glowing blue numbers next to me: "10:42." *Aaaah, this is perfect. What more could you ask for in a day?* I'd get to cap off my evening at my favorite neighborhood dive bar— a scant 122 yards away—with some Pabst Blue Ribbon and Pop-a-Shot. Maybe get in a game of bubble hockey if they'd fixed it: the USA's left defender couldn't spin and the Soviets' center could only move halfway along his track. Angeline would be trekking out in about 10 minutes, so I could be at the Mauna Loa by 11 p.m.

The doorbell rang. *Billy, my man!* I snatched the sweatshirt from on top of the answering machine and hustled it over my head. I grabbed the last pair of clean shorts in my drawer—a pair of novelty Stars and Stripes Bermudas that I really only ever wore as a joke ("Here, I thought I'd wear these to the barbecue, honey...").

I jogged the 70 feet to the front entrance, dancing around a couple articles of my clothing in the hallway. "Yo, broooooo..." I bellowed as I opened the door.

"Is Angela here?" intoned an unknown voice from a face I didn't need to squint to recognize. Trevor.

Now the real saliva crisis began, as my tongue sucked up all available spit in an instant. My heart rate had never spiked so high in a period of three seconds. "Wait here. I'll tell her you're outside," I managed, as I began to close the door.

"No, I'd like to come inside." His foot was in the door, blocking its closure.

His foot is in the door. His foot is in the door! What the fuck is this? This is not real.

He actually started pushing on the wooden edges of the frosted glass door.

He's pushing on the door. He's pushing on the door! What the fuck is this? He was breaking and entering, or at least entering. I had to either slam my shoulder into the door and break his foot—or let him in.

I eased up on the slight bit of pressure I was exerting on the 80-year-old door and let it open. "You wait right here."

He looked into the living room to his immediate left. Cushions. Shoes. Wine bottles. Smoldering fire.

"Angela!" He tried to walk past me. *He's trying to walk past me. He's trying to walk past me! What the fuck is this?*

He advanced down the entry corridor six feet and peered into the dining room. A crumpled tablecloth. A belt.

"Angela!" I could hear the faintest "Oh, God" from the bathroom 30 feet away.

He tried to walk past me again. I angled back into the flat's main corridor.

What the fuck is this? This is right out of fucking COPS! Is this MY life? I'm about to fight this guy! I'm about to fucking fight this fucking guy in my own fucking house!

I put my hand on his chest. *Am I doing this? What the hell am I doing?* "You *are not* going back there. I let you into my home, but I'm telling you—you're staying right here."

And so there we were. My heart thudding its way through my ribcage—his doing the same. I could feel it. My hand was still on his chest. He looked down at my hand. *God, he might do the Terminator move and bend my hand right back. Did Angeline mention anything about Kung Fu?*

There we were. Him in his San Francisco standard issue mid-thigh length leather jacket and heavy, almost boot-like shoes. Me, in an inside out and backwards sweatshirt, the washing instruction tag tickling my chin. Wearing my red, white and blue "Uncle Sam goes to Miami Beach" shorts. Barefoot. Smelling of tannins and vanilla and blue cheese and smoke and sweat and everything else.

He looked to his right at the one askew frame on the long wall of pictures. Cinque Terra. He must have recognized it, whether he ended up going, or just researched the trip on the Internet.

I wondered if that image would set him off. After the evening's activities, I was nowhere near prime fighting condition. *If he makes a move, I'm going to have to smash his face with Cinque Terra. He is not going a step further into my house.*

My hand was still on his chest. I could feel his heart start to quiet down and sensed him easing up on his forward push. I pulled my hand away.

He stood there, looking down, silently, his jaw periodically clenching. My hand was still raised, but slowly moving in a sort of "just stay cool" gesture. Still raised, just in case I needed to do a "wax-off" defensive move. He was just two feet away. *Can he tell I'm still gimpy from surgery? Will he go Cobra Kai on me and try to sweep the leg?*

Silence.

I was still shaking, but I almost started to smile, as the first hints of humor in the scene dawned on me. The sensation of rage, of animal territoriality, started to drift away.

I looked at the crown of this head as he focused on the floor. *You stupid sonofabitch. You fucking ballsy bastard. You beautiful idiot.*

I hoped that if ever a situation required such a profoundly stupid gesture on my part, I would jump in with both feet like Trevor did. I hoped that I would pursue what mattered to me so decisively, scrapping all rationality and going with the gut. It was a magnificent and brave move.

Except for a brief glimpse at Cinque Terra, I had not taken my eyes off of him. He raised his glance from the floor and looked up into my face for a split second, before starting to stare at the white wall opposite the pictures. "I'm sorry," he said, his breathing speeding up. "I'm so sorry for this."

"I..."

"Trevor!" interrupted Angeline as she emerged from the bathroom. She'd only been in there for about five minutes, but she looked perfect. Lipstick even. It was hard for me to judge time, but I think the doorbell had rung less than two minutes before. "What are you doing?"

"It's all right. We're just chilling out here. Everything's OK," I inserted.

"I really need to talk to you," he proclaimed past me toward Angeline, still a few feet up the hallway.

I turned to her and she looked up at me. I gave the smallest hint of a nod to her, even though she hadn't asked my permission for anything.

She shook her head. "Let me get my things. Just a second..."

"Could you wait outside for just a minute?" I asked Trevor. My hand was still up in the "it's cool" gesture. He nodded and walked toward and out the door. I didn't push it closed behind him.

Angeline was gathering up her shoes and her purse from the living room.

"You don't have to go if you don't want to...or you could stay here and talk...that would be weird."

"Yeah, I'll be OK. Don't worry."

"You'll call me when you get over to your friend's, right?"

"Uh-huh...I'm sorry...this is just..."

"It's all fine. It was different, though..."

"Yeah, different..." We were standing by the door, all her scattered belongings either on her body or in her purse. Trevor had advanced a flight down the outside stairwell. Angeline gave me a hug and silently kissed me on my now-stubbly cheek. She was trembling. After a moment, Angeline pulled away, shaking her head and laughing. "Different..."

I closed the door behind her and walked back up the hallway, intending to wash up. Or to at least splash some cold water on my face.

I bent down to pick up my shirt, wadded up in the corridor. I then backed up a few steps, and, looking only out of the corner of my eye, straightened out the picture of Cinque Terra.

33

Girl We Couldn't Get Much Higher

My alarm woke me much earlier than my sleep-deprived body deserved, but it was for a good cause: football. Earlier in the week, I had taken the lead in organizing a group for the Oakland Raiders' final regular season game, but the gathering storm outside my window seemed to rule out the delightful day of friendship, tail-gating and bone-crushing tackles that we had envisioned.

I walked past the mess of clothes, baguette crumbs and cheese wrappers Angeline and I had created 10 hours before and flipped on the TV in the living room. Local weathermen, basking in their self-importance now that they actually got to report on some *truly* inclement weather, foretold of monsoons, typhoons and deluges the likes of which are rarely seen in our little slice of the world.

But I still wanted to go, and I was pretty sure this latest Storm-of-the-Century-of-the-Week would just be a minor annoyance. In order to rally the crew, I needed to lock in an early commitment…an anchor tenant, so to speak…so I called the one person I thought to be impervious to the assault of the elements.

"Y-elloooooooooh," boomed Beef.

"Yo, it's JT."

"Yo."

"Yo. Are you about ready to roll? We should head to Safeway in the Marina to get some beers and maybe some stuff for tail-gating." My tone was telling. I might as well have been saying, "I just assume you're going to the game because I know you're not a little punk ass bitch, Beef. You're not going to let a little sleet, a modicum of hail and a petite shower of locusts get in your way of enjoying the Raidahs."

Unfortunately, I sensed immediately that Beef was wavering. I could hear him fight his hangover, straining to get up and pull the blinds so he could peer out at the black clouds over the Bay. "Aaaaah…uuuuh…maybe we should just watch this one at a bar. Get some Bloody Marys at the Bus Stop or the Mauna Loa…"

I'm sure he could almost hear my thoughts penetrating through the phone lines. *Weak. WEAK! WEEEEAAAKKKK!* Too many days of fun and sun in NorCal had thinned out the blood of this man who had played hockey a thousand times on the frozen surface of Minnesota's ten thousand lakes. "I understand," I told him. "It'll be cold out there. We may even have to wear wind-breakers."

My words were designed to sting, but I felt no guilt. I just didn't want him to chime in with the tried and true "Home Depot" excuse.

But then, unfortunately, he brought out that old standby. "Besides," he began, "Renee is moving in here in a few weeks and I need to buy some shelves for her stuff and maybe get a new towel rack…"

He was dangling in the bitterly cold wind. I couldn't let him go on. "That's cool. Just look for us on TV. I'm sure we'll all be wearing our silver and black face paint. Later."

It looked like the plan was doomed, but, nonetheless, I called the rest of the crew as well.

Billy: "Duuuuuuude. Are you on crack?"

EZ: "Yeah, right. I'll meet you in the parking lot. Are you crazy, JT?"

Dennis: "Oh, it was *this* Saturday?"

Carson: "Anyone else rallying? No? Why don't we go to the game tomorrow? Maybe they'll call a rainout." *There's only ONE football game a week, you loser. And there are no rainouts in football, you wanker.*

I had one more call to make, just a formality to notify the final member of the group that we would not be attending this final regular season game. But my phone buzzed just as I was dialing her up.

"So are we getting this show on the road or what?" Erica asked me.

"Are you fucking with me?"

"No, why?"

"Because all the fair weather fans bailed. It seems that when the weathermen start using phrases like 'wind chill' and 'flash flooding' and 'cold front from Siberia' they just get scared off. It looks like it's just you and me, kid."

"Good. That's the way I like it anyway. Come get me in an hour?"

"Done."

An hour later I hydroplaned through the mean streets of San Francisco to pick up Erica. She popped out of her place in an instant and was brutally pummeled by Mother Nature during her 20-foot scamper to the Probe. I'm talking gale force stuff here.

"Are you still up for this?" I asked her as she fought the wind to tug the door closed behind her. "We can always go shoe shopping."

"You're not getting an excuse from me to chicken out. Just point your Probe toward Oakland and start driving." Erica was always good at Probe humor.

❋   ❋   ❋   ❋

I spent a good chunk of the slog to Oaktown recounting yesterday's events to Erica—the whole wine and cheese and home invasion episode that I wrote about from 11 p.m. to 4 a.m.. Judging from her cogent analysis of the situation—"Sounds like a lovely fucking soap opera you're writing there, Jake"—she didn't seem to be as entertained by the series of events as I was. But seriously, in just one night, I was able to get it on in every room in the whole flat *and* enjoy some manly pre-fisticuffs posturing. What's not to love?

❋   ❋   ❋   ❋

The Oakland Coliseum—actually, it has some ridiculous corporate name attached to it that I choose not to dignify by including here—is an eyesore, a concrete monstrosity with next to none of the modern amenities that make attending a sporting event today like visiting an adult Chuck E. Cheese. When the Oakland Raiders' capricious owner Al Davis—to some a reviled figure of pure evil, but to others, a lovable figure of pure evil—decided to move the team back to the Bay Area in 1994 after a 13-year reign in Los Angeles, the Coliseum was "upgraded." Some assemblage of geniuses decided to build a new section of seating so high that that the "nosebleed" seats are actually just a base camp where you prepare for your final assault on the summit. A section so high that you need a sherpa to help you tote your foam "we're number one" finger to the top. This was "Mount Davis."

I took special care to ensure that the tickets Erica and I bought from drenched scalpers just before the game were indeed on the face of Mount Davis. If we wanted a guilt-free pass to jump on the bandwagon for the team's unstoppable Super Bowl march, we would have to overcome all of the trials of the most die-hard member of the Raider Nation. Our search was rewarded when we found seats on the 50 yard line—at the very pinnacle of Mr. Davis' monument, the very edge of the stadium's escarpment.

The wonders of Mount Davis are truly breathtaking. The white water rapids that course down its stairwells during a maelstrom like today's carry veritable flotillas of beer cups and cardboard food trays. From its summit, you can *almost* see the game through the viscid haze below. But most awe-inspiring are the many types of precipitation you are privileged to behold. I've been pounded by globs of rain during Indiana's summertime thunderstorms. I've walked through Boston's omnipresent mists, the kind that hang in the air, circumvent all umbrellas and leave you sopping wet. I've been assaulted by powerful barrages of precipitation, rain and sleet driven horizontally by Chicago's vicious winds, an onslaught that renders any protective barrier useless.

But I'd never faced all of these forms of precipitation at once.

Plus new ones. The design of Mount Davis seemed to shape the very wind itself, driving rain *straight up* into our faces. And some sort of malevolent aerodynamic effect created by the Coliseum's bowl structure smacked us from both sides simultaneously with sleet and hail. My God, the brilliance of the design. The exquisite torture of it all. The trial by fire—or by water, actually—which only the most dedicated bandwagoneers could hope to endure. That Al Davis is, indeed, an evil genius not to be trifled with.

✻   ✻   ✻   ✻

The only thing worse than *sitting* in drenched clothes on a gusty 33-degree day is *running* in drenched clothes on a gusty 33-degree day. At least when you're sitting you can hunker down, ball up and minimize your surface area, huddling next to the other miserable soul at your side for a little bit of warmth. If you sit still, the water next to your skin heats up and actually starts to form a protective barrier.

But once the Coliseum started to empty, Erica and I were forced to give up the comparative comforts of the fetal position and had to brave the brunt of the storm once again. We couldn't know for sure, but judging by the lack of brawls on the way out, it appeared the Raiders had won. As we ran through acres of parking lots dodging drunk drivers and designated drivers (those imbibing only six beers), it was impossible to tell the one-inch deep puddles from the 6-inch deep potholes. I didn't think it was possible to get wetter than "drenched," but we were positively saturated by the time we made it to the friendly confines of the Probe.

Our neighbors in the parking lot must have thought someone had convened an orgy in my car. The windows steamed up within a few seconds and the car rocked like we had a *ménage-a-twenty* going on inside. Erica and I started stripping off our "waterproof" outer layers immediately, but had to help each other with the adhesive, waterlogged inner layers. We crashed against the fogged-up windows, smacked our hands against the roof and the rear view mirror, and banged our heads as we peeled feverishly.

Now, I've had bouts of chattering teeth before, but with a moment's concentration I could silence the teeth immediately. On this day, neither Erica nor I had a chance to stop the dental rattling. You would not believe how painful it is when your body is wracked with simultaneous chattering, sneezing, coughing and laughing. And, in Erica's case, farting. I'm sorry—but I gotta tell it like it is.

"Th-th-th-this is the mo-mo-most fu-fu-fu-fun I'v-v-ve ever-r-r-r had-d-d-d, Jake. Wha-wha-what are we doing f-f-for our second d-d-date?" asked Erica as she shed her sodden fleece.

"Y-y-you gotta be k-k-kidding. This is l-l-like our t-t-two hundredth date. I thought th-th-this was all f-f-foreplay for hot-t-t monkey s-s-sex in the backseat," I replied as I put the driver's seat into full recline and rolled into the aforementioned backseat. Actually, I just needed a little more room so my numb, claw-like hands could unpeel my socks.

Once we were both down to our skivvies, I confirmed my status as the greatest planner of all time by grabbing the bag of dry, warm clothes I had packed for both of us. Actually...there was *one* gap in my plan. I had to jump out of the car in my boxers and scurry around to the hatchback in my bare feet in the midst of the tempest to retrieve the bag of dry, warm clothes. But it was worth it.

Erica immediately slipped into my red Indiana sweatshirt and then, with a series of well-honed maneuvers, proceeded to extract her bra—à la Jennifer Beals in *Flashdance*. A truly *strong* performance that I admired out of the corner of my eye. As I prepared to pull on my sweatpants, I worked through the physics of trying to remove my Calvin Klein boxer shorts in a similar manner, but determined it scientifically impossible. I probably should have just pulled my arctic underwear right off, but I didn't want Erica's "first impression" of me to be under such extreme conditions, such...*unflattering* circumstances.

With our drenched clothes balled up in the backseat and our new dry leisure wear rapidly returning our core body temp to normal, we laughed as we examined the empty, flooded parking lot around us. We were the last Raider Nation refugees in the area, we proud nomads who had completed our pilgrimage to the top of Mount Davis and back. I put the Probe in gear and we headed away from the Coliseum.

As the adrenaline rush of our hurried strip tease wore off, I began to feel the tug of sleep coming on. The long trek, the penetrating cold and the altitude amplified the exhaustion I would have felt anyway after a long night spent writing about my trip to Napa and all of the subsequent adventures.

"I *cannot* believe how bone-tired I am. Do you…" I looked over to Erica and she was asleep already, curled up in her cozy mismatched outfit.

I turned away to check the road signs and then looked back over to her side of the car. Passing headlights illuminated the passenger-side window. I allowed myself a little smile.

I steered us onto the exit ramp that would take us back to the Bay Bridge. I peered back in her direction and broke into a wide grin.

After merging into San Francisco-bound traffic, I turned toward Erica again and began to laugh out loud. I wish I had a camera handy to take a picture of the precious moment: the angelic Erica leaning against the fogged-up window and—on display for me and all passing drivers—her flawless ass-print on the glass, an impermanent souvenir of our perfect day together.

34

Dropping the Ball

At 7:20 p.m. on December 30 I decided that the New Year's Eve pickings in San Francisco looked pretty slim. By 7:24 p.m., I had found an astoundingly low fare to New York City on a semi-reputable airline. At 9:42, I was removing my shoes to go through security. And at 10:47 p.m., it was "wheels up" on the way to Money's New Year's Eve bash.

Angeline had left two days before to spend a few days in Vail with her group of friends. Both of us thought that my joining up with their little group would probably be a little too much, too soon. The girls would have their ski bunny sorority house in full effect—pillow fights, hair braiding, hot-tubbing—so it probably would not be the best venue to meet her friends for the first time (at least not in her estimation). We planned a lower profile, more gradual introduction into her social set in the New Year. Besides, with my knee preventing me from skiing, I would probably have nothing to do in Vail besides crossword puzzles.

I hoped I could get in a couple hours of sleep on the flight, and I did. Almost exactly two hours worth of sleep, as a matter of fact. As I trudged like a zombie through Newark International Airport toward the rental car shuttles, I knew I would not be at my best for the New Year's Party. I just hoped that the time zone arbitrage would work in my favor and I'd be able to stay reasonably awake and alert until midnight.

✳   ✳   ✳   ✳

"So, did you have a great Christmas?" I asked the desk attendant in Kenneth's building as he flipped through the collection of Lilliputian mustard-colored envelopes for the keys to Kenneth's apartment.

"Oh, of course! It was the first Christmas my wife and daughter were able to join me for here in New York. It was beautiful," said the doorman.

"That's great. Well, here's to many more of those!"

"Thank you, sir."

"So, did apartment 6-J take good care of you on the holiday bonus?"

"Yes, thank you. He is a good man. Very generous."

"Because if he didn't, I could go steal a few twenties. He leaves an awful lot of money lying around," I winked as I wheeled away from the reception desk.

Kenneth's apartment was just as I left it almost three months before. I checked the freezer and found the Barbecue Beef Hot Pockets I had procured in early October. It was only 8:45 a.m., but my time-shifted body would hardly notice the difference between the saturated fats in bacon and eggs and the saturated fats in Hot Pockets.

Once my Hot Pocket was fully irradiated, I journeyed over to my couch. *God, I really have destroyed this thing. I probably owe him a whole new sofa.* The Jake crater remained in the tan couch, slightly less pronounced than when I packed up to leave in early October, like an ancient meteor impact partially worn away by millennia of wind and rain. Of course, my periodic visits prevent nature from ever returning the couch to its unspoiled state. I grabbed the panoply of media center remote controls, inserted myself into my custom molded cushion, and watched as SportsCenter flared to life before my eyes.

✳   ✳   ✳   ✳

I ended up getting *maybe* one hour of sleep in the next 10 hours. Unfortunately, even my work couldn't put me to sleep. I read all three journal articles I needed to get through—all on product development processes in the bio-pharmaceutical industry—without nodding off even once.

Just a little after 7 p.m., I started the rally process to get ready for Money's event. A hundred push-ups. A hundred sit-ups. Shower and shave.

As I got dressed, I tried to get the blood pumping. I turned up the stereo and blasted the Metallica CD I had bought Kenneth a year earlier for just this purpose. Other than crying, utter exhaustion has probably been the major recurrent theme of this little narrative I've been pecking on the last few months. I just hoped I could stay awake until midnight.

I'd spent enough New Year's Eves in New York to know that the evening can be utterly ruined by poor logistics. In my twenties, my New York New Years celebrations were always intense social campaigns, concerted efforts to hit three or four venues over the course of a six hour period. My audaciousness and hubris ultimately led to my downfall—I spent New Years 1993 in a line outside of the China Club, 1994 in a cab and 1995…in another cab. Since that time, I'd adopted a new philosophy: Get There, Stay There.

Money had been on my case for several years to get out to NYC for his New Year's Eve party. For better or worse, this year I didn't have the "West coast entanglements" complicating my travel schedule.

"JT! Get the hell in here! Great to see you!" said Money as I entered The Naked Lunch, the SoHo bar he had rented out for the night. "Dude, taking the red eye…*you* are hardcore!" Our man hug had a couple of extra slaps on back—I guess my reward for traveling 3,000 miles.

"Any wayward traveler's discount on the festivities?" I asked, as I pulled out my wallet.

"C'mon, a high roller like you? You're going to do so much damage here, I should charge you more," Money laughed. I laughed, too. But I *was* serious about the discount. I tugged on his belt just above his hip and inserted a $100 bill into the waist band of his boxers. "You better be worth it, Money!"

Only about twenty partygoers had shown up by 8:30. Most of the early arrivals were women. Across the room, Nick's fiancée of a month captivated a covey of unmarried Manhattanites with her show and tell on the 4Cs. In my corner of the bar, a scrum of Money's former college rugby teammates watched the NBA games on the televisions above the bar. I ordered up a vodka tonic and joined the large gentlemen near the plate of crudités.

To break into a group of guys, it's never hard to come up with an opening line. "Hey, what's the score?" I asked a particularly large fellow munching on watercress.

"Pacers are up by 4. I'm Greg by the way," he said as he extended a massive mitt.

"Hey, I'm Jake, a friend of Nick's from grad school. I think I'm the lone member of the San Francisco delegation that made it out here."

"So, what do you do for a living, Jake?"

I was truly and utterly surprised by the question. In San Francisco circa 2002-03, *no one* asked this question. It *simply* isn't done. The genteel poverty that pervades the City infuses conversations with tales of triathlon training, yarns of yoga technique and protestations of our pecuniary standing. I couldn't remember the last time I had to answer this question phrased as such.

I stumbled and rambled, but, after about one minute, had managed to assemble a pretty good explanation of my "current professional situation." I left out the part about taking conference calls in my boxer shorts.

"So, Greg, what do you do here in the big city?"

"High yield," he said as he took a sip of his beer and returned his gaze to the Pacers game. "High yield," as in "junk bonds", as in raising debt financing for distressed or risky companies. I could only nod in admiration at the power of his two-word answer, and pondered how fantastic it would be to have a two-word answer to a question about *any* part of my life.

I stayed at the periphery of the rugby crowd for about twenty minutes. Money came by a couple of times to check and see how the appetizers were doing. Money's fiancée came by a couple of times to check and see how the appetizers were doing, as well. By the time Greg had finally polished off the watercress (most accomplished watercress eater I've ever seen, by the way), a familiar voice shouted out from behind me.

"JTeeeee! Huge move, brother, getting out here for the bash!" It was Balls, already swooping in for his New Year's Eve man-hug.

"Well, you flew in from Beantown…"

"Dude, the trans-continental party commute is pretty damn *hardcore!*" I was pleased to see my friends think I'm pretty hardcore. Which is nice.

"JTeeeeeeee!"

"Yo!"

"Yo, JTeeeeee!"

Monkey, Dog Breath and Wonger emerged from the coat check area, joining Balls and me by the bar. A cascade of hugs and fist knocks soon followed, and a cascade of drink orders soon followed that. Money's invitation for the New Year's Eve extravaganza included the tagline "All You Can Drink." However, with Money and the rest of the crew, this wasn't an *inducement* to get people to attend, it was a *commandment* for those who ventured inside the venue.

After each of us had accrued about four drinks toward our blood alcohol content requirement, the guys began looking for some updates from the visitor from far away. "JT, what's this we've been hearing about some new woman? Billy said you're playing way over your head, man!" said Balls.

"Yeah, Carson said you've got some ballerina on the line, JT!"

"JT, what's up with that? How the heck did you meet a ballerina?"

"You gotta see if she has any ballerina friends for your pals, JT!"

"First of all, she's not a ballerina, she's more of a gymnast," I said, eliciting a bunch of pushes and punches to the shoulder from the gang. "Secondly, yeah, things are going pretty well. I think we're at the stage where we're trying to figure out what 'it' is, you know. But I think it's going to be fun."

"Nothing wrong with that!" stated Balls as he patted my on the back. Then, turning back toward the bar, he said, "Bartender! Another round for all of the boys!"

To be honest, in the days since the Trevor break-in, my picture of the whole situation around the new relationship with Angeline had become a little cloudier. When she called me from her friend's house an hour after the episode to let me know she was OK, she also passed along an apology from Trevor. He promised her he wouldn't pull anything like that again, but I still wasn't sure. I didn't know if I was prepared in any sense of the word to be a part of any soap opera-like love triangles.

❋   ❋   ❋   ❋

"Bartender, another round for all of the boys!"

For those of us in the Eastern Time Zone, the final hour of 2002 was underway. A few minutes before, the great metropolises of the Atlantic Time Zone had welcomed the New Year to North America. I could only imagine the revelry as the Canadian version of Dick Clark presided over the celebrations in St. John's, Newfoundland or Halifax, Nova Scotia.

Already, a few noisemakers and party hats were being dispersed amongst the now bustling crowd. Over 250 people (and counting) were jammed into The Naked Lunch. I was exhausted and smashed, thanks to my hard-drinking friends. The mirror behind the bar displayed for me the reddish glow I boasted. My movements were slow but my mind was sharp—well, sort of sharp. And a powerful, irresistible idea crept into that mind of mine.

I'm gonna get me a New Year's Kiss! Fuck, yeah!

OK, I added the "Fuck, yeah!" just now for emphasis, but it *was* a powerful thought. Without a word, I parted company with the fellows I'd been drinking with for the previous two hours and ventured out into the crowd.

It was 11:24 p.m. I had 36 minutes.

While I had been yucking it up with the chuckleheads at the bar, most new New Year's romances had already taken shape. Of course, many wouldn't last past 12:15 a.m., but some would last until the

Rose Bowl pre-game show on January 1. There wasn't much liquidity in this marketplace. I had 32 minutes.

Just then, a group of young women came into the bar. This was my opportunity. While they checked their coats, I moved toward the front of The Naked Lunch, snapping a party hat off the top of Wonger's head as I blew past my friends. One of the women turned toward me, coat check receipt still in hand.

"Hi. I'm Jake," I said, of course. I had 30 minutes.

"Hello there. I'm Cara," said Cara.

"I'm a part of the official unofficial welcoming committee," I told her. "You are extremely lucky...I managed to get you the last hat."

"I think they're passing around some more—" She gestured back toward the center of the room.

"Ah, but, those are counterfeit hats. Low quality. This is the last of the real ones!" I explained as I put it on her head.

"Well, thank you. I guess I owe you."

"Think nothing of it. So..." I'd forgotten her name already. "So, what's you're connection to the whole scene here?" I directed some quick snaps to the four corners of the room, in the general direction of the "scene."

"My friend is friends with Nick Monroe's fiancée. And you?"

"Nick's a good friend from our days up at business school. I flew in from San Francisco for this mega-bash, if you can believe it. So, what do you do here in the big city?"

"I'm a doctor...a pediatrician, actually," she replied as she adjusted her party hat. "And you? How do you fill your time in San Francisco?"

"I'm a novelist," I answered. If you're reading this, it was about the truest thing I could have said at the time. If you're not reading this, then my terrible lie will never be revealed.

"A novelist? Really? It's not something I would expect someone who went business school to do..."

"Well, I guess you could say I'm an 'MBA novelist'. It's sort of like a 'real estate novelist,' except you start out $100,000 more in debt." I wondered if she got my Billy Joel reference.

"Oh, my God! You're funny!" she said as she put her hand on my cashmered shoulder and laughed away. She got it—she was after all, a New Yorker. Game over. New Year's Eve kiss successfully procured. I had 28 minutes to spare.

For the next 26 minutes, we talked about the Hamptons, the SoHo eatery Balthazaar and the 1999 Pollock exhibit at the MOMA. By 11:58, the music of the Chemical Brothers had been replaced by the chemically preserved Dick Clark. Dick was omnipresent; the countdown had begun.

One of my intended's gaggle of friends suddenly teleported into view, champagne bottle in hand. "Cara come here." *Cara! That's right!* I thought. And just as I remembered her name, her friend teleported her away. They vanished into the crowd.

The crowd cranked and blew their noisemakers like there was no tomorrow. The glowing Times Square ball was descending. And, there I was as the final seconds ticked off the clock. No kiss to be had. No champagne. Not even a hat. The ball had dropped and I just had Dick.

"Happy New Year!" the masses screamed.

Oh well, just another cluster fuck New Years Eve in NYC. Par for the course.

Within seconds, the vibrating message indicator on my cell phone went off. I extracted the handset out of my pocket and retreated to the back of the bar, where it was a little quieter.

"Hi. It's Gabrielle. I wanted to be the first to wish you a Happy New Year. I don't know if you ended up going to New York, but if so: 'Happy New Year.' I want you to have a great 2003, Jake. OK? I hope we catch up soon. Bye."

I was incensed. I immediately deleted the message and made my way back through the crowd. Cara's group of friends was around the bar—actually bordering my group of friends—finishing off their bottle of champagne. The little doctor was nowhere to be found.

"Break?" I'll show you a fucking "Break!" I'm embarrassed as I type the words, but those were the thoughts pinging through my skull at the time.

I doubled back through the throng. Some people wished me a "Happy New Year," and I nodded and did a quick wave back over my shoulder to each, but I never broke stride. Finally, I returned back to the spot where Cara was torn away from me. And there she was.

"I was kidnapped!" she laughed, just before taking a sip of her champagne.

"I'm just glad you're OK!" I yelled over the crowd noise. I leaned closer to her ear. "I was pretty worried about you."

"You were? Why's that?"

I leaned in closer. "Because you didn't get that New Year's kiss you had your heart set on," I told her.

Her left hand wrapped around my neck while the plastic champagne flute in her right was crushed up against my back. Our New Year's kiss, though delayed, was happening in earnest. It was 12:04 a.m.

"We should dance," Cara declared.

I felt like I really needed to beg out of dancing with her. "Oh, y'know, I just had ACL surgery five mo…five weeks ago and I'm not much of a dancer right now."

"Really? You're moving very well for someone five weeks removed from surgery. You must have a great physical therapist," said Cara. "Well, then, let's get out of here." She took my hand and pulled me along gently, away from the crowd.

"Where are we going?"

"Why don't you come with me…to a party for a little bit?"

"OK. Sounds good, but don't you want to get your coat?" I asked as we exited out the side door.

"My friends will know to get it. C'mon!" She raised her hand and the first taxi we saw stopped for us. I had to respect Cara's sense of New York New Year's logistics. During the first few minutes after New Years, taxis were plentiful as partygoers sang "*Auld Lang Syne*" or waited in lines to retrieve their coats.

She stated the address even as Adam West—the 1960s-era Batman—welcomed us into the Yellow Cab and urged us to buckle up for safety. She removed a $20 bill from her miniscule purse, one, it seemed, just big enough to hold an ID and a few folded twenties.

"This should get us there," she said as she tossed the bill into the front seat. Immediately, we reinitiated our New Year's kiss. It seemed like she might want to keep it going until the Central Time Zone rang in 2003. I wasn't about to argue with her.

After about 15 short blocks and four long blocks, we arrived at our destination. She exited the cab without a word. I paused to say "Thanks", but I don't think the cabbie cared either way after his $14 tip. Cara was already unlocking—*unlocking*? I thought she'd just be buzzing—the front door of the apartment building as I ascended the stairs to join her.

"Hey there," I softly asked her neck as she unlocked the second set of doors inside, "Just curious: did you say, 'Come with me to *a* party.' Or did you say, 'Come with me to *party*'?"

"Whatever. Do you really care?" she smiled back at me as she walked into the elevator. The three-floor ride barely provided enough time to move from knowing stare to deep kiss. We exited the elevator and she began reading the tiny door-mounted metal plates bearing each apartment's number. I heard music playing inside as she unlocked this door. *Oh, so this is a party...* I thought.

...or not, I re-thought. MTV's New Year's broadcast played from the TV until she turned it off on her way to the kitchen. The apartment obviously *had been* the site for some sort of party during the previous couple of hours. Dozens of cups, beer bottles and tomato sauce stained plates littered the fashionable apartment. "So, it looks like everybody left us," I said, "Or is this a surprise party?"

"My friends and I had about 15 people over for dinner and drinks earlier. *And*, yes, it *is* also surprise party...for you," she winked from around the door of her refrigerator. "Can I get you a drink?"

I decided to have a little fun. "No thanks, there are plenty around here," I replied as I lifted a clear yellow plastic cup filled with some sort of brown liquid and topped off by a very visible extinguished cigarette.

"No!" she screamed as she bounded out of her kitchen. Like a Secret Service Agent on detail with the Bush twins, she literally jumped and knocked the drink out of my hands, and we both fell onto her futon. If I had actually been only five weeks removed from surgery, this would have definitely been a violation of her Hippocratic oath. The corner of her off-white rug became extremely *off*-white after the mystery drink splashed down onto it. We continued on with our own little "tradition" as we embarked upon version 4.0 of our non-stop New Year's kiss.

"Here, come with me," she said after two minutes, getting up and heading further into her apartment. She kicked off her high heels and unclasped her earrings. She walked right past her light switch and came to a stop right next to her bed, clinking down her earrings onto her desk and then doing the same with a heavy bracelet. We fell onto the bed and continued with the rolling, kissing and other assorted maneuvers.

She pushed herself up from the bed and started to remove her top. All of a sudden, I started to think again. I started to think about vanilla and *dreidls* and heated seats and impromptu slugs to the stomach. And that's when Cara and I had our first fight.

"Hey, hey, hey," I said as I reached out to hold one of the unbuttoning hands, "You know what? I think we should maybe take a nap or something…"

"Wha..?" she asked as she moved her free hand toward my buttons.

"Yeah, yeah. You know what? That was, like my best fucking New Year's kiss *ever*. It was like art! We should just have the kiss, y'know?"

"What? Why are you saying..?" Her hands stopped fumbling with her buttons and mine. Even with just the faintest glimmers of streetlights piercing her Venetian blinds, I could tell her eyelids were weighing heavily. Within a few seconds, she collapsed like a heap onto my left arm. I let her rest there a minute, and then whispered over to her. "Hey…hey…?" She was already asleep.

I leaned over to try and execute the "hug and roll." But, my new friend's hair seemed to be caught in my metallic watchband. I thought I might have to stay in this position for a while. My eyelids were starting to collapse on me as well; the red-eye flight from SF had taken its toll. I gave one last look at my watch before surrendering to sleep.

It was 12:24 a.m. Happy New Year.

35

Resolution

I awoke just after 6:30 a.m. on January 1, 2003. My body clock was a disaster. Cara had rolled over at some point during the course of the night, so I was free to rise. I picked a few long orphaned hairs out of my watchband as I shuffled out of her bedroom.

I winced when I flicked on the light in her bathroom. I took a long swig of cold water from the sink and then washed my face in the frigid stuff. On her sink was a tube of Aquafresh, so I squeezed a healthy dollop onto my index finger and worked it around my mouth. I knew the white was for cavity fighting power, and the blue was for minty fresh breath, but I couldn't remember what the red stripe was for.

As is to be expected for New Year's Day, my head was pounding. I knew it was a breach of hook up etiquette, but I needed to check to see if she had any analgesics in her medicine cabinet. Behind the mirror was a well-organized cache of toiletries and assorted girl things. I grabbed the industrial-sized tub of Advil from its top shelf position and opened the cap. It was a new container, so I had to pierce the tamper proof packaging and remove the cotton ball. As I swallowed the three orange pills, I noticed the green topped Mennen Speed Stick that had been hidden—or maybe lost—behind the new bottle of Advil. It seemed misplaced given the line of three light blue Secrets on the bottom shelf.

Cara's living room was even messier than I remembered it— probably because we messed it up even more. I picked up my sport coat from the floor and dusted off the remnants of a couple of crushed water crackers. In her kitchen, I found a bottle of club soda and poured some on the still-damp brown stain on the corner of her rug. Then, I set about gathering up the array of multicolored plastic cups, emptying the melted and decarbonated remains into a large plastic pitcher left on her coffee table. Finally, I collected the last vestiges of what looked like a delightful Italian dinner, tossing about a dozen plates and an assortment of plastic utensils through the swinging door of her large kitchen garbage can.

So…

So…

What to do. What to do.

In the cubby hole of the end table nestled next to her futon lay a stack of magazines. I pulled out the thick pile and searched out some solid reading material. Most of the periodicals were medical journals—*JAMA, The New England Journal of Medicine* and *Pediatrics Today*. Some were fashion mags—*Vogue, Marie Claire* and the like. And one was *Sports Illustrated*. It was about three weeks old; I had already read it in the gym. The magazine had been mailed to a subscriber—a Dr. So & So who, according to the address on the corner of the cover, made his home about twelve blocks away from Cara's apartment. It seemed she had done yeoman's work in cleaning out *nearly* every last reminder of Dr. So & So from her home. I certainly knew how hard it could be to root out those final few pesky remnants.

I settled on *The New England Journal of Medicine,* poured myself a massive glass of water and read for about an hour.

After I had finished the cogent and thought-provoking "An Analysis of Outcomes of Reconstruction or Amputation after Leg-Threatening Injuries" and conquered the mysteries of "Herpetic Encephalitis and Acute Retinal Necrosis," I decided to check on my own patient. I poured Cara a glass of ice water and procured her a few Advil from the medicine cabinet. She was still asleep, lying on her side with her mouth almost wide open. She groaned for a moment and repositioned her arms. It was almost 8 a.m.; I figured if I stared hard at her for a few seconds, she would probably wake up.

And she did. Try it sometime—it almost always works.

"Happy New Year, Cara," I said from the doorway to her bedroom.

"Hey...hi...good morning..." she said as she rubbed her eyes. I had double-checked her name on the address labels on her medical journals. I didn't mind if she'd forgotten my name.

"I brought you some powerful medicine," I said as I put the water and Advil M&Ms down on her bedside table. "I thought I might need to check you for gene polymorphisms associated with myocardial infarction, but luckily you're awake and alert." I thought I'd bust out some of the knowledge I'd just gleaned from *The New England Journal of Medicine.*

"Wow. You're way more advanced than a 'real estate novelist,' aren't you? You don't get that kind of stuff watching *ER*," she said as she shuffled out of her room, pulling down her bunched up skirt. She got her first look at her living room, which had returned to some semblance of *feng shui*ed order. "Oh, my...you didn't have to...I can't believe you..."

"No worries. There's no good football on for a while, so I figured I had some time to kill. Besides, you still have your work cut out for you with that kitchen."

"Well, you...I..." Yes, she was pretty much speechless. See, I was already just *busting* with good deeds in this New Year. What a *mentsch* I am. Fucking salt of the earth is what I am. "Here...uh...let me give you a baked ziti." She made a beeline toward her refrigerator and extracted a massive disposable aluminum platter. "I made it. I was going to give one pan to my mom and dad, but they decided to stay in New Jersey...so..."

Her arms quivered as she held out the covered but obviously heaping pan. "Thank you. This is really great. Now, I can afford to 'buy' my host dinner." We laughed. I took the pan from her. I could see why her arms were quivering—baked ziti is a pretty damn heavy food.

Cara and I chatted for a couple of minutes. We talked a little about what my New York New Year held in store for me: some combination of football and friends. Cara was envious; she actually had to pull a shift in her hospital later that day—no Leisure Circuit in the medical profession.

Then, it was time for me to leave. "You know, I really think you're going to have a great New Year," I told her. We said goodbye and hugged briefly. And I left—with no phone number, but *with* a platter of ziti.

Eight hours later I was watching a meaningless college bowl game out of the corner of my eye while eating a meaningful and delicious bowl of microwaved ziti. I mean, seriously stellar ziti.

I checked my voicemail. Angeline had left a message just after midnight in Vail. Gabrielle had left another voicemail, this time passing on New Year's greetings just in case I had remained in SF. Kenneth called to inform me he was driving out to his parents' house in the 'burbs with his new girlfriend; the apartment was all mine.

Rain tapped on the 12-foot high window in Kenneth's loft apartment while I pecked on the keyboard. I had thought about venturing out to meet up with friends, but the nasty weather and vicious hangovers were discouraging everyone from leaving their apartments. Besides, I had a couple more days in Manhattan. Dark, cold, somber rainy days—there's no time better to write.

Sooooo…interesting times last night with Cara, eh? I think I need to get my act together.

I don't know if I did what I did last night because of my confusion with my "Gabrielle situation" or uncertainty around my "Angeline situation." But, I don't like living a life with so much confusion or uncertainty. I need to change it.

Angeline is such a tremendous woman. Even in just the two months I've known her—God, it's *truly* hard to believe it's been just over two months—I've been transformed. She's done *so* much for me, without even trying. I don't think she appreciates how much.

But for as much as we've done and said over the past two months, what's more notable is what we've left undone and unsaid. Some of the things are downright pedestrian. I've never been to a movie with the woman, for God's sake. We've never danced together. I've never cooked for her…and I love to cook.

Angeline and I just seem to have been wrapped up in this drama. I'd really like to see us in a more normal setting. She and I need to just hang out a little more to get to know each other. I feel like I just know the "crisis mode" Angeline; we've had a sense of urgency during almost every moment we've spent together. Hey, maybe we can chalk part of that up to the undefinable concept of *chemistry*, but I hope even with all the sparks that shoot of our eyes every time we see each other, we can also develop some sort of *comfort* level and a sense of our *compatibility* as well. Wow, I think I just discovered some new "3C" relationship framework…I'll have to check out the self-help section of the bookstore to see if I can patent that.

We need to have a number of conversations we haven't had yet. I have only the sketchiest information about how and why she broke things off with Trevor, and obviously this week's unexpected face-off brings a lot of new questions to mind. I would even look forward to a "where is this all going?" conversation—for the first time in my life.

I've attempted not to look too far forward as I've tried to manage my life over the last couple of months—looking too far ahead opened me up for a world of hurt with Gabrielle. But, it seems to me that Angeline is looking ahead, at least a little bit. I mean, for the love of Abraham, Isaac and Jacob, she asked me a few weeks ago to set up an *appointment with a rabbi* to find out more about my religion. I *think* that means something. No one has ever asked me to do that—it was especially surprising given we had only had a grand total of around 50 days together. She broke off the relationship with her boyfriend of two years within one month of meeting me. I didn't ask her to—at least I don't think I did. When something like that happens, one experiences a tremendous rush of emotions ranging from guilt to fear to pride to sadness; it's all very difficult to sort out. I need to understand what she saw—in *me*, in the potential of *us*—that led her to do that. *Maybe*, it wasn't even brought on because of anything she saw in *me*, or in any special potential she saw with *us*. So, I just need to ask her why she's made the choices she's made. I need to know.

We haven't said, "I love you." We haven't even said that meaning-filled statement's precursors, like: "I love spending time with you" and "You know what I love about you?". I don't think we've used the terms "boyfriend" or "girlfriend" yet. I sometimes laugh at the way we verbally weave our way around those descriptors.

There's a *process* to falling in love. I don't write this because my mind is packed with business minutiae about processes and procedures; I write it because I want to be careful. There are things you want to know about someone you want to give your heart to, and there are things you want her to know about you. I write it because right now, frankly, I'm still hurting. I write it, because I want to be smart.

Is there a *process* to falling out of love with someone?

Wow. That might have been the most difficult sentence I've typed into this collection of stories and experiences. I've been staring at that line for ten minutes. I can't deal with that right now—maybe in a few weeks.

Right now, my mindset basically boils down to this: to the best of my ability—when I get back to San Francisco, when I'm with Angeline—I need to stop thinking of myself as "the guy on the break."

OK, now I think I deserve to drink a beer and watch some football. I'm calling Money.

36

Life Moves

In spite of my sterling record as a logistician par excellence, I
was cutting it a little too close with my Sunday morning flight
out of Newark. I hadn't put in much quality time with Kenneth on
this trip to New York, so I decided to answer the call when he challenged me to an early morning squash match. A street closure in
Manhattan and a missed exit in New Jersey had eliminated the cushion in my timetable.

I hustled from the Hertz rental car bus like…that guy who used
to run through airports in the 1970s. It was 10:30 a.m. and I was just
reaching a packed security area. Although the crowd was moving
through relatively quickly, I knew it would be tough to make my
11:10 a.m. flight. I reached the baggage scanner and went through
the whole routine: putting my bags on the conveyor, removing my
shoes and belt, taking the change and keys out of one pocket and
removing the cell phone from the other. In the middle of the juggling
and disrobing, my mobile phone buzzed. It was Gabrielle.

"Hey, G, how are you?"

"I'm good. How are you? Where are you? There's a lot of noise."

"Yeah. I'm actually just getting to the—"

The Transportation Security Administration interrupted. "Sir?"
the woman said, funneling me with her arms through the metal
detector.

"Hey, G. G? Just…just hold on ten seconds, don't hang up…"

I put the cell phone in a plastic tub on the conveyor and walked
on through. I should have just called her back when I got to my gate;

I don't know what I was thinking. The fellow manning the scanner moved my bags back and forth a few times on the conveyor to inspect my luggage more closely. It was almost a minute before my cell phone emerged from the lead-lined tunnel.

"Gabrielle? Are you still there?" I asked as I began to work my belt back through the loops.

"Yeah. What happened?"

"I'm sorry. I'm at the airport and I was just going through security. But, you'll be happy to know you just went through the X-ray unit and you're perfectly safe and approved for air travel," I told her as I tried to poke my feet into my still tied shoes.

"So, how was your New Year's Eve? You were in New York?"

"Yeah," I answered as I cradled my phone against my shoulder, balancing against my rolling bag and striking a one-legged pose like a flamingo. "Nick's party was pretty packed. Saw a bunch of the guys." I tried to get the knot out of my shoe, and stymied by the daunting double knot, used both hands to try to force it on my foot. "So, how was Toronto?"

"Well, my mom really..." she began. My phone slipped away from my ear and I tried to catch it. Still flamingoed up on my bad leg, I lost my balance and slammed my tail bone into the stainless steel structure that formed the terminus of the X-ray conveyor.

"Mother fu..." I almost said as I finally worked my shoe onto my foot and retrieved my phone from its landing place.

"Jake, are you still there?"

"Yes, I'm so sorry. I dropped the phone, but I'm OK now. I'm headed away from security and toward my gate. I'm sorry, you were talking about the trip home."

She told me about Christmas with her family and New Year's Eve with an assortment of Toronto friends, most of whom I had met once or twice. I listened as I approached a McDonald's. I was starving and dehydrated—squash had taken a lot out of me and I hadn't eaten anything since a granola bar at 6:30 a.m. "So, what else has been up with you?" G asked as I approached the counter.

"Well, I was pretty psyched this morning. Kenneth challenged me to a squash match and I haven't played since before the surgery, like almost six months. So, it was our...hold on. I'll have the Egg McMuffin meal with an orange juice, thanks...it was our one hundredth match. He keeps track of them all. So, I'm sure he thought...no, no coffee, just the orange juice, please...he would win the one hundredth match of all time and just walk all over me. But I was actually moving surprisingly well and I...what? You don't have Egg McMuffins? G, can you believe it? I missed the Egg McMuffin deadline—someone just got the last one..."

"That's funny."

"Yeah. So, I actually played pretty damn...OK, I'll have the Quarter Pounder with cheese meal...pretty damn well. The knee was feeling really good."

"Well, I'm glad for you. Sounds like you're making a good recovery."

"Yeah, it's been pretty good; I'm trying to...no, don't Supersize it. Just regular size—I'm trying to watch my figure. Thank you. So, overall I'm really very...Diet Coke, yeah...I've been..."

"Are you still talking to me?" she asked.

Finally the McDonald's take out bag was pushed in my general direction. I grabbed it and started to roll my way to the gate. "I'm so sorry. I'm just really rushed and I haven't eaten today. My plane is boarding and I'm just hustling to get there."

"I thought we said we were going to talk on New Year's...You got my message, right?"

"Yes, thank you. I was going to call you when I got back to SF and things settled down a bit. Because I do really want to...hold on, I need to grab my ticket out of my—" I stepped toward the gate agent.

"This is a little ridiculous," Gabrielle said. "Why don't you just take a minute to—"

"Just a second," I said to the gate agent as I stepped out of the line. I set down my briefcase and released my rolling bag. I stopped moving for the first time in the last hour. "OK, G, I'm all yours."

"It's just a little annoying. It seems like you don't want to talk to me."

"Gabrielle, I think you know that there is no one in this world I'd rather talk to than you. I think you know there is nothing I'd rather do than talk to you two or three times a day rather than once every two or three weeks. I'm sorry, but I *was* busy in New York, trying to live my life. But I *was planning* to call you from San Francisco. Remember: this was your choice."

"I know."

"You know, right across from me is a flight to LAX," I said as I gestured with my McDonald's bag toward a gate for a flight to Fort Lauderdale. "I will get on that flight right now if you want me to. Then we can talk a lot. We can talk every day. We can talk whenever you want to. It's your choice."

"You know I'm not ready," she said icily.

"Well, G, you know, life moves. A lot has happened because of your choice to go on this break. A lot more will happen. You know, it's *my* deepest wish that none of this ever happened, but I'm just trying to cope with the hand I've been dealt...the hand you dealt me."

"I know."

"I do want to catch up. Why don't we talk tomorrow or the next day?"

"OK. I know. I'm sorry."

"No, I'm sorry. You know I...I just have to get on the flight. Tammy, the gate agent, looks like she wants to body slam me. I'm just lucky I got my own Quarter Pounder because I think they would poison my complimentary peanuts." We both laughed. I think we were looking for any excuse to laugh. "I just have to go now."

"OK. Goodbye."

"Bye."

As I handed the gate agent my ticket, I realized I hadn't wished G a Happy New Year.

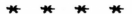

Right now, I'm on a long, long trans-continental flight. I think we're above Indiana right now. Since I skipped most of the New Year's Day bowl games, I finished all of the work I had stacked on my plate. So I have not a thing to do except type into this little chronicle as I cross this great land of ours. It's either that or read the special advertising sections in the in-flight magazine.

If one reads at a 3rd grade comprehension level or above, it's fairly easy to see that I'm still very much in love with Gabrielle. I wish our conversations could be easy and breezy…actually, I'm not sure I do. That would require either acting, or being completely done with each other. At least the strained conversations are real.

For the last few minutes, I've typed and erased, typed and erased. All because of verb tense. It started when I wrote the sentence "Gabrielle *was* the love of my life." *Was? Is? May be?* I can't figure out which tense to use. Can the term "love of my life" even be confined within the temporal brackets of verb tenses? Do I even really know what it means to have someone be the "love of my life"? Is *my* definition at all similar to *your* definition?

What I do know is this: I really wish you had gotten to know Gabrielle better. She may possess the truest, purest soul I will ever know. I very much wish I'd written different stories—I had certainly planned a whole slate of different chapters for this book.

One would have been the moment I knew I loved Gabrielle. I was really looking forward to penning that anecdote.

Within the three months after we met, Gabrielle and I had been on two trans-continental dates, traversing borders on interminable flights like the one I am on now. We had spent some fantastic times together on our weeklong "dates," but in a way, I think we still viewed each other as interesting, but impossible, companions—more like pen pals with benefits.

Late one night in September of 1998, we were talking on the phone. She was in Toronto; I was in Boston on business, my body, per usual, riddled with jet lag. Near the end of a two-hour conversation, she asked me, "May I read you something?"

I almost begged out, nearly asking her if we could do it the next day, or if she could e-mail it to me. But, instead, I told her, "Sure. Whatcha got?"

She prefaced her reading by telling me that a few days before, her friend Annie, the performer from EuroDisney, had been in a terrible auto accident. She was, at the time, in a coma, with spine damage that might lead to paralysis. Gabrielle had written Annie a letter, one which she hoped Annie could read when she emerged from her coma. But, in reality, it would probably be read to her by a relative while she was still unconscious.

Gabrielle started reading me the letter. To be honest, I don't recall much of the language; I wasn't taking notes for a book at the time, after all. What I do recollect, however, is that this was the most moving phone conversation I had ever participated in. I recall lying back on my hotel bed with the scraps of a terrible room service dinner on the tray next to me (this was before I was relegated to the Couch Patrol) and seeing flashes of the muted SportsCenter from the room's TV, not knowing what to say to her. I remember the feeling of falling in love with her the instant she finished the letter, and being utterly surprised when a tear emerged from my eye.

"So, what do you think? Is that OK?" she asked me.

Now, I'm supposed to be the writer, but I'd never written anything like it. She had spent hours writing a letter knowing it might only be read to a young woman *in a coma*. "I wish I could do that," I told her. "It was really beautiful."

I'll skip forward twenty minutes in the story now. I pulled the notepad out of the desk drawer in the hotel and started composing a letter myself. A younger colleague from my old firm McKay had withdrawn from Stanford business school a few weeks earlier because of some quite serious personal issues. This was a woman who usually came across my radar screen once or twice a year at most, but I always thought well of her. Actually, the last time we had talked was when she called after her grad school admission to thank me for helping her with her essays. That was almost a year and a half earlier.

I started writing a letter having no familiarity with what she was going through and no idea what I could possibly say to her. But I wrote my two-page letter anyway, and mailed it the next day. Three years later, I ran into her in San Francisco. She had returned to business school and graduated the following year. She told me that though a few classmates had written or called her, I was the only one of her professional colleagues to send along a note. It had meant a great deal to her.

I loved Gabrielle on that day in September 1998 because she inspired me—in, yes, a small way—to be a better person.

So, now back to lying in a Boston hotel room at 2 a.m., being dumbfounded that this woman seven years my junior—my e-mail and long distance phone call buddy—could move me so much. I wanted to tell her I loved her right at that moment, while I still had the tear on my face. But I decided to wait, because I wanted to see *her* face when I did it.

So, a few weeks later, I was with Gabrielle in Toronto on a warm October evening. There, at sunset, sitting on a log by the side of Lake Ontario, I told her.

"Thank you," she said, "I'm sorry. I don't know what to…" I didn't mind that she wasn't there yet, not in the least. And I told her I didn't mind that she didn't know yet. *I knew*, and that was enough at the time. Eventually, she knew.

And then, four years later, she didn't know. I guess that's how life moves.

Which brings us to today. A few months ago, I had nothing but a foolhardy plan, an hours' worth of research on the 4Cs and a few printouts of possible itineraries for holiday travel to Canada. But you know me and my plans. In spite of the potential risk of frostbite, I wanted to return to that spot on the lake (or maybe a warm spot within comfortable viewing distance) and wish Gabrielle a Happy New Year 2003—by asking her to marry me.

I planned on giving her a few short stories and anecdotes—maybe even professionally bound into a book—detailing how we met, the moment I knew I loved her, the time she gave me that sponge bath after my surgery and maybe a couple of other moments from a fall and winter I thought we would spend together. A Halloween, Thanksgiving, Hanukkah and Christmas I thought we would share. It became a very different story, as you know.

So, now it's New Year's 2003 and I'm flying from Newark to San Francisco instead of from Toronto to Los Angeles. I guess that's how life moves.

✱ ✱ ✱ ✱

This all sounds very dramatic and emotional, but I was actually just laughing at myself as I transcribed the last few bits of the preceding paragraphs—written an hour ago on my McDonald's take out sack and a United air sickness bag. Hey, it was the only paper I had available after I stowed my briefcase in the overhead. But now, we're at a comfortable cruising altitude, so I'm back at it on the laptop.

So, is it the brave thing to do, or is it the cowardly thing to do? Is it the smartest thing I could do, or the dumbest thing I could do? Is it the strong thing to do—to admit that despite everything, Timing is indeed against Gabrielle and me—or is it the course of action followed by a weak person? Is the Break a "time out," or is it a less painless phraseology that still spells the end of a relationship, as so many people have told me? When Gabrielle dropped me off three and a half months ago at the Southwest terminal at LAX, was that the last time I will ever see her?

I don't know.

But what I do know is this: an absolutely astounding woman is picking me up at the United terminal at SFO tonight. It's strange to say, but after just two months, it seems Angeline in many ways "knows" more about me than Gabrielle ever did. At least that's what I glean from the hints. It's the inkling I get from the conversations we *almost* have. We certainly seem to dance around a lot, but I think I'm starting to assemble a picture. She and I have some work to do—we have a lot to figure out. But, I'm looking forward to it.

I don't relish that I'm writing about Angeline and Gabrielle on the same page. It hurts, actually. But it's just a little glimpse of what cycles through my mind a hundred times an hour. They are both on my mind all of the time. But right now, what I'm looking forward to is being with and thinking about Angeline more and more.

When I met Angeline, I was a heap of emotional wreckage. Hey, in a lot of ways, I probably still am. But to the extent I've healed at all, it's because of her. She is the most energetic person I've ever met, and bestows a zest for life on anyone in her proximity. And I'm lucky enough to be the one in her proximity. Every minute with her is pure art, like a ballet; I can't take my eyes off her for a second for fear of missing the graceful way she opens a jelly jar, or the elegant way she sharpens a pencil and blows off the shavings.

I'm looking forward to discovering other things that I'll love about her. I can't wait to see her.

My laptop's battery is down to its last few minutes of power. I think we're above Nevada right now. I can almost hear the sounds of "Vegas, baby, Vegas," even though Vegas is very, very far away. San Francisco and Angeline are about an hour distant. Almost home.

37

Random

Well, this is exactly *not* what I thought I would be doing at 10:22 p.m.—two hours after Angeline picked me up at the airport. I spent a good chunk of the day in front of this computer and I thought the old Dell would get a chance to rest while Angeline and I rang in the New Year—albeit a few days late. But, somehow that didn't happen.

Once again, my connection through Chicago was delayed, which gave me plenty of time to polish up the preceding stories. It ended up being a much longer and more taxing day of travel and writing than I anticipated. Angeline was a sight for sore eyes—literally—when she picked me up at SFO a couple of hours ago. I tossed away my makeshift McDonald's and United Airlines notepads and walked out the sliding glass doors near the baggage claim to join her. We shared what I thought at the time was an incredibly strong New Year's kiss, and I was looking forward to more belated Happy New Year's festivities when we returned to Union Street.

She looked fantastic with the remnants of her ski tan. I was even digging the subtle reverse raccoon look she was boasting. Angeline was feeling a little tired, so I drove her car back home from the airport. We shot smiles back and forth as we talked about our recent holiday travels. She played with my right ear most of the way back, almost rubbing it raw. Every once in a while, she would take a break from bending my ear and deliver a couple of kisses to my neck. All seemed pretty normal.

When we arrived back at my place, we immediately paid our favorite couch a visit. A few minutes later, our stomachs gurgled in unison, prompting uncontrolled laughs from both of us. "We really are in synch," she said.

"I guess I timed my Quarter Pounder perfectly. I wanted to reach the 'absolutely starving' point at exactly the same moment as you," I replied. "Let's get some food delivered."

She agreed, and I proceeded to order a feast fit for a Shogun from a sushi joint a couple of miles away. "Hey, look what my flatmate gave me," I said as I returned to the living room. He had been in SF for New Year's and had left me a pretty damn good bottle of wine to welcome in 2003. "Should we uncork this?"

"No, let's not…it'll put me right to sleep," she answered.

We don't want that now, do we? I thought as I placed the bottle on my mini wood peg "glue it yourself" wine rack. *I need to get him something. Maybe a variety pack of Chunky soups.*

"OK, enough of this 'it'll put me right to sleep' stuff. We need to wake you up a little bit." Next came a bit of tickling—contrived, I know, but she has such a great stomach, I'll touch it with just the slightest excuse. I thought the 15 seconds of tickling would easily transition into 15 minutes of kissing, couch tussling and the other associated activities. As it turned out, it was only 13 minutes.

For the first time since I'd known her, Angeline pulled away from our embrace. "This is…I can't…Jake, I think I'm just going to go home now," she said as she leaned back to the far side of the couch.

"Oh. Are you not feeling well? We could just chill…" I was in the process of scooting toward her—just to put my arm around her. She stood up from the couch while I was in mid-scoot and walked toward the dining room to retrieve her purse, without even looking at me. I got up from the sofa and followed her into the next room. "Hey, hey. You need to talk to me for a second here. Are you OK? Any recent development I wasn't apprised of while I was in New York? I don't quite understand what's happening right now."

"I don't either. I mean what are we *really* doing here? I mean, what is this that Jake and Angeline are trying to do?"

"I *thought* they were trying to start something really great. That's what I thought, but I'm really not getting this 'moment' we're having here. Everything was *peachy* 30 seconds ago, and now you're packing up like…hey, *hey!*" She was already putting on her coat, flinging her sleeve right pass my face as I was in mid-sentence.

"I'm sorry, but I'm leaving. We can talk tomorrow, Jake."

I grabbed her arm. "You have to tell me what the hell has changed in the last *minute* of our lives. Angeline, I'll come over to your place and we can talk about this. I'll come right back here afterwards, but I just want to know you're OK. Why won't you tell me what's wrong?" I asked as I let go of her arm, moving my hand toward her ear and starting to rub it as she had mine a little while earlier.

She almost broke a smile…I think. She leaned her cheek toward the hand that was rubbing her ear, and let it rest there for a moment. But it was literally just a moment; she reached up slowly and pulled my hand away. "We can talk tomorrow. I *want* to talk to you tomorrow, but I really need to go now. Please…I'm just going to go now."

I took a step back. She put her hand on my chest for two seconds, looked downward and away from me and then walked out the door without another word.

✳   ✳   ✳   ✳

So, now it's 45 minutes later, and I'm writing this story, randomly inserted, it seems, into an interesting storyline I *thought* Angeline and I had been crafting. What fun.

Earlier tonight, we had made plans to have lunch in her neighborhood tomorrow. I don't even know if she still wants me to show up at her place.

Fuck it. I don't care. I'm going.

Next to me are the remnants of what I *thought* was going to be our dinner tonight. It was exceedingly expensive and I was extraordinarily hungry, but a rasher of raw fish and a bushel of rice remain. There's nothing less appetizing than sushi-for-two…for one.

I feel like such a fool. Did I misread something? Am I following my normal path of under-observing and over-analyzing? Have I been concocting grand plans for the future while not even correctly reading the reality that surrounds me in the present? Have I been acting—and dreaming—like a little kid? Have I just been playing with Popsicle sticks, again?

38

Defenses

Angeline has cancer.

That took me two hours to write.

✳   ✳   ✳   ✳

It's now about two hours after I typed those two lines and six hours after I visited Angeline at her apartment.

She's been diagnosed with uterine cancer.

Angeline is so young. I just can't comprehend what's happening. I can't comprehend what she's feeling right now. How can this happen? Does this happen to women this young? What happens next? My mind has never raced like it's raced over the last six hours, but it's never felt like such a feeble instrument to me in all of my life.

I couldn't believe I came back to my flat after an emotional two hours with her and the first thing I thought of was going over to my computer. God, am I so narcissistic that I have to chronicle my every emotional tremor? What the hell have I become?

Should I even be writing about this? This isn't a part of my life. Is this a part of my life? Can I talk to other people about this? I don't think I can talk to anyone about this. I have no idea what I should do. I have no idea what I *can* do. I have no idea how I can help her.

I literally can't write anymore. My shoulders and neck have cramped up. It's impossible. It's impossible.

✳ ✳ ✳ ✳

Ten hours ago, it was 12 noon, and I arrived at Angeline's apartment. I hadn't the vaguest notion why she seemed so upset the night before, but I had resolved that I would know before I left her home.

I sat down on her couch in her living room, the whole area bathed by the light streaming in through her southward facing windows. She sat down on the couch but again positioned herself far away from me; I tried to make light of the situation by stacking up my own fort of pillows in front of me. I was glad when she laughed for a couple of seconds, but it was painfully obvious that her defenses were still up—and they were much more formidable than my castle of cushions.

"Angeline, *Jelly...*" I began, citing the nickname I created for her over three weeks before but hadn't employed until just that moment. She smiled for a few seconds again. "...please help me with this. I'm not sure what might have changed between last week and now. I'm not sure what changed between the time you picked me up at the airport and the time you hustled out of my place. I'm not sure what happened between the time we ordered dinner and the time you drove home. You stuck me with an awful lot of edamame."

She started laughing again, but then buried her face against my pillow fort, obscuring her expression. When she raised her head, it was obvious she'd been crying for a few seconds. "Jake, I don't think we can do this."

"Yes, you already told me that last night. But you know my inquisitive nature, and that statement alone doesn't help me understand this Dr. Jelly and Mrs. Hyde transformation."

"Well, here it is then. Maybe you can understand this," she said in the coldest tone I'd ever heard her utter. Actually, the only cold tone I'd ever heard her speak. "You've recently broken up with someone. I've just broken off a relationship. There's just so much going on. So much. Jake, the timing just doesn't work out for—"

"OK, OK. Please just stop with this 'Timing' thing. That's a line...that's a piece of dating bullshit I refuse to accept. It's overused, it's trite and the least we owe each other even after just a little bit of time together is—"

"I have cancer, Jacob. I have cancer."

I don't think any portion, any sliver of my experiences in relationships and life in general prepared me for those words. I felt every emotion at once, but still felt nothing, like they all drowned each other out. My shoulders and neck, mildly strained from all of the time I had spent in an airline seat and in front of the computer the day before, immediately and painfully cramped up, the twinge also extending itself into my numbing tongue. And my knee, bent beneath me in my awkward position on the sofa, began to throb as it hadn't done in months.

I reached across the wall of cushions and cradled the back of her neck with my right hand. "How did you…when will..?" I began. I wanted to know everything. I wanted to know what kind of pain she was feeling, what sort of fear she was experiencing and what cauldron of emotions was roiling in her head and heart. I wanted to know timetables, treatments, survival rates and side effects. But, I didn't know how to begin. I didn't know if *I* should begin. Should I be questioning, probing? I decided to let her tell me whatever she wanted me to know.

Angeline told me she had gone to the doctor with some health issues months before, prior to our meeting. Though at the time the physician prescribed drugs for what he thought was a minor affliction, new tests and retests later confirmed the presence of cancerous cells. A specialist had recently informed her that they had caught the cancer fairly early, so a non-surgical course of treatment could be pursued at first; surgical options with this form of cancer made bearing children impossible. Though the therapy she would be receiving over the next several months was the only hope of preserving both her life and her ability to have children, her capacity to have a baby might still end up being severely compromised.

I sound like an intern going on rounds with an attending physician on some TV hospital drama. A kid in scrubs antiseptically describing the condition of the patient lying beneath the ultrawhite sheets and the faded blue hospital-issue blanket. But unlike that intern, my knowledge stops there. And I have no crusty doctor with years of experience to tell me what to do.

All I knew to do was to still cradle her perfect neck and to pull her closer to me. Her forehead rested against mine, and we sat silently for a few minutes. I listened to the sound of her breathing and stared with no purpose at the sheen and texture and imaginary patterns of the velvet cushions that separated us. And then I asked her.

"Angeline, please tell me, why did you say what you said last night?"

She was silent for a few seconds. I think I could feel the muscles in her face straining though our only point of contact remained our foreheads. "I wanted to give you a way out," she said quietly.

"Jesus Christ, Angeline," I managed, shaking my head in frustration even as our skin stayed in contact. I then felt the familiar surge of tears attacking my eyes and elevated myself from the couch, walking toward Angeline's fireplace. I rested my arm on the mantle but still kept my gaze away from hers. "I don't understand. Why would you do that? Didn't you think I'd want to be there to help you?"

"I don't know," she said. I wasn't sure which of my two questions she was answering.

"God, with this thing you're going to go through…you have to let people be there for you. Give me a 'way out'? You have to know I'll be there for you. You have to know your friends will be there…" I trailed off. I knew that Angeline had met most of her friends in the City through Trevor, a lifelong Californian. My neck cramped up, delivering another wave of pain.

Angeline was still sitting on the couch, her legs tucked beneath her small frame, her body propped up against the stack of cushions and her eyes looking down toward her lap. I reassumed my position on the other side of the couch, and lay my head down on the still formidable fort of pillows. I looked up at her and tried my best to smile. She grinned back, exhaling a tiny chuckle through her nose. She rested her head on the cushions as well.

There we remained for the next half hour, staring at each other's upside-down faces while we lay on the soft ramparts of the fort I built when we first sat down. We smiled at each other periodically and

wiped away each other's tears before they could work their way diagonally down our noses and onto the pillows. Angeline nearly drifted
off to sleep a couple of times.

Eventually she rose, declaring she needed to get ready for her 3
p.m. doctor's appointment. I almost suggested that I should go with
her to the office, but instead I just offered to drive her and pick her
up. Should I have offered to do more? Should I have insisted on getting involved? I don't know exactly what I am to her—what my definition is. What my place on the relationship spectrum is. Am I her
boyfriend? Am I just the guy she finds herself in this situation with?
God, does she even consider me "with" her in this in any way? I
offered to drive, and at that moment certainly was ready to do more
if she asked.

"No, I'm OK going over there myself. Besides, I'm going for a
jog in the same neighborhood with a friend afterward," she told me.

"Oh? Well, that's good...that you're still feeling strong like that.
That's excellent," I said as we started walking together toward her
front door. "But the offer is good anytime you need it."

"Thank you."

"And some day I might actually insist on driving you. So don't
try to resist."

"Thank you," she laughed.

"And right now, I'm insisting we have our lunch tomorrow"

"It's a deal. We'll do it." We kissed, and shared an extraordinarily long hug, and then I left.

It's 6:30 in the morning in San Francisco. I didn't sleep a wink
last night. I tried to lie down a few times in between different sessions
at the computer, but it was no use. I even read a few articles I needed
to get through for work on reforms in Pentagon procurement practices advanced weapons systems. Even after two billable hours with
those articles between 3 and 5 a.m., I was still unable to fall asleep.

Almost half an hour ago, my cell phone rang, and I answered.

"Oh, hello Jake; I expected to get your voicemail." The surprised
voice belonged to an editor at a magazine based on the east coast. I

had submitted a revised article—the one about the retailing maverick who had made me cry—to her about four weeks earlier, but had not heard anything from her since.

"Yeah, I just happened to be up a little early today. How are you?"

"Good, good. But, we're going to need to do some work on this piece. We're going to press today and, frankly, some of the parts of this article don't have a tone appropriate for our publication."

Then why are you calling me now, almost a month later? Aren't editors supposed to be the ones who know the publishing schedule?

All of a sudden, the exhaustion and sleepiness I had wanted to embrace all night grabbed hold of me. "Well, maybe we can talk through a couple of things over the phone."

"Well, first, you use the word '*chutzpah*.' I replaced it with 'entrepreneurial verve,'" she informed me. I've never uttered the word "verve." I had never even typed it until just now.

"You know, that's fine. I'm sure anything you want to do—" I began to tell her before she cut me off.

"And when you talk about the opening of their new stores, you wrote: 'It was an *orgy* of organic soy—'. Now, we can't have any mention of 'orgies' in our magazine."

Oh, the horror! Maybe every reader will picture all of the customers rolling around in 100% organic vegetable oil and licking off inviting dollops of 100% organic macrobiotic whipped soy cream. "Yes, you're right. Please make any changes you see fit."

"Well, I've highlighted a number of sections that really could use a rewrite to make the tone—"

"I'm afraid that will be impossible today with my schedule. I wish you had contacted me earlier. Please do whatever you feel necessary; I'll understand. Thanks. Take care."

✳ ✳ ✳ ✳

It's nearly 9 a.m. and I think that within the next couple of minutes I might actually fall asleep. It would be good to get in a few minutes of rest before I go meet Angeline for lunch.

God, any emotional defenses I may have built up over the years, any intellectual defenses or rationalizations I may have constructed about the world of "relationship *realpolitik*" have all been useless to me today…yesterday. All of my defenses and experiences were just like the Maginot Line— completely circumvented and totally ineffectual. I have no idea what to do. I have no idea how to act. I have no idea what to feel.

Please let me sleep now.

39

Comfortable Silence

Late Thursday, Angeline and I got together to see a film. I picked her up and we traveled to a movie megaplex in SOMA. "I'm so excited! This should be really good," she said as she looked down at the printout with the showtimes and vital statistics for our chosen movie. "Reviewers alternatively describe the movie as '…Astounding…,' '…Breathtaking…' and '…Spellbinding….'"

"Did they include the usual ellipses around the word…or did they go with the exclamation point?" I asked as I drove down Van Ness Avenue.

"Ah, they chose the three little dots."

"I don't trust reviews with too many ellipses, 'cause…you know…it seems like they might be leaving out something really important."

"Of course. They might be leaving out critical data and factoids that could be useful in one's assessment of said theatrical endeavour," said Angeline. I think she'd appreciate I spelled "endeavour" with a "u".

"Exactly."

We parked in the megaplex's megagarage and journeyed to the entertainment complex. Once inside, we approached the automated dispensers to collect our pre-ordered movie tickets. Angeline—who had ordered our tix a few hours earlier—inserted her card several times, but was rebuffed by the heartless machine. I dutifully wiped off the magnetic strip and tried again, but I too was unsuccessful in persuading the electronic sentinel to grant us entry.

"Here. Let me see that printout; maybe we can take it to the…" I began. Then I saw why we had both been unsuccessful. "Hey, Jelly, we're at the wrong theatre." The tickets she had actually paid for resided in a ticket machine several miles away.

"Oh, my God. I'm sorry. What should we do?"

We scanned the massive display of red letters and numbers to our left, but unfortunately our chosen flick started over 30 minutes before and wouldn't be lighting up the screen again for another two hours. As a matter of fact, our film options for the next hour were very limited and for the most part utterly undesirable; many of the selections could have been entries in the Ishtar Film Festival.

"Uh, we could see the new *Star Trek* movie," I suggested. I had never been to such a hardcore science fiction film with a woman, but it seemed like the final frontier was begging to be crossed. "It looks like it's pretty much the only halfway decent movie we haven't seen that will be starting in the next hour. Hey, my treat on this one, since you got the last one," I smiled as I pointed to the computer printout.

"Well, make it so," she laughed.

We sort of watched the movie for the next two hours. I think Captain Jean Luc Picard was menaced by some evil clone or something—probably the twentieth evil twin the folks behind *Star Trek* have rolled out. And Commander Data gets blown to bits in the end. Sorry if I ruined it for you.

Neither Angeline nor I were too engrossed in this tale of Romulan political intrigue, so we just kept staring at each other. At first, we alternated; I could just sort of tell when she averted her gaze from my left ear, so I would then take my turn staring at her right ear. Eventually, we got so bored with the predictability of the film, we just commenced staring at each other at the same time.

I know—we just did a lot of staring in the last chapter. I understand that writing about staring is not exactly exploring new literary worlds, but, I'm not scripting this thing, I'm just narrating it. We've been doing a lot of staring and gazing in the last few days. I think she finds comfort in our moments of just watching each other. I do, too. The silence is comfortable—the silence of the moment. Maybe it's because I have no idea what to say to Angeline about the next moment, the next day, the next week or next month. Our silent, thin smiles are comfortable; the whole galaxy of things left unsaid is still daunting and intimidating. So, we smile, touch hands, breathe together and stare.

40

In-N-Out

This afternoon we both busted away from our hectic schedules for a field trip. Angeline had lived on the West Coast for a year and a half and had not partaken of one of its true pleasures, a situation I decided to rectify immediately once I became aware of this gap in her base of life experiences.

Though *the* best thing about living in California is being able to wake up on Sunday and start watching NFL games almost straight away, the *second* best thing is In-N-Out Burger. It's a "regional delight" which only the residents of California, Arizona and Nevada get to enjoy. For those of you in the Midwest, your regional delight is White Castle. For those if you in the South, think Krispy Kreme Donuts in the decades before they started fattening up other regions. For those in the Northwest, hearken back to the time when Starbucks was yours alone, before they started popping up in gas stations in Branson, Missouri and strip malls in Miami Beach, and that gives you a sense of the regional flavor imparted by In-N-Out Burger's fresh-cut fries and secret sauce.

Angeline had loaded up into my car at noon before picking out our lunch destination. We cruised by a McDonalds, and I made some remark comparing the burgers at the Golden Arches with the lunchtime fare of the Golden Arrow (In-N-Out's logo has a giant arrow, one that sort of suggests your path as you drive in n' out of the joint). When she mentioned she had not yet visited an In-N-Out Burger, I immediately set our course toward the sole San Francisco location of the chain. When I considered that that particular location lay in the heart of SF's hypertouristic Fisherman's Wharf, I set a new course and bearing, toward the Golden Gate.

Across the Bridge and a few miles north on Highway 101 in Marin lay the Mill Valley In-N-Out. It's pretty close to a place where you can get copious amounts of blackberries during the summertime.

In-N-Out boasts a huge line during prime lunch and dinner hours. Today was no exception; we waited in line for 15 minutes, the queue stretching well beyond the building's front door.

"I can't believe I haven't been here until now. I'd heard so much about it, but just never got around to it," said Angeline. Then, she molded her face into an expression of mock wonderment. "Jacob, I can't believe how much you've changed my life. I could never thank you enough."

"Well, you're buying, so that would certainly be thanks enough." I had forgotten my wallet in my flat. I might have had enough parking meter quarters stashed in the Probe to buy one combo meal, but my sugar mama volunteered to foot the bill for our lunch today.

Our time together in line afforded me the opportunity to explain to Angeline some of the intricacies of ordering at In-N-Out. Though the burger and fries-only menu is simplicity itself in this day of McRibs, McSalads and nonfat soy mochafrappacappucinos, there were hidden, unwritten rules in this restaurant. Reciting one code word instructed the white-and-red togged crew to grill the normally raw onions on your sandwich. Another secret command told them to serve your meal without the bun, but instead swathed in extra lettuce leaves. I told her I usually kept it "old school" and just went straight from the menu.

"Well, since you're my host today, I'll keep it old school, too," she replied.

We waited for our order among literally dozens of other diners as number after number was called out. I think there were over 200 patrons eating in- and outside the restaurant. Finally, our number came up.

I won't bother trying to extol the virtues of the food itself. There's just some subtle, unquantifiable and unknowable sprinkle of genius mashed into those little burgers, each of them packaged up tightly in small brown paper wraps.

We ate and smiled and talked about the football playoffs and upcoming art exhibits we might see. It was ultra-pleasant and ultra-comfortable. It's in the writing of this story...in the last few minutes...that I've become uncomfortable and discomfited.

What am I doing? Am I trying to build this little relationship here, or navigate it into a perfect little holding pattern? Did I do this whole day with Angeline so I'd have a nice example of how I was trying to build my familiarity and comfort level with her? God, did I take her on this quaint little trip across the Golden Gate to this cute, fun "those of us in the know really like it" restaurant so I'd have a cute, fun anecdote to prove to...you...myself...that I'm doing the best I can in spite of the huge revelation a few days ago?

And this huge revelation doesn't even have to be huge for me. She didn't even really ask me to be a part of it—as a matter of fact, she gave me an out. But I decided to stay in. Actually, did I really decide anything, or am I just letting my momentum keep me going forward until I get a little tired or decide it's too hard or the situation gets too complicated or it all gets too real? Am I *truly* in this?

My, internal monologue certainly is ugly. Every once in a while I scroll back and look at the diatribes I penned and tangents I followed on karaoke and ripped jeans and New Year's party logistics, and just look at myself as this little person with insignificant, irrational thoughts. I made sense to myself at the time, but now I feel any notion of good sense and honor and intelligence and propriety are moving around on me from day to day and anecdote to anecdote.

Internal monologue is embarrassing. Our verbal statements, our e-mails, our memos, our essays and all of our other communications are packaged up for the rest of the world. Or at least tweaked and checked and molded during half second pauses in conversations and moments sitting idle in front of our keyboards. With this thing you're reading right now, I left all notion of packaging behind long ago. I still don't know if I should even be writing about this. I still don't *know* if I should be a part of this. I have no idea what comes next. How ugly and how weak would I seem if I told you there were moments when I wished that I had been less persistent questioning Angeline? Every moment with her is pure joy, and I'm happy for those, but am I prepared for the moments that aren't pure joy? I don't know what to do.

If I had known Angeline for two weeks, I would know what to do in this situation.

If I had known Angeline for two years, if I had been *with her* for two years, I would know what to do.

I had known her for just over two months when she told me. "Two months" is what it is in the discussion of building relationships. It's not a long time, but it's not a cup of coffee, either. I've seen some friends chastised for not taking things seriously enough after seeing someone for two months. I've seen others chided for overthinking and taking things way too seriously after two months.

Two months. I don't know what two months means. Our level of commitment and obligation to other people in this world isn't merely a function of time, is it? Maybe time is a part of it, but it's also measured in things said, moments shared, mental visions weaved, actions taken, decisions made and the like. Some people measure things— and I'm not sure whether they're right or wrong in doing this—based on sexual boundaries crossed.

Is this all something that can be added up, summed and totaled to show us our level of commitment and obligation to someone else? Does *Cosmo* have some grid with a scoring system that lets you know how committed you should feel when the complex formula of lapsed time and milestones achieved is tabulated? I mean, I *feel* the tug. I feel like I want to do whatever I can for her. That tug scares me. Is it totally irrational, is it another case of playing with Popsicle sticks, making decisions and crafting plans about things I shouldn't be?

I was having just the best time when Angeline and I drove back over the Golden Gate Bridge a couple of hours ago. I insisted on exhausting my supply of parking meter quarters in order to pay the $3 toll on the San Francisco side of the span. We were giggling at how hard I fought her off when she tried to foist her crisp one-dollar bills upon me. I was in such a good mood. When I sat down to write, I was in a completely different frame of mind than I am now, as I finish.

41

Grand Plans

I truly believed that my mind had gone out of control a couple of months ago when I was musing, cogitating, ruminating and fuming non-stop about "Break" or "break up" or whatever we might choose to call it. I had an ample helping from the smorgasbord of emotional pain.

But this last week has been a whole new sort of experience. In October, I merely experienced different flavors of sadness: gloom, despondency, melancholy, wretchedness, etc. At least I had a comforting consistency, a steady baseline from which I might deviate *a bit* from day to day. Now, I feel like a tetherball being smacked by rowdy kids from extremes of happiness, contentment and comfort to the depths of confusion, guilt and desolation.

I cannot stop thinking. Hour upon hour, when I should actually be devoting some portion of my mind to earning my living, I try to think through the grand plan, the mechanisms I might employ and the steps I might follow to best help Angeline. I want to *do* something. *Do* something. Do *something*. But, so far, all I can think of to do is just *be there*. *Be there*. Is that all I can do? Is that the best I can do? What would you do?

I think all the time about what it must be like to have your own body turn against you. At times I allow myself to think about…myself. I want to be happy. I would love to be in a place where I didn't have to sort out from moment to moment the mix of emotions whirling in my brain and heart. I would love to have a simple day—where I experience one emotion, or maybe two, or maybe even three. God, I seem to remember days where I felt happiness for a good 10 or 12 consecutive hours. That seems like another epoch, a different millennium.

Nearly two weeks ago, I made a New Year's resolution. I wanted to see if Angeline was a woman who could make me happy, and I wanted to see if I could be the man who could make her happy. There were things I wanted to know about her, things I wanted to ask her and things I wanted to experience with her. I'm not a bad person for wanting this, am I?

I feel incredible sadness and sympathy for what Angeline is going through with her disease. I think about this every day, and I feel it twisting my guts hour by hour. But, I also feel a sadness that we will not experience the month or two or three that I had envisioned. I know life is not perfect, and maybe it's never "normal." But, I just wanted to see how we functioned as a couple in *more* normal times. I wanted to see if we could be happy together. Just the two of us, with no—or at least *less*—relationship baggage cluttering and complicating the situation. I just wanted to see if we could be happy when it was just the two of us.

I'd never embarked on a quest for happiness as such before, but I thought it would be a nobler quest than the search for the perfect Manolo Blahniks. Maybe the quest for happiness is too boring for a book on the Technicolor shelf, but I'd love nothing better than to bore you to tears. I would love nothing better than to experience a day of happy boredom right now.

✳   ✳   ✳   ✳

Last night, I had dinner with Billy at an Irish bar. Over a meal of fish and chips, shepherd's pie and Guinness, I told him about Angeline's diagnosis of cancer. I don't know if I had any right to do this, but I had to talk to someone about it. Thus far, these little stories have been my only outlet for discussing the situation, and my laptop has been an exceedingly unsympathetic companion.

With just a few sentences, I recapped the series of revelations and events that have stacked up since the start of the New Year. Billy stopped chewing his shepherd's pie and sat stunned, motionless. Finally, he finished his mouthful and spoke.

"Dude…" he said quietly, shaking his head slowly. We sat in silence for a minute; I was hoping his brain, the generator of a Phi Beta Kappa and an Ivy League graduate degree might see some nuance or some wrinkle I had missed. Maybe he knew someone or had heard of someone who had gone through a similar situation—a situation which at least *I think* is fairly complex, given that it's taken me almost 85,000 words to explain it thus far.

Of all my friends, Billy knew Angeline the best, having spent a grand total of about 45 minutes in conversation with her. Maybe he had some insight about her personality gleaned from his small bit of time talking to her. I looked over at him, but he was still just shaking his head while looking down at his beer. We sat in silence for another minute.

Then he spoke. "Dude…" he said, as he shook his head with a new and distinct rhythm.

"Exactly," I nodded.

"So, what are you going to do?"

"I don't know."

"And, how does this factor into the whole thing with you and Gabrielle and the break?"

"I don't know. I try not to think about that. I'm just trying…to figure out what I can do for Angeline."

"What about her friends…and her family?"

"God, man, I think most of her friends are people she knows through her ex. There are a couple of people she still hangs out with I know of…but I actually don't *know* any of them. Her family, well they live pretty damn far away, but I imagine someone will eventually come out here. But she told *me* about it before she told her family. I don't know if there's something going on there…I really don't know who she has to support her."

"Have you been spending a lot of time with her since she told you?"

"Yeah, tons. More than ever. I see her much more frequently now. It's the strangest thing. I'm more drawn to her than ever."

"JT, are you in—"

"I don't know," I interrupted. "I just can't figure out what's friendship, what's empathy, what's...you know...physical attraction, what's guilt, what's just some general urge to do good in the world and what's...what *may be*...love. I just can't sort it out. All I know is I feel this compulsion to be with her all the time."

"JT, I feel bad saying this, but you know a lot of people would bail. You haven't even known her three months."

I sat silently for a few seconds. "To be honest, I think, in some way, she wanted me to bail, at first. She sort of positioned it...she tried to give me an out. I just didn't want her to be alone. It's hard to explain."

"Well, you're a good man, JT. But, as your friend, I just have to say, you may be in for a world of hurt. And again, speaking as your buddy, you're not exactly the strongest I've ever seen you. Dude, you need to weigh what you can do for her against what it might do to you. I mean: what can you really do for her?"

"I guess I can...just *be there*."

"JT, c'mon, what does that mean?"

"I don't know! I don't know! Maybe I give her a massage some time. Or maybe I kiss her on the forehead. Maybe I go and rent a movie and cook her dinner with some recipe from some cookbook written for cancer patients. Maybe I clean out her cupboards of food that nauseates her. Maybe I find some kind of tea that fights nausea in patients undergoing chemo or radiation, and I come by and brew her a pot every day. Maybe I clean up puke from her bathroom. Maybe I sweep up hair from around her apartment. Maybe I get her a blanket some time when she's cold and maybe I lie under the blanket with her to keep her warmer. Maybe I let her listen to me do interviews on the phone with America's premier business leaders. Maybe I make her a sandwich. Maybe I drive her to the doctor. Maybe I walk her to the elevator. Maybe I go with her to her appointment and ask all of the tough questions. Maybe I slam my fist down on his desk and say, 'That's not good enough, damn it; you can do more!'. Maybe I research exotic treatments available only in Mexico or Switzerland or Myanmar. I don't know."

Billy nodded his head and flared his nostrils as he took in a deep, knowing sniff. "Well, JT, sounds like a plan."

We both burst out laughing uncontrollably as I wiped tears—from laughter or emotional desolation, I don't know—away from my face. And as we continued our laughing, I exhaled the first snot bubble of my adult life.

Stop

Over the last few days, I've come out of my bunker a little more. I've sought sage counsel from a few other friends and family members, thinking maybe someone had some experience or perspective that might prove helpful. I talked to Kenneth, Garrett and my mother. After hours of hashing through the issues, their recommendations included the following:

"You've done the right thing."

"It's difficult. But, you're doing the right thing."

"You're a good person; you'll know what to do."

I have no idea what I've done.

I have no idea what I'm doing.

I have no idea what I can do or will do.

Tonight, I shared dinner with Erica in a small Italian restaurant in North Beach. For the last couple of weeks, I had been a ghost to her, avoiding any discussions of the current reality and exchanging only the most feeble and emaciated conversations. Tonight, though, we talked in great detail about the current events that dominate my every thought.

Erica virtually gushed empathy, but again, in my quest for some shred of wisdom to help me figure out *what to do*, I was left empty handed.

"You seem pretty fixated on that," Erica asserted.

"What?"

"Doing something. *Doing something.* Maybe it's a man thing. She's probably just looking for you to be with her, be a good friend and be understanding. To be someone she can talk to. It's sounds like you're doing that. If you ask me, you've been great. So many guys would freak out."

"Don't get me wrong. I *have* freaked out. I just have to deal. I just have to do…" I stopped myself. "OK, I just have to be there, *you say…*"

"Which you're doing."

"…and being 'someone she can talk to.' Should I be forcing her to talk about it? I mean there's still so much left unsaid."

"I don't know," Erica said. "You'll figure it out. You'll both figure it out."

Erica offered to pick up the bill after our uber-somber dinner. "I am worth it, aren't I?" I asked. "When have you ever had such an interesting dinner conversation? Definitely not with…what's his name?"

"Bailey! For the tenth time!" she exclaimed as we walked out of the restaurant and toward the bus stop. "C'mon, hurry up. Our bus is just coming up!"

"I'm sorry, I'm sorry! You know, there are so many guys competing with me for your attention sometimes it's hard to…wait, what's going on?" As we walked through the cross walk, amidst the rush of commuters getting off, getting on, and transferring between the buses of the 45 and 15 lines, we saw him. On the elbow of the sidewalk at the vertex of Columbus and Union Street lay a man. Another guy, brandishing a cup of Starbucks, a laptop computer case and a small MP3 player, stood above him and seemed to be making a modicum of an effort to help the prostrate man.

"Hey, what happened here? Do you need help?" I asked. All around us, commuters scurried like ants from a destroyed anthill, a few looking down briefly at the scene as Erica and I approached.

"You folks got this? Great…thanks. I gotta catch the 45," said the commuter as he took his cappuccino and consumer electronics and hopped away to get on the packed bus just as it released its air brakes.

And then there were three. On an otherwise barren street corner, Erica and I took up positions on either side of the man, both squatting down so we could talk to him.

"Hey, darling, are you OK?" asked Erica as she patted the moaning man gently on the chest. "What happened to you?"

"Where is it? Where did it go?" he asked. He picked up his head from the cold cement of the sidewalk and craned his neck to look for something. That's when I noticed the paperback-book-sized pool of blood beneath his head, neck and shoulders. In his weakened state, his neck could obviously not support the weight of his head, which quickly slammed back down on the pavement.

"Oh, my God. Sir, sir, stop, don't try to move..." But he was already lifting his head up again. His hair was pulpy and bright red. In a moment, his head slammed back down in the growing puddle of blood, sending a shower of crimson droplets onto my shoes and the bottom of my pants. "Sir, sir..." Already, I could see his neck muscles tensing for another attempt. "Erica, do you have a newspaper?"

Even before I completed the sentence, Erica was pulling a copy of *The Wall Street Journal* out of her oversized purse. She folded the paper over a couple of times, giving us a makeshift pillow for our patient.

"Hey, friend. Hold on, let us make you more comfortable," I told the man. I cradled the back of this neck and the base of this skull in my hand as Erica slid the small cushion through the pool of blood. "There, now we're set. Sir, what's your name?"

"Where is it? Please help me find it." He tried to get up again, and again was foiled by gravity, dizziness and weakened muscles. At least this time, the paper prevented further damage; his blood adorned the smiling pointillist portrait of Warren Buffett on the front page.

"Sir, what are you looking for? Erica, do you see anything like a wallet..?" I said as I rose slightly from my squat to examine the surrounding sidewalk for some unknown possession that belonged to this unknown man. I squeezed my hand in below his back, his buttocks and his legs in order to find some mystery object, and then repeated the operation on the other side as Erica stood up and expanded the search radius.

"Sir, I'm sure we could help you if...oh, gosh, I found it," she said from about ten feet behind my back. Erica reassumed her position on the man's left side and showed me the token she had found on the sidewalk: a wedding band. "Here, honey, I have your ring. Let me put it on you."

Like a new bride, she slid the surprisingly shiny band onto the man's fourth finger. The man moved his hand only slightly, and the ring was set in motion again, rolling toward a sewer grate. Erica fell backwards out of her squat to catch the rolling band. She regained her balance and pushed the ring down the man's knobby knuckles again. Either this man had come by a ring that was not his own and had bestowed some special mystical meaning unto it, or else his hand had withered significantly since the time the wedding band had been placed upon it by someone who meant a great deal to him.

"OK, we have your ring back on you, but we need to be careful," said Erica. She folded his fingers over and closed his hand. "You'll let me hold your hand, won't you?"

"Sure...you're nice," the man said.

Erica winked at me and smiled, but her expression soon became flavored with bittersweetness as she continued looking over at me. She knows I spend inordinate amounts of time writing these days, stringing together uneloquent but sentiment-laden quotes and tracking the histories of mundane daily objects that are inculcated with layers and layers of meaning as they cease to be spatulas and planters and ripped jeans but become instead symbols in the story that's overwhelming my life. Erica knows I'll get 2000 words out of this, easy.

"Anything like this ever happen to Bridget Jones?" I asked Erica as I waved to her, my fingers coated with the man's blood. The man's breathing had eased and his muscles had relaxed once Erica had put the ring on his hand. "Sir, what's your name?"

"I'm Walter. What's your name?"

"Well, I'm Jacob, and this is my friend Erica."

"Jacob and Erica. You're a really good looking couple," he said as his eyelids started to bob up and down.

"Well, thank you, Walter, but she's been rejecting my advances for years. Walter, I want you to talk to us," I told him. I thought I remembered that in the case of possible head trauma, you're supposed to keep people talking. Was I right? "I'm calling the ambulance right now so people can help you."

"Walter, where were you going? Should we call your family or friends? They'll want to know where you are," Erica said as I talked with the 911 operator.

"I was going home," said Walter.

"Oh, where is your home?" she asked.

"I don't know."

"Oh…do you remember a phone number?" Erica inquired.

"I don't know."

"Hey, Walter," I interrupted, "We have an ambulance on the way. It'll be here in just a couple of minutes. So you keep your eyes open and keep talking with us, OK?"

"Jake, are we supposed to elevate his head or something? I think you're supposed to move the area that's bleeding above the heart," said Erica quietly.

"I don't know. Aren't you supposed to keep them as still as possible, in case there's a skull fracture or neck injury?" I whispered as we leaned back away from Walter's line of sight for a moment.

"Should we apply direct pressure to the wound?" she asked.

"I don't know. I don't think you'd do that if there's a skull fracture. But then again, the full weight of his head is resting right on top of the wound. God, should we raise his head to lower the pressure on the skull?"

"What are you talking about over there?" Walter asked.

"We're deciding how to cure you, darling," said Erica.

"Yeah, you ever watch *ER*? We're just like those guys," I laughed.

"Naaah, I'm OK," Walter told us, as he started to lift his head up again.

"Yeah, you're gonna be OK," I said as I pressed gently down on his chest. "But you're bleeding, so we have to keep you still and wait for the ambulance."

"What, I'm bleeding?" he asked as he felt the back of his head with his right hand. His hand re-emerged crimson and shiny underneath the corner streetlight. "Oh, well, thank you for helping me. You're a nice fellow."

Walter emphasized this "thank you" by patting me on the back of my as-yet unbloodied hand and on my knee as I squatted next to him. His ruby fingerprints lay thick on my hand, and his palm print added a certain purplish flair to the knees of my three-month-old pre-ripped blue jeans.

"And thank you, too," Walter said as he turned his eyes and slowly rotated his body toward Erica. I softly snatched his bloody hand at the wrist as he prepared to impart to her his pat of gratitude; she still clasped the hand with the wedding band.

"You're very welcome, Walter. We're just glad we could be here for you," Erica replied just before she mouthed me a "thank you" for saving her pantsuit from a bloody ruin.

Erica continued on with most of the chatting duties in an attempt to keep Walter conscious and alert. I just held his blood-stained hand and took in the scene. The clothes he was dressed in seemed to be of an 80s vintage, well-worn, but clean (before the intrusion of a few drops of blood and a couple of recent smears of street grime), pressed and even creased. Though it might have been because he was slumped on the ground, Walter seemed a size too small for all of his clothing. On our bus ride home, Erica told me he wore a watch that didn't move.

Walter's skin was loose around his presumably shrunken form. He was weathered, ruddy, but his skin appeared relatively soft, smooth and unchafed. His face was clean-shaven, though I noticed a couple of nicks on his neck, one covered by a tiny, thin bandage of toilet paper.

Less than four minutes after I got off the line with the 911 operator, a fleet of public safety vehicles converged on our location—so many I feared for the safety of the rest of the City. Two police cars, an ambulance and a fire truck came to a halt at the bus stop within 30 seconds of each other, and 14 (!!) uniformed heroes came to rescue Walter, and to relieve Erica and Jake. An EMT put a brace around

Walter's neck while another took his pulse. I briefed an ad hoc huddle of cops, EMTs and firefighters on the events of the previous five or six minutes as Erica remained with Walter.

My group broke its huddle just as EMTs elevated Walter's stretcher. I turned around just in time to hear Erica ask, "Can you guys do something about his wedding ring? It's been falling off and he really wants to keep it on." An Asian-American EMT extracted a roll of medical tape from a nearby bag and wrapped up half of Walter's ring finger. Out of the corner of my eye, I saw a couple of firemen mop up pools and splatters of blood, and pour some sort of solution over the spots, presumably to neutralize any infectious agents. It didn't occur to me until much later that I probably should have asked for a few spritzes of the stuff myself.

"He told me he was going home, but couldn't remember the address or the telephone number…probably because of a concussion, right?" I said to the assemblage. "You guys might want to find his address."

The EMT felt Walter's pockets and dug out a rubber banded wad of folded papers: about ten $1 bills, 20 bus transfer slips, some Safeway coupons and an assortment of notes written on strip club pamphlets, the sort that the touts on nearby Broadway hand out to passersby every night. He thumbed through the sheaf. "I can't find any identification in here right now. I'll have the folks at the ER take another look," declared the EMT as his colleagues pushed Walter into the back of the ambulance. "You guys did a tremendous job here. You handled it perfectly."

The bus stop on the 45 line is right across the street from my flat. I said goodnight to Erica and hugged her with my unbloodied hand. When I got inside the place, I sat down on the couch and pulled out my cell phone. I wanted to call both Gabrielle and Angeline. Because I wanted to call both, I called neither. Instead, once again, I sat down and started to type.

Last night (it's almost 3 a.m. now), it was so easy to be a good person. Believe me, there were plenty of people who literally hopped

over Walter as we approached the scene on that crowded street by that
bustling stop. People who probably accidentally kicked around his
wedding band...who might have cursed the bum when they got
home and realized they had tracked his blood onto their hardwood
floors.

I was glad we could do something good. We didn't know what
the hell we were doing—elevate or not, direct pressure or not?—but
it was so easy to do what was right.

Right now, my only agenda item in life is to do right by Angeline,
to help her—to do good—to do right by her. I'd love to be happy,
but it's so secondary for me right now. If the best thing for me to do
to help Angeline was tell her every last scrap and every last detail of
the truth about my life—though I don't believe I've deceived her—I
would do it. If, in some way, she would be best served by my lying to
her, I would do it. If I could help her by staying with her, I would do
it. If I could best aid her by getting out of her life, I would do it.

I just don't know what to do. She's starting her treatment soon,
and I don't know what to do. Other than "be there."

In this darkened kitchen office, Walter's fingerprints shine with a
mix of black, purple and red under the blue-gray glow of Microsoft
Word. Even in the faint light, I can see the darkened palm print on
my knee. I think it's time to wash my hands, and maybe throw away
the jeans.

43

Slow Dance

Angeline and I stood at the counter at a deli a few doors down from her apartment building. She conversed in Spanish with the fellow operating the meat slicer, or at least tried. God, she's freaking adorable, bad Spanish and all.

"All right, my friend, what will you have?" asked the head guy and sandwich maker after he finished with the customers preceding us.

I examined the short menu board. "I'll just go with the turkey sandwich."

"With?"

"Eeehhh, with whatever comes on it..."

"And you, my lady?"

"*Por favor...*" she began. What ensued was a Spanish monologue and interpretive dance dedicated to sandwich making—the likes of which I'd never seen before. Even I could follow the progression of extra-thin slicing, chopping, grating and condiment spreading which she so ably demonstrated. It looked delicious.

Once she had finished, I piped up. "Hold my order. I'll have what she's having!"

"No, no, no," said Angeline as she patted me on the chest. "We should get you a different one so we can split our sandwiches. Allow me..." She worked her imaginary-sandwich-making magic again. It again involved horrific Spanish and an evocative dance with a little bit of toasting, melting and julienning—plus a pinch of some sort of spice that she added by rubbing her fingers together over the imaginary sandwich in her left hand.

After watching her bravura performance, I rotated around the end of the aisle to get us some drinks. When I returned, the sandwiches were in their final stages, and I pulled out my wallet to pay. "How much for everything?" I asked.

"Oh, my friend, the lady already paid," the head guy said as he snapped open a virgin white takeout bag. He inserted the tightly wrapped sandwiches.

"Damn, you, lady! When are you going to stop doing this?" I joked as I feigned kicking at her shins.

Angeline countered with a "ha-yah" and a karate chop to my shoulder. "Don't fight it. You, Jacob, are my kept man! You are my bitch!" She grabbed the take out bag, took my arm, and did a little "We're off to see the Wizard!" sashay as she led me out of the store.

✴   ✴   ✴   ✴

"'Nob Hill…an attitude, not an address,'" I read aloud about halfway through our meal. I had found a copy of the *Nob Hill Gazette*—a 30-page "newspaper" and social register—in Angeline's kitchen and was investigating how the other half lived in San Francisco. It seemed like a non-stop progressive dinner filled with art, wine, opera openings and grande dames wearing animal print hats filled with feathers. "Geeez, I don't know anybody in here."

I scanned a few of the pages, noting the overly posed pictures and the bolded names throughout the various "articles." Eventually I ran across a few familiar names, ones which Carson bandied about from time to time. There were Tammy and Julie at the zoo benefit, and there were Rex and Delilah at the opening of the symphony.

"Hey, I think I at least know someone who knows someone in here. So, I got that going for me…which is nice."

"Don't worry," said Angeline as she mussed up my hair before going to the sink with her plate, "We'll get you in there some day."

"Nah, you're the one who needs to be in there. A few shots of you would really boost the circulation of this thing. It looks like we just need to get you the right hat."

We retired to Angeline's living room and just hung out on the couch for a while. The stereo in her living room played some relatively easy listening alt rock. She read *The New Yorker*—I should really read that thing...I hear there are some short stories in there—and I settled down with a fascinating piece on the value chain dynamics of the optical internet router industry. For half an hour, she rested her head on my stomach—I think she may have dozed off for a few minutes. Then, for half an hour, I rested my head on her stomach, reading and trying to isolate patterns in her digestive gurgling.

"Hey, Jelly, I need to get back for a conference call," I said into her abdomen. I pushed myself up. "Sooooo...I'm going to bid you a 'good afternoon' and head back."

"OK."

"So, thanks for buying me lunch, but most of all, thanks for *ordering* me lunch," I said as I hugged her and kissed her on the ear. "It was *muy* entertaining."

"As always, my pleasure," she offered as she stood up with me.

Green Day's "Time of Your Life" was playing on the stereo. I wrapped my arms around her in the junior high dance configuration. Angeline and I started swaying to the music during the second half of the song. Our first slow dance. I felt a little guilty, given the lyrics of this anthem are often misunderstood; more bitter than sweet, it's actually a song about endings. But sometimes we don't pick the soundtrack, we just dance along.

We continued our slow dance as the next song came on. The tune was "Longview," also by the three punker lads of Green Day—it must be "Twofer Tuesday" or something. In this song, the Bay Area rockers don't explore the complex world of relationships and break-ups. No, "Longview" is a loud, fast-paced ode to masturbation. Angeline smiled up at me as we rocked back and forth slowly, totally out of time to the beat; she obviously knew the song's meaning.

Angeline and I started swaying faster and faster. About a third of the way into the song, I did my manly duty and took the lead on the dance, assertively moving Angeline into good swinging position. And we swung. We danced. We dipped. I picked her up and even did the move they did in *Grease* where they flung their chicks to one side of their legs and then the other. Angeline squealed, and I danced despite the pain.

It may seem like a scene cut and pasted out of incredibly sappy works across many genres. But, please bear with me for including it; it's the first time I'd danced in...God, seven or eight months. It wasn't *really* swing music, but sometimes we don't pick the soundtrack.

44

Making the Call

Last night, Money was in town. Carson, Beef, EZ, Billy and I were going to join our visitor from NYC for the kind of night we used to enjoy quite frequently in business school: the prototypical (or stereotypical, take your pick) boys night out featuring steaks and cigars—California's anti-smoking laws be damned. We were gathering to celebrate Money's recent engagement. I thought I might be writing about that testosterone fest today.

But I'm not.

✳   ✳   ✳   ✳

At about 7:15 yesterday evening, I was in the final stages of getting dressed. My home phone rang, and I wedged the receiver between my shoulder and my chin as I buttoned my cuffs. "Hello?"

"Oh…hi, Jake…it's Angeline." This was the first time she had called me on my home line; both of us seemed to be more tied to our mobile communications capabilities. "I thought you were heading out at 6:30…"

"Ah, that's when I was going to have to pick up my friend at the airport," I told her, "But he's on the company dime, so that *schlub* can cab it into town. Whatsup? Are you getting ready for the birthday *fest-eeee-vaalll*?" She was joining three girlfriends for a little birthday celebration for one of them…

…or so I thought. "Yeah…no…yeah. I'm not going out tonight," she began. "That's actually why I'm calling. I wanted to tell you that Trevor is coming by here tonight, about eight o'clock."

"Oh."

"He heard from a mutual friend that I was sick. But he doesn't know the details…and I think I owe it to him to tell him. I don't want him to…get the full story…from somebody else," she said quietly. "We were together two years, and he was with me during an earlier health issue and I just want to—"

"Of course, of course. I totally understand," my voice smooth and understanding in spite of the acidic taste bubbling up in the back of my throat. "No, that's good. He should hear it from you directly."

"Right, that's what I thought."

"I mean, with something like the situation you're going through, it's good to have all the people you can in your corner. And he obviously cares about you a lot. I mean—*obviously*."

We both chuckled a little bit at the reference to the awkwardness of the last month—what with the breaking and entering and all. "He was *so* sorry about that. When we talked afterward, he really felt bad and was so apologetic—"

"No worries, really. Please…I don't know…I guess just tell him, 'No worries' about the whole episode." I wondered if she'd been in contact with him since that break in and confrontation a few days before New Years. I wondered if he'd been calling her, or if she'd been calling him, since that profoundly stupid, insanely idiotic, utterly brave and entirely magnificent break-in. "So, Jelly, have you and Trevor…been talking much—"

"Oh, no. We haven't talked since that night. He just heard from a friend."

"Right. Right."

"So."

"So."

"So, have a good time with your friends tonight, and tell them I said 'Hi'. Tell Carson that he needs to learn some new moves if he wants to keep up with you in the swinging department. And say 'Hi' to your visitor. This 'Money' sounds like a nice fellow," she said.

"Yeah, he'll be here a week. Maybe you'll get to meet him. He just got…" I paused for a split second, "…a new co-op in Manhattan. I hear it's beautiful. I think he could use some decorating ideas."

"All right. Hopefully we can do that. So, I guess that's—"

"Hey, Jelly?"

"Yes?"

"You know I just want you to do whatever it takes to make your-self healthy and well, right? You know that. I mean, that's all you should be doing: everything necessary to make yourself healthy and well. Y'know what I mean?"

"Yes."

"Good. I just want...I mean, have a good night," I told her.

"Sure, sure. We're still on to meet up for Saturday, right?"

This was Thursday evening, and my Friday would involve a series of conference calls and a Herculean exertion to labor though several of the large pillars of undone work so that they could be moved away from my kitchen table/desk. I had done virtually no paid work since the New Year, and the paper pillars and pyramids of tasks undone were indeed enormous.

"Saturday...definitely...yes," I responded.

"Well, then, I'll miss you tonight. Have a good time with your friends."

"You, too. I mean, *I'll miss you, too.* Have a great time tonight, Angeline. Bye." The hollowness and inappropriateness of my part-ing words struck me immediately. *"Have a great night" while you're telling Trevor about your cancer. Fantastic, Jake. You stupid...*

I don't know if I'd ever experienced a "cold sweat" in my life until that very moment. I thought the cold sweat might have been some literary device used by writers of detective stories, or a cinematic con-trivance used to illustrate the extreme stress of kids taking the SATs in some John Hughes movie or something. But there I was, alone, in some of my finest hitting the town regalia and accoutrements, sweat-ing like one of the devotees of the bikram yoga studios that dot the Marina.

The acid—the bile or whatever it was—that had been gurgling up my throat had turned my mouth into a chemical wasteland. My tongue tasted like a combination of jabanero peppers and that fluo-ride solution dental assistants used to dab on my molars and tongue with extra long Q-tips when I was a kid. I had a difficult time taking in a breath for the extremely sour taste which accompanied each inhale.

I sat down at my desk—it was either that or double over from dizziness. My elbows rested on a stack of articles I had printed out over the last three or four days. Journal articles on cancers of the reproductive system. Stapled. Sorted. Highlighted. Dog-eared. Book marked. I looked over at the recipe for chicken soup—the Jewish remedy for everything—that I had found on the 'Net and printed out a few hours before. I had never made chicken soup before, but I planned on cooking some for Angeline, something mild she could eat in case her treatments made her nauseous. Chicken soup. My cure-all for her. My wonderful, small, half-in, half-out, pathetic demonstration of my healing powers.

As I sat at the desk, I thought aloud. I don't mean I talked to myself, I mean that my breathing was labored, and I grunted and—to be honest—whimpered periodically. My toes tapped incessantly on the linoleum minute after minute.

I got up from the desk and paced around the kitchen, searching out some futile, stupid gesture I could commit at that moment to symbolize how I felt. The kitchen's white walls seemed particularly inviting. I had never punched a wall before, but I was sure the walls of this circa 1908 dwelling would give way to my fist. The towers of work-in-process surrounding my desk seemed to virtually invite me to kick them and send their contents showering all over the room, a blizzard of consulting minutiae, a flurry of neat and clean 2-by-2 matrices and strategic frameworks.

I settled on smacking the roll of paper towels that rested on the edge of the counter next to the sink. The roll was held by a stainless steel Williams-Sonoma dispenser, which cut my hand upon contact and then shattered into its component pieces when it hit the doorframe on the opposite side of the room. My Bounty kept rolling—or I should say unrolling—through the dining room and living room until its cardboard core lay bare near the couch.

At that moment, I wished for five seconds I could change the point of view for my whole life story. Actually, just for the last few months. Couldn't I just be the omniscient narrator for five measly

seconds? Couldn't I see, just once, the facial expression of the person
on the other end of the telephone line with me? Couldn't I hear, just
one time, the italicized thoughts which run through someone's brain
during the half second pauses in conversations? Couldn't I just once
precisely gauge the tensile strength of the cables that bind all of us in
this narrative together and accurately measure the height and thick-
ness and structural integrity of the walls that keep us apart?

I knew so very little of the facts dominating my life—or the lives
of people joined with my life or bordering my life or whatever you
might want to say. I didn't know anything. I could barely keep track
of my own emotions from minute to minute, and I realized I possessed only the smallest speck of understanding of other's feelings.

At the beginning of the month, I *decided*—of course, weighing all
of the known variables and projecting future scenarios from just a
smattering of data points, as is my wont—that Angeline and I had
real possibilities as a couple. Of course, I also *decided* that there was
a lot more I needed to test, figure out, ascertain and otherwise divine
about her and about us. I just wanted to know.

And I definitely still don't know. Does anyone ever really *know*?
I don't know. Maybe *someone* knows. Maybe someone *knows*.
Maybe there's someone with no doubt, no hesitation.

I took a sip of water from the faucet, and then I dialed.

"Hello?" said Angeline, almost 15 minutes after we said goodbye.

"Hi," I responded. I hadn't checked my watch and I didn't have
any idea if Trevor was over at Angeline's apartment yet, but I wasn't
going to ask. "I just wanted to say…I'm not sure if you knew what I
meant when I said I wanted you to do everything necessary to make
yourself 'healthy and well.'"

"Yes?"

"I wanted you to know I can do anything you need me to do—
I'm not going anywhere. I also wanted you to know that if you think
you made a mistake a few months ago—if you have a flicker of a
thought that you wish you could undo things you did—I would
understand. You and Trevor have so much history…you know each
other so well…if you decide he's the best person to support you
through this, I would understand. We're so new, and I realize even we

don't know what we have, or what we might have. I can be your friend, and just your friend, if you need me to be that, and I promise, I will be."

On the other end of the line, I heard Angeline sniffle. "Thank you. I understand why you said that. There are reasons Trevor and I aren't together beyond all of this with you and me. But thank you for calling back. It actually...means a lot that you called," she said softly.

"You know how important you are to me." I realized my words were probably watered down substitutes for what I should have said.

"I know. And you're so important to me," she said. "You're right, I need to do everything I can to get better. So other than getting healthy, I'm not going to worry about any life altering decisions, right now. I don't know if after the last few months, *either of us* is ready to make any huge decisions. There's been a lot of excitement...just a lot of huge stuff thrown at us," she laughed.

"Yeah, some things much huger than others, Jelly. You know I just—"

"I know," she said. "I also know that you should get going, and I *really* know I should get going."

"OK. Have a...have a good night. Bye."

"OK. Goodbye."

I didn't know if it was my better instincts or my weaker instincts that caused me to call Angeline back. I might never know.

I re-brushed my teeth, changed my undershirt, and left the flat. I was glad I got the chance to congratulate Nick on his engagement for the second time, and I was particularly exultant that I had to the opportunity to witness Carson lose at credit card roulette.

45

Three

Late Saturday morning, Angeline and I went to the gym to build up a good appetite for our early afternoon brunch. Titan Fitness bulged with sweating venture capitalists, technology gurus, housewives, househusbands and a smattering of the familiar quasis, pseudos and semis. We were only just over three weeks into the New Year, and most fitness-oriented resolutions were still in full effect.

"What are you today?" asked Angeline. "Arms, legs, chest…"

"Legs today. A gimp's job is never done."

"Legs…good. Let's do it," she said as she took off her fleece.

We had worked out together four times since the New Year. I didn't know the nuances of her disease, but it seemed to me a good thing that she was staying active. Plus, it always provided her a fantastic opportunity to show off her midriff. She would be commencing her treatment in a matter of days; I wondered how it would affect her and if we would be going to the gym together many more times.

Angeline and I started with leg curls, a critical part of my rehab routine for almost six months. Three sets of 12, 10 and 8 reps, pushing the peg two notches further down on the weight stack each time. Just a few months before, the weights I put up during my sets of leg curls wouldn't have stood up in a kindergartner's weight-lifting contest. Now, the deep, resonant "clang" of the weights on the last set bore testament to the full healing of my repaired joint.

"I remember when I had to *raise* the weight when we shared a machine," joked Angeline as we traded positions. She lowered the poundage by moving the metallic peg about halfway back up the weight stack and then pinched my cheek. "Look at you. You're so big and strong. I'm so proud of you!" she exclaimed in a voice befitting the most effervescent of preschool teachers.

"Well, thanks, but it was just a ploy all along. To get the hottie to feel sorry for the poor convalescing patient."

"And did you find one?"

"I don't know. It's kind of hard to tell who to go for in this gym. Too many of the wives take off their big diamond rings."

"We have to work on your targeting skills," Angeline grunted as she completed her last rep.

Leg extensions were the next stop on the rehab circuit. This exercise was excruciatingly painful for me. Both my doctor and my physical therapist had told me, "Every patient heals in his own way and at his own pace." Evidently, it was going to take a while longer to build up the strength and smoothness of motion for this type of exertion, even with my bionic anatomy—my new anterior cruciate ligament, created from a filet of my own patellar tendon, anchored by wires and bone screws to holes drilled in my tibia and fibula. Three painful sets of lifting and jaw clenching left both my patella and my mandible throbbing.

"Hey, I'll be back in a sec," said Angeline as she finished her last set on the leg extension machine.

"All right, I'll be right here, pressing away."

The next routine included three sets on the leg press, the exercise by which I really gauged my recovery. During my first couple of months of rehab, this apparatus was without fail the site of an exercise in extreme masochism. Over the next several weeks, however, the pain had diminished dramatically and the stacks of weight had grown much more prodigious. I knocked out one smooth easy set, and knew I could boost the weight way up there on the next one.

"Hey there," said Angeline as she returned, a bottle of red Gatorade in either hand. She offered me one. "Here. For a toast."

"A toast to what?" I asked as I extended my bottle toward hers.

"To our third anniversary. We met right back here, in this corner, three months ago *today*."

"Wow, three months. You're right! Happy Anniversary then!" I said as I chinked my PET bottle against hers. We drank of our cocktail of electrolytes, artificial flavors and artificial colors, smiling and winking at each other over the plastic bottles. We both finished our gulps and smiled again, the effect on her face—maybe mine, too—amplified by a cherry red Gatorade mustache.

Three months. It was really hard to believe that it had only been three months. Increments like days and weeks and months seemed like inadequate units of measurement lately. I'd lost track of the time.

46

The Score

Angeline and Carson were chatting about football, much to my amusement.

"It's sort of an 'irresistible force' meets 'immovable object'-kind of thing. The Raiders are near the top in almost every offensive category, but the Buccaneers probably have the toughest defense in the league."

"Uh-huh."

"I mean the Raiders have Jerry Rice and Tim Brown at receiver—both future Hall of Famers—and Rich Gannon at QB...and that guy's the Most Valuable Player of the NFL this year."

"So that's good, right?"

"Of course, but you see Tampa Bay has Jon Gruden coaching them, and he was the Raiders coach until this year. So, he's probably come up with some great game plan to exploit Oakland's weaknesses, because he knows them better than anyone else."

"Wow," replied Carson.

Angeline's football tutorial helped the host of the Super Bowl party get up to speed fairly quickly. Her research sessions on Google over the previous few days had made her quite the expert on all things Raider. While she ran the special education session for Carson, I ate. A lot.

Even though his knowledge of football equaled that of your average Laotian schoolgirl, Carson did succeed in laying out quite an elaborate spread for this gathering. Angeline and I were planning on hitting the party at Billy and EZ's for the second half, but I had no doubt that the sumptuous buffet in front of me would provide ample opportunity to even the score with Carson. Nearly five months after the short-changing in Vegas, I would have my recompense, and Carson would have his comeuppance. My vengeance would be complete, my *vendetta—finito.*

The cracked crab provided the swiftest means to complete my task. I had downed a drift net's worth by the end of the first quarter. And, I polished off another plate near the beginning of the second as I watched "highlights" of the Buccaneers' woeful early history, when they were clad in uniforms that captured all the possible hues of orange—tangerine, mandarin, apricot and even peach.

Unfortunately, the 2003 edition of the Bucs—now clad in a manly deep vermillion—were opening up a Costco-sized can of "Whoop Ass" on the Raiders as I went back for a final run at the buffet. But, *again* unfortunately, the last of the crab had been polished off.

"Hey, Carson. Is there any more of the cracked crab?" I asked as the host passed by.

"Isn't that stuff great? I get it at this little Chinese market and the guys there have these spices that…"

"Yeah…right…cool…I'll have to get the recipe. Just wanted to see if there was a little more."

"Well, I have a couple of containers in the fridge, but we have a bunch of new people coming over for the second half. And you know, when Beef is in the house, you gotta have plenty stocked up," he replied with a wink. "Have some of the cheese. It's great. There's this little place on Polk Street…"

"Thanks. It's cool. I should probably keep a little room in my stomach for pork rinds at Billy and EZ's, anyway."

So close. Drat…foiled again. Another day, Carson, another day.

As the first half wound to a close, Angeline and I made the rounds, receiving mock kisses aplenty as we bid the other attendees goodbye. By the way, this was a sacrilege—there should be *no* kissing at Super Bowl parties.

We climbed the hillside of Pacific Heights to get back to my car. I aimed the Probe straight up Broadway and we motored toward Telegraph Hill. We started up Lombard Street, but as we neared our second half party destination, Angeline tapped me on the arm.

"Do you mind if we make a quick detour?" she asked.

Requests like that from a gorgeous woman send the male mind into overdrive. "Sure, where did you have in mind?"

"How about up to Coit Tower?" she said as she pointed up the road. Coit Tower was at the terminus of Lombard Street, just three blocks ahead of us.

"Sure thing. Let's go," I answered as I sped past Billy and EZ's house and looked longingly in the rear view mirror at the perfect parking spot right in front.

A minute later we pulled into a spot at the nearly deserted Coit Tower. Usually teeming with tourists, it was quiet and serene during the Super Bowl.

"Put the game on the radio," she suggested as we started to get out of the Probe. We sat down on the nose of the car and Angeline reached into her large coat pockets. "Y'see, I packed us a little picnic…"

From one pocket she pulled two beers and from the other a couple of plastic forks and a small Tupperware container with more of Carson's cracked crab. "I didn't get to have any crab at the party and I heard it was *delicious*. You don't think he'll mind that I took a little, do you?"

"Of course not," I assured her.

"Good," she replied as she handed me the Tupperware, slid off the front of the car and moved around toward the passenger-side wheel. Angeline wedged the beer caps underneath the Probe's hubcaps and popped both off at once. *Is there no end to this woman's talents? It's positively mind-boggling.*

We were encamped in an ideal spot for our impromptu picnic. Across the bay to our east, was Oakland, where fleets of cars would probably burn tonight, win or lose. Directly in front of us, Alcatraz. To our left, at the extreme western edge of the continent, lay the Golden Gate and, of course, Vista Point.

She offered up some crab to me, but I insisted she partake first. "I already had a little bit back at Carson's; you go ahead." While we sipped our beers, we talked a little about our plans for next week. We talked a whole lot about football as the Super Bowl play-by-play streamed out from the car stereo speakers behind us. She seemed to have an insatiable appetite for the most arcane football knowledge.

The drubbing continued as the Buccaneers ran up the score. The Super Bowl meant that January was near its end, and we probably should have been talking about what February and March and April may be like. Those months are on my mind a lot. But that may be a conversation for other days.

"Here. I'm stuffed. I insist...you need to polish this off so we can go catch the fourth quarter," Angeline said as she loaded up a large last forkful of crab and moved it toward my mouth. I took the last helping of the gourmet fare, a final serving that evened the score.

"Yummmm. Thanks, that *is* delicious," I said after I swallowed.

"Where do you think he gets it?" she inquired.

"At a great Chinese grocery. I know the place. We should really go by there sometime," I suggested as I opened the car door for her.

"We really should. And Jake, you'll return the Tupperware to Carson for me, won't you?"

"Of course. After this great picnic, I owe him."

47

Driving
and Parking

I hadn't pulled out my golf clubs in five months. My last visit to
the driving range at China Basin had almost earned me a lifetime ban. I threw the sticks in the hatchback of the Big Red Probe
and then smacked the dust off the "McKay & Associates/Winter
Retreat 1994/Golf Outing/Scottsdale, AZ" travel bag that had covered the clubs for almost half a year. After wadding up the duffle-like
travel bag—a reminder of times both fancier and schmancier—and
tossing it into the back seat, I backed out of the garage and drove
across town to the driving range.

Three of us were gathering at China Basin on this fine Monday
to mark a couple of very important milestones. After six months,
Billy was graduating from the Leisure Circuit, moving on to the
strange and crazy world where people receive checks twice monthly in
exchange for work they carry out for the benefit of some sort of company. How exotic. We were also initiating a new member of the
Leisure Circuit. After three years with the same firm—a mind-blow-
ingly long tenure—Beef was now dipping his toe into the world
where we rarely get dressed before noon and have to ration our stolen
office supplies for years. I was looking forward to passing on my
storehouses of knowledge to my good friend.

"JT, we're looking forward to a goooood show today," Billy
laughed as I plopped my clubs behind the emerald green faux turf hit-

ting surface. "I told Beef about your awesome display of athletic prowess a few months ago, J Train."

"Don't worry, JT. I believe in you," said Beef as he donned his old hockey helmet before accelerating his Big Bertha through a 300-yard slicing drive. "Jus' show us wha' u ga'," he said through his rubber mouth guard while teeing up is next range ball.

If I remembered my driving range habits correctly, I usually started by swinging through a few nice, easy chip shots with my pitching wedge. Since that particular wedge had been decapitated and remained unhealed, I pulled out the trusty 5-iron from my basic array of clubs.

"Ten bucks says he whiffs or bashes it into the metal divider," said Billy.

"C'mon, you gotta give me some odds on that one. That's not a straight up bet," retorted Beef through his Plexiglas face protector.

"Take the bet," I said without looking up as I addressed the ball. I waggled a moment, wound up, transferred my weight from my nature-made right knee to my scientifically-regenerated left, uncoiled my trunk and hips and smacked the little white range ball 185 yards in the air, straight and true.

"JTeeeeee!" Beef bellowed as he snatched the ten from Billy's hand.

"Taaaasste it, punky!" I smiled and growled in Billy's general direction. Beef hopped over the metal divider to knock fists, his newly acquired $10 bill clenched within. I quickly teed up the next small white recipient of my perfectly reconstructed golf swing. "JT is back. It's all good, all the time, my friends." I swung.

Crik-fwam!

✳   ✳   ✳   ✳

Where five months ago I displayed such an impressive consistency in my awfulness, on this day I was bad in just so many different ways it was astounding. It was a regular cavalcade of crappy hacks out there. That some shots were perfect—straight and true—might just have been due to the law of averages. A myriad of imperfections canceling each other out to deliver a near perfect result—every once in a while.

It served as a reminder that even before I had my knee for an excuse, I had absolutely no game at all.

After enjoying one beer in the afternoon sun with my fellow sportsmen and slackers, I cloistered myself at the Grove for several hours to write a few things. As soon as I finished tapping out some tracts about visits to the gym and the driving range, I cleaned up bit, changed shirts and drove across town to Angeline's apartment.

I dialed her number on my cell, "Yo!"

"Yo, yourself!" she replied before hanging up. Thirty seconds later she was skipping down the front steps of her apartment building.

"Yo!" she smiled as she plopped down into the passenger-side seat.

"Yo, yourself," I said before I kissed her.

I sped—yes, at times the Probe can actually *speed*—south. We were driving to Palo Alto, about 35 miles south of San Francisco on the Peninsula. I had been invited by a PR firm I'd worked with in the past to be their guest at a technology industry panel discussion. There would be a lot of crudités being nibbled, an abundance of nobs trying to hob, and a virtual swarm of business cards fluttering about trying to find new Rolodexes to call home. It would almost be a living time capsule, a theme park of sorts. We could call it "Silicon Valley World"—the magical land where it will be 1999 forever. The place where Webvan delivers a bountiful harvest to our doors each week and E-Toys sends along the latest Hotwheels, Play Doh playsets, Barbies and Easy Bake Ovens just as our children are tuning out yesterday's amusements.

The PR firm had asked me to shoot the breeze with some of their clients before and after the main presentations. "Just talk about some of the new ideas you've been generating. You know, the stuff you've been working on recently. They'll love it," said the PR exec. "New ideas", eh? I wasn't sure I'd been creating any; I thought I'd just been writing about orgies of organic soy products. And, of course, about my karaoke strategies. Oh well, I guess it's all in the eye of the beholder. Anyway, I told the firm I could only come down if I could bring a guest.

"So, I read the last *week's* worth of *The Wall Street Journal* today. And I even found some of those techno-babble bulletins that you love so much and read a couple of those," said Angeline. "I'm going to be ready."

"Ugh. If you can wade through all of that stuff, you must really be committed," I said. "Maybe we can get you in on the panel discussion."

"I have ideas aplenty. Just let me at 'em," she said.

It took us almost an hour through rush hour traffic to reach our destination; three years before, it might have taken twice that on a *good* day. The hotel ballroom teemed with investors and engineers. I could feel the enthusiasm that sloshed through the room, but I couldn't tell if this was the rearguard of a powerful movement that would soon be fighting its way back to victory, or more like the 1885 convention of grizzled, hardscrabble gray-clad Civil War veterans, remnants of an era that would never rise again.

"Jake, over here!" the PR exec yelled from about 40 feet away. He waved us over toward two seats saved at a table of ten currently populated with eight. When we arrived, he gave me a two-handed shake—maybe the secret handshake in the PR industry? "Here, let me introduce you to everyone." I had heard of half of the executives seated at the table, all CEOs or Chief Technology Officers of firms in the Valley. I introduced everyone to Angeline; she, too, received a lovely two-handed shake from our host.

The gray-haired fellow next to me nudged me. "I read your piece on the transformation in health care diagnostics. I really agree with what you wrote. We do cardiac pacing implants—subcutaneous defibrillators and such. Do you see any of the same dynamics going on in our industry?"

I started to answer even though I couldn't remember what exactly my health care article had been about and despite the fact I knew virtually nothing about cardiac implants. I recalled seeing something on PBS a few years before about the future of implant technologies and weaved the threads into the argument of the article I wrote, which was starting to drift back into my mind in bits and pieces. I wrote it seven months earlier, a long time ago—even before I started this little collection of anecdotes.

As dinner was served, we continued our little round table discussion in the corner of the ballroom. We talked about artificial bone implants, nanotechnology, gene therapy, optical data storage and biometric security tools. I couldn't wipe the smile off of my face during the conversation, and not just because of the absurdity the scene—these C-level corporate officers listening to a guy who had earned a grand total of $420 during the first four weeks of 2003. I also smiled because I loved the fact I got to look over at Angeline every few seconds. She was kicking ass in her discussions with the CEO seated next to her…I think they even came up with a few new product ideas.

"So, Jake, what about the data networking arena? I mean, with the current trends in storage area networks and—

"Whoa. I drove all the way down here so I could listen to *you guys*. You folks are the doers. I want to hear what you're up to. I'm just a guy who sits in his sweatpants all day and works out of a kitchen office in Cow Hollow," I told them, stirring a burst of laughter from our entire table.

Of course, I lied. I never wear sweatpants.

Angeline and I drove back to the City at about 9 p.m. The trip up the sylvan path of Interstate 280 took only 30 minutes at this time of night. At times, it seemed as if we were the only ones on the road.

The Probe squeaked to a halt in front of Angeline's building at about 9:30. We already knew we were going to part company here. We each had 6 a.m. flights out of different airports—hers a trip back to see her family in between rounds of her treatment, mine a two-day trip up to Seattle for a little more corporate strategizing and brainstorming. We both had to pack, get to sleep and get out of our houses by about 4 a.m.

"So."

"So."

"Yeah."

"Yeah."

We both leaned in for our kiss good night, which was interrupted all too soon as we heard a family with young children approach the car. We broke off the embrace and just contented ourselves with listening to the radio for a few moments. She and I approached each other for our re-kiss and were again cut short by a cadre of folks strolling the sidewalk. We were very close to a streetlight, and the interior of the car was lit up almost as if it were daytime.

"I've never seen your street so busy. What…is there some sort of carnival around here or something?" I asked her as a third posse of people moseyed by.

"They're so intrusive," said Angeline. "Don't these people know we want to make out?"

Light bulb. "Uh, I think I may have a solution," I said, already stretching into the backseat of the Probe. I returned with the almost dust-free McKay & Associates golf travel bag. "This can give us some privacy."

"What are you—?"

I unfurled the bag and spread it out above us in its full duffleness. We stared at each other in almost complete darkness, our nylon retreat virtually impervious to the intense glare of the nearby streetlight. Even though the citizens of the world continued walking by and chatting, we were totally separated from them.

Within our cocoon, our kiss recommenced, with much more urgency and intensity than I anticipated. We immediately both began to sweat as the heat built up under the layers of synthetic fibers and padding. I felt it on her forehead, cheeks, neck and stomach. I wanted to feel her heart pound. I kissed all the way down her neck to her collarbone and beyond to her chest, pausing there a moment to let my sweaty forehead feel a few beats.

Such urgency, yet such total comfort. I closed my eyes for a moment, perhaps yielding a bit to the relaxing halcyon effect brought on by the building heat. After a few minutes of kissing, our cocoon stopped writhing. We just looked at each other again in the darkness for another minute or so, each of us dabbing the beads of sweat on the other's face. I then lifted up the large duffel and placed it again in the back seat. The bracing feeling of cold late-January air struck both of us immediately, as did the bright buzzing streetlight above us. We squinted for the few seconds it took her to gather her belongings.

Angeline and I grinned at each other, indulged ourselves with one final peck—and then another final peck—and then said goodbye.

48

Circle

Last Thursday, the morning started out fantastically. I took part in an excellent meeting in the City. The confab was about nothing, really, and little was accomplished, but you could have lit up a medium-sized town with the energy in the room. Afterward, a gay gentleman complimented me on the outfit I was wearing. Definitely a first—the flattery put me in an even better mood.

I got into the Probe, sparkling red on the outside and freshly vacuumed and pine scented on the inside. Checking my watch as I departed the bloc of modern and minimalist live-work lofts in SOMA, I knew I had plenty of time to get to the airport.

Traffic on the Bay Bridge connecting San Francisco and Oakland was light. The only brake taps were due to the presence of the work crews, cadres of which had occupied the bridge during my entire tenure in San Francisco. One wonders if the work will ever end.

Traffic sped southward through Oakland. Not a delay in sight; I would get there even sooner than I had originally expected. As I pulled into the entrance of the airport, my cell phone buzzed to life on the seat next to me. Angeline's caller ID lit up the LCD screen.

"Hey there!" I said.

"Hi."

"So, how the time with the fam going?"

"It's been really nice. My brother and sister came in, too. It's been great to see everyone together…"

"Oh, before I forget: are you joining us for dinner on Monday night?"

"Jake," she said quietly, "Are you sitting down?" I could have written the rest of the chapter in that instant.

"Yes, I'm sitting," I answered as I swerved back into my lane to avoid a semi in the next.

"Jake, I'm engaged," Angeline uttered softly.

I was surprised by my lack of surprise at the pronouncement. Immediately, twenty possible responses leapt to the verbal processing center of my brain. The speechwriters in my subconscious must have been working overtime during my sleeping hours—all of it was right there, queued up in my brain's teleprompter.

One part of me wanted to say: *You can't. I can still hear the thud from when you hit me in the heart the night you and I sat together in the park with the moon. It still reverberates through me. And I know it reverberates through* you.

Another part of me wanted to ask her: *Have you really forgotten our time in the cocoon so quickly? Hiding from the people and the harsh light from the streetlamp? I know you didn't want to leave it. I know you wanted to stay inside with me.*

Another part of me wanted to declare: *We need to dance again. We didn't have near enough time just to spin around and dip and jump. I know you want to dance again.*

I wanted to tell her that she deserved to be fought over. I wanted to tell her so much more. I still wanted to *ask* her so much more.

Instead, I picked the simplest response. Angeline had experienced more than her share of drama in her life recently, and she deserved to have at least a few peaceful moments. Or maybe I was spent and exhausted. Or maybe I didn't think anything on the teleprompter was particularly profound.

"Angeline, I'm really happy for you. I mean it," I told her. It was true, as were all of the italicized thoughts I recounted above.

"Thank you. I have a ring and everything," she said. She sniffled and then emitted a small laugh. "I'm sorry it's such a surprise. I didn't want to—"

"No, no. I mean it: you deserve everything, you deserve *everything!*" I said as I began to drive around the circle at the Oakland Airport. I was joined by many other drivers who instead of parking, chose to navigate the circuit slowly until their guest or loved ones appeared on the sidewalk outside the airport. "So...when did this all happen?"

"Trevor called me the day I arrived home. He flew out the next day..." she began, very coolly, almost in a rehearsed manner. I urged her to tell me details, even though I really didn't want to hear them, and she shared some. I allowed myself to feel no stings from anything she said. Instead, I chose only to feel joy for them. I thought about Trevor: *You brave, ballsy bastard. You are a freaking man among men. Good luck.* I kept circling

I was a little surprised when we began to reminisce about some of the times we spent together. Her voice remained cool, a little weary and—again—well rehearsed. We discussed our little scrapbook of anecdotes quickly, but we discussed them, almost like they transpired years ago instead of in weeks and months just past. I kept circling.

And then I said, "Angeline. I still want to be a help to you in any way I can. I care about you so much, and that's not going to change. I meant it when I said that I can be your friend. I can be a good friend to you."

"No," she sniffled, "We can't do that."

"Why not?" I asked, allowing the first tiny trace of bitterness to enter my mouth. "Did he say we can't?"

"No, I'm saying we can't," Angeline replied. My eyes stung immediately, but I held back any tears. I had learned some techniques for stemming the tide over the last couple of months.

"Please tell me why." I wanted to be a friend to her, and help her, but I don't know why I pressed her. Did I want to prove what I said to myself, when I plucked a couple of kernels of decisiveness out of acres and acres of fear and indecision and "I don't knows"?

For the first time she changed her tone, breaking from the rehearsed cadence and cold timbre. "Oh, Jake. You have to understand. You have to. I need to get you out of my head. I have a very busy life right now, and I can't be thinking about anything but what's right in front of me. I have to get healthy. I have to try to live—to beat cancer. I have enough 'ifs' in my life right now. I don't want to have any 'what ifs.' Don't you understand?"

"I do." I did. Nothing scared me more than being 40, 50, 60 years old and having a brain echoing with "what ifs?". She shared a little more with me, but I think I might keep that bit for myself, the only significant sentences I haven't shared with you over the last six months. I kept circling.

But I knew the circling had to come to an end. "I just wanted to tell you how much you, and my experiences with you have affected me. It was just a short time, but you really will be with me forever. I think I might just keep you in my head, if you don't mind."

She laughed. I continued.

"I want you to know that I think you did the very best thing you could do. I only want to see you happy. But I won't try to see you. I understand everything you've said." I applied the brakes and put the car in park. "I just want to say, you're an amazing woman, and you're going to be an amazing woman for a long time. I've seen a strength in you that I don't think even you know about. I drew on it. And I just wanted to thank you for that."

I cracked open my car door and undid my seat belt. "So, I guess we'll say goodbye now," I whispered as I got out of my car.

"Goodbye, Jake."

I flipped my cell phone closed and walked around my car. "Hi, Dad. Happy Birthday," I said as I immediately hugged him. My sister and I had flown him west for his 60th birthday; she and her fiancé were joining us up in Lake Tahoe in four hours. I held on to the hug a second or two longer than usual, as the one tear I would shed that day streamed out of my eye and onto his navy blue jacket. I gave my father a hearty slap on the back to disperse the tear, and picked up his suitcase. "Welcome to California."

Have I told you the full story? I have, to the extent that I know it. As I drove with my father through Oakland, we joked about the coverage of '77 El Caminos and '82 Caprice Classics ignited after the Raiders' loss in the Super Bowl last Sunday, just four days before. But my mind pondered how little we know about our own lives at times.

The last six months have shown me how amazing and incomprehensible life can be, how utterly unpredictable.

Dad and I discussed the chances of our Indianapolis Colts making the Super Bowl next year (and the possibility of car burning in Indy if they did), but I still contemplated the conversation I had concluded just minutes before. Was I just a speed bump in the relationship of Angeline and Trevor? Or, were there other possibilities that just weren't allowed to develop and evolve? Was I just an annoyance, a person getting involved where I didn't belong? Or did I end up doing something with some trace of right, with some measure of good? I don't know. And only God knows how long I'll analyze these last few months.

I know the hints and the clues—I've seen them, too. I know the possible interpretations of the multiple subtexts. Friend—and I truly hope I can call you that after the last six months we've spent together—I wrote all of the lines that you've been reading between. If I were the omniscient narrator, there would be no subtext and no interpretation, would there? But maybe that's what makes life interesting.

In the end, I don't know if I tapped out a love story of almost 3,000 paragraphs, or one of 1,500 paragraphs, or one of just several hundred words. I *do* know I indeed wrote about a love story—I just don't know if I wrote about one, two, or three. I may never know, because I'm the most fallible of narrators.

At that moment, all I knew was that the conversation my dad and I were having had moved on to the upcoming NCAA Basketball Tournament. Our Indiana Hoosiers had made a valiant run at the highest prize the previous year, when they reached the final game and *almost* eked out a victory. Did they stand a chance this time?

I don't know.

49

Why

This morning the Space Shuttle Columbia disintegrated as it tried to complete the final 3,000 miles of its 10 million mile journey.

Late last night, we arrived back in San Francisco from Lake Tahoe. Early this morning, my father, my sister and her fiancé drove out to Napa County to spend a day and a half in wine country, but I stayed behind because I have an extraordinary number of tasks to complete for work and around the house. I poured myself a bowl of cereal, switched on the TV, and immediately realized I would be accomplishing very few of my tasks today.

Early in the day, experts were saying that they believe the shuttle's breakup started over the skies of California. By the time Columbia reached Texas, pieces of the superstructure were falling off and lighting up like shooting stars in the pastel morning sky. Almost immediately, television coverage showed Texans examining shuttle remnants that had fallen into their yards or onto their farms.

A few hours later, one of the networks broadcast footage from Columbia's liftoff two weeks before. It depicted some foreign object—maybe ice, maybe insulating foam—striking the leading edge of the shuttle's wing. A few commentators and former astronauts began to speculate that damage to the craft's thermal tiles caused by that impact may have contributed to the accident. Gaps between the ceramic, heat-dispersing tiles can leave the shuttle's aluminum frame and delicate electronics unprotected from the massive heat of re-entry.

Writing about this seems very strange to me. But the two rules I've had since I started writing again after that night in LA are that I should write what I feel, and I should never delete anything.

✳   ✳   ✳   ✳

I was in the fifth grade when the Space Shuttle Columbia took off from Cape Canaveral on its first mission. Millions of school children across the country watched the takeoff on televisions wheeled into their classrooms by legions of audiovisual department professionals. It sure beat another filmstrip.

Ms. Sweet, my teacher, had prepared our class for this event weeks before by having us all compose reports on various aspects of the shuttle and the space program in general. Some kids were assigned to write the biographies of America's newest heroes, shuttle astronauts John Young and Robert Crippen. Others were asked to write about other prominent astronauts, and therefore dutifully paraphrased the encyclopedia entries of people like Neil Armstrong, John Glenn and Indiana's own Virgil "Gus" Grissom. Some kids wrote about subjects like gravity, the planets, the sun, the moon, the stars, etc. Others were asked to examine the effects of weightlessness and the food astronauts eat in space. Ms. Sweet asked me to write about the shuttle's protective heat tiles.

I had wanted to profile one of the swashbuckling astronauts, but obeyed Ms. Sweet's dictate because I was in love with her and looked forward to engaging her in yet another intellectual exchange. She was a fashion plate of the styles that bridged the 70s and 80s, frequently sporting small scarves tied around her neck—similar to the kind stewardesses used to wear. Ms. Sweet also had the most exquisite blackboard style. Her *click tap swoosh* routines were unparalleled, and the sound of her writing on the chalkboard gave me chills. I don't think her masterfully handled chalks emitted a screech all year.

Eager to please Ms. Sweet, I investigated the shuttle's thermal tiles to the best of my ability. I used a microfiche machine for the first time at the public library, employing a pile of dimes from my ceramic basketball bank to obtain newspaper and magazine articles from the machine's chemically driven printing mechanism.

The tiles, I read, were marvels of modern engineering. They were composed of a silicon-based ceramic that could resist heat in excess of 3000 degrees Fahrenheit. The material was extraordinarily light-weight; with 28,000 of them necessary to cover the craft's surface, Columbia could not have taken off if the tiles were composed of a heavier material.

But I also read the silicon material was very fragile, easily shat-tered. Losing several dozen strategically placed tiles within Colum-bia's mosaic could cause the craft to burn up upon re-entry. High on acetone fumes from the microfiche printer, I was horrified when I saw the picture of the shuttle atop its 747 piggyback carrier, stripped naked in places of its heat-dissipating tiles. I read that Columbia had lost 40% of its most critical tiles during the comparatively mild trip between California and Cape Canaveral. The shuttle carried no machines for creating new tiles, and no robot for replacing lost tiles in the vacuum of space. How could the system possibly stand up to the trials of takeoff and re-entry?

I wrote my report, stopping just short of calling for a suspension of all shuttle flights three days before the first flight of Columbia. I turned the paper in, but knew there were a lot of questions I wanted to ask Ms. Sweet when we discussed the mission later in the week.

✳   ✳   ✳   ✳

Over ten years later, I ran into Ms. Sweet in a supermarket when I was back home after my college graduation. Transformed by the power vested in some priest by the state of Indiana, she was now renamed Mrs. Mientkewicz —such a travesty…she'll always be Ms. Sweet to me. Mrs. Mientkewicz and I had our unexpected ren-dezvous as she traveled down the cereal aisle at Joe O'Malia's market with her three children. At the time, she was maybe one or two years older than I am now.

We discussed my recent graduation. "I knew you had it in you. When you built that recreation of the Battle of the Alamo out of Pop-sicle sticks, I knew you were on your way to great things," she said, with all sincerity.

We caught up about her life. She was still at my old elementary school, and married to a gym teacher who came to the school the year after I left. And then we discussed the first mission of the space shuttle Columbia. She remembered my paper, and the discussion we had in front of the class.

"You and I had never spoken that way before. You always asked a lot of questions, but they were always specific. Other kids at the fourth or fifth grade level just like asking 'Why?' a lot—*all the time*. But you never really did that.

"I think you knew *too much* about those shuttle tiles; you had thought too much about them. All you asked me was 'Why?'. It was the only time you ever did that."

✳   ✳   ✳   ✳

"...so when Columbia comes back down tomorrow, there will be a large fireball. The heat is caused by *friction* when the shuttle runs up against the earth's *atmosphere*. But the astronauts inside will be fine, because they have a layer of *thermal tiles* to suck up the heat and keep it away from them," said Ms. Sweet.

I raised my hand. "Jacob," she called.

"I don't like the thermal tiles. Why would they go up with a system like that?"

"Well, class, Jacob wrote an excellent paper on the tiles. He wrote that there have been a lot of problems with the tiles over the last couple of years and *NASA* has taken a lot of time to try to fix them."

"But they haven't fixed everything with the tiles. Why would they go up?"

"Well, Jacob. The astronauts want to orbit the Earth, and, if they used a heavier layer of protection, the shuttle might not be able to fly. It can be dangerous sometimes if you want to fly into space, can't it?" The class nodded. Ms. Sweet had already discussed the death of Indiana's own Virgil "Gus" Grissom during a training accident.

"But I don't understand why they'd fly up there if all of the tiles might just fall off. Why would they do that?"

"Well, maybe because there are some things about *science* and *astronomy* and the *human body* that we can only learn in space. Some day, the space shuttle will be used to launch satellites, so we'll all be able to *communicate* better. Maybe, they will be able to conduct special *scientific experiments* and what they learn will help us cure a *disease*, or will help us go to *Mars* one day."

"But why would they go up if they know they might not come down safely."

"The astronauts love their *country*, and they love their *families*. They think they can help everyone by what we learn in space. People in the United States and all over the world. And they have important personal goals, challenges they want to face and achieve. So they go up, in spite of the *risks* they face."

"Why?"

"Because, they're brave, Jacob. They're brave."

✳   ✳   ✳   ✳

I don't know if I'm brave. I would like to think that I am...that I would be...that I will be. I would like to think I was prepared to be a rock of support to someone afflicted with cancer, but now I'll never know for sure. Maybe it was easier to investigate my priorities when it was simply a matter of cogitating on them in the privacy of my apartment. Maybe it was simpler to *craft* grand plans than it would have been to *stick with them* when put to the test. But those are tests in life I won't be facing now. But, maybe...probably...someday, there will be other tests.

I think Trevor was brave. I think he'll help Angeline be brave. Of this, I'm fairly certain.

Our world is dominated—inundated—by a flood of unknowns, uncertainties and incongruities. The unrecognized, unobserved and unexplained can overwhelm those looking for any measure of security. In reality, a lot of us spend the majority of our time dwelling in the enormous space between the hard facts in our lives. We see events unfold in front of us and around us, sometimes even decisively shaping them, but often we only know enough about these episodes to fashion imperfect descriptions—a flawed anecdote here and an incomplete short story there. We analyze and overanalyze our anecdotes, but still come up with little that we can *know* for certain. Ours is a world crammed with "I don't knows."

Maybe bravery is the quality of latching onto those few things we actually know—that we *know*—and holding on tight as we wade through the things we don't know and may never know. Of this, after my recent experiences, I'm fairly certain.

50

My New Place

Now, it's Sunday. When I returned from Lake Tahoe late Friday night, a good portion of my Union Street flat was packed up. Towers of freshly formed boxes surrounded the couch and the dining table and my kitchen table/desk. The long corridor was stripped of six continents' worth of framed photos.

In the kitchen, beneath a couple of used cans of Chunky Soup, a vacant Hot Pocket box and three empties of Diet Coke were a $20 bill and a note:

"Hi! My movers are coming over Sunday about 2 in the afternoon. Probably best if you're out before then so we don't trip over each other! Kitty and I are in Napa for two nights until then. One last Bay area experience before the big move! Oh, and we need to show you her ring!"

I might have forgotten to tell you: I'm moving. It had sort of slipped my mind.

The trip to the beautiful U-Haul lot SOSOMA (South of South of Market) this morning had taken longer than expected. I had done a little bit of packing Saturday, but had been distracted and physically drained by the Columbia tragedy; I was still looking at cramming about a day's worth of packing into an hour.

Luckily, I have quite a totable life. No major appliances. No large pieces of furniture. No expansive collections of wall-mounted photos. I managed to make quite a dent in my set of tasks within my hour-long window.

A knock on the open front door, and a query. "JTeeeee? You here?" called Billy.

"Yeah, guys, I'm right back here in the bedroom. Just...finishing up a last...few things," I said as I looked at my room, basically still arrayed as the same set piece from the first scene of this book. I ran out to the front of the flat before they could see my poor preparation. "Billy! EZ! Thanks, boys. I really appreciate it."

"No worries, brother," said EZ as we transitioned from a high five to a snapping handshake and then a fist knock. "So, what's the plan?"

"If you guys can get started on the stuff in the kitchen, that would be great. Basically, anything in a brand new, beautiful moving box is my flatmates'. Anything in a recycled box that looks like it was stolen from outside a liquor store...that's mine," I instructed them. "Just toss 'em in the van. It's the big orange one in the driveway, in case you didn't notice it."

"We just thought you got a sweeter ride to replace the Probe, JT," EZ deadpanned.

I hustled back to my bedroom to "finish" the packing process. The space beneath my bed was like a clown car full of smushed duffel bags and suiters. My entire collection of hanging clothes was unhung and deposited into handy carrying cases within sixty seconds. Every drawer of clothing was unceremoniously dumped into a cavernous duffle; I'd have two weeks of extremely wrinkled undershirts and boxers, but I could live with that. My limited collection of shoes burrowed themselves into the unoccupied nooks and crannies in the duffels.

Legions of milk crates—some stored in the garage, some masquerading as quasi-furniture until hours before—then sprung into action. Within two minutes, one platoon of crates had collected and packed away nearly 300 alphabetized CDs. Another squad had grabbed all photo albums and stowed them for transport. A final detachment fanned out to reconnoiter all books, efficiently segregating the tomes of business buzzwords from the biographies and histories and separating the fine literature from the mound of Technicolor fiction. Once packed, they stood along the wall of the long corridor in formation.

I then returned to my bedroom to retrieve a couple of final plastic crates, lost for months at the back of my closet.

Once EZ and Billy had finished loading the items in the front of the house, we made quick work of the milk crate formations and the rest of the stuff at the back of the place. Years of living were dispatched within about 15 minutes. Billy and I pushed my mattress down the longest hallway in the City toward the front door.

Somebody blocked our path. "Hey, buddy! Long time no see!" said my soon to be ex-flatmate Dale as we almost collided with him at the front door. "Whew. It's been like four or five months hasn't it?"

"You know, man, I'm pretty sure it's been six months…just a few days *over* six months as a matter of fact," I said as I gave him a quick, sweaty handshake. "That's life in big business, eh?"

"Ain't it the truth? So, what's been going on? Surgery turn out well?"

"I think so. Guess I'll know by the end of the day, eh?"

"So, all's good?"

"Pretty good."

"And how's Gabrielle?"

"Pretty good, I think. Hey, we should get our van out of the way. Your movers will be here any minute."

"Yeah, that would be good. But let's catch up soon! I think I owe you a beer."

"I'll take it," I told him as Billy and I maneuvered the mattress down the twisting staircase.

✳   ✳   ✳   ✳

I am now the third member of a most august triumvirate. We live in a house on a hill. An estate far removed from the mundane concerns of those who populate the lower regions. A villa with inspiring vistas of the City we rule.

But it's an incredible pain in the ass to move into.

Billy, EZ and I wound my caravan of possessions up seven flights of stairs (four outdoors, three inside) to reach the final destination. Our new place…well, their *old* place, *my* new place.

During our exertions, I was afforded ample time to update them on the events of the last few weeks. In between the huffs and groans of lifting and carrying, they questioned, I answered and we discussed.

"Shit...duuude..." EZ said a few times.

"Dude...fuuuuck..." said Billy a few more.

✷   ✷   ✷   ✷

By five o'clock, we had unloaded and I had returned my U-Haul. Sitting in my bedroom, I was surrounded by a small fortress of possessions: walls of mattress, box spring, cardboard containers and milk crates. Inside the outer wall, a balustrade of books awaited reshelving. I had a good laugh when I spied the one on top: the volume of short stories Erica had given me just after my surgery. The inscription captured all of the eloquence we've come to expect from our Erica: "Get well soon. Don't worry. You'll walk again someday...I think...maybe..."

I had already unpacked my small appliances, implements and other accoutrements downstairs in the kitchen. A quick accounting of the kitchen tool drawers revealed that I now inhabited a house with a grand total of 13 spatulas. Some were sparkling, nearly new and relatively unspoiled. Others bore individual scars, pronounced and distinctive. One was marked with the oversized thumbprint of an electric burner. Two others were warped and crenellated by the heat of gas flames. Another was disfigured by baked-on blemish of egg yolk. I rearranged the drawer so that it could accommodate all of the new implements.

All in all, it was an incredibly successful move. Even with my last minute preparations and the paucity of padding, only *one* item was broken. Usually my moves are marred by much crunching, scratching and mangling.

Billy and EZ had already showered and were enjoying a couple of pre-dinner cocktails in the penthouse/living room with their girlfriend and fiancée, respectively. I had accepted a beer from them and socialized for a moment, but soon retreated to my nearby bedroom to start to bring some order to my chaos.

"JT, we're getting ready to head out, my man!" said EZ. "We'll be seeing you!"

"OK, catch you guys later!" I said as I continued transferring CDs from their milk crates to their new home.

I heard men and women whispering in the other room. Just as I had finished unloading the soundtrack to this book onto my newly reassembled collapsible and highly portable shelving unit, EZ and Billy popped their heads into my new bedroom.

"Dude, you should come with us, bro," said EZ.

"Oh, thanks. But, isn't it a total couples thing?" I asked.

"Yeah, but dude, just come along; it'll be good for you to get out," stated Billy.

"Hey, thanks, but listen, I have about 31 different flavors of dried sweat and gook on me right now," I returned. "Plus, I want to return your home to at least some level of livability by the end of the night. My stuff is freaking everywhere."

"You sure?" asked Billy.

"Totally sure."

That being said, I didn't do much more unloading that night. I ended up taking a break right after they departed, and watched the sun set from my new deck while finishing off the warm beer I had started almost an hour earlier. A few minutes after that, I sat down to finish this book, leaving far too much unpacking undone.

I've mentioned before that I'm terrible with endings. I think I wrote that at the beginning. For the last several months, I've wondered how it would all end. I've pondered when I would stop writing.

Sometimes, I pictured some very literary ending, the stuff of your finer hardcover novels. Maybe Jake running through the streets of San Francisco on a cold, misty—maybe even rainy—night. We don't know what exactly he's looking for as he sprints and stumbles. He splashes from puddle to puddle, some displaying shimmering reflections of the constellations of stars, others, the rippling portrait of a half moon. I hadn't exactly ascertained how you could see the reflections of the heavenly bodies so well on such a misty and rainy night, but now I guess I don't have to figure it out.

I'd pictured some endings inspired by film—Hollywood endings. Cut to the scene…a party on a beautiful night…Chinese lanterns are lit up like…well, like *Chinese lanterns*. We don't know exactly who's there or what they might be celebrating, but we can see piles of immaculate *hors d'oeuvres* and mountains of the finest cheeses. I still hadn't considered precisely what types of cheese would be served and I hadn't thought through exactly who would be at said celebration— but I probably would have invited Warren Buffett, Sheryl Crow and Eddie Vedder for kicks.

Y'know, I'm pretty content right now to go with a short story ending. I mean, it sort of fits in this book of short stories and anecdotes that never was…well, *almost* was.

I've told you before that their…excuse me, *our*…Telegraph Hill house has one of the best views in the City. And on this night, the sunset was unlike anything I had ever experienced in my life. In the foreground, a solid glacier of fog cut diagonally across the Bay. I'd been up on this deck before a dozen times as a fog rolled in, but this was nothing like the weak mists that added to the grayness of gray days. Today was a perfectly beautiful and clear day, one that was transforming itself into a perfectly beautiful and clear evening. The fog, though welcome, seemed out of place. This was a powerful wall of fog that moved over the water with a certain solidity, not a tendril of vapor extending out from its borders. The perfect wall totally obscured the small island of Alcatraz not even half a mile away, an island very visible from this spot even on the foggiest of days. A ferryboat returning from Marin county suddenly appeared out of nowhere as it moved beyond the obscuring borders and onto my side of the curtain. There was no creeping transition—it just materialized out of nothing.

That solid gray partition in the foreground cut off only the tiniest corner of the most beautiful background I'd ever seen. Someone must have invented a few new shades of orange for this sunset. I certainly don't know *all* of the names, but a few shades of orange I *could* recognize were tangerine, pumpkin, peach, rust, frozen creamsicle, melted creamsicle, Play-Doh, 1979 Tampa Bay Buccaneer and 2003

Tampa Bay Buccaneer. I don't know if you can buy all of those colors at your local art supply store.

An extraordinarily powerful revelation hit me as I watched that sun set behind the Golden Gate Bridge. I'd seen a documentary about its construction and had absorbed a truckload of facts. I was aware of all the political wrangling around the plan and the socioeconomic impact of the project during the height of the Great Depression. I knew how much it cost, how many miles of cable were lain for its spans and how many men died in its creation. I'm an educated man, probably an over-educated man, but it never dawned on me until that moment why they had painted the Golden Gate Bridge in orange vermillion. On this night, though, it all blended together perfectly.

I decided to crack open a second beer and take a seat on one of the terrible, white mold-stained plastic chairs on our deck. The sunset was worth watching to its completion. Don't look for any symbolism in there. I just thought it was pretty.

When most of the orange had vanished, I looked away for the first time in minutes. I peered down, actually, toward the one item that had been broken during my move. The planter—the one which had occupied the corner of my bedroom for years—was laid out on the planks of the deck like an artifact from a lost Greek city-state. In death, the amphora was displayed in a structure that mirrored its anatomy in life. Pieces of the mouth lay furthest away from me, then came the shoulders, the belly and finally chunks of the planter's solid foot. In spite of my careful packing, the pot had been smashed by a falling bed frame in the back of the moving truck; I loaded the pieces into a couple of milk crates and brought them up here once the van had been emptied of every other item.

You'd think, after all of this time, I wouldn't be so clumsy, wouldn't you? I should have all of the necessary experiences to execute flawlessly. But the shards of the pot prove how maladroit I can still be, both with moving and with symbolism.

I don't know what it all means. All I know is that at that moment, I was in more pain that I had ever felt in my life. And I was loving it. I've amply documented months of taxing rehabilitation. At this particular moment, I was feeling the pain brought on by my day of skiing in Tahoe, my first attempt at that sport in two years. I felt the ache of packing and carrying and then climbing the equivalent of the Empire State Building loaded down with hundreds of pounds to get myself into this new place. I had gained an intimate understanding of the pain of weakness and the pain of recovery over the last several months—I preferred the pain of exertion.

I grabbed a heavy piece of the pot's base with the hand that wasn't holding my Anchor Steam Ale. I chuckled as I examined it. What does it all mean? I don't know. I'll think about it tomorrow. I set the chunk of clay down, elevated myself gingerly from the deck chair and walked inside to my collection of anecdotes. Tonight, I think I might just keep typing until my third, muscle-relaxing beer of the evening runs dry. And then I'll press "save."

Acknowledgements

If it takes a village to raise a child, it must take a township or at the very least a kibbutz to create a book. I owe a great deal to so many great people.

Two artists went well above and beyond the call of duty to help me. I would like to thank my friend Michael Walsh for his hard work on the painting for the cover of *Anecdotal* (more of his paintings and sculptures can be seen at www.walshart.com). Lucas McCann also provided a tremendous addition to the book; his maps hopefully aided readers in following Jake's far-flung journeys through the wilds of Cow Hollow, the Marina and other exotic regions of the San Francisco Bay Area.

I am very much indebted to a patient, thorough and creative group of readers, both friends and strangers who became friends. Their thoughtful recommendations often served as the missing pieces of the puzzle in the development of many of the book's characters and themes. Plus, they helped me learn many important lessons about life...like that a "sachet" is a packet of potpourri that one might throw in an underwear drawer, while a "sashay" is a quick, gliding, sideways step. So, I once again send along a hearty "thank you" to Rahul Banta, Mark Casey, Christine DeLeo Cline, Trish Gardner, Anthony Gellert, Lisa Krim, Andrea Leon, Brandt McKee, Jillian Richardson, Joe Ronayne, Tod Sacerdoti, Sally Moody Schedler, Carolyn Spaht, Pankaj Talwar, Susan Tunnell, David Wright and Hannah Wright.

If a copy of *Anecdotal* has made its way to you (and correct me if I'm wrong, but I believe it has), it is in large part due to the help of people who helped me spread the word about the novel early on. I am extraordinarily grateful to a group of people who believed in this novel, believed in me and/or just wanted to be in a book's acknowledgements section; they are Amy Andersen, Kevin Barenblat, Catie Chase, Ravi Chiruvolu, Tyler Cormney, Jeff George, Jim Goldfarb, Amanda Harvey, Marcie Hatch, Jay Haynes, Scott Hilleboe, Auren Hoffman, Sean Jacobsohn, Steve Matloff, Susan Matloff, Kara

McCarthy, Laurance Narbut, Gordon Rubenstein, Cami Samuels, Lisa Schahet, Fran Seegull, Kimberly Twombly, Jim Underwood and Bill Walsh.

Other friends who provided valuable information, counsel or couch space along the way include Monica Keany, Tom Morgan, Alex Panelli, Lawrence Steyn, Ryan Turner and Adam Shaywitz. I would like to express gratitude to my parents, Patricia Hester and Dixon Dann, who furthered my intellectual and creative development by never ordering cable television until I went to college.

I also want to thank a group of people who took time out to talk to me about the ins-and-outs of the book publishing process: Geetu Bedi, Jennifer Joel, Greg Dinkin, Dorothea Herrey, Brad Meltzer, Stephen Quinn, Rob Reid, Scott Smith, Jay Schaeffer, Jacques de Spoelberch and Matt Williams. They all helped—some by accident, but most, on purpose. I would additionally like to extend thanks to Dog Ear Publishing of Indianapolis for their support of this book.

And now, to round out my patented *Acknowledgement Marketing* © campaign, I would like to recognize the contributions of another 100 million or so people. Since *Anecdotal* was written in large part "on location," I wanted to acknowledge the citizenry and café owners of the following locales for their hospitality and inspiration: San Francisco, Oakland, Palo Alto, Napa County, Sausalito, Mill Valley, Los Angeles, West Hollywood, Beverly Hills, Paris, Las Vegas, New York City, Greenwich CT, Stamford CT, Newark NJ, Boston, Cambridge MA, Chicago, Indianapolis and Pascagoula, MS. Without you, none of this would have been possible.

JBD
26 February 2005
jbrooksdann@gmail.com

Printed in the United States
26936LVS00003B/43-459

9 780976 660354